The Things That Last Forever

A Vic Lenoski Mystery

Book 3

THE THINGS THAT LAST FOREVER

The Vic Lenoski Mysteries

by Peter W. J. Hayes

Janet –
All the best –

LEVEL
BEST BOOKS

Quote from Burning Bridges by Chris Pureka, from the album, Driving North, copyright 2004, Sad Rabbit Music (ASCAP)

First edition

ISBN: 978-1-947915-56-5

This book was professionally typeset on Reedsy.
Find out more at reedsy.com

To my father, who lived his beliefs through action, not words, which turned out to be about the best lesson a novelist could have

A champion is someone who gets up when he can't.

—Jack (The Manassa Mauler) Dempsy,
World Heavyweight Champion, 1919-1926

This is a story of burning bridges
And allowing time to pass
This is a story of forgiveness
And breaking things in my hands
This is a story of understanding
You can't choose who you love
And this is a story of soft skin
And rats in the walls

— From the song *Burning Bridges*
by Chris Pureka

Contents

Praise for The Things That Last Forever

In *The Things That Last Forever*, Peter W. J. Hayes delivers the goods in masterful fashion: a compelling plot populated with complex characters in an atmospheric setting, capped off by a gut-punch of a final twist you won't see coming. Throughout it all, Hayes paints a vivid picture of Pittsburgh detective Vic Lenoski's emotional struggles that will resonate with every reader. A terrific novel!

—Alan Orloff, Thriller- and Derringer-Award winning author of *I Know Where You Sleep*

Chapter 1

Sometimes you walk into a room and what's inside changes your life forever. That sense stopped Vic just inside the doorway. A woman with skin the color of dark amber lay on the only bed, her bandaged arms shockingly white among the shadows. She was reflected in a large window in the far wall, the outside sky as black and still as the inside of a tomb. He smelled disinfectant and blood. Numbers and graph lines flared on grey-eyed medical monitors. Somewhere in the vast empty spaces of the hospital a voice echoed.

He'd never visited a burn ward.

Never had a partner so close to death.

Never thought a room could seem as hollow as he felt inside.

The feeling was so disembodying that when he reached the bed and looked into the woman's face, he half expected to see himself. But it was Liz, her forehead and knobby cheekbones smeared with ointment, eyebrows and eyelashes burned away. A bandage covered her left earlobe where her favorite earring, a small gold star, usually sat. It seemed like every breath she took pained her.

He wanted to take her hand but the bandages made it impossible.

"Liz," he said softly, her name almost lost among the beeps and clicks of the monitors. Liquid dripped into a tangle of IV tubes at the back of her fist.

Her eyelids fluttered.

"Liz. Doctor told me I could talk to you."

Her eyes opened. He watched her pupils widen and narrow as they absorbed the distance to the ceiling and distinguished shadows from feeble

1

light.

"Vic?" A hoarse whisper.

"I'm here."

She turned her face to him. "You got me out."

Relief rose in Vic's throat. "Yeah. But the house didn't make it."

"Cora Stills?"

Vic squeezed his eyelids shut and rocked on his heels. He didn't know where to start. Cora Stills. The one person who knew something—anything—about his missing teenage daughter. Liz on her way to arrest her. Instead, Liz, handcuffed to a radiator pipe as flames lathered and stormed through Cora's house. Cora's burned-out car found two days later on a crumbling stone dock next to a deserted warehouse, the Allegheny River emptying westward.

Cora, alive and moving through that tomb of darkness outside the window. Free.

"Vic," Liz said something more but he couldn't make it out.

He bent closer.

She forced her words from somewhere deep inside, and as she spoke, he knew this was what she saved through all the fear and pain to tell him.

"Someone told Cora I was coming."

Chapter 2

When Vic stepped from the room his wife, Anne, waited for him, her arms folded. She hadn't left his side during his four-day stay in the hospital, the longest they'd been together since she'd moved out of their house. That was right when he was at his drunkest, just six months after their daughter, Dannie, disappeared—the morning after he brought his service Glock to their bedroom and slept with it fully loaded on the bedside table.

"How is she?" Anne asked. Somehow, despite those days in the hospital, her blond hair was smooth and brushed, her yellow crew-necked sweater unwrinkled, her blue eyes clear. Only her forehead, clutched in concern, showed anything amiss.

"Talking. Her mind seems clear." Vic worried about his own mind, about how he felt when he entered the room. The fear that he had crossed to a new place and lost the path back.

"You did a wonderful thing." Anne pressed his forearm through his sling. He felt her touch all the way up to his shoulder, where the doctors had popped his arm back into joint.

"I lost Cora Stills. I saw her at the end of the driveway. I could have caught her."

"And leave Liz to die? You couldn't. You're not built that way."

Vic didn't say anything. He pictured Cora, her short red hair, her eyes hooded as if she was staring into a sandstorm. Again, he heard her laughing at him. The flames leaping from the house windows. Liz's piercing scream.

He shivered, aware of Anne's gaze. He knew what she waited for, what

3

she wanted him to say.

Instead he said, "Crush stopped by. Said the police union required I take two weeks disability. Then back to work."

"He couldn't act like he was glad you got time to recover? He's an idiot."

"Maybe. I'm just a detective, he's my commander. You know how it goes."

"Vic. What are you going to do?"

He was avoiding the question and he knew it. He stared at her. He was amazed she stood in front of him at all. He knew how he'd acted when Dannie disappeared. It was unforgivable. And yet here she was. He wondered if it might be different now, if she might come home. He hoped so.

He took a breath. "I'm going to find Cora."

"Good." She didn't take her eyes from him.

Vic knew she wanted more…she wanted to be sure he meant it. She'd carried Dannie; Dannie was their only child. He felt the night around him, the yawning emptiness of the hospital halls. He wondered vaguely what time it was. Two a.m.? Three? Yet in all that space and silence it was just the two of them together. Here. Barely a foot apart.

He met her gaze. "She'll go to ground somewhere she feels safe. We just need to figure out where. Levon's helping." He breathed, thinking about Levon, the private investigator he now counted as a friend. "Cora was in the military. So was Levon, he's working that angle. I'm going to circle back on everything in Pittsburgh. Do all the document searches. Figure out what she owns and what neighborhoods she knows."

Anne nodded. "That's better."

He thought about telling her what Liz said and decided not to. Finding Cora was one thing. What Liz told him was something else completely. He needed time to process it. To understand what it might mean.

"I can give you a ride home, Vic. If you want."

"Where are you going to stay?"

She stared at him. Vic felt the night tighten around them. He remembered the darkness outside the windows, its stillness. How it seemed to be waiting.

"With my mother. Where I've *been* staying." Her voice was brittle.

He knew he'd overstepped. This wasn't the time or place to bring it up. It was him being thump-footed again. Whatever possibilities might have sprouted during her stay with him in the hospital, he hoped he hadn't just trampled them.

"You're tired, Vic. You've been in hospital for four days." Her voice was firm, the voice she used when she made up her mind and was ready to do something. It was more of an attitude than a tone, and it was among the first things he ever loved about her.

"You're right." He tried a smile and knew he failed at it.

She raised a small knapsack to him. "I put your stuff in here. Let's go."

He took the knapsack with his good arm and followed her down the hall. They passed a nurses' station and took an elevator to the ground floor.

Halfway across the lobby the front doors shushed open and Levon Grace stepped into the building, the creamed-coffee color of his skin tinged yellow under the LED lights. He half grinned at them, looking at Anne. "I heard tonight was the night he gets out." He shifted his gaze to Vic. "Good to see you upright. You talk to Liz?"

They all stopped in the center of the lobby.

"I did," Vic said. "I thought it was going to be earlier but the doctor wanted to give her a few more hours because we aren't family. That's reserved for you and Jayvon."

"Well, Jayvon is family," Levon answered, referring to Liz's fourteen-year-old son. "Liz and I still have a ways to go."

"Only if you're slow about it." Anne stared at him pointedly.

Vic frowned. "Where is Jayvon?"

"I signed for that apartment Liz liked, and he and I moved in yesterday. He can start school on Monday. My Mom's staying with him now."

Vic didn't know that Levon's mother lived in Pittsburgh. Levon was so self-sufficient and contained it almost seemed possible he never had a mother. It was odd to hear him talk about her.

"Liz talked to me," Vic said. "Her mind is clear, given all the pain killers they've got her on."

Levon shook his head. "She asked them to back off on those. She doesn't trust them."

"She looks pretty good, given everything, don't you think?" Vic knew he was asking a different question. He didn't know the extent of Liz's injuries and how they might affect her recovery, and the doctor refused to discuss it with him. He guessed that Levon knew.

Levon hesitated long enough for Vic to know he understood the real question. "Scars on her thighs and forearms, when everything heals. Maybe a few around her cheeks and forehead. You got her out just in time, Vic." From the relief in his voice, Vic understood how much Levon cared for Liz. That, perhaps, the two of them did have a future.

"I'll pull the car around." Anne touched Levon on the arm and left them in the lobby.

As they watched her go Levon said quietly, "I might have something."

"What?"

They turned to each other. "I tracked down a guy I know. He was an MP and transferred to NCIS. He did a records search and Cora Stills came up."

"The same Cora Stills?"

"Right. We're that incompetent. *Yes* the same Cora Stills. You told me she did a tour in Africa. Dates match up. Gets better. He knew her. She was named in an investigation a few years ago. He said he'd call me tomorrow. With a little luck we'll have something."

"He can just tell us what he knows?"

"Depends what it is. We'll know tomorrow."

"Call me as soon as you talk to him."

Levon nodded. "You got it."

They shook hands, awkwardly, using their left hands. Vic carried his knapsack outside. The air was cool, the darkness moist, as if it carried the morning dew. The hospital sat atop a steep hill above Pittsburgh near one of the universities, but he couldn't see the city skyline. It was right there, he knew, on the other side of the parking garage. As he waited, he saw Cora Stills in his mind again, the way she flexed onto her toes and called up the driveway to him just before he plunged into the burning house to find Liz. He heard Cora's voice, as clear as a day's first bird call.

"Me or your partner? Which one? Which one do you want?"

He drew the black night air as deep into his lungs as he could. "I want both of you," he said out loud to the image of her. "I got one and you're next."

Chapter 3

They drove in silence, Anne with the seat pulled close to the steering wheel, her body tense as she peered through the windshield. She picked her way along residential streets toward Greenfield, parked cars on both sides of them. The houses were dark.

As they drew close to their home, Anne said, "I stopped by and picked up the mail. I knew you were getting out today, so I left spaghetti in the refrigerator."

"You okay getting back to your mother's?"

She didn't say anything for a moment. "I'll be fine." She pulled the car to the curb and waited.

He hesitated, wanting to thank her for staying with him in the hospital, but he couldn't find the words. He knew it was important to say it the right way, and he didn't know how.

"Something else," she added. Her firm 'get on with it' tone was back. "I got a job. I started a week before you went into hospital. I need to be back there tomorrow. They let me take a week off right after starting. Nobody does that. I need to prove this won't be a regular thing. Do you understand?"

Vic felt himself nodding. "Great." He winced inside at how insincere the word sounded. He didn't mean it that way. "Where are you working?"

"Front office of the Penguins. Their marketing department."

"Wow." He was glad to hear more enthusiasm in his voice. He thought that perhaps the note of pride in hers put it there. "Then you need to go home and get some sleep."

He busied himself opening the car door and leveraging himself out of the passenger seat. The porch light was on, again Anne anticipating his return. He struggled through unlocking the house door with his left hand, turned and waved. Anne pulled away and he watched the taillights disappear.

Inside, the house was black and still. He dropped his knapsack just inside the door and turned on the living room lights. In the kitchen he checked the refrigerator and spotted a plastic container of spaghetti, but he didn't feel hungry. He noticed that Anne had replenished the milk and orange juice. He turned out the light to move upstairs, but stopped at the doorway to the dining room. He hesitated before stepping inside and switching on the corner standing lamp. Light flooded the documents taped to the longest side wall; different colored Post-its with his hand-written comments jumped out at him. He breathed carefully, staring. At the center of the wall, like a bulls-eye amid all the police-file documents related to Dannie's disappearance, were three photographs. He walked over and studied them. The red-haired Chrissie Stutz, Carole Vinney and the Asian woman, Susan Kim. The three who, working as strippers, disappeared at the same time as Dannie. It was their missing person's reports that had led him to Cora Stills. He glanced at the documents from the police file on Dannie's disappearance. A perfectly thorough investigation, and yet it was those three seemingly unrelated photos that provided the break.

He rocked on his heels, aware of the still darkness outside the window, and how patches of it clung to the inside corners of his home. Working his arm out of the sling, he gingerly tested his shoulder, registering the stiffness as he rotated it. He already had two days of physical therapy under his belt, but continuing the exercises was up to him. Tiredness washed over him and he lowered his arm straight at his side, exploring the feel of not using the sling.

It was only as he turned to go upstairs that he noticed it, or rather the lack of it. The fifteen photographs of Dannie he had arranged on the windowsill—one taken each year of her life—were gone, save one. Only the photograph of Dannie at fifteen— just a few months before her sixteenth birthday—remained. The empty space raged at him.

Anne was the only person with a key to the house. He thought about the meaning of that, why she might take them and leave just the one. He felt the house around him. The emptiness of it. It was as if his memories of Dannie's presence in the house were evaporating. Her whispering footsteps on the stairs, her laughter soaking down from her upstairs bedroom. The clatter as she washed the dishes after dinner, her one daily chore. Her voice as she called out to Anne or him with a question. All fading.

He turned out the light.

Upstairs he lay on the bed fully dressed, too tired to change. The sheets smelled freshly washed.

Anne again.

He remembered when he and Anne first met, the ink on her University of Pittsburgh diploma still wet, her working for some kind of company that organized events. It was a fundraiser for the Golden Gloves and Vic was invited, a newly minted cop, ex-Golden Gloves boxer. He was drawn to the way she kept the hotel staff moving, her competence and quickness. Her confidence. The direct way she looked at him. Her legs in that short shiny dress.

Sometime during the night, he tracked down a business card to the event company and the next day, after thinking about it all morning, dialed them and asked for the woman who ran the Golden Gloves fundraiser.

She answered almost immediately. He stumbled out a few rehearsed sentences—hoping she would remember him—and ended with an invitation to coffee.

When he finished, she was silent for a few beats, and then said, "Oh you! The hunchback!"

He remembered his surprise and confusion, until she added, "You're the one with the big left shoulder. Someone said you had a bandage under there. You're the policeman someone wounded."

"Oh. I didn't think people knew." He hadn't mentioned the shoulder or the bandage in his preamble to her.

A few days earlier a bullet had grazed his shoulder during a drug bust. Through the pounding of his body's adrenaline he'd hardly noticed. The shooter threw his gun and ran, and Vic had chased him over a couple of backyard fences and tackled him. The bullet furrow needed fifteen stitches, and during the Golden Gloves event he was still wearing the bulky compression bandage recommended by the doctor.

"Coffee would be great," she'd added.

Later that day, thinking about their conversation, Vic realized that Anne must have asked about him. Why his one shoulder was so large under his sport coat. He took it as a good sign.

Two months later, after a number of dates and their first few nights together, he went out drinking with another officer, a friend, a round-faced black man nicknamed Moon. He'd regularly sparred Moon in Golden Gloves and they trusted one another, understood each other in the way of guys who have tested each other in the ring, and Vic always liked how quick he was with a joke. After a few beers Moon kidded him about the smile that Vic couldn't wipe from his face. Feeling confident about his relationship with Anne, he told Moon the entire story. The fundraiser, her legs in that shiny dress, how she must have asked about him, the coffee, the dinners, her confidence, the movie, her legs, the nights together.

"Shit," Moon said, slopping beer from their third pitcher into Vic's mug. "You been shot and survived, caught the bad guy and won the girl. Shit."

Another pitcher and two shots later Moon convinced Vic that only he could be his best man. Vic knew he was absolutely right. They sealed the deal with another shot.

Vic shifted on the bed and smelled the freshness of the sheets. Looking back on that conversation, he knew it started then. The mixing of the bad with the good. The truth of that. Five months afterwards, Moon knocked on a front door to serve a warrant. The door was answered by a shotgun blast and Moon bled out on the house steps, December rain freezing his face.

A few months later mesothelioma finished ravaging his father's lungs and Vic buried him next to his mother in a Homestead graveyard.

The cemetery overlooked the mill site where his father worked his entire life. The mill was gone now, overtaken by strip malls, a mini-casino and a garish Chuck E. Cheese. Anne pressed herself against his side for the entire ceremony, her hand tight on the crook of his elbow.

Then a wedding, his best man another officer. Yet, as beautiful as Anne looked, despite the bright love he felt for her, he couldn't shake the feeling it should be Moon handing him the rings. A few years later Dannie was born, something that made him so happy words failed him. But the truth had hold of him by then: that for every good there is a bad. How it didn't work the other way—there isn't a good for every bad. How the good things are a moment and then flicker into memory, bits of glitter, but the bad things cling to you like clothing, walking with you, tight on your movements, binding you. How the bad passes into the new good things and back into those glittering memories, like the way whenever he thought of his wedding day, he remembered Moon not being there. The way his pure memory of holding Dannie for the first time was now blackened by the fact she was gone. Lost.

The bad just gathered weight, an unrelenting gravity, pulling you to the ground. The place we all end up.

He fell into an uneasy sleep. He dreamed, vivid and breathless. There was Cora Stills, calling up the driveway to him.

In this version of it, she was holding all the photographs of Dannie that were once on the windowsill. It was sunny, she was laughing, but when Vic tried to spin and run inside the burning house, he couldn't move his feet. They were rooted. Liz's scream shredded his heart.

And Cora dropping each photograph to the ground, one at a time, each a year of happiness gone forever.

Chapter 4

Vic rose at dawn and made coffee and toast. To push back the overbearing silence, he turned on the radio, half listening to the news. After breakfast, he went into the basement and ran through the exercises the physical therapist had taught him to strengthen his shoulder. He stared at his heavy boxing bag as he worked, wanting to slip on his gloves and work out properly.

His phone rang just after seven-thirty.

"Vic?" Levon asked, "I got something."

Vic went tight. "Let's hear it."

"That guy in NCIS. I got him on hold but he won't talk to me, only you. Professional courtesy or some bullshit. Like I'm not professional."

"Put him through."

The phone clicked a couple of times and Levon's voice returned, asking for someone named Skiv.

"Speaking," came a new voice through the phone. It was deep and he spoke the word quickly, smartly, as if he was responding to a general. Levon introduced them and dropped off the call.

"Good to meet you," Vic said. "Levon introduced you as Captain Steven Klein, but he called you Skiv?"

"Long story, before I tell you, you got a badge number or something? Just covering my ass. In case I get called upstairs for talking to you."

"Sure. It's Vic Lenoski." He gave Skiv his rank and badge number.

"It worked this way," Skiv said, following a moment of silence when Vic guessed he wrote down his ID and logged the call. "Levon and I were in basic together. I hated getting my fatigues wrinkled because the drill instructors ate you alive for that. I sat around in my skivvies a lot. You can figure it from there."

Vic grinned at the explanation. "And Levon said you have something on Cora Stills?"

"I do, but tell me what you got. Levon said she skipped town. You guys want her for trafficking or something?"

Vic hesitated, unhappy that Skiv wanted an exchange of information and annoyed that he didn't have any choice. "We came across her while investigating some cold cases of missing women. She was the common denominator, boss to all three women at a strip club here in Pittsburgh."

"Three strippers disappeared?"

"Right. But we're looking for four people. My daughter was taken at the same time. She was almost sixteen. She walked to school, and her route went right down the street where Cora Stills lived. Too coincidental."

"Christ. I have two boys, can't imagine losing one."

Vic didn't respond. The comment was the type people often made when they learned his daughter was missing. He knew the sentiment was real even if their understanding of the horror wasn't. He squeezed his eyes closed and started again. "We were in the middle of a different investigation, murder of a public defender, and we had a suspect who looked good for it. We flexed on her, and that scared her boyfriend. He's an accessory to the crime and didn't want jail, so he offered an information trade."

"Wow, isn't love grand."

"Exactly. He told us that his girlfriend and Cora trafficked four women through their farm. Turns out his girlfriend and Cora Stills go way back. From that we got a warrant for Cora, but when I got to her house, she'd set it on fire, with my partner handcuffed inside. I helped her get out but Cora escaped. So, add attempted murder to trafficking."

"She's graduated to the big leagues. Your partner okay?"

"Not great, but she'll pull through. That's the short version of it. You said she's graduated?"

Skiv was silent a moment. "I can tell you one thing. We pulled her in twice when she served in Africa. Somalia. This part is just between you and me, right?"

"Sure."

"Military supplies kept going missing and showing up on the black market in Mogadishu. That got us investigating, and we found a link to smuggled African artifacts. Warrior shields, masks, traditional rug weaving, baskets, that kind of stuff. Someone was trading our supplies for artifacts that were then shipped back to the U.S. The local warlord was pissed, he wanted it to stop and refused to work with us unless we got the artifacts back. Stills was one of four or five people we thought were involved."

"I can confirm she stole the art."

"What?" Skiv responded so quickly the end of the word disappeared.

"I was in her house. She had African art all over the place. One of those cowhide shields you mentioned, some kind of rug hanging below the stairs. African masks on the mantelpiece. You'd have to make sure they're not copies, but from what you're saying, I bet not."

"Damn. We figure they traded away half a million dollars' worth of Uncle Sam's supplies."

Vic switched the phone to his other ear, wincing at the complaint from his right shoulder. "I didn't see the whole house, but she's got some of it."

"I damn well knew it. That was one of my first cases, and it pisses me off I couldn't close it. You didn't get pictures, did you?"

Vic chuckled, recognizing in Skiv's voice his own frustration when he couldn't solve a case. "Sorry. I was over to see her twice and I commented on them the first time. Second time I went, she'd packed them away. I thought that was weird but the way you explain it, I get why."

"Well, if you track her down, I want them back. The big problem is the local warlord. Every time we try and get him to do something, he asks for the artifacts. And get this, he was the one had his guys trade the stuff to get our supplies. He was trading artifacts for our supplies, selling those supplies on the black market, and now he wants the artifacts back."

Vic stared at the floorboard joists above him and decided not to say anything about the artifacts being returned because they belonged in Africa, not as bribes to a warlord. "Anything else you can give me? Her background? Any relatives in her file?"

"Yeah, yeah. Sorry."

Computer keys clicked. "North Dakota."

"What?" Vic squeezed his phone.

"Where she's from. Some tumbleweed town near Williston. Only parent listed is a mother. A Nadine Stills. I got an address."

Vic told him to wait, climbed the stairs to the dining room and found a paper and pen. He wrote down the address. His mind swirled. "Nothing in Pittsburgh?"

"Nope. Makes you wonder how she ended up in your town, huh?"

"Exactly."

"I'm not seeing anything. We just have the mother's name and address. Don't even have a phone number."

"Tell me about her career in the military."

"Let's see. Basic at Fort Benning. Couple training programs. Reached the rank of E-4. Specialist in logistics."

"Moving military supplies?"

"Exactly. That's how they made it work. She had access to the base supplies and could ship the artifacts back. She knew the transport pilots and did the document prep for all the shipments. Her unit even packed the loads. When you think about it, it's easy to see how she did it. She just needed someone stateside to collect the shipments."

"Makes sense. Anything in there that might tell you where she'd go to ground?"

Again, the sound of tapping on a keyboard. "I can give you a list of her postings. Won't be anywhere outside the country, because she's on the watch lists now. Her postings in the U.S. are next door to nowhere. I don't know where she lived in the five years since she left the army. Want me to email the list?"

"Sure." Vic gave him his email address.

"Okay," Skiv said when they were finished. "I got one serious request. You come across those artifacts, you let me know. We need them back."

Vic couldn't help himself. "Africa needs them back?"

"You know what I mean. The Mogadishu mission is national interest. If you find them make damn sure you let me know, or you'll be in shit with us and the FBI."

The call over, Vic stood in the dining room, staring at the documents hanging on the wall. He thought about Cora's job managing the strip club, wondering if he could see her job application again. But that made him think of something else. He didn't know where she worked after the strip club.

And that felt like a very good place to start.

Chapter 5

An hour later Vic was showered and inside his ten-year-old Toyota Corolla, his key ring threaded onto his index finger. He flipped his keys back and forth from the front of his hand to the back.

He could return to headquarters and use his system access to find Cora's last workplace, but he didn't like the idea. It wasn't the risk of being dragged back into casework, or of angering his commander, Crush, who expected him to stay on disability leave. It wasn't even the thought of sitting across the aisle from Liz's empty desk.

Finding Cora was so personal he needed to do it himself, on his own terms.

He flipped the key ring again. The arrest warrant was out. One forgetful use of a credit card, ATM withdrawal or a speeding ticket and databases would churn, notifications pop up and emails fly. They would have her. He could wait for that mistake, but he guessed she was too smart, ruthless and disciplined for that.

He didn't have it in him to wait.

It was like the nervousness before a boxing match. He needed to get in the ring. To get going.

He turned the key in the ignition, lips clamped against the stiffness in his right shoulder. An ungainly reach over the steering wheel with his left hand put the car in drive. Moving, he wondered how the left-handed ten percent of the population dealt with driving every day.

The Strip District, a lick of land along the southern bank of the Allegheny River just east of downtown Pittsburgh, was named after the four-block-long storage building where trains once unloaded produce to supply the city's grocery stores. The area was now a mass of floor-creaking specialty food stores, restaurant patios, and one-way streets. He directed his car through the alleys, alert for pedestrians. Foot traffic was so heavy that people felt emboldened, sometimes popping into the road from between parked cars, as entitled as politicians.

He trundled over the railroad tracks and parked outside a modern four-story square office building, out of place among the red brick—and recently renovated—warehouses built at the turn of the last century. Inside, he strode past a dozing security guard and took the elevator to the fourth floor. He knew that arriving without notice was a risk, but his experience was that people caught by surprise were often more helpful.

The receptionist on the fourth floor was new. He guessed she was in her fifties, her hair impeccable, competence clouded around her like perfume. Vic introduced himself and asked for Mary Monahan. She smiled, the reflex somehow authentic despite a mouthful of teeth so startlingly white Vic almost ducked.

"I'll see if Mrs. Monahan is available." Her hand snaked for her telephone. She said a few words, hung up, stood and presented her hand as if it were a gift. "I'm Alison, but everyone calls me Allie."

"Good to meet you, Allie."

"I've heard so much about you, Detective Lenoski. How you investigated what happened to Mr. Monahan. Saved Mrs. Monahan." She leaned over her desk. "Caught the bad guy." Her brown eyes twinkled.

"I had some help with that," Vic said carefully, remembering the stabbing pain in his side, Levon Grace crossing the office floor with his pistol leveled, the shattering glass of the conference room window when he fired. Liz pulling Mary Monahan to safety. He blinked himself back into the present.

The smile on Allie's face didn't falter. "And humble too."

Vic looked at the door that led into the offices, hoping she would get the hint. She did, and managed not to look annoyed.

"Follow me." As they reached the door, she called over her shoulder, "There's a bit of a celebration going on. We just did a stage-three funding of a startup."

"Exciting." He hoped it was the right thing to say.

Allie held the door for him. "It's the first major position in a company Mrs. Monahan's taken. It's a really big deal." She whispered the last sentence as he passed her, as if she wanted to have secrets between them.

The workspace was essentially the same as his last visit—the center a large room of open work stations, with glass-walled offices and conference rooms along the side walls. The largest office, which Vic knew belonged to Mary Monahan, was engulfed in a low roar of conversation and packed with people holding half-full plastic champagne flutes. Balloons swayed back and forth along the door frame.

Vic nodded his thanks to Allie, who beamed and turned for the lobby. He glanced into the crowd and caught the eye of Erica Lauder. Her cheeks were pink and blue eyes alight. Was it really less than a year since Erica discovered Drake Monahan's body on his office floor? He knew she had quickly become Mary Monahan's confidante, and he guessed she was the driving force behind this new investment.

Erica waved and left the man she was talking to, who barely looked old enough to drink. A crooked smile on her face, she grabbed him, thankfully, by his good arm. "Detective Lenoski." She pulled him into the office and around a couple of slim men in open-collar shirts who were talking over each other so loudly the conversation was nonsensical.

Mary Monahan was perched on the edge of her desk facing the crowd, a flute of champagne in her hand. She was listening to a tall man in his thirties with a shaved head, broad shoulders, olive skin and a light beard immaculately trimmed to look five days old. He was standing at an angle, as if protecting Mary from the rest of the party, or keeping her from it. From the intensity in his posture, Vic guessed it was the latter.

The moment Mary spotted him, she called his name and hopped off the desk. She put her hand on the crook of his left arm, stretched up and gave him a lingering kiss on the cheek. The young man's gaze shifted from surprise to confusion to burning anger in the space of an eye-blink.

The noise of the crowd dipped, and Vic knew everyone was watching them.

"Mary," he said. "Sorry for just showing up."

"You know you can stop by any time. You should do it more often." She stepped back and Vic tried not to gawk at her dress. Almost skin tight and sleeveless, the electric blue of the material radiated from her.

Slowly, as if remembering a boring detail of courtesy, she turned to the young man. "Vic, meet Connor Fariz. He runs a company we've decided to support."

Vic stuck out his hand, which seemed to confuse Connor, as if a request to be civil was too much to ask. Vic watched him recover and relent to the handshake. His gaze barely shifted from Mary.

Vic understood what Mary was doing. She already had Connor wrapped around her little finger, and now she was crooking that finger and squeezing the air out of him. Vic felt vaguely sorry for him.

He warmed to the dynamic. "Pleased to meet you, Connor. Heard your company is stage three." He had no idea what that meant but was interested in the reaction he might get.

Connor's gaze swung onto him, eyes burning. "Remind me again, what is stage three?"

"Connor," Mary said carefully. "It would be bad strategy to try and embarrass Detective Lenoski. I've watched him break someone's nose. Or he might arrest you. As your largest investor I wouldn't find that amusing."

Connor looked from Vic to Mary and back again. The skin along the knife edge of his jawline reddened.

Before Connor could say anything more, Mary smiled. "Vic, unfortunately, you only stop by when something serious is going on. What can I help you with?"

Vic saw the smile in her eyes and knew he'd guessed right. She was using him to push Connor back into place. And because it was Mary, he didn't mind at all.

"There *is* something. Do you remember those employee files I reviewed not long ago? I'd like to take another look. It's important."

She smiled. "Then I have a surprise for you." She gestured to Erica Lauder and said something in her ear. Erica slipped away between the guests.

"Erica will set you up in one of the conference rooms. If I wasn't in the middle of this, I would do it myself." She paused, and Vic knew her last sentence hit Connor like a club. She smiled. "Oh, and I saw my father the other day. He sends you his personal thanks."

Vic thought about that. Mary's father, Dom Bandini, was a retired gangster-turned-businessman who once ran all the loan sharking, numbers, and cocaine that kept Pittsburgh's mill workers awake, cash-strapped, and under thumb. But in the last fifteen years he'd bought into legitimate businesses and survived two federal money-laundering investigations. There was no reason for Bandini to thank him.

Mary leaned in close, a small smile on her lips. "You'll see why. It's something good."

"I'll trust you on that," Vic said, as she gave him a quick kiss on the cheek. He glanced at Connor, but he was glaring at Mary's desktop hard enough to burn the wood.

Outside the office, Erica waved him into an empty conference room on the other side of the floor.

"I asked someone to join us."

Vic grinned at her. "Tough life. Champagne at ten in the morning. I'm guessing you had something to do with that?"

She nodded, her eyes bright. "Connor and his team have a neat idea. They call it deep crunch AI. They've figured out how to make computers teach themselves to get better at facial recognition. Department of Defense and Homeland Security is all over them. They're going to be huge."

"And you found them?"

"They started at Carnegie Mellon University. I knew some of their friends, so I heard about it. The idea is solid. Pretty sure they'll sign a government contract in the next year. When that happens, the stock will go Amazon."

Vic opened his mouth to speak, but a middle-aged woman entered the room. Vic had to stop himself from lurching back in surprise.

"Detective Lenoski." Her green eyes twinkled at him, enjoying his shock.

"Barbara Stutz," he blurted out. The mother of Chrissie Stutz, the redhead whose photograph still hung in the center of his dining room wall.

"Isn't it great?" Erica beamed. "You suggested Barb might be a good hire and she's turned out to be fantastic! She saved our lives with the personnel files. She's got everything organized and up to date."

Barb didn't break her gaze. Vic nodded slowly, absorbing the situation. Barb wore a green wool suit and cream blouse, her suit and hair styled in a way that seemed impossible after their first meeting. On that day she matter-of-factly told him about her husband dead in Afghanistan and the disappearance of her daughter. He remembered her baggy and stained sweats, her ancient farmhouse. The overwhelming sense of how run out everything seemed. Her house alone amidst untilled fields, the crush of the low grey sky, the watching, stalking wind.

He pulled himself back from the memory. "Glad to hear it."

"I have to thank you for recommending me," Barb said.

Vic shook his head. "No need. How is Maya doing?"

If it was possible, Barb's smile widened in appreciation. Maya was Chrissie's toddler daughter, Barb's granddaughter. "Mary and Erica helped me get her into a wonderful daycare. She's doing well. Thank you."

"Good."

Erica touched Vic lightly on the arm. "Okay, I want to get back. I'll leave you guys to it."

Vic thanked her. They shook hands and Erica darted from the room. Barb and Vic sat down. The surprise of the meeting over, a shadow of discomfort settled over him. Barb had as much at stake in his investigation as he did. Worse, he hadn't been honest with her the first time they met.

She sensed his hesitation and the smile slid from her face. "How can I help you?"

Years ago, Vic had learned that when he was unsure, the best direction was straight ahead. "I'm sure you know about the HR files that Mary's father dumped on her?"

Barb nodded. "She told me the story, or at least some of it. Somehow, she made him give his entertainers medical and retirement benefits. After he agreed, he dumped all the personnel files on her. Said she needed to do the work of tracking and delivering the benefits."

"That's pretty much it." He then understood why Bandini sent his thanks. It was likely that when Mary told her father about hiring Barb, she mentioned Vic had recommended her.

"Okay." He took the plunge. "I'm guessing you know that one of those businesses is Bare Essentials."

The corners of Barb's mouth tightened. He wasn't surprised. If she managed the files it was likely she'd spotted the ones from the strip club where her daughter last worked, and disappeared from.

He kept going. "When I came to your house, we talked about Chrissie's boss at Bare Essentials. Her name was Cora Stills. I need to see her file. It looks like she was involved in what happened to your daughter." Vic hesitated, knowing it was the time to be honest. "And mine."

Barb's green eyes narrowed. "Your daughter is missing as well?"

"Yes. I didn't mention it when I visited you, but one reason I was investigating Chrissie's case was because she disappeared about the same time as my daughter."

"Vic, I'm sorry." A second later she sat back and crossed her arms. "Well, that makes a hell of a lot more sense. I knew there was no way you'd driven out to Portersville just to ask about Chrissie's case. Not all those months after it happened."

Vic waited a few moments. "I can't excuse that, but talking to you gave us both a lead. And that's why I need to see the Cora Stills file."

She clutched herself tighter. "Can you tell me anything at all about Chrissie?" Her voice faded to a whisper. "Where she might be? What happened?"

"I can, but I don't know much, and I have no proof. All I know is the shape of it."

"Tell me."

He took a slow breath. "It looks like Cora Stills and a friend abducted four women. Three of the women worked at Bare Essentials, including Chrissie. The fourth was my daughter. Her connection is the fact she walked past Cora's house every day on her way to school."

"How old was she?"

"Almost sixteen, then. Seventeen, now."

She shook her head, her face tight. "Why were they abducted?"

"I haven't confirmed this, but one witness said it might be trafficking."

She blanched. Laughter and excited voices drifted by them from Mary Monahan's office. Finally, slowly, Barb drew a long breath. "Do you have any other leads?"

"No."

"All right." She gathered herself. "Then you need Cora's file. I'll be right back."

Vic waited, looking at nothing in particular. On the other side of the floor, the party was breaking up. Connor circled Mary as if he was attached by an invisible rope. Vic thought about how a woman as beautiful as Mary could arrive on the doorstep of Connor's struggling company and write a check for millions of dollars. Make his dream come true, in effect. He wondered if Connor understood that—for Mary—it was simply business. Or, did he take it personally and interpret the situation as validation from a beautiful woman? He wondered if Connor could separate the two—if he could see Mary's investment for what it really was. It would be bad for him if he couldn't.

Barb appeared in the doorway with a file. She sat down and pushed it across the table.

"That was fast."

"I knew where to find it."

Vic heard the way she moderated her voice, as if she didn't want to give something away. He opened the file, took out his phone and swiped open his camera.

"You have to understand." Barb shifted in her seat, uncomfortable. "I saw the story about Cora burning down her house on TV. When I heard the name, I remembered she was Chrissie's boss. I heard about the cop who was trapped inside. How you got her out." She fell silent.

Vic finished taking photographs of each page in the file. He checked that he could expand the photo and read all the words on the sheets. He put away his phone.

He looked at her. "So, you looked at her file?"

"Yes. By then I knew we had the files for Bare Essentials. And for Chrissie."

"Did it help you remember anything else?"

She shook her head. "No. But I have to ask you. The TV said you ran into the house instead of chasing Cora Stills. How could you do that? Knowing what you know about her? That she might have taken your daughter?"

Vic wasn't sure how to answer. Finally, he said, "Maybe this: I had a boxing coach once. He used to tell me all the time, 'Don't box anything in your head. Your mind always comes up with all kinds of crazy crap. Don't fight any of it. Only fight the things you can hit. The things you know for sure.' I had theories about Cora, what she did. I still do. But Liz was right in front of me. Flesh and blood. My partner. I chose her."

Barb stared at him. "I was so angry. Knowing you let Cora get away when she might know something about Chrissie. I couldn't sleep."

"I can understand that."

"But now I know." She stood up. "You chose right, Vic."

Vic rose as well. He patted the pocket that held his phone. "Thanks, Barb."

"And you keep me updated. As soon as you know anything?"

"I will."

He came around the table and they shook hands. A bit awkwardly, as if after their conversation a handshake was inadequate but a hug too much.

"Vic." She dropped his hand and leaned toward him. "You get Cora Stills." Her voice hardened. "You get every piece of her. Do you understand?"

"I will."

He didn't like or trust promises, but he was fine with that one.

Chapter 6

I t hit him as he threaded his car back through the Strip District. Reflexively, he banged his right hand on the steering wheel and a withering clutch of pain shot through his shoulder. He couldn't believe he hadn't thought of it. A full-blown search for Cora was already underway. Of course. She'd injured a police officer. Half the city's detectives would be ripping apart her life, her photo taped to the wall of every ready-room in the city.

He cursed his self-absorption, how he always needed to do things himself. He'd underestimated how fast he needed to move. By now the task force would be closing in on her. But their job was to jail a would-be cop-killer, not solve the problem of what happened to Dannie.

He was going to be shut out. Once they busted her, interviewing Cora was out of the question. The prosecutors wouldn't want him on the same coast. Too much anger, too much conflict of interest. Too big a chance Vic might poison the prosecution.

He had to find her first.

He worked his injured shoulder, forcing himself to accept the pain, to let it clear his thinking. He needed a direct line to the task force's findings. And a fail-safe, maybe a deal with someone for a heads up if her arrest was imminent. Plus, a way to stay low and approach the group sideways, so Crush and the DA didn't know he was bird-dogging them.

In an alley parallel to Penn Avenue he parked nose-in to a dumpster. He thought about it, and grinned.

Dave Norbert.

The murder case of Gretchen Stall—the public defender—had led Vic to Cora, but when the DA took Vic and Liz off the case, it went to Dave, an Allegheny County detective. Dave would know who was running the search for Cora, whether it was Crush or Allegheny County. And Vic had leverage. Dave had admitted to an affair with Gretchen. He should have started as a suspect, not as investigative lead. Vic and Liz knew about that particular pile of dog mess, but Marioni, the DA, didn't. He bet Norbert still didn't want anyone catching a whiff of it.

He dialed Norbert, who answered on the first ring. "Vic? They let you out?"

"It isn't jail."

"Day ain't over yet."

Vic shook his head. For all of Dave's faults, and despite his checkered work history and willingness to skirt rules, nothing seemed to get him down.

"Dave, I have a couple of questions."

"Shit. Work. Okay."

"Can you help me out? Who's running the task force on Cora Stills?"

"Beats me. Not out of our shop."

"You didn't hear about it? I mean, Liz was attacked."

"Strange, now that you mention it. But no." He fell silent, then added, "Maybe the DA threw it to the FBI. Interstate stuff and trafficking is FBI."

Vic thought about it. The first thing Marioni said when Vic told him about the trafficking was how the case should go to the FBI. His heart sank. Getting anything from the FBI was as likely as time travel. He strained, wondering if Dave might have anything on Cora Stills.

"Wait. Dave, you told me in the hospital the DA wasn't going to cut any deals with Lily Bauer and Denny Halpin. He wanted a show about catching Gretchen Stall's killers."

"Right."

"Did you take statements on what they knew about the trafficking? Especially Denny? He was the one who offered it."

"No. DA didn't want to go there."

Vic frowned. A sour smell was thickening inside his car, he guessed from the dumpster. "I don't get that. The DA said he was going to file an arrest warrant for trafficking. That's why Liz was at Cora Still's house to arrest her. I'd think he'd want statements on it."

"His warrant on Cora Stills is for abduction and assault of a police officer. I read it."

Vic squeezed the steering wheel with his left hand. A nasty thought came to him. "Did he *ever* file one on Cora for trafficking?"

"Give me a minute."

The sounds of clicking from a keyboard, and Dave was back. "He had one but rescinded it."

"When was it posted?"

"Last Wednesday. Eight in the evening."

Vic stared down the alley. He didn't understand. Marioni had agreed to file the trafficking warrant when Vic visited his office at three o'clock that same day. But Norbert was saying he actually filed the warrant once he and Liz were in the hospital. The implications unspooled. If he and Liz had arrested Cora Stills that afternoon it wouldn't have held up. She would have walked.

Vic tapped his thumb on the steering wheel. "When did he delete that warrant?"

"Two hours later. Ten o'clock that night. Makes no sense."

"No, it doesn't. And then he told you not to question Denny about trafficking?"

"Not exactly. But you got to understand things have changed since I talked to you in the hospital. Now he absolutely wants deals for Denny and Lily. But only for Gretchen's murder. He gave us the rah-team speech on nailing down the evidence on Gretchen's murder, not getting distracted, keeping strictly to that case, blah blah. He didn't say don't look into trafficking, specifically, but the message was there."

Vic tried to absorb this change of direction. "Where is Denny now?"

"Still in County. Lily Bauer is there too."

"Maybe they'll talk to me. Any restrictions on visitors?"

"Let me check." More chittering from a keyboard.

29

Vic made a bet with himself.

"Only their lawyers, case investigators and prosecutors. Huh. Your name isn't on the approved visitor list."

"Nor Liz's?"

"Nope."

Vic sat back, disgusted at winning the bet.

Several moments passed until Dave said quietly, as if he didn't want anyone around him to hear, "You're going to ask me to do something I don't want to do, aren't you?"

Vic nodded to himself. "Probably."

"Can't talk you out of it?"

"You want me reminding the DA about you and Gretchen?"

Silence for a few heartbeats. "Okay. But after this we're even. Let me know when. And when you're done make sure you tell me. I'll need to take you back off the list."

"Thanks, Dave."

"Screw it. Anyway, this is your daughter we're talking about. And Marioni is an asshole."

"I'll let you know when I'm going to visit them. It's going to be soon. And I'll need to talk to both of them. Any sign Lily might confess?"

"No. She's tight-lipped. And like I said, Marioni seriously wants a deal with her."

"Like he doesn't want it going to trial?"

"Exactly. It goes to trial it comes out that Gretchen was taking bribes to throw cases. The press will run that story for months."

"And it's an election year for Marioni." The smell from the dumpster reached pungent levels. He started his car.

"Yes, it is."

"Thanks, Dave. I'll call you."

He dropped the phone on the passenger seat, drove along the alley and took the first dumpster-free parking spot he could find. He turned the conversation in his mind. It made sense the FBI would handle Cora's case. He didn't like it, but it was by-the-book. He was back on his own, about to start kicking at dirt clods the FBI had already turned. A waste of time and energy, and when he showed up to ask questions, people would be angry about doing a second interview. They'd want it over as quickly as possible. He sighed. Nothing to be done about it. Except find out where Cora Stills last worked and get on with it.

He went through his phone's address book and pressed the number for Craig in the Bureau's Tech Center. He waited as the phone rang.

"Detective Lenoski?"

"Craig, how's the basement treating you?" It was a standing joke because the Tech Center was below ground.

"You must be out of the hospital. How's Detective Timmons?"

"She's recovering. I got out last night. She's probably going to need a couple more weeks. But I need a favor. Can you keep it between us?"

"Sure." His voice lowered to a conspiratorial level. Vic liked him, not just because Craig's father was Vic's first sergeant after the police academy, the man who taught him what to look for on the street and how to keep safe. Vic appreciated that—like his father— Craig approached his job as a craft and looked past the shape of things to their meanings. It was a rare quality.

"I have a social security number for Cora Stills, the woman who burned down her house and hurt Liz. Can you run it? I'm guessing you know the SDNH?"

"The new hire directory? Sure, I've used it before. I thought it was to track down guys skipping alimony payments?"

Vic toggled his phone onto speaker. "Right, but they list where people work. I want to know Cora's last job." He recovered the photographed employee file on his phone and read out Cora's social security number.

"Cora Stills," Craig said, the distant sound of mouse clicks coming over the phone. "Didn't think you would let this go. My dad didn't either when I told him about it. Here we go." He was silent for a few moments. "Last workplace was Premium Tile and Granite in Monroeville."

"Thanks, Craig."

"Sure, no problem. When do you come back to work?"

"Maybe a week or so." As he spoke, Vic realized he wasn't looking forward to it. That feeling was new to him. Even after Dannie disappeared, when he was lost inside himself, going to work was a relief.

"We need it. Crush is screaming about closing cases. We need more people. I know I do. I've got like a three-week backlog."

"I won't keep you on the line, then. Thanks again."

"No problem, Detective Lenoski."

Vic caught the tone of respect in Craig's voice and found himself smiling as he checked the location of Premium Tile and Granite.

Chapter 7

Premium Tile and Granite sat across from a ski and snowboard shop halfway down the stretch of strip malls and fast food outlets known as Monroeville's Miracle Mile. Inside, Vic asked to speak to the manager and flipped open his badge wallet. A voice in the back of his head chided him about presenting himself on official duty while on leave, but he ignored it. The elderly woman behind the counter didn't blink. Except for the black roots, her permed blond hair was the color of straw, the skin around her eyes and on her upper cheeks crisscrossed with shallow wrinkles.

"You're a long ways from home," she said, her brown eyes locked on his ID. Her words were followed by the stale smell of cigarettes.

"You never know where life will take you."

"Ain't you the philosopher." Before he could respond she picked up a phone, pressed a button and said something about Vic to someone on the other end. After hanging up she looked him up and down. "We got a sale going on Terrazzo tile. Stuff lasts forever."

"Not remodeling right now."

"Save it for when you do. Lasts forever."

"Thanks anyway." He nodded at the phone. "Whoever you talked to coming out?"

"He probably ran out the back door." Her voice was so deadpan, for a second Vic thought she might be telling the truth.

"Happens to me a lot," he said gamely, trying to keep it light.

"Pittsburgh Police?" asked a male voice behind him. The words contained a waver, as if the speaker could think of several reasons the police might

33

need to interview him. Vic turned to a man about five feet eight who looked as if he hadn't slept in a week. It was mid-afternoon, but Vic caught a whiff of whiskey.

"Yes. I have a question about a former employee. It's related to an ongoing investigation."

The man's shoulders loosened. "Oh, sure. Cora Stills? C'mon back. I'm Jeff."

They shook hands and Vic chose to pretend he hadn't noticed the lack of a last name. He followed Jeff past displays of tile and into an office near the entrance to a warehouse stacked with slabs of granite.

The office was dominated by a desk topped with papers and bulky sample books. He tasted the dry cool of stone dust. Filing cabinets lined one wall, the other held photos of different people, the frames out of alignment and askew. In the center of the wall was an African mask, dark brown, the features twisted into a scowl.

After they took their seats, Vic pointed at the mask. "You were right. I'm here about Cora Stills. I understand she worked here?"

"For a while. Stopped coming in last week." Jeff's gaze darted to the mask and back to Vic. A frown crowded his forehead. "She gave me that. What's up?"

"She's wanted for assaulting a police officer."

"I heard. All over TV."

"So, walk me through it. When did she start working for you, when did she leave, everything in the middle."

Jeff licked his lips as if he needed a drink. "So, I hired her maybe eight months ago, but she needed a couple of months to finish her old job. Worked until last week. She was supposed to be in Tuesday, but didn't show. I called her and she asked for a sick day."

"What did she do here?"

"Commission sales. She was good to start with, then fell off. Turned out she was a discount queen."

Vic raised his eyebrows, asking for an explanation.

Jeff shrugged. "You work here three months you get a forty percent discount on merchandise. She hit three months and a day and put in a big order for herself. Top end stuff, special order from Italy. When the order arrived, she took all her earned vacation days. After she got back, she sold like one order. I figured she was about to quit. Discount queens. They take the job to get the employee discount. I get someone like that every few years."

"And you've been doing this long?"

"Twenty years."

"How big was the tile order she made?"

Jeff sank into his chair. "Beats me. I'd have to look it up." Vic waited, but Jeff made no move to check his records. Vic pushed on.

"So, she made the order, and when the tile came in, she took a vacation. As if she took the tile somewhere?"

"Yeah." Jeff spoke quickly, back on solid ground.

Vic waited, and finally asked, "So where did she go?"

"Beats me. But she talked about North Dakota, and she took like eight days off. I figured she went there."

"With the tile?"

"With the tile. She had some white van. I told her she's nuts. That product is heavy and you're gonna be buying gas every fifty miles, if you know what I mean. And she had enough to tile Heinz Field. But she took off."

"And when did she give you the mask?"

Jeff glanced at it. His face flushed. "Maybe after she'd been here a few months."

"Nice of her. And how big was the tile order? I mean what did she pay for it?"

"I said I don't remember."

"But it's written down somewhere."

Jeff shrank a bit deeper into his chair. "Well, sure. Order forms, that kind of thing." He looked everywhere but at Vic.

Vic tested his right shoulder, glad to feel only stiffness and no real pain. "Okay, Jeff, this is how it's going to go. I know that mask hanging on the wall is valuable. I would hate to think she gave you that mask in exchange for the tile, because that would mean the state lost a nice chunk of sales tax. The easiest way to put my mind at rest is for you to give me an inventory list of the tile she bought. Then I know there's a paper trail. When that happens, I won't worry about the payment details. We on the same page?"

Jeff hopped out of the chair and disappeared toward the front of the store. "I'll get it," floated in his wake. Vic took out his phone and snapped a couple of photos of the mask, from different angles. He slid open the drawers to Jeff's desk. Despite the piles on top of the desk the drawers were empty, except the deep lower right drawer, which held several bottles of cheap whiskey. The bottles set off a memory and disgust rose in his throat. He closed the drawer and retook his seat. A few moments later Jeff appeared and handed him a Xeroxed copy of an order. Vic glanced over it.

"You need to explain this to me. It's just numbers and stuff."

"Easier if I show you."

Vic followed him into the showroom where Jeff pointed out three different types of tile, explaining how the blue painted one was decorative, the tan-colored was for flooring, a third for a backsplash. Vic photographed each one. When they finished, they were standing at the front of the store, near the doors. Vic knew that wasn't an accident.

"One last question," Vic said. "The white van. How was it tagged?"

Jeff frowned. "What do you mean?"

"Did you see the license plate? What state was it from?"

"Beats me. She came into my office and said she was going to load up. That was it. I let her do it."

"Texas."

Vic turned. The blond woman was leaning against the counter, her arms folded. "I was outside on smoke break when they pulled up. Her and some guy."

Vic crossed to her. "Texas?"

"We don't have front plates on our cars, so you notice when a car has one. It was Texas."

"And the guy?"

She shrugged. "I didn't get a good look at him. Tall, blue jeans. Some kind of cowboy shirt. You know, they have those points on the chest at the front? Snap buttons and stuff? But he was from here."

"How do you know?"

"How he talked. He might live in Texas now, but he was born here. Said the van needs *warshed*, that kind of thing. Not a real heavy accent, but it was there."

Vic stared at her. "You didn't hear a name, did you?"

She shook her head. "No. They just gave me shit about smoking. Which pissed me off. Cora was a pain to work with, she was always acting like she had a plan and the rest of us were losers. Attitude. She had attitude. But with Jeff she was always smiling and sticking her boobies out."

"Hey," Jeff said.

"Tell me it ain't true." She fell silent, as if she realized she might have overstepped.

Vic thought about what he'd learned. "Anything else? Anything at all. Was the van new or old? Do you remember the make? Maybe the license plate number?"

"Oh right. I have a photographic memory." She caught herself just before she rolled her eyes. "But it was one of those Dodge delivery vans. It looked pretty new; I just don't know what year."

Vic nodded to her. "That's very helpful, thanks."

She straightened and dropped her arms. "She really tried to kill a police officer?"

"Yes, my partner."

Her eyes widened. "You're the one who got her out? Paper said her partner got her out."

"It would have been better if I got there sooner."

"Still." She smiled, and Vic was surprised at the warmth in her eyes.

Vic placed his business card on the counter. "Thanks again. If you think of anything else about that guy or the van, call me on my cell."

"Sure thing."

"Sure thing," Jeff echoed, holding the door open for him. He avoided Vic's eyes.

Outside, Vic turned back before Jeff could close the door. "Hey, thanks for not giving me grief about talking to me after the FBI took you through it."

Jeff frowned. "FBI? What are you talking about?"

Vic stopped in the parking lot, halfway to his car.

"The FBI didn't interview you about her? Has anyone?"

Jeff shook his head. "You're the first."

Back in his car, before starting the engine, he wondered how it was possible no one had interviewed Cora's coworkers.

Family and coworkers were the start of an investigation, usually.

Chapter 8

Driving toward Pittsburgh, Vic considered texting Skiv a photo of the African mask in Jeff's office, but he couldn't stop thinking about the FBI and their disappearing act. He didn't understand it. He considered asking Crush, but after Crush suspended Vic on trumped-up charges, they'd settled into a kind of polite neglect. When they had to talk, Liz mediated, which was out of the question now. In truth, he was in no hurry to fix that particular problem. He liked the distance they kept from one another.

As he inched along in the rush hour traffic toward the Squirrel Hill tunnels, he dug out his cell phone and pressed the number for Dave Norbert in the DA's office. The call went to voicemail. He started a terse voice message, but his phone rang before he could finish.

"Dave?" he asked, taking the call.

"Sorry, I was in a meeting. I had to step out."

"I'm thinking I'll visit Lily and Denny tomorrow morning. Can you put me on the call list at nine? I think they do male visits first, women afterwards. If I time it right, I can do them back to back."

"Sure."

"Something else. Are you sure the FBI is investigating Cora Stills? I just visited her last workplace, and no one's been there."

"After we talked, I asked around. Turns out it's you guys, not the FBI. Word is Marioni told Crush to do it, it was his detective, blah, blah."

Vic was silent a moment. Crush wanting to run the case made sense. Liz reported to him. But if Crush was running the investigation, someone would have interviewed Cora's coworkers by now. Crush was pedantic and political, but his investigations were thorough. He had the documents on his dining room wall to prove it.

"How the hell did Crush get that nickname?" Dave asked suddenly.

The tunnels were about half a mile ahead. Vic inched another few feet closer. Distracted, he said, "Goes back to one of his early staff meetings. You know he's a health nut?"

"One look at him says that."

"He eats healthy, works out, but he's one of those guys can't keep still. Not comfortable in his own skin. Always needs something to play with. So, he shows up at a staff meeting and he's got this orange. He's playing with it as we go around the table. Some point he gets mad, he starts shouting what a bunch of useless assholes we are and slams his fist on the table. Forgot he was holding the orange. Pieces went all over, he had a chunk sitting on top of his head. Done. We called him Orange Crush for about a week and then it was Crush."

Dave chuckled into the phone. "Suits him."

Vic tried to blink away the oddity of Crush running the task force, but he thought that might give him a better chance to get information. "So, you good for tomorrow morning?"

"Yep. Not a problem. Text me when you're done so I can take you off the list. In case Marioni checks. You know DAs."

"I do. And where is the case? I mean where are you guys with Denny and Lily Bauer? It would help when I talk to them."

Dave hesitated before launching into a minute-long update. Vic listened carefully, but it sounded like a stalemate. The DA had made a couple of early plea deal offers, but neither had bitten yet.

"Thanks, Dave," Vic said when Dave finished. He felt alive inside. If neither of them had cut a deal, he had a chance.

"Just make sure you text me when you're finished."

When Vic ended the call, the tunnel opening was still a quarter mile away. The driver in front of him was shouting into his phone. His original problem was back. He needed a way inside the task force, and in a hurry. He checked the time and pressed the number for Craig in the Tech Department. At least Craig could access the case-file software and find the name of the lead investigator. But when Craig answered a deafening roar of conversation came over the phone.

"Craig?"

"Yes, can you wait a second?"

A moment passed and Vic passed into the tunnel. Suddenly the din of conversation disappeared like a candle put out. "Sorry, Mr. Lenoski, I'm at a restaurant."

"That's what you guys call bars now?" Vic kidded him. The last case he worked, Craig was routinely at his work bench until midnight.

"Kind of. I got asked."

Vic grinned as the gap between him and the car in front widened. The last few times he visited Craig, Eva, Crush's new administrative assistant, was with him.

"Say hello to Eva for me," Vic said.

"Yes, sir." He sounded like a kid caught stealing candy.

"I won't keep you. I'm trying to track down who's running the Cora Stills task force."

After a pause Craig said, "I don't know. I haven't seen it on the case file list." He hesitated and Vic heard a truck rumble through the phone. He realized Craig had walked outside to avoid the restaurant noise. "You know what, though? Eva might know. I'll ask her."

Before Vic could say anything, the noise thundered back. As Vic waited, he popped out of the tunnel into a bright sunset. The traffic was running at fifty miles an hour, and he realized he had missed his exit. He was headed home, not to the office. He hadn't needed to go through the tunnel at all.

"Detective Lenoski?" It was Eva's voice.

The background noise dropped.

"Yes, how are you?"

"I'm glad you're out of the hospital, Detective Lenoski." Vic heard a slight affectation to her voice as if she felt the need to speak formally.

"Me too," he said warmly, trying to soften her a bit.

"Craig told me what you're asking." Her voice dropped to just above a whisper. "I know Detective Timmons is your partner and I thought you should know. I sit right outside Crush's office? He had a big argument. He was really mad. I thought I should tell you."

Something tightened in Vic's chest. "Okay, what happened?"

"The DA called him. I know because I took the call and connected them. It started quiet but I never heard Crush get so mad. I mean he was shouting. Anyway, after the call he closed his door for like half an hour. He was that angry. And then he called Kevin in. Closed the door. And Kevin is doing the investigation into Cora Stills."

"What?" Vic swerved and brought his car back into his lane. "Kevin couldn't detect ketchup on a hamburger. It should be Doug or Amy. One of the guys who've done this a million times."

"I thought so, too."

"I mean Liz was almost killed. She almost died. She won't work for weeks. And he put Kevin in charge?" Vic guided his car onto the downtown exit beside the county jail. He made himself unclench the steering wheel. "Who's helping him? Tell me he put someone good on it as well. A team."

"No, that's the thing. That's what Crush was so mad about on the phone. He wanted to pick the investigator, put a team together."

"The DA *made* Crush pick Kevin?" Vic jammed the brakes at the exit ramp's stop sign.

"I don't know if he said Kevin exactly. But Crush was shouting this wasn't the case for an inexperienced detective. Like the DA wanted someone new to the job."

Vic closed his eyes and opened them. Behind him a car honked. He pulled away and guided the car into a nearby gravel lot underneath an overpass. He didn't bother to shift the transmission into park; it was too complicated to reach over with his left arm.

"Anyway," Eva said, "the detectives keep stopping by to ask who's leading the investigation, they want to be on the team. They thought a bunch of them would be involved. I mean everyone wants to help. But Crush said Kevin only."

Vic breathed through his nose, his heart thumping. "Okay, Eva. Thanks." She was helping him and he needed to appreciate that, not get angry at her. He forced his voice back to normal. "Thank you for telling me this. You should get back to Craig. You guys enjoy yourselves."

"Are you going to do something? I mean someone has to."

Vic steadied himself. Eva might be right out of college—and new to the department—but her instincts were good. "I am. I just don't know what."

"Sure, Detective Lenoski. Craig says I should trust you. I told Craig about it, and he wanted me to tell you."

Vic blinked, wanting to end the call without being rude. "You did the right thing, Eva. Thanks again." He pressed the disconnect button before she could say anything more. Cars whizzed by. It was dim underneath the overpass.

Kevin, he raged. The last remaining member of Crush's *New Techniques Team*, as he called them. Guys right out of college, put on cold cases and moved to detective desks without the minimum five-year patrol stint, all because of unspecified college-taught modern investigative techniques. The only skill he'd seen Kevin employ was reporting back to Crush everything Vic and Liz did.

There was nothing modern about being a snitch.

He cleared his mind and waited for his breath and heartbeat to slow.

Just like Crush, he thought. He'll work like hell on an investigation, turn every stone he finds, but he caves in a second to anyone he thinks will help his career.

His detectives and everyone working for him be damned.

Chapter 9

The next morning, Vic found a parking spot in the same gravel lot as the day before. He walked the hundred yards to the front door of the county jail, minimizing the swing of his right arm. After working out, he had decided to again forego the sling, and so far, apart from a cobwebby stiffness, his shoulder felt strong.

At the thick bulletproof glass inside the door, he showed his ID and was passed through the metal detectors. A few minutes later he was led to a room with a line of booths. He sat down to a reinforced glass window and a black telephone hanging from a cradle. He waited, listening to the murmur of voices. The room was unnaturally bright from the overhead fluorescent lights. When he angled his head, smudged palm and fingerprints showed up on the glass. He wondered idly when the glass and phone were last cleaned.

A few minutes later a guard led Denny Halpin into the room on the other side of the glass. Vic studied him as he was directed to his seat. Denny had agreed to meet, and that suggested he was desperate. Nothing in his looks changed Vic's opinion. Vic had decided when they first met that Denny was insecure; someone who blustered and postured as a defense mechanism. Now, gaunt in his orange jumpsuit, his gaze darted nervously along the backs of the prisoners seated at other booths. He walked with a shuffle and slouch, as if trying to stay invisible.

Denny eased himself into his seat, adjusting to the straight back and the way the chair was bolted to the floor. Vic unhooked the phone and held it up. Denny was so slow to understand that he wondered if he was Denny's first visitor.

Denny gently placed his own handset over his ear and near his mouth.

"Hey, Denny. How you holding up?"

"How the hell do you think? It sucks in here." His voice was an angry rasp.

Vic chose not to point out that Denny was in jail because of his own decisions and as accessory to the murder of Gretchen Stoll.

"I asked you for a deal," Denny said. Vic heard a small boy's whine in it.

"And I told you then. I can't make a deal. That's up to the DA. But they've offered you one, right?"

"My lawyer says I'm looking at ten to fifteen years! In here!" Desperation ran his words together.

"They'll send you to Somerset or somewhere like that. Chance of parole sooner."

"Right, like that's goin' to happen."

Vic strained his mind for a way to bring the conversation around. "I wanted to thank you for what you told me about Cora Stills. You know we almost got her?"

"I heard she screwed up a cop."

"She did. My partner." Vic rested his right forearm on the narrow shelf in front of the window, taking some of the pressure off his shoulder. "We'll get her. But I'm hoping you can help me with some information. About the women you kept in your barn?"

Denny sat back as best he could against the rigid back of the chair. "If I do, how does that help me?"

Vic waited. The way Denny phrased the question made it sound as if he had more to say. He knew that without anything to offer, there were only two ways to get him talking. He decided to try the least likely approach first and use it as a stepping stone to the second.

"Denny, I said I can't make a deal. I've said that from the beginning. I'm just looking for help. My daughter was one of the four women in your barn. She's gone. My wife and I are lost without her. I want to find out what happened to her."

Denny picked a spot about a foot above Vic's head and stared at it. He clasped his right shoulder with his left hand and Vic saw how Lily's bullet wound pained him. Despite that he jutted out his chin. Sympathy wasn't going to work. Vic shifted to the second approach.

"I hear they've told Lily she can get a plea deal, but so far she isn't talking."

Denny blinked. "So what? They talked about a deal with me as well. I'm thinking on it."

"You planning to counteroffer?"

His mouth moved but he caught himself before talking.

Vic pressed. "A good lawyer should be able to sweeten the deal."

"My lawyer said I'll only get one offer." Denny glanced at him, looking for confirmation.

"Maybe. But it doesn't stop you from making a counteroffer."

Denny shifted in the immovable chair. "Your daughter was the blond one, right?"

"Yes." Vic waited.

"She was okay. She helped the red haired one. That one was a mess. Wanted to see her daughter. But that Asian chick. She messed up one of the guys came to take them away."

"Tell me about it." Vic's heart thudded in his chest and he strained to keep his voice even. Just two guys shooting the shit.

Denny leaned closer to the glass, his knuckles white around the phone. His gaze was desperate. "What do I get out of it?"

"I've only got one thing I can give you."

"What?" Denny hissed.

"What I've been doing all along. I won't lie to you. You need someone to trust. Your lawyer will want you to take a plea, he wants this over more than you do. But I understand how the system works. You need that right now, Denny. You need someone who doesn't pull punches with you. It's the only way you get through this."

"I want out of here."

"Denny, you're a party to murder. You were in Gretchen Stoll's house. You drove the car. That makes you an accessory. End of story. I can't change the facts."

"What if Lily says I did it?" he hissed. "Puts it on me?"

Vic knew that was the bottom of it. That was Denny's fear. Denny lived every day waiting to hear that Lily's testimony made him the killer. Tagged him as the one who tied Gretchen Stoll down. The one who put a match to the gasoline-soaked bedroom carpet.

It might even be true, something the DA didn't seem to care about.

"Get in first, Denny. That's my advice. Make a statement. Ask to do it under oath. Tell them you'll take a lie detector test. Put it all out there. Insist on it. And don't lie about a thing, or they'll find it and throw out your testimony."

"And screw myself?"

"The first person to give a statement is always more believable. Offering to do it under oath and with a lie detector tells them you're not lying. The last thing you want to do is try to clear your name after Lily accuses you. You won't have a chance. Look, your version fits the facts better. Lily spent most of the day with Gretchen Stoll. You didn't. Find a witness who can say you came to the game late. Make the point that Lily shot you because she couldn't let you live as a witness. Your story holds together. Better than hers. And when you've done that ask for a better deal."

"It's not a story."

"Just keep saying that. Keep saying it's the truth. I can't describe it, Denny, but when I hear people tell me what they've done, true stories always sound right. Things fit. That's what you've got going for you. Use it."

Denny angled his face downward. His eyes brimmed with tears but somehow, he held them back. "You'll come to see me?" His voice quavered.

"Regularly. Until your plea deal is signed. And I won't lie to you, Denny. You can count on me to tell you everything straight. Which you won't get from your lawyer and the DAs office. They're gonna try to manage you. They want this over and buried."

Denny pressed back in his chair but the metal wouldn't move, trapping him upright. "Okay. I see what you're saying."

Vic kept his face blank. He didn't feel like he'd won. He felt like a cheat, taking Denny for everything he had. Screwing him. The moment Denny gave testimony it would last forever. Jail was just the start. He didn't think

Lily would try to pin the murder on him. From everything he'd seen, Lily was too smart and tough to go that route. She'd know it would come across as desperate. It was more likely she would force the defense to prove their case at trial. And if the prosecutor tried to use Denny's testimony to convict her, he was sure that Lily's defense would be that Denny was lying, in revenge for being shot.

He felt dirty.

"Denny," Vic heard himself say. "What else do you have on the four women?"

Denny rubbed his free hand over his face as if he was trying to get his mind to change direction. "Not much else. I was so pissed when Lily told me she had the women out there, I hardly talked to her."

"How long were they there?"

"Four days, maybe. Then some guys came and took them."

"Tell me about that."

Denny shifted in his seat. "They showed up late on the fourth day. They stayed the night at some hotel nearby, took them the next morning."

"How did they take them?"

"White van."

Vic forced himself to breathe. "Okay. Let's start there. Did you see the tags on the van?"

"Sure. Texas. Don't ask me the plate number. I have no idea."

"That's fine. Now tell me about the guys. And you said the Asian woman—her name is Susan Kim—messed one of them up?"

Denny hesitated, his eyes inward. "The one guy was tall, wore some beat-up cowboy hat. Like one of those straw ones? Had a huge belt buckle and cowboy boots. The other guy was short and real stocky. Mexican, looked like. Black hair, brown eyes. He had cowboy boots, too."

"Catch any names?"

"No. Like I said, I stayed away from them. They looked like guys would mess you up."

"Did the tall guy have a Pittsburgh accent?"

Denny frowned. "Beats me. I never talked to him."

Vic nodded, encouraging him.

"Yeah, so, that night after they go to the motel they come back to the house. The tall guy, he's inside talking to Lily. He wants some kind of supplies and I think he was paying her. They're downstairs. The short guy, he goes out to the barn. About fifteen minutes later he staggers back, I saw him from the upstairs window. I went downstairs to see what was up. His nose is broken, blood all over his shirt, he can't move his wrist. Turns out he decided to give the Asian woman a go. Try her out, he said. Lily had handcuffed them inside this storm fence cage I had inside the barn, place I used to keep generators and equipment I didn't want stolen. I guess he figured no problem, small woman, he'd uncuff and do her right there, in front of the others. Soon as he turned the key on her cuffs, she lit into him. Worked him over before he got a punch in and backed her off enough to get out of the cage. The tall guy had to go in and lock her back up. Lily said it took a gun to settle her down." Denny stopped talking and shrugged.

"Susan Kim knows Tai Kwon Do. She's a fifth-degree black belt. Her brother told me."

A small smile crept over Denny's face. His chest heaved a couple of times as if that was the funniest news he'd heard in months. "That's good. That guy was an asshole, one of those cocky guys always wants to make up for how short he is."

"Did he go to the hospital?"

"No. He wanted to, but the tall one said no way. He didn't want anyone to know they were in town. Told him he'd have to gut it out home."

"Did he say where home was?"

Denny squinted, thinking. "He said some town, but I don't remember it. I'd never heard it before."

"Keep thinking about that, in case you remember."

Denny shrugged an okay.

"Anything else?" Vic asked.

"Not really. They left the next morning. Put the girls in the back of the van, handcuffed them in there on some mattresses and took off. That was it."

"Did Lily talk about them after that?"

"No. She knew I was pissed. That we'd argue. She didn't bring it up."

"Okay, Denny. That's helpful. Think about everything you said. Next time I stop by, if you think of anything more, let me know. Doesn't matter how small it is. Everything helps."

He tried to straighten his shoulders. "When do you think you'll come next time?"

Vic didn't know. "Just depends how things go, but I'll be here once a week at least, okay?"

Denny nodded.

"Take care of yourself. Remember what I said."

Carefully, Vic hung up the handset. It took Denny a moment to do the same, as if he was listening for someone else on the line, anyone. He raised his arm and a guard crossed to him. Vic watched as he was led away. The pool of disgust in Vic's stomach stayed with him.

Chapter 10

While Vic and Denny talked, the room had emptied out. It was refilling now with visitors for the female inmates. Vic watched the last of the male inmates file out. He guessed he had another fifteen minutes before the women were shown in. Everyone was waiting, the room rustling with low conversations punctuated by the sharp scrape of chair legs on linoleum. Vic sensed an unusual intensity underlying the sounds, as if everyone wanted to stay silent and shout out at the same time. He wondered if Lily Bauer would meet with him. The last time he saw her, he had tried to bulldoze her into giving him more information on Cora Stills, but she had stood up to him.

Despite that, he bet she would want to meet.

She hadn't given a statement yet, and he liked the idea that she would make the DA's office prove its case. The only way the DA could counter that strategy was by limiting her information. They needed her imagination to take over, to work on her, to force her to lose perspective and nerve. If she broke, she would take a plea deal. But Lily was tough. He guessed she knew what the DA was doing. Her best way to fight was to glean information wherever she could find it.

From someone like him.

He waited, working his injured shoulder slowly. The movement was already smoother, the stiffness and pricks of pain pushed to the corners. He guessed another day and he could start working out on his speed bag.

A guard led Lily into the room on the other side of the glass. Her head was high, her eyes alert. She'd pulled her hair back into a pony tail. Without

51

makeup, Vic thought that her skin was rougher, the vertical crease from the bridge of her nose into her forehead presenting a hard look of anger. The baggy orange jumpsuit hid her figure.

She sat across from Vic, never breaking eye contact. Vic lifted the telephone receiver and she did as well, but was faster to speak than he was.

"So. The Polish Prick."

Vic let a smile break his lips. Part of his earlier attempt to bulldoze her was to force her to call him that, but she'd hung tough and given him nothing.

"Yes it is. How are you doing, Lily?"

"Wondering why the hell you would want to talk to me."

Vic sat back. "You know why. Your friend, Cora Stills."

Lily smiled. They were close enough now that Vic saw scarring on her cheeks, as if she once had acne. He guessed that normally she covered it with makeup.

Lily shifted her hand downward on the telephone receiver. "I heard she messed up your partner."

"And I have no idea where to find her."

"Good luck with that." She smirked.

Vic knew what she meant. The last thing Lily needed was for Cora to be arrested. If Cora admitted to trafficking the four women, it gave the DA's office leverage on Lily.

Vic switched tactics. "I know you don't want her found. That just means more trouble for you. I get that. Honestly, I don't much care if she's arrested. I just want to find my daughter."

"You want sympathy? While my son sits in jail because of a crooked public defender? Nice try."

"Sure. But if I find Cora first, I could offer her a deal. Just between her and me. She tells me what happened to my daughter, I forget to arrest her."

Lily's gaze exploded in merriment, and she looked at the ceiling. "Honey, you couldn't lie your way into an R movie."

Vic wasn't surprised she saw right through his statement. "I thought you might need some entertainment right about now."

She lowered her face to him. "I do. But I also saw Denny on his way out of here. You talked to him as well."

"I did."

She frowned in concern. "Is he doing okay? I worry about him."

Vic didn't believe her for an instant. "And you couldn't act your way into an elementary school play. You don't give a shit about Denny. Last time you saw him your shot him."

They locked eyes and finally a small smile moved the corners of her mouth. "I guess we understand one another. So why are you here?"

"I'll start with a question about Cora. Did she ever talk about the DA? Did she know the guy?"

"Marioni?" Her gaze turned inward for a second. "She never said anything to me about it. Why?"

"Just trying to figure stuff out. Cora lost her job because she ran a lot of private parties using the women from Bare Essentials. Her boss told me that. I'm thinking that she might have met a lot of guys in her travels. Maybe even the DA." Vic wasn't about to tell her that Marioni might have warned Cora about her arrest warrant. He also didn't want Lily to figure it out, but if that was what it took, he might go there.

"Beats me. Like I said, she never mentioned it, and I worked a couple of her events. I didn't like them. Guys expect a different level of shit at those private parties. Some girls don't care. I do."

"But you had no problem climbing into bed with Gretchen Stoll. When she asked."

Lily stiffened. "I'm not talking about anything like that. If it even happened."

Something clicked in Vic's mind. He leaned forward. "Sorry, just thinking, those private parties, did Cora have a guy work security?"

Lily didn't move for a moment. "You do need someone," she said finally.

Something warmed in Vic. "Same guy?"

Lily shook her head. "Nah. She used whatever bouncer was free from the club. Paid them cash. I worked three of those events. We had a different guy each time."

"You needed the money."

"Why else would I do it?"

Vic nodded, trying to form something from what she was saying. He knew Gretchen Stoll asked Lily to sleep with her for a lighter sentence for her son. He'd worked that out earlier. "Wait a minute." His breath turned short. "You told me Gretchen never asked you for money to free her son. I believed you."

Lily stayed silent, but a smirk rose into her eyes.

Vic smacked his fist on the shelf. "You lied to me."

"Maybe I'm a better liar than actor. Maybe."

"She did ask you for money." A new narrative formed in his mind. His stomach tightened. "That's why you trafficked the women." He could barely get the words out. "You needed money to pay Gretchen Stoll. I bet you didn't raise enough, so you offered to sleep with her. That's why it didn't happen until after your son was convicted. First, she wanted money, and you tried to raise it by trafficking. You got Cora to help. She had the connections. But you didn't get the money fast enough, or Gretchen wanted more, so you offered to sleep with her. Or she added the bedroom requirement after you paid her."

Lily sat back as best she could against the chair. "Do you really think I'm gonna say anything?"

"No. But the timeline works. It's the first thing I can understand about all of this."

They watched one another. Vic took a quick breath. "How about if I give you a piece of advice. If you think it makes sense, you tell me if that's what happened."

"Look, Lenoski, I'm not admitting a god-damned thing."

"Hear me out. I'm gonna give you some advice." Vic swallowed. "You and I both know what you're doing. You aren't going to give an inch to the DA until you find out how strong his case is. You'll learn that in discovery."

Lily crossed her arms, watching him.

"You're going to find it's a tight case. Maybe not a slam dunk, but good enough to hurt you. But there's a witness who knows more than you think they do. That's what'll kill you."

"Sure. Denny."

"Nope. Someone else." It was a lie, but he wanted to plant a seed of doubt. He drove the index finger of his hand onto the shelf a couple of times for emphasis. "But keep this in mind. The DA needs a plea deal more than you do. Whatever he offers, I bet a gag order is part of it. That's how you'll know. He wants to say he solved the death of a public defender, but he also wants to keep all of Gretchen Stoll's bullshit out of the press. How she sold sentences, screwed the people who couldn't pay, like your son. He wants all that to go away. It's an election year. Putting you in jail is just plan B. So here's my advice. When he offers a deal, say no and insist on going to trial. Keep saying it. Line up someone from the papers. You'll scare him to death, and in the end, he'll offer a deal you can live with. Like taking a second look at your son's sentencing and reducing it to time served. You understand me?"

Lily's gaze was unwavering. "This is some pretty weird advice coming from a cop."

"Right now, my plan A is finding out what happened to my daughter. Plan B is being a cop."

Lily raised and lowered the handset like it was a lever attached to her ear. "I don't know where Cora is."

"I want to believe you. Not sure I do."

She shrugged. "I don't know. That's a fact. But I get what you're telling me. And I get that you want to find your daughter." She broke her gaze from him and glanced down at the corner of the window. A moment later she said, "Remember my ex? The asshole who knocked me up and then took off for a fracking job? About five years later the fracking company moved him to North Dakota. He's still there."

Vic's muscles were so tight for a moment he couldn't move.

"What was his name?"

"That's all I'm saying." She licked her lips. "Asshole didn't come up with a dime to get our son out of jail."

For a second, Vic thought that she was going to apologize about Dannie, to say she was sorry it was his daughter. Instead, she loosened her hand on the handset.

"Take it easy, you Polish Prick." Her voice was warm. She hung up and motioned to the guard. Without a glance at Vic, she stood and waited for the guard to instruct her what to do.

Slowly, his mind feverish, Vic hung up. He left the room and followed the center white line down the hallway to the front of the prison. Inside his car he texted Dave to take him off the visitor's list. He rested his head on the car's headrest.

He was angry he hadn't thought about Lily's ex. Of course she would have called him for money when their son was arrested. She'd given him the next link in the chain, but he should have figured it out himself. And he hadn't.

He pursed his lips. Despite what Lily had done to him, done to Anne and their marriage, he could begrudge her a hair of respect. She was tough, and he guessed she was strong enough to hold out for her son's release as part of her plea deal.

He breathed, a feeling overcoming him. It was the same feeling he had when he saw Liz in the hospital, how he felt like he had crossed to a new place and lost his way back. It had happened in that room with the rustling conversations and Lily sitting on the other side of the glass. He knew why. He didn't know the exact law, but his discussion with Denny—and his advice to Lily—were more than enough to get him fired, perhaps arrested. If it ever got out, his days as a cop were over.

Forever.

He closed his eyes and steadied his breathing. Cars whisked by. He sensed the grey of the sky underneath his closed eyelids. It felt wide, high, and as hard as iron.

Chapter 11

Vic called Anne to update her, but only got voice mail. She didn't call him back until just after four o'clock. She agreed to meet him at a restaurant at seven, her voice over the telephone efficient and quick in a way he hadn't heard since he first met her, before she left her job to raise Dannie.

"You're lucky there's no game tonight," she told him. "Otherwise I'd be here until midnight."

"I appreciate that," he answered, annoyed at how little the sentence sounded like something he would say. His words felt filtered through some new formality between them.

Anne arrived half an hour late. Vic had chosen an Italian restaurant in the Strip District, knowing it was near her offices at the arena. When she sat down, she eyed his empty soup bowl.

"Italian wedding soup?"

"Yep." He purposely didn't mention how late she was, or that his annoyance about it meant he barely tasted the soup.

She sat back and let out a sigh. "Do you mind if I have a glass of wine?"

"No. I'm good. Go ahead." He gestured at his glass of water. His annoyance softened. From her tone he knew she asked the question out of respect, not as a test to see if he'd fallen off the wagon. She genuinely wanted to follow his lead about ordering liquor. He appreciated that.

They ordered and he asked about her job. She talked about her work for the city's pro hockey team, and as the wine warmed her, she told him about her new colleagues and the things she was required to do. He listened, unable to shake the feeling the meal felt like a date. They were still married, and Anne had never used the word divorce, but the feeling of being on a date lingered. He didn't like it.

As they finished their entrees, Anne followed a pause in the conversation with a guarded look. "Vic, I'm doing all the talking. Why did you want to meet?"

Vic pushed the last of his pasta around the plate and put down his fork. "A couple of things have come together about Dannie. I wanted to tell you."

She carefully placed her own fork on her plate, the last of her chicken parmigiana unfinished. Vic knew from the way her lips tightened that she was preparing herself.

"Okay."

"I've interviewed some people over the last few days, and Levon set me up with someone he knows in the military. I've got a direction."

"What does that mean?"

"You know Cora Stills is at the center of it. It turns out her mother lives in North Dakota, and Cora grew up there. And I have another lead from North Dakota, it involves the people who might have transported Dannie." He didn't remember if he had used the word 'traffick' with Anne, but he knew he didn't want to start.

Anne's shoulders tensed. "What do you know about this person in North Dakota?"

Vic tried to keep the conversation level. "There's a guy named Kent Bauer who grew up in Western Pennsylvania. Years ago, he married Lily Bauer and they had a son. Lily was the one who helped Cora Stills kidnap Dannie and the other women. Right now, Lily's in jail for killing Gretchen Stoll, our public defender, and her son's in jail for drug dealing. Lily believes Gretchen purposely let her son go to jail. Kent, he moved to North Dakota years ago and didn't help Lily raise their son. I spent some time tracking him down this afternoon. I've got an address for him, the same for Cora's mother."

"But, is this Kent guy really involved?"

Vic thought of Lily saying that Kent never sent any money when his son was arrested, leaving Lily to traffick women to raise cash and sleep with Gretchen Stoll to perhaps shorten her son's sentence. Perhaps, just perhaps, it was only a grudge that led Lily to mention him, but he guessed it was deeper than that. Vic was sure Kent was connected to the trafficking somehow. He had to believe that Lily pointed her finger at him for more than just revenge. "I'm sure of it. Or at least he knows something about it. And who knows, maybe Cora was stupid enough to contact her mother. That's an interview worth doing."

"Then you have to go. Do you have the money? I'm guessing the department won't pay for it."

"I'll figure it out."

"When will you go?"

"As soon as I can." Saying the words made him realize how little he knew about North Dakota, how alone he would be.

As if reading his mind, she asked, "Do you know anyone out there?"

"No." He grabbed at straws. "I'll talk to the local cops. I can't start interviewing people without them knowing. I might get some help from them." As he said the words, he knew the chance was tiny. He wasn't likely to help someone who showed up in Pittsburgh on a private case. He was sure the detectives in the Dakotas would feel the same way.

Anne pushed the last of her food around her plate. She'd stopped listening. Vic sensed she wanted to tell him something, and was debating whether this was the right time.

"Is there something else?" he asked carefully. He guessed it was a topic he didn't want to face, but he knew he needed to.

She raised her eyes to him. "Vic, what do you want from this? I mean when all this is over? You understand we can never be the way we were."

Vic heard the depth in her voice and saw the focus in her gaze. They were something that never existed in their early years of marriage. From that time, what he remembered was her lightness, the ease in how she accepted her life, the way she laughed and was excited about the smallest things. But this last year, she'd developed a gravity, a kind of sober strength, as if her emotions had toughened into muscle. He liked it, but he also knew its meaning. Her expectations of him would change and her new job would accelerate that process, changing her perspective and suggesting new ways she could live her life. He wondered if that new version of her future might not include him.

"Yes. I understand that." He breathed through his nose so his lungs were empty and he was starting from bottom. "I'd like to find a new way for us, but I don't know what it is. That's a large part of why I want to uncover what happened to Dannie. I agree with you. We both need to know. Honestly, I don't think we can find a way to be together until that's done. When we get to that point, I think we can see what that means to each of us, and to us together. Does that make sense?"

She watched him for a few moments. "It does." She glanced at her plate. "In a logical way. But I guess you answered the most important question. You know it can't work the way it did."

"I do. I also think that what happened to Dannie is something we'll never get over. But you can be sure about one thing…if I do discover what happened to her, I'll still want to find a way to make it work with you. To try, at least."

She drank the last of her wine. "Then go get us to that point." She leaned toward him. "But I can't make any promises, Vic. That's a fact."

He pushed his water glass an inch away, more for something to do. "Is that why you took the photos of Dannie from the windowsill?"

"No. There were two reasons for that." She answered so quickly, he knew she'd expected the question.

Vic waited, watching her as she glanced about the restaurant.

Her gaze settled on him. "The fact is I don't have all of those photos. I wanted to make copies. I'll give them back when it's done."

"And?"

She blinked, as if committing to something she'd thought about but had yet to say out loud. "You're finished with what's in our dining room. Everything you hung on the wall needs to come down. It isn't just about Dannie any more. It's about Dannie and the three women who went with her. Those three women were shortchanged when they disappeared. No one really searched for them. You saw the difference in follow-up between them and

Dannie. They're owed something as well. Their families certainly are."

Vic saw the way she held herself erect as she spoke. The iron in it. She wouldn't duck from it. He thought about telling her how he'd found a job for Chrissie Stutz's mother. How he set a parole officer chasing Carroll Vinney's abusive stepfather. But that wasn't what she meant, although it showed they thought along the same lines.

"I agree," he said, quietly.

Chapter 12

At home, Vic sat in the dining room with the lights off, the documents on the wall pale, almost glowing in the ambient light from the kitchen. He swirled a single shot of whiskey in the bottom of a water glass, steadied it and sipped. He'd bought a pint bottle on the way home and was surprised he didn't like the taste, given how easily it went down several months earlier. He was glad he didn't. Glad this pint was an exception. As the liquor warmed his stomach, he drank off the glass and rose. Carefully, one at a time, he removed the documents from the wall. He kept them categorized. Witness statements in one pile, timeline documents in another, interview summaries in a third. He ended with seven piles. In the basement he scrounged a cardboard box, clipped each pile together and packed them so they would be easy to recover and search.

He took his glass into the kitchen, poured another meager shot and returned to the dining room. He sat behind the empty card table and stared at the only things still hanging on the wall: the photographs of the three missing women.

He repeated their names out loud, aware how the silence of the house rushed in after each word.

The whiskey smudged the room's corners. He thought of Anne sitting across the table from him at dinner, her happiness as she talked about her new job. The good and the bad. For her, the job was a new good. A chance for something positive. At the same time, he was the walking embodiment of the bad. He knew that. The living, breathing reminder of their life together with Dannie.

He couldn't see a way to become a good for her. He saw no way to squeeze the bad so hard that it became a good.

He shrugged back the last of the whiskey. Stared at the photographs of the missing women.

His phone's shrill ring filled the empty house. He blinked and looked at the time. Almost midnight. Levon's name headlined the screen. He slid the button to accept the call.

"Did I wake you up?" Levon's voice was gruff.

"No. Sitting here thinking." He wanted to laugh at himself, at how pathetic he sounded, but the truth of it squelched the laugh in his throat.

If Levon caught the tone, he ignored it. "I figured you'd want to know."

Vic blinked his eyes, shaking away the funk. "What?"

"They just moved Liz out of the burn ward. She's in a step-down unit. Talking more."

"Good news."

"And she was asking about you. Wants to know where you are with Cora Stills. I figure I might be able to keep her in bed a few more days, and then she's gonna be on your doorstep. She wants that woman."

"Me and her both. And I got something." Vic struggled to sequence his thoughts.

"What?"

"Two leads. Both of them in North Dakota. Cora Stills grew up there and her mother never left. And Kent Bauer, the husband of Lily Bauer? He's out there too. So I'm going. I need a face-to-face with them."

Levon was silent. Vic stood, hoping to clear his mind.

"Wish I knew someone out there." As Levon spoke his voice turned distant, as if he was speaking from memory. "You'll need help."

"Sounds like you know someone."

"Kind of." He breathed out, releasing something more than air. "Guy from Iraq. But he's in South Dakota, I think."

"Tell him to drive up."

"He doesn't have any legs."

Vic squeezed his eyes shut against the aching silence. "Fuck me."

"I haven't talked to him in a while. I need to." Levon's voice was one-sided, as if he was chastising himself, calling out his own failure. "This gives me a reason to call."

Vic let the silence widen for a moment. "I'm flying to Williston tomorrow. Right after I meet someone."

"Text me the flight times." Levon's voice was sharp, back in the present. "Also, Liz wanted me to pass on a message."

"Okay."

"She said you have to understand. Cora knew she was coming. Cora was ready for her, had a sidearm, she was waiting."

Vic was sober again. "Tell her I heard her. I'm meeting someone tomorrow about exactly that. No one gets the drop on Liz unless they have an advantage. That's a fact. I've worked with her long enough to know."

"Good. And lay off the booze."

He was bothered that Levon spotted his drinking so easily. "That's the only thing I'm gonna lay off." Then he realized what he'd said: he sounded like a tin-cup tough guy, and felt silly.

They ended the call. The house was still, the sky outside the dining room window black as death. He crossed to the wall and stared at the photographs of the three women, turned and gazed at the single framed photo of Dannie on the windowsill. He wanted to say something to them about what he planned to do next, to promise them something. He felt it then, again, the sense he had crossed to a different place. That he was far away from where he started. Promises are just another way we lie to ourselves, he said to himself. He couldn't bring himself to do it. Not anymore.

He turned off the kitchen light and went to bed.

Chapter 13

The meeting place was the same Starbucks where Vic met Hana Richards several weeks earlier, while investigating the murder of Hana's colleague, Gretchen Stoll. Like Gretchen, Hana was a public defender, and it was her recordings of Gretchen's clients that proved Gretchen was throwing cases.

Vic arrived early, but Hana was waiting for him. The Starbucks was inside a venerable Pittsburgh hotel, the pressed tin ceiling twenty-five feet above the floor, the plaster crown molding as thick as an elephant leg.

Hana watched him, her hands around a large clear plastic cup that contained some kind of coffee drink Vic couldn't fathom. He pointed at the cash register and she nodded. After collecting his coffee, he crossed to her. She was absorbed in her cell phone, her well-manicured fingers tapping the screen.

As Vic sat, she looked up and smiled, and Vic was taken again with her looks. Rich brown hair perfectly cut at shoulder length, deep green eyes, a high forehead showing the slightest trace of lines, just enough to give her words and thoughts stature and weight.

"I'm glad to see you up and around again, Vic."

"Me too. And Liz is out of the burn ward."

She smiled, her lips moist somehow, but not obviously made up. She waited a beat, and in that second her intelligence was almost palpable.

"So," Vic said, gathering his thoughts. "I wanted to talk to you about something."

"Last time you said that I almost got my ass handed to me."

65

Vic grinned, he couldn't help himself. That was the other thing he liked about Hana; she was always straight to the point. "And somehow you figured your way out of it."

"If you only knew. But good job catching Lily Bauer, Vic. I've seen the evidence against her, we pretty much have her. Gretchen was a lot of bad things but she was one of ours."

"Only by job title. After that I don't think so." He hesitated. Something in Hana's words set off a warning bell, but he couldn't identify it. "What I wanted to talk to you about is our friend the DA, Frank Marioni."

"Ah." Hana sat back. "What'cha got?"

Vic tasted his coffee, but it was still too hot and he put the cup back on the table. "I'm not sure. That's why I wanted to talk to you." A thought crossed his mind. "Hey, is Lily Bauer using a public defender, or did she find council?"

"She retained council. Some two-dollar lawyer from the North Hills." She tossed off the comment, and Vic knew she thought he was stalling. Her eyes bored into him.

Vic collected this thoughts. "Here's what's bothering me. Once the doctors cleared it, I talked to Liz. You know she was hurt trying to arrest Cora Stills, who is a friend of Lily Bauer and likely trafficked my daughter and three other women."

"I heard something like that."

"Just before Liz went to arrest Cora, I talked to Marioni. He promised to prepare an arrest warrant for Cora Stills."

"I heard about that meeting. The whole floor did."

Vic couldn't help but smile. "It was that loud?"

She waved a hand. "Prosecutors talk more dish than what's in a kitchen cabinet."

He hesitated. He had to trust that Hana would stay quiet about what he said next. The risk she took to obtain the recordings suggested she would, and he knew she felt strongly about the integrity of the public defender's office. He waded ahead. "Here's my problem. When I talked to Liz, she said Cora Stills knew someone was coming to arrest her. She was armed and waiting. I know Liz, she isn't sloppy. She would wait for backup before attempting an arrest. If Cora got the drop on her it's because she knew ahead of time Liz was coming."

"Okay."

"Second, Marioni promised to cut a warrant for Cora Stills, but he posted it a few hours after we went to arrest her. And rescinded it two hours later. Basically, if Liz did arrest her, any judge would have thrown it out of court. The warrant wasn't in place."

Hana tilted her head. "There could be a bunch of technical reasons for that, all of them procedural. Tough to say Marioni did that with intent, if that's what you're implying."

"But he was the only one who knew I left his office to arrest her. The warrant posted several hours later and he deleted it two hours after that. Does that make sense?"

She shrugged. "Anything else?"

"Yep. He isn't pursuing any of the trafficking charges he could bring against Lily and her boyfriend. The boyfriend even offered his testimony for a deal, but Marioni refused. The only charges he'll consider relate to Gretchen Stoll."

"You think that Marioni is protecting Cora Stills?"

"I can't say that for sure. But I'm certain that Marioni and I, and Liz, were the only ones who knew Cora was going down. On top of that, normally when a cop gets hurt like that, our investigation goes all out. Every cop who can walk, talk or breathe pounds pavement. From what I hear, but I need to confirm this, Marioni leaned on my commander to slow walk that investigation. At Marioni's direction, Crush put the weakest investigator in our department on it, and never formed a task force. Basically, Marioni's pressure on my boss means we really aren't searching for Cora."

Hana frowned, the lines in her forehead centered just above the bridge of her nose. "Wow. I see your point. You're suggesting he warned Cora Stills and is now impeding the search for her."

"I'm just saying it could look that way."

Hana drummed her fingernails on the tabletop and took a sip of her drink.

"Any thoughts?" Vic asked.

"Well, full disclosure. You're talking about my boss."

Vic's heart quickened. "What? You work in the public defender's office. That doesn't report to Marioni."

"I used to. Monday, I started in the DA's office. I'm an assistant DA now. A prosecutor."

Vic folded his arms. "You tell me this now? You let me say all that?" He almost spat the words at her.

She held her palm toward him. "Easy, Vic. I'm not going to run to him and tell him what you think."

Vic knew he was glaring at her and reined himself back.

"And by the way," she said tartly. "It's partly your fault."

"How does that figure?"

"Remember the tapes I made for you? You gave one to Marioni, remember that?"

"Yes."

"Guess what. He listened all the way through. I'm betting you didn't take the time. You were moving too fast. A couple of times on the tape, the person I'm interviewing called me by name. He figured out I recorded it."

Blood rushed to Vic's face. He felt foolish. She was right, he'd been moving too fast and had put her in jeopardy. He hadn't listened to the whole tape, only enough to confirm Gretchen's crimes.

"I'm sorry," he croaked.

She flashed a broad smile of straight white teeth. "Don't be. Like I said, he hired me."

"It can't be because he liked your initiative. He doesn't work that way."

"Damn right, he doesn't. He hired me to get control of me. You think I don't understand that? Think about it. I know about the tapes and what Gretchen did. If I'm in the public defender's office I can talk about it. But, since I'm working for him, he can order me to stay silent, which he did, and if I talk, then he has me on insubordination. He fires me. If I release the tapes then or talk to the press, I'm just a vengeful, disgruntled worker. I have no credibility."

"He decided to keep his enemies closer."

"Exactly. But think about it from my point of view. I came out of law school, worked three years in a law firm, moved to the public defender's office for four years, and now I'm in the prosecutor's office. I do three years there and every law firm in town will be recruiting me. It's tough as hell to get experience as both a public defender *and* a prosecutor. And that's why I know how good the evidence is on Lily Bauer. I'm on the prosecution team running her case."

Vic sat back. He had to hand it to Marioni. It was a clever move, and kept the worst evidence against Gretchen buried during an election year. "And I bet he reminded you about how good it would be for your career if you worked for him."

"Of course he did. Carrot and stick." She smiled and sipped her drink.

Vic watched her. "And where does that leave us?"

She leaned in close to him. "It leaves me in a place where I can watch Marioni like a hawk. He asked me not to speak about the tapes on Gretchen. We both know he doesn't want that coming out in an election year. But he didn't ask me to stop thinking. I wouldn't do that anyway. And now you have someone in the DA's office who can figure out if he really is covering for Cora Stills. He never told me not to do that."

Vic crossed his arms. "You like this shit, don't you?"

She cocked her head, her face serious. "I have my own reasons for keeping my eyes and ears open, Vic. If he's covering for a known criminal, he needs to come down. The DA *is* law enforcement in our county. He has to be squeaky clean. Otherwise all law enforcement is a joke."

Vic watched her. Where she got her hard muscle of honesty he didn't know, but he was glad he'd found her.

"Okay, then I'll tell you what I'm up to."

"You mean you were thinking you wouldn't?"

"It crossed my mind, just now."

"Trust, Vic. It's good for relationships."

"Is that what we have?"

She grinned. "You wish. Let's call ourselves coworkers. That'll do."

Vic flipped his hands over so the palms faced up on the table. "Works for me." He took a breath, and gave her the account of his progress searching for Cora, leaving out the advice he had given to Lily Bauer and Denny Halpin. "I'm going to North Dakota. See if I can track down Cora and Lily's ex-husband."

"And I guess Lily gave you his name?"

Vic stared at her, not speaking. He couldn't tell her that he had snuck into jail to meet Lily.

"Relax." Hana blinked her eyes at him. "I'm on the prosecution team, but I'm low person on the totem pole. They have me doing all the crap work, like setting up jail visits. I track the visitor's log and everyone she talks to. Funny that, how you weren't approved to visit her, then you were, and now you're not. Magical, kinda."

"Must be coincidence."

"Right. That's what I figured. It's why I forgot to list you with her other visitors on the official court record. I have to work so late, sometimes, I get tired and make mistakes."

Vic felt warm all over. He couldn't get over how smart she was. He wanted to thank her, but he knew that was a statement of collusion. He stayed quiet a moment longer. "Coincidences. They do happen. Can I say something?"

"Sure."

"You know, if I was Lily Bauer, I would keep saying I want a trial. I wouldn't cut a deal."

"She's figured that out. She's no idiot. She knows Marioni doesn't want Gretchen's dirty laundry coming out at trial. We're deadlocked."

"Exactly. You need to offer her something big, like getting her son out of jail. I bet she would make a deal on that."

Hana sat back. "That's interesting, Vic. I'll have to see if we can actually do it."

"Everything Lily did, sleeping with Gretchen, killing her and trafficking my daughter, it was all for her son. Pick your time and suggest it to Marioni. Then, when he reorganizes the department after the election, which he always does, maybe you won't be the first one out the door." He smiled at her. "Just a thought."

She sipped her drink. It was half empty now, the cream melted to a white puck on top of the caramel colored liquid. She gazed at him, her eyes bright. "I do like our coffee meetings, Vic."

"I'm starting to like them, too." He rose and she did the same. He held the door for her on the way out. They stopped in the alley outside, facing one another on the sloped sidewalk. With her advantage of being uphill and wearing high heels, they were at eye level.

"Have fun in North Dakota, Vic."

"Is fun the right word?"

A bus thundered by on Grant Street, echoing down the alleyway.

"No." She gave him a wry smile. "I just hate saying 'take care.' That sounds so boring."

"And you'll keep an eye on Marioni?"

She smiled. "Life will be more exciting if I do, don't you think?"

Chapter 14

The plane trip to Denver was a squeeze of people, seats, air and light. Everything was cinched tight, even everyone's politeness. To reach the regional airline gate for his North Dakota connection, Vic walked the length of Denver airport's B Concourse, passing trim women wearing technical outdoor gear, bearded young men in T-shirts and tight jeans, and the usual collection of pasty-faced office workers, head-phoned college students, and preoccupied parents chasing youngsters.

The Williston gate was at the end of the concourse, around a narrow corner and down an escalator. Here the hallways narrowed and ceiling lowered, as if they were moving underground. At the gates, the rows of seating were so compressed that everyone had to move their legs for people to walk the aisles. The men were mostly young, tall and beefy, baseball caps low on their foreheads, their snap-button cowboy shirts stretched over bulging pecs and aggressive stomachs. They laughed hard and radiated themselves into the air around them, demanding space. Natural gas and pipeline workers, Vic guessed. Sprinkled among them were a few thin, middle-aged men in metal-framed glasses, chinos and button-down shirts. The young men showed them the impatient deference reserved for bosses and technical experts. With only a few exceptions, the women among them were in their twenties and thirties, sleeveless blouses revealing swirling arm tattoos, their blond-streaked hair in severe pony tails, the grip on their phones implacable.

At the sight of those women a hard weight settled through Vic's insides, crushing his stomach. Breathless, he sagged into the nearest seat and closed his eyes. Dannie. What would she have looked like at that age? Tattooed? The same death-grip on her phone? Or something else. One of those trim, outdoor-geared women in the concourse above? One of the distracted mothers? He breathed, but it was like drawing air through a coffee stirrer.

He waited, the image from the photograph on his windowsill moving through his mind. His heart slowed and he opened his eyes. Distracting himself, he watched the arrivals from Montana and Wyoming flights. They were wiry men with large belt buckles and cowboy hats, middle-aged women who walked briskly, their hair swept back from their faces in no-nonsense, pragmatic cuts.

It disoriented him. He'd lost this—all of this—he knew suddenly. What Dannie would have become. Until now he'd struggled against the enormity of losing her; now he saw that was only the beginning. Gone was everything she would become. Everything she would be. And with it, his own years of watching it unfold.

The sounds around him swelled into an unintelligible din. He stared at the gate for the Williston flight and tried to focus. A gate attendant was checking people through. He lowered his gaze, staring at the floor. He didn't care. Nothing mattered. He breathed again and it was like trying to lift a stone from his chest. Unable to look up, his gaze skimmed the feet of everyone around him. He registered cowboy boots, trail sneakers and heavy-lugged work boots. His gaze settled on his own shoes…black lace-up leathers with Christy soles.

Poor damn choice where I'm going, he thought to himself.

It lightened him somehow, as if it was better to be unprepared.

Numb, he rose and crossed to the gate.

The airplane was so small he crouched as he sidled down the aisle. The large young men bumped into him and one another like billiard balls as they squeezed into their seats.

Ninety minutes later, Vic stared out the window on their final approach into Williston. The ground was littered with oil drilling pads, each a livid red square cut from the plains grass, red dirt roads like scars leading to the platforms. Flame spewed from exhaust vents.

They touched down in Williston at one in the afternoon. Everyone angled, crouched and sidled their way from their seats and down the aisle, silent, as if escaping an embarrassment. The airport was so small the baggage claim was just inside the terminal. It was a large chunk of stainless steel that looked like a misshapen playground slide, perhaps fifteen feet wide and four feet higher at the back than at the front. Directly behind it was a wide garage door that Vic guessed could be raised to deliver their luggage. The terminal's front entrance was barely fifteen yards away, flanked by car rental desks. His gaze settled on a man standing underneath a screen of flight departure and arrival information. He was about five foot ten, his long black hair strewn across rounded shoulders. The tanned skin of his face was tight over high cheekbones, his brown eyes so dark they appeared black.

He held a sign that read *Lenoski*.

There was no plan for Vic to meet anyone. Knowing the luggage would be a few minutes, he crossed the terminal and arranged himself in front of the man. "I'm Lenoski."

"Vic Lenoski...Pittsburgh?" There was an off-beat pause between the two questions.

"I already said that." Vic shrugged out of the day pack he'd used as his carry-on and squared up to him.

The man looked him up and down. When he finally spoke, his words carried an undercurrent of humor, or sarcasm. "Yeah. You got that look."

Still hollow from his thoughts in Denver, Vic didn't want to put up with it. "You need to do better than that. At most three people know I'm here."

Again, pauses, first before he spoke and then in the center of the sentence. "I'm supposed to meet a Vic Lenoski...don't know much more than that."

"Try." It was one short word, but Vic said it like a slap.

A small smile turned the corners of his mouth. "Heard you're a cop." Another pause. "And right now, you got that situation working for you...I also heard words like mill-hunky-type."

The last remnant of Vic's patience evaporated. "Hasn't been a working mill in Pittsburgh in thirty years."

The man's almost-black eyes met Vic's gaze. "Hasn't been a working Sioux war chief in more than one hundred and fifty years…I win that one."

Somehow, the statement shook Vic out of his torpor. Oddly, he felt a smile eddy near his lips, but he tightened his mouth and kept his voice level. "Look. Okay. I wasn't expecting anyone to meet me, so we need to figure this out. Who sent you?" Vic took in the man's scuffed suede boots, blue jeans, and blue checked cowboy shirt.

A shrug. "I wasn't expecting to be here today…holding a stupid sign…but Charlie Running Bear asked me to come."

Vic tried his own delay to see if the man needed to fill silences, but he seemed to relish the quiet. He remembered Levon's phone call from the night before. "Charlie Running Bear, huh? Tough name to live with if he's the guy I think he is. He missing his legs?"

The man folded the sign twice and worked it into the chest pocket of his blue jean jacket. "That's Charlie."

"And your name?"

"Jimmy Pronghorn."

"How'd you know to meet me?"

Jimmy tilted his head, and a sly humor rose from his voice to his eyes. "Charlie Running Bear asked me, so, smoke signals?"

Vic had to glance away not to laugh out loud. This time he let the smile show. "Fair enough. Maybe a stupid way for me to ask the question. How about this? Why did Charlie Running Bear ask you to meet me?"

"It's a mystery." Jimmy looked over Vic's shoulder and frowned. "You check baggage?"

He nodded, and didn't mention he needed a checked bag to transport his Glock.

"Then let's get that. We can talk…while we wait."

Vic heard what sounded like a garage door clatter up and guessed the luggage was arriving. He liked the idea of doing two things at the same time, rather than this disjointed conversation.

"Sure."

Jimmy followed him to the baggage return. The door was up but the luggage had yet to arrive. They took up a position at the corner of the ramp with their backs to the windows, keeping the airport in front of them. They both chose the spot without discussing it and Vic liked that as well.

He looked at Jimmy. "Let me see if I can put this together." He spoke lightly, so Jimmy knew he wasn't taking anything personally. "I told a friend in Pittsburgh I was coming out here, and he said he knew a guy from the military, but he lived in South Dakota. He lost his legs in Iraq. I didn't think that would help me, but my friend wanted to talk to him anyway. I thought my friend might feel guilty for not calling him more often. He didn't give me the guy's name, but I'm guessing it's Charlie Running Bear. And you say Charlie's the one who asked you to meet me."

"Sounds right."

"So what's the deal? You supposed to just meet me or what?"

Jimmy shrugged. "Meet you...show you around. You'll need taking care of." He said the last sentence in a softer tone and Vic sensed there was something behind it.

"I just need to drive around and talk to a couple of people. No big deal. I do that kind of crap for a living."

Jimmy looked at him. "I grew up around here...you ever read Sophocles? You're a stranger in a strange country."

Vic didn't know who Sophocles was, but stopped himself from asking. Instead, he watched a worker position a luggage trailer behind the ramp and thought about Jimmy's words. He could use the help, but he didn't know Jimmy and it made him uncomfortable. The first few suitcases slid to the bottom of the ramp and were snagged by waiting passengers.

Vic looked at him. "Charlie Running Bear expects you to do a lot. I'm just saying. I'm staying in Watford City, which is like ninety minutes from here. That means you have to drop everything and lose a bunch of days out of your life to shadow me around. Do you work for Charlie Running Bear?"

"No...he just asked me to do it. I said sure."

Vic felt himself beginning to understand the rhythm of the pauses in Jimmy's conversation, or at least grow comfortable with them. He spotted his suitcase sliding down the ramp. The moment before he stepped forward to retrieve it, he said, "You and I know there's a hell of a lot more to it than that. You want to stick with me, you need to tell me."

He swung the bag off the ramp, stood it upright and extended the handle. He turned to Jimmy, spread his feet and waited.

Jimmy nodded slowly, his gaze inward. "Charlie Running Bear lives on the Standing Rock reservation. That sits in North and South Dakota. I'm on the council of the Fort Berthold Rez, that's not far east of Watford City. Charlie is real active on his reservation. Fought the pipelines, fights just about everything whites throw at us. We talk a lot. Help each other out…and your friend said one of the guys you're going to meet works for an oil company."

He fell silent so quickly Vic wondered if he'd exhausted himself. "Still not really an explanation. Except I can see why you might be interested in oil companies, if they were the ones wanted to build the pipeline."

Jimmy shrugged. "There's something else…Charlie trusts your friend." His gaze shifted and bored into Vic. "Which is weird…Charlie never trusts white guys…so the fact he wants to do a favor for a white guy interests me."

"Levon is half black. Only his father is white."

"That would make Levon fifty percent more trustworthy."

Vic ignored the insult. "Levon and this Charlie guy were in the military together…that'll have more to do with it." He blinked as he heard himself imitate Jimmy's way of speaking.

If he noticed the mimicry, Jimmy ignored it. "I know that. What is this Levon's last name?"

Vic waited a beat. He didn't want to tell him, but he thought if he was honest, maybe Jimmy would be honest back. It felt like they were dealing with each other at that level. "Levon Grace."

The skin around Jimmy's eyes tightened. "Sergeant Grace?"

Vic shrugged. "Yes. I checked his military file once. You know him?"

"Of him." Jimmy's voice turned soft. "I was military too…Iraq at the same time. That's a name you remember…ironic as shit."

Vic stared at him. "What do you mean?"

Jimmy shook his head as if dislodging a weight. He nodded at Vic's bag. "Kinda small…traveling light?"

"Needed to check a bag."

"So, you're traveling heavy." Jimmy met his gaze. Vic knew he understood the bag was to transport a weapon.

"Something like that."

Jimmy squinted at the front door of the terminal. "Good talk. Let's go get your car...and see that?" He pointed at the bag. "Now I know for sure I need to stick close. Looks like you came out here hunting."

"Just being careful. Safety first."

"White man with guns been giving us that bullshit for two hundred years." Sarcasm freighted Jimmy's voice. He turned for the front door.

With Jimmy gone, Vic signed the paperwork for his car at a rental agency near the terminal's front door. He found himself smiling. For whatever reason he liked Jimmy. The shots at Vic's race hadn't carried any anger or insult. It was more as if Jimmy was describing a room, his room.

He thought about that as he walked to his rental car. It was as if Jimmy wanted Vic to be sure about the location of each chair, table, and lamp. Which knick-knacks were passed down from generation to generation within the family, which were the new ones he'd bought. Why the doorway and windows were in specific locations. It was as if he was saying don't fall over that chair or bump into this. Be sure where the drafts come from and how to leave. Know where to come in. Respect this and laugh about that. It was an odd way to get to know someone, but Vic liked the openness. The offbeat honesty of it. Somehow it even matched Jimmy's pause-laden way of speaking. It was as if Jimmy was saying this is who I am. Take it or leave it.

Vic decided to take it.

At least long enough to understand Jimmy's comment about Levon.

Chapter 15

Vic found his car and stood beside it until Jimmy swung around the lot in a beat-up Ford Ranger pickup.

"Follow me to Watford City?" Jimmy asked.

Vic nodded and got into his small purple Chevrolet. It was uncomfortable no matter how he adjusted the seat. At least his right shoulder didn't complain as he shifted the transmission lever.

Another ten yards and they cleared airport property. Vic opened the maps app on his phone, pressed the GO button underneath the name of his motel and placed the phone in the nearest cup holder. Just to be sure about where Jimmy was leading him.

They headed south on Route 85, Jimmy's pick-up crouched in its lane, never faster than sixty. Vic's mapping software told him they needed ninety minutes to reach Watford City. When they cleared the Williston city limits he called Levon.

"You make it?" Levon asked, without a greeting.

"Yep. And there was someone waiting to meet me. A Jimmy Pronghorn. He said a guy called Charlie Running Bear asked him to meet me. Is that who you called after we talked?"

"I did. Well, Marines called him Charlie Bear. That's about as flexible as the military gets with names. How's this Pronghorn guy?"

"Thinks he's a jokester, and he's on me like glue. What did you tell Charlie? It feels like they want in on this, but I can't figure out why."

Levon was silent for a moment. "I said you needed to talk to a couple of people. One of them works for a fracking company, and he might know something about Dannie going missing. I told them Dannie is your daughter. I also said a woman pointed a gun at my girlfriend, tied her to a radiator and tried to burn her alive. That woman's on the run, and you want to talk to her mother, see if she knows where her daughter's hiding."

Something clicked in Vic's mind. "Maybe that's it. You and Charlie go way back, right? If you told him about Liz, maybe Charlie thinks this is personal for you. He's thinking that if he gives me Jimmy, he's helping you. Charlie's trying to help you, not me."

"Maybe. I hadn't thought of it that way."

"Tell me something." As he talked, Vic stared at the countryside, the rolling hills covered by grass so low it looked like a lawn. Light green bushes he'd never seen before dotted the landscape. "Turns out Pronghorn was in Iraq too. Seemed like he'd heard of you. He said he thought the name Sergeant Grace was ironic."

After a moment, Levon said, "Probably just means it's ironic that my name would come up in North Dakota, now. Vic, I need to tell you something."

"Sure."

"Liz went back into the ICU. It's her lungs. The burns are healing okay, but they're saying some of the chemicals she breathed damaged her lung tissue. They're running more tests and she's back on oxygen."

"Christ. Doctors say anything else? Can I call her?" He heard the croak in his voice.

"Wait and see. Anne called me. She said she's planning to visit after work. I'm taking Jayvon when he gets out of school."

Something skated away from Vic, lost into the rearing sky. The car wheels hummed, the highway an afterthought. "Okay. Keep me updated." He exhaled.

He didn't press the disconnect button, and sensed Levon hadn't either. They were linked, but neither said anything, as if all that mattered was the connection between them. He understood suddenly how far away he was now, how everything at home was fragile and diminishing.

The screen on his phone flickered back to the map.

Through his hands he felt the earth roll away under his tires.

Ahead, the horizon line wavered against the treeless, rolling hills. As he drew close it receded into the towering sky, the spaces cartwheeling around him, only to form again in the distance. The green here was light and indefinite, close to the ground, unlike the dark, looming green and interspersed shadows that coated the rearing, tree-covered hills and jagged valleys of Pittsburgh's Allegheny Mountains. Everything felt indefinite, as if driving wasn't toward something, or away from it. He was simply one more in the stream of white pick-up trucks, panel vans and tanker trucks, all of them moving through a landscape littered with drilling platforms, the plumes of fire from exhaust vents piercing the sky. He poked the screen of his phone—again and again—to check the blue dot that marked his position on the map. It told him nothing, until finally Watford City appeared a scant quarter inch away. Soon afterwards his phone rang, shrill in the small car.

"You hungry?" Jimmy asked.

Fifteen minutes later Jimmy's truck slowed and took a left turn at a traffic light, onto a new two-lane concrete road easily the width of a sprawling four lane highway. Some distance later, the road passed a strip mall and led up a small rise. On the hill-top, sidewalks appeared. Restaurants, bars and retail stores crowded against the road for the next two hundred yards. Jimmy picked a parking spot and Vic pulled in behind him.

Jimmy led him into a restaurant called the Roosevelt Saloon. It was deserted, except for a man at the end of the bar nursing a draft beer. He stared blankly at one of the television sets.

"Local place," Vic said, once they were settled at the bar.

Jimmy shrugged. "This street is pretty much Watford City. The old one. I take the road east from here to my Rez…I stop here sometimes. You see the same guys. Oil people don't eat here…they eat at those huge convenience stores along the highway…or the malls we got everywhere now. Your first time out here?"

"It is. I guess I haven't travelled much."

"Real Pittsburgh guy."

"Seems that way."

"That explains your shoes…they wouldn't last five minutes here."

A man with a paunch, overgrown mustache and slack, pasty face walked through the swinging door from the kitchen. He spotted them and brought menus. He nodded to Jimmy.

Jimmy thanked him and placed his menu on the bar. As the bartender went to refill the other man's mug, Jimmy turned to Vic. "Who do you want to talk to, and when?"

Vic scanned the menu to avoid looking at his shoes. His head still down, he said, "I want to start with a guy named Bauer. He's here in Watford City. Today, if I can do it." He placed his menu next to Jimmy's and the bartender retraced his steps to them.

"Fries and a salad," Jimmy said.

"Hamburger basket," Vic added. As the bartender collected the menus, Vic noted a blurred tattoo of the words *Semper Fi* on his forearm.

"Drink?"

"Water is fine."

The bartender turned from them toward a kitchen pass-through. A long, bright white line angled down the back of the bartender's head and onto his neck. A scar.

Jimmy shifted on his seat. "Watford City is pretty small. You said you're staying here tonight?"

Vic nodded.

"After we eat you can check in, then we'll head over to Bauer's house. You got an address?"

Vic gave it to him. Jimmy stayed silent for a moment. "That's a couple of blocks from here. The old Watford City. I was expecting one of the condos put up for the new timers."

"New timers?"

"New to the area. Only here for a short time...the drilling companies bring guys in on a two or three-year's contract. Usually they take off after that."

Vic let his gaze stray behind the bar. "People who were born here appreciate that?"

Jimmy was quiet for a moment as the bartender placed glasses of water in front of each of them. "No one's arguing with the money that's coming in. We go out of town east and you'll see a brand-new high school, landscaped and everything. That's oil and gas money." He sipped his water. "Watford is pretty much a boom town. Some of the people who lived here for generations don't like it much. It changed the scenery, that's for sure. But the money helps."

Vic's survey of the bar stopped on a high shelf near the kitchen door, where two triangular wood and glass boxes held folded American flags, the kind given to widows and family after a serviceman's death. Either they were new, or someone dusted them regularly.

"You still haven't told me why you're so interested in what I'm doing."

Jimmy shrugged. "Charlie asked me to do it. He's a big deal with us...he asks you to do something, you do it."

"Still doesn't answer my question."

Jimmy glanced at him. "Charlie told me a woman almost killed Levon Grace's girlfriend...you think she might be hiding near here. He also said your daughter is missing, and this woman might know about that...and all of it might connect to the oil companies. You get that we're not on good terms with them, right? So, if you're investigating them, we want to know what you find."

Vic relaxed. He was right about two things. Jimmy was open, you just had to get him talking. It also did look like Charlie Running Bear thought he owed Levon. Whatever Jimmy and Charlie discovered about the oil companies would be gravy.

"You could have said all that when we met at the airport," Vic said carefully.

Jimmy turned to him, eyes sharp. "Not the right place to do it...plus I figured you would call that Grace guy once we were on the road. Get his side of the story. See if what I told you checked out...how'd I do?"

"You're making more sense."

Jimmy leaned toward him and lowered his voice. "But let's understand each other. I know you aren't out here officially...and a missing daughter and injured partner don't make for a clear head. Charlie also wants to make sure you don't get yourself screwed up."

"What I decide to do is up to me."

"Maybe...but understand something. This is big country and there's no back-up...my tribe knew that two hundred years ago and we still had it handed to us. You gotta play things differently...pick your spots...stay level-headed. Out here there's a million places a body could end up lost, forever."

Vic stared at him. "You thought I was coming out here to shoot someone?"

His eyes flashed. "That's the whole problem...I don't think *you* know for sure. You're gonna talk to some people, find some stuff out. Maybe it changes how you think...how you react to things...what you choose to do. Maybe you find things run deeper than you expected...that you're facing something bigger than you thought...or that you're in over your head. That's the thing about being out here. All the wide-open spaces, big sky, it doesn't seem like much is going on. But it is. Big time it is."

Vic stared at him. Jimmy *did* meet him for another reason, he was sure of it, now. Jimmy and Charlie Running Bear were after something. He just didn't know what.

The bartender arrived with their orders. Vic pushed his aside. "I still don't think you're telling me everything."

Jimmy spooned ranch dressing onto his salad. "I'm telling you what you need to know. You see how pretty this country looks? That's for tourists in bad shoes. In real life? This place is small, grubby, mean and hard...that's why it's called the badlands. Whites out here, all they ever did was squeeze money out of the ground...doesn't matter how. First it was land for farming...they screwed us over that...then coal...now it's oil and natural gas. Everyone plays for keeps...you need every friend you can get." He mixed the dressing into his salad.

"And right now, you're the only friend I have? I don't like convenient."

Jimmy turned to him. "No. We're just aligned...but that's better than nothing...and might even keep you alive."

Vic sat back. "I see what Charlie Running Bear likes about you."

Jimmy picked up a French fry. "He'd rather call me He Who Talks Too Much." He pointed the French fry at him. "After this we check you into your motel, then we go talk to this guy."

84

"Sounds good to me." Vic took a bite of his hamburger. As he chewed his mind drifted back to the drive from the airport, to the undulating hills and towering sky. How the horizon was always shifting into the distance. The constant stream of oil and gas pads. Jimmy's words made him see something else. How birds flying into that raging emptiness could disappear to the naked eye, migrating bison shrink to brown dots and evaporate. How the shifting horizon could erase anyone determined to reach it.

He chewed but didn't taste anything, the food a weight in his mouth.

Chapter 16

Their meal finished, Vic and Jimmy paid and returned to their cars. Vic was tired, and the feeling matched the day's fading light. Jimmy led Vic down a hill and turned right onto a gravel road that took Vic directly to his motel.

Inside his room, with Jimmy waiting outside, Vic stared at his black leather shoes and their flat soles and shook his head. There was nothing he could do about it. He removed the case holding his Glock from the checked bag, unlocked it and loaded the weapon. He clipped the gun and holster to his belt, covering it with a windbreaker. When he returned to the parking lot, Jimmy was standing next to his truck, his arms folded over his chest. Vic saw him check if he was carrying his weapon. As Vic took the passenger seat Jimmy climbed behind the wheel, silent.

Barely three minutes later, a few blocks behind the main street, they turned left onto the street where Kent Bauer lived.

Flashing red and blue lights from a pair of parked police cars and an ambulance flared at them. Jimmy made a noise that sounded like 'huh' and parked down the street from the nearest cruiser.

"Looks like it's Bauer's house," Vic said, and slid out. As he walked to the police cars, it registered that he was passing fully grown trees, the first he'd seen that weren't growing inside narrow gullies between hills. He confirmed the house number on the mailbox, stepped into the next-door neighbor's yard and stood near a thick tree trunk.

The front yard of Kent's house was cordoned off in yellow crime scene tape, bright in the fading light. Inside the perimeter, parked in the driveway, stood a large white Dodge pickup truck. A slim police officer leaned against the driver's side door, talking through the window to someone. Vic counted another officer at the front door, and from the silhouettes moving against the windows of the house, two more inside. A pair of paramedics lounged beside the open back doors of the ambulance. From the way everyone moved, he knew the scene was fresh; he doubted the police had arrived more than twenty minutes earlier. He scanned the perimeter formed by the crime scene tape, surprised to see it tied off at the front corners of the house. The backyard wasn't cordoned off.

He thought about that.

He set off across the neighbor's lawn, staying well outside the tape, until he could see the lawn behind Bauer's house. It was barely the size of a tennis court, edged by a ragged line of pine trees that separated Bauer's property from the house directly behind it. Still wondering at the lack of crime scene tape, he crossed to the pine trees, stepped between them and into the rear yard of the house directly behind Bauer's. A few more steps brought him to a garden shed. He wrapped his hand in a handkerchief and tried the door. It opened. He flicked on his phone's flashlight and pointed it inside. A lawnmower, fertilizer spreader and garden tools took shape. Footprints marred the dust near the only window. He closed the door, swiped off his flashlight, circled to the window and stood with his back to it. The window looked through a gap in the pine trees directly onto the rear of Bauer's house. As he watched, two officers stepped through the back door, framed in light. One was older with a white shirt straining to hold his heavy stomach. The other was chunky, middle aged, his uniform shirt untucked, as if he had been kneeling or lying down. Vic couldn't hear what they were saying, but the conversation was short and, moments later, they went back inside.

Vic stepped closer to Bauer's backyard, ticking through a list of possible reasons why it wasn't considered part of the crime scene. He couldn't think of any he liked. He scanned the grass and spotted something sticking six inches out of the ground near the tree line, almost lost in the shadows. Staying in the neighbor's yard, he moved along the row of pines. Closer, the object looked like a large eye screw set into the ground. A silver chain ran from it to a dark lump underneath an untended shrub. He walked into the yard, and found a German Shepherd flat on the grass. He placed his palm on the dog's side. Its body was warm, its breathing shallow and quick.

Vic retreated between the pines and circled through the neighbor's lawn the way he had come. As he passed the white pickup, he glanced inside and saw the pale face of someone watching him from the passenger seat. He couldn't see the man's features. He hurried to the road.

Jimmy was talking to a stocky man next to a newly arrived car. The man wore a sport coat and open-necked shirt. As Vic watched, he and Jimmy bumped each other lightly on the chest with the flat of their knuckles. Jimmy sauntered toward his truck. The man retrieved a fabric briefcase from the trunk of his car and started for the crime scene. As he passed the ambulance, the paramedics straightened and nodded to him.

From the width of the tires and spotlight on the driver's side, Vic knew the man's car was police issue. A detective, he guessed. He watched him duck under the crime scene tape. The lean officer next to the pickup strode over to shake his hand. The detective shook it briefly without breaking stride.

Vic crossed to Jimmy. "Who's that?"

In the wash of blue and red lights Jimmy looked thoughtful. "State police investigator."

"Did he tell you what happened?"

"No. Why would he tell me?"

Vic hesitated. If Jimmy wasn't going to tell him that he knew the man, this wasn't the time to ask. "Look, I need to talk to him. I was around the back of the house. He's got leads back there and the local guys haven't spotted them. Can you get him? I need to talk to him."

Jimmy frowned and didn't move. Vic saw one of the paramedics watching them.

He leaned closer to Jimmy. "You know him. I saw you guys together. I need to talk to him. I do this shit for a living."

Jimmy shrugged. "Not sure I can help."

In frustration, Vic spun away and crossed to the crime scene tape. The lean cop was back talking through the driver's side window of the truck.

"Hey! Officer!" Vic shouted. "I need to talk to the state police investigator."

The officer didn't respond, beyond a languid look in his direction.

"Do you hear me? I need to talk to the state police investigator. Now! It's about what happened here."

The officer pushed away from the truck, annoyance settling onto his face. He made no move to step closer. The truck's passenger door opened and a man slid out. Given the height of the pickup bed, Vic only saw a blue baseball cap moving toward the tail of the truck.

"What do you know about what went on here?" the officer barked at him.

"I need to speak to the investigator," Vic repeated.

The passenger came around the truck bed. He was of medium height with shoulders that sloped up to his neck. He looked like an arrowhead, with a sagging stomach that hid his belt buckle. He pointed at Vic. "Lou, that's the guy I was talking about. He was in Kent's back yard. I saw him."

The officer, or Lou, pointed at Vic. "You. Stay there." He started toward him.

Vic slid his hand into his pants pocket for his badge wallet.

"Hands!" Lou shouted. "Show me your hands!" He moved his right hand to the butt of his gun.

Vic realized his mistake and spread his arms away from his body. His windbreaker flapped open.

"Gun!" Lou shouted.

Too late, Vic remembered the Glock under his windbreaker. Lou leveled his gun at Vic, his eyes wide. In his peripheral vision, Vic saw the officer at the door launch toward them.

"Gun!" Lou shouted again, his voice notched higher. "Get down!" Lou stopped five feet away, his body sideways and aligned behind his revolver. "On your knees!"

All Vic could think about was how stupid the situation was.

"Now!" Lou shouted.

His arms stretched away from his body, Vic carefully kneeled on the grass.

"Lie flat!" Lou shuffled closer. Vic heard a new note of superiority in his voice, as if Vic's compliance made him bolder. "Face down!" The officer from the doorway stepped next to Lou. Somewhere in Vic's mind, he registered their mistake. His own training was to stay spread out, to make it harder for anyone armed to hit multiple officers.

Without hands to help him, Vic angled his body to the ground and used his left elbow to break his fall. He hit the elbow nerve and felt it all the way to his shoulder.

Moments later the officer from the front door dropped onto Vic's back, using a shin to pin him down, yanked his arms behind his back and snapped handcuffs onto his wrists. The ground was damp, Vic's left cheek pressed against gravel. His view was up the street. About twenty yards away Jimmy leaned against the driver's door of his truck, watching, his arms crossed over his chest. His lips were shaped into a half smile.

This *would* be funny, Vic thought, if it just wasn't such a damn waste of time.

Chapter 17

The handcuffing officer slid Vic's Glock from underneath his coat. Vic twisted his neck and angled his head to see above Lou's cowboy boots. "I'm a police officer."

Lou looked at the man from the passenger side of the truck. "You said he was hiding in the back yard?"

The man watched Vic as he replied. "I saw him come out of the back yard. Absolutely."

The driver of the pickup slid to the ground and slammed his door. He was a second version of Lou, but taller and more heavyset in the shoulders. His eyes were thoughtful. He hitched his thumbs onto his belt, comfortable in his skin. Even at rest he exuded command.

Anger slid into Vic's throat. "Hey. Officer Lou. You're screwing up your investigation. There's evidence in the back yard and you're ignoring it."

Lou nodded to the other officer, who kicked Vic in the side. "Shut up." It wasn't a hard kick, more of a reminder that something worse was possible.

Vic fought back his anger. "Okay, Larry and Moe, cut the crap and get me the state investigator."

Lou backed closer to the driver of the truck. "Shut up or you go to jail."

Vic bit off what he really wanted to say and talked through a small gap between his teeth. "Check my ID, Lou, and get me the state investigator. Don't be a stooge, make a career move."

Through the wash of red and blue lights on Lou's face, Vic saw a flicker of uncertainty.

"Check that," Vic called, "just leave me here while your investigation goes to shit. Last thing your department needs is you promoted."

Lou's face froze. He glanced at the driver of the truck, who shrugged, an amused look on his long face.

"Can't think for yourself?" Vic taunted. "My ID is in my pants, left front pocket. Check it."

"What the hell is going on?" Walking toward them was the white-shirted man Vic had seen by the back door. A star glinted on his chest. He stopped above Vic, looked down and after a couple of quick breaths, asked, "Who are you?"

"Detective Vic Lenoski, Pittsburgh Police. I came here to talk to Kent Bauer. You guys got here first." The chief was so close Vic couldn't strain his neck enough to see beyond his boots.

Lou's boots appeared next to the chief's. "He was in the back yard. He's got a gun."

"Was it holstered?"

"Well, yeah."

The chief's toes shifted toward the other officer. "Get his ID out." Vic watched him step back.

Vic rolled onto his side.

"Anything I can stick myself with in your pocket?" the officer asked, as he leaned over.

Vic looked him in the eye. "You already stuck yourself with being stupid."

The officer grunted a 'sorry' and dug Vic's badge wallet out of his pocket. Vic wasn't sure if he was apologizing about the kick, taking the wallet, or for being stupid.

The chief studied Vic's ID and squatted down to compare the photo to Vic's face in the slurring red and blue lights. "Stand him up," he said.

They didn't remove the handcuffs. Upright, Vic found that he looked down on the chief. He was in his late fifties, he guessed, with a flattop haircut of thinning grey hair. Old for an active officer, but he didn't know how the rules worked in North Dakota.

"You're a long way from home," the chief said, patiently. His eyes didn't give anything away.

"I came to talk to Kent Bauer. It's related to a case in Pittsburgh. Is he here?"

The chief studied him. "Okay. Two things. One, you should have stopped by and told us you were here investigating."

Vic opened his mouth to say something and the chief flashed his palm to silence him. "Second, Mr. Bauer is indisposed." He gave a smug smile, as if enjoying a joke.

Vic waited until the chief lowered his hand. "First, I just got here less than an hour ago. I was planning to stop by tomorrow morning. Second, and this is what matters, there's evidence in the back yard. You guys missed it. That's why I want to talk to the state police investigator."

"You can tell me."

Vic forced himself to relax. He hated this kind of gamesmanship. "I'm telling you. Cordon off the back yard and half the neighbor's property. Make sure you include their shed. You need to protect all that. There's a dog out there as well. I think someone drugged it and it needs a vet. You'll want to know what drug was used, and I doubt you want the dog to die."

"Cinders is back there?" The driver of the pickup stepped closer.

The chief automatically shifted his body to include him in the conversation.

The pickup driver added, "Chief, I asked Lou where Cinders was when you guys got here. Made no sense he wasn't around. The doors were all closed. He shoulda been inside."

The chief licked his lips. His pale tongue reminded Vic of a turtle. He said something to Lou that widened his eyes and sent him toward the house at a fast walk. They stood in silence. From the corner of his eye, Vic saw Jimmy had moved to a tree in the neighbor's yard, neatly within hearing distance.

Vic looked at the chief. "Tick, tock."

The chief moved his lips as if he wanted to spit, then said, "You're already on my shit list, so shut up. Otherwise I ask why you were sneaking around the back yard and charge you with screwing up a crime scene."

"It wasn't cordoned off, so it wasn't part of the scene. Don't bullshit a bullshiter. And I've done a lot of investigations. I was there exactly because it wasn't cordoned off. You pretty much invited me."

The chief looked as if he might say something, but stayed quiet. Vic appreciated him more for that. He was smart enough not to take the bait.

Vic glanced at the pickup driver. He was a physical presence, but held himself in a relaxed way. Despite the cool of the evening he only wore a T-shirt tucked into jeans. The words above the pocket were the same as on the side of the truck: O&G Supply.

Lou appeared with the state police investigator in tow. They crossed the yard, the investigator with his head tilted down, studying the ground. Vic knew he was looking for evidence and liked his investment in the case. When they reached the group, he pinned Vic with a gaze, his blue eyes set well apart in his face. From the way his blond hair was combed back, Vic wondered how it stayed in place.

The chief threw a thumb in Vic's direction. "This guy says he came to interview our vic. ID says he's a Pittsburgh Police detective. He has a theory about the back yard."

The state investigator shot a glance at the chief, and Vic saw anger in his eyes at the chief's slip. He'd just told everyone that Kent Bauer was dead. He turned back to Vic. "Have you done homicide investigations?"

"I have. But that's not why I'm here. My partner was attacked, and I thought Kent might know something about it." Vic waited to see if that information might win him some cooperation.

The investigator tapped a large hand against his thigh. "Kent Bauer didn't have a record. He was clean. I checked on my way over here."

"I didn't say we had him sized for anything, I just wanted to talk to him. I was guessing he knew something without realizing it. His ex-wife is in jail in Pittsburgh for the murder of a public defender."

The investigator's gaze stayed on Vic's face. Vic could see he wanted to ask about that, but instead he said, "Tell me about the back yard."

"I saw it wasn't taped off, so I went for a look."

"And?"

"Only reason I can think you *wouldn't* tape it is because when you arrived the back door was locked, no sign of forced entry. You assumed your perp came in the front. You'll dust the door, sure, but it's low priority."

"Keep going."

Vic knew from the investigator's tone that he'd guessed right. "But when I got there, I found two things. A neighbor's shed with a view of Bauer's house. Good place for someone to hole up while they waited for Kent to come home."

"Okay."

"And I found a dog knocked out cold on a chain." He looked at the chief. "Do you know if Kent came directly home from work today?"

The chief glanced at the driver of the pickup truck, who spoke up. "Kent worked today. Like I told Lou, we decided to have a few beers tonight. He wanted a shower, we stopped by to pick him up."

"It fits." Vic returned the investigator's gaze. "The grass is worn near the dog. My guess is he gets chained up there regularly. I'd line it up this way: the perp waits in the shed until Bauer comes home, it's a good way not to get noticed by the neighbors. You might find trace evidence. Perp watches Bauer bring the dog into the back yard, tie him up and return to the house. Perp then tosses the dog some pills wrapped in hamburger, or something, waits until he keels over, then goes to the back door. Now, you put a dog outside like that, you don't lock the door. Why bother, you have to bring the dog in later. I bet the door was unlocked. Perp goes in, does whatever with Bauer, leaves the same way they came in. Locks it on the way. Done. If there was a deadbolt on the back door, check Bauer's keychain, I bet his key is gone because your perp locked up when they left. You need to tape the back yard."

The red and blue lights washed over everyone's faces. The investigator nodded slowly and cracked a small smile. One of the paramedics coughed in a way that sounded like he was trying to hide a laugh.

"Chief." It was the pickup driver. "Kent usually tied Cinders outside when he came home. I gave him shit about it all the time. Told him to walk the damn dog, give it some exercise."

Still watching Vic, the state investigator cocked his head to one side. "Show me."

Vic shifted both his arms to his left so the handcuffs showed from behind his back.

"Little help here?"

Chapter 18

The chief nodded to the officer who kicked him and a few moments later Vic's hands were free. Vic held out his palm for his ID and the chief returned his badge wallet. The state investigator waved at him to lead the way.

Vic pointed at Lou. The chief followed his hand and saw Lou holding Vic's Glock and holster.

"You got a permit for that?" the chief asked.

"Pennsylvania permit. If that isn't good for North Dakota, let me know."

The chief hesitated. Vic knew the math. State gun laws were so inconsistent that working out state-by-state alignment and reciprocity was a pain. He was betting the chief would just hand it over.

"After we look at the back yard," the investigator said. Vic caught a slight smile, as if he understood what Vic was doing. He waved for Vic to lead the way.

Vic started around the outside perimeter of the tape toward the back. The investigator ducked under the tape and followed, as did the chief, the two men from the truck and Lou.

Halfway down the neighbor's side yard the investigator said, "Hold up." He turned to the chief and Lou. "We got this, guys. Head back. I don't want four more sets of footprints back there." He pointed at the two men from the truck. "Especially you two, unless you want to end up suspects. Stay in your truck. I'll interview you after this."

The chief opened his mouth but snapped it shut and started for the front of the house. The pick-up driver frowned, but followed him, as did the others.

Vic could tell he didn't like following someone else's lead. The investigator turned to Vic and held out his hand.

"I'm Detective Karl Swenson."

"Detective Vic Lenoski."

They shook.

Swenson nodded toward the backyard. "Okay, show me what you got."

Vic led him past the scraggly row of pine trees, pointed out the shed, and waited as Karl swept the inside with an LED flashlight. The beam lingered on the floor beneath the window. When Vic pointed out the German Shepherd, Karl slid out a walkie talkie and told the chief to cordon off the area plus ten feet of the neighbor's backyard. He instructed the paramedics to transport the dog to a veterinarian. He waved at Vic to join him, and started toward the neighbor's house, his head down, his flashlight sweeping the ground in front of him like a metronome. Vic sidled several feet to his left and walked beside him, helping with the search. He knew Karl assumed the perp walked through the neighbor's property and waited in the shed.

They walked past the house and reached a wide street.

"Well, doesn't that take the cake," Karl said.

Vic followed his gaze. Facing them loomed a three-story brick building that looked like it was built in the early 1900s. Engraved on a sandstone slab above the front door were the words *Municipal Building*.

They crossed the street and looked through a high chain-link fence into a parking lot.

"Anyone could park there," Vic said, gesturing at an open gate.

"And I bet anyone did," Karl answered softly, under his breath. At almost the same instant they both turned their gazes to the side of the building that faced the parking lot.

"Shit," Vic said.

"Damn right. No cameras. And why am I not surprised? This is where the city council meets. You ever notice politicians like working where no one can see them?"

"But they love being on TV so much."

Karl huffed. "Don't get me started." He took several photos of the lot. Vic liked that. He knew at some point Karl would track down the owner of every car parked there and ask them what vehicles they remembered seeing that night.

"Took some balls, though," Vic said. "Is the police department in that building?"

"It is. But this is someone smart enough to hide in the shed and drug the dog. And parking here is hiding in plain sight. They obviously plan ahead." He pursed his lips in annoyance.

Vic knew what he was thinking. Most criminals weren't that bright. This one was, and it would make catching him a heck of a lot harder.

They returned to the line of pine trees behind Bauer's house. The officer from the front door was stringing yellow tape through the neighbor's backyard. He avoided Vic's eyes. Vic and Karl walked around the perimeter.

"Anything you can tell me about what happened to Kent Bauer?" Vic asked.

Karl didn't say anything for a few steps. "You know I can't. Even with the chief screwing up. Professional courtesy doesn't extend that far."

"Jimmy Pronghorn tell you that he brought me here?"

Karl stopped. "No."

Vic turned to him. Red and blue lights skated across Karl's pale face. "You guys know each other."

Karl stayed quiet. Vic knew he was considering how much to tell him. Karl let out a short breath. "We both grew up out here, Bismarck, unlike ninety percent of the people living here now." Vic guessed he was talking about Jimmy to avoid discussing the case. "Back then it was a real small place. You got to know people."

"But you guys know each other pretty well."

"Is that any of your business?" Karl's voice turned gruff.

"No. But I flew in and he was waiting at the airport for me. Never met the guy. He was sent to me as the friend of a friend. Don't know how much I can trust him."

"You flew into Williston or Bismarck?"

"Williston."

"And you drove out here with him?"

"Yes."

"Seems like you already decided that, haven't you?"

"Not really. Just haven't seen anything that warns me off. So far."

Karl smiled, his teeth flashing, his eyes bright. "You won't. Not with Jimmy. He's native Hidatsa Indian, on his mother's side. That gives him claim. He reads too much for my taste, but that means he respects his tribe's history. Do some research on that, it'll tell you a lot about how he really thinks, instead of all the shit he gives you for being white. Plus, we played high school ball together. We both served. I'd take him beside me any time it got sloppy."

"And what about the chief and those guys from O&G Supply? They frat brothers or something?"

Karl didn't answer for a few seconds. "Kind of wondered that myself." He turned and walked toward the front of the house.

Vic followed. "Any chance I can see the reports on what happened? I mean I can't interview Kent anymore, and I flew all the way out here."

They reached the tape at the front of the house. The ambulance was gone, and with it Cinders, the German Shepherd. Karl turned to him. "Maybe you should have called before you got on a plane."

Vic held his gaze. "Where's the fun in that?"

He thought he saw the glimmer of a smile before Karl held out a business card. "Got a card? I'm gonna need to talk to you. If you're out here because someone took a run at a cop, and Kent might have known about it, I need to understand what you know. Might lead me to a new group of suspects. Where you staying?"

"Days Inn." Vic held out his own business card.

Karl took it. "I'll be here most of the night. But we need to talk before you leave. When is that?"

"I figured at least four days."

"Let's talk tomorrow. I'll call you. Don't leave town until we've spoken." They shook hands.

Now he did smile. "Pittsburgh, huh?"

"Born and bred."

"I was a linebacker in high school. Used to watch game film of the Steelers back then. Loved your linebackers. Lloyd. Lambert. Those guys."

"Until the last few years."

He waved his hand in the still air. "Look around. See a pro team anywhere near here? You gotta pick your spots." He ducked under the tape, said something to Lou and crossed to the front door of the house. He didn't nod or make a gesture toward the men inside the pick-up, and Vic was glad about that.

Without a word Lou walked over and handed him his Glock.

As he returned to Jimmy's truck, he thought about the last thing Karl said, about picking his spots. It was the same sentence Jimmy had used at the diner.

A little too convenient, he thought.

Chapter 19

Vic found Jimmy slouched in the driver's seat, arms folded on his chest, staring at the steering wheel.

"Sorry." Vic slid into the passenger side. The dome light didn't turn on with the opening of the door, and Vic wondered if that was on purpose.

Jimmy worked himself upright. "Looks like this Kent Bauer's going to be a tough interview."

"Conversation would be one-sided, true."

"Timing is tough for you."

"Yes. It is," Vic said, not liking that coincidence.

"Where to?"

"Motel." He was tired, suddenly, even though it wasn't that late. Then he remembered the time difference between Pittsburgh and North Dakota.

Jimmy executed a three-point turn. Once they were moving, he said quietly, "You figured out a lot about the back yard."

Vic glanced at him. "Drugging the dog makes it premeditated, unless someone always carries around raw hamburger and some kind of sleeping pill. That means the person thought about how to get into the house without being seen. Go in the front and a neighbor might spot you. Odds on it was the back door."

"When you put it that way."

Something else turned in Vic's mind. "Do you know those O&G Supply guys or their company?"

"Some…I can ask around. I saw how buddy-buddy they were with the cops."

"That's exactly what bothered me."

They stopped at an intersection, Jimmy taking his time, the same way he paused between sentences. "I know they used to be a drilling company, but maybe five years ago they switched to supplying the drill sites and their crews. Drilling is elephant hunting. You have to stay in business long enough to get the kill. Equipment and servicing aren't sexy...but you get rich. Slowly."

Vic let the silence drift between them, thinking about the next day. He couldn't spot a single star in the sky. "Tomorrow I want to check the house where the mother lives."

"Nearby?"

"Kind of. Arnegard. It's west of here, but I'm guessing twenty minutes to get there."

Jimmy smirked. "We drove past it."

"We did?"

"Blinked and you missed it. But that's not the best part. A few weeks ago, their town council voted to fire their two police officers...that's after the cops brought charges against two of the council members. Worse than tribal politics. We can drive all the streets in about six minutes, if we go slow."

"We'll go slow."

The Days Inn loomed ahead. Jimmy turned into the parking lot and Vic guided him into a parking spot below the window to his room. Jimmy's movements were smooth, and Vic had the feeling he was parked perfectly between the lines. Jimmy killed the motor.

Vic didn't get out. "That Karl Swenson guy talked about you. Said you guys played ball together. Football."

Jimmy left one hand on top of the steering wheel and hooked the thumb on his other hand over the bottom of the steering wheel. "We both made varsity in ninth grade. Only three of us from our class. We got picked on that year, but it made us tight. Senior year we should have won state, too."

"You guys made the championship game?"

"We did, and lost. Coach said it was my fault. I had a pass interference penalty called on me late. Afterwards Karl found me and apologized. He knew what really happened. He missed his assignment and I had to cover his guy. Meant I couldn't play the right way and took the foul. But he owned up to it. I was only eighteen, but I understood how important that apology was. Didn't surprise me he decided to be a cop."

"Usually you lose because a lot of little things go wrong. It's hardly ever one play."

"Tell that to an eighteen-year old…or a locker room full of them. My penalty gave the other team a first down and they ran out the clock."

Vic let the silence gather. He'd never played team sports, but he understood team dynamics, how everyone had to do their job. Behind them on the road a tanker truck thundered past.

"Where you staying?" Vic asked.

"Right here." Jimmy opened his door and slid out. As he walked in the direction of the motel's office, he called over his shoulder, "if they decide to rent me a room." He was being sarcastic, but Vic guessed he'd been turned down before.

Vic left a gap between his curtains, so he could look down and see the grill of Jimmy's truck. He flipped on the television and placed his Glock on the bedside table, next to his badge wallet. Cars whizzed by outside, the sound sometimes deepened by the roar of an eighteen-wheeler. He linked his laptop to the hotel's Wi-Fi and checked the O&G Supply web site. The company founder was in his forties, with a square face, thick lips and arrogant brown eyes that bored into the camera. He looked familiar, but Vic couldn't understand why.

He searched on Jimmy Pronghorn, Charlie Running Bear and the Hidatsa Indians. On the Hidatsa Tribe website, he found Jimmy in a group photograph of the tribal council. Charlie Running Bear's photo appeared in a string of articles about the Dakota Pipeline protests of 2016. In one, he sat upright in a manual wheelchair, thick chested, his face set, jawline prominent. His long black hair was parted down the middle. Vic guessed he was in his early forties. No electric wheelchair for him, Vic thought. Not the type.

He read the history of the Hidatsa Indians, and how their captive, the Shoshone Indian Sacagawea, took part in the Lewis and Clark expedition. In a stunning coincidence, he read how she helped Lewis and Clark survive a meeting with an angry Shoshone chief because she turned out to be the chief's sister. He also read how the Hidatsa never went to war with America, and remembered Karl's comment about ignoring Jimmy's pot shots at white people.

He glanced outside. The grill of Jimmy's truck was still there. He closed the curtains, prepared for bed and lay down with only the television for company. He turned it almost all the way down, the images flickering on the walls like firelight in a cave.

As he drifted toward sleep, he thought about Anne and how their marriage hung by a thread, as fragile as the call he and Levon left open that afternoon. Outside a truck drowned out the murmur of the television. He'd come all this way, taken the chance of talking to Kent Bauer, and already that was gone. He knew he'd be lucky to get three minutes with Cora Stills' mother. The air thickened in his lungs. If she didn't talk to him, he'd have nothing, he would have travelled this distance and failed. He knew the meaning of that. He needed to bring something back for Anne, some explanation of what happened to Dannie, a truth about her. Then, they might have a chance. But if he was empty-handed, Anne would turn away and Liz's sacrifice would be for nothing. Somehow, he sensed, even Pittsburgh would be lost to him.

He stared at the popcorn ceiling, then the television. The people on the screen seemed silly and forced.

His phone rang.

Anne.

"Vic?"

"I was just thinking about you." He hoped she ignored the catch in his voice.

Silence for a moment. "I visited Liz tonight. I just got back. She's struggling."

"I talked to Levon. Is she doing any better?"

"The nurse said she's not getting any worse. I guess that's good." She paused. "How about you?"

Vic didn't know where to start. "Different country out here. Levon found me some Hidatsa Indian to take me around. He thinks he can do standup."

"Maybe he can. Or maybe you aren't getting the joke." She said it quickly, tartly, as if she wanted to change the emotional frame of the conversation.

Vic chuckled to himself. "Wouldn't be the first time."

"Have you ever even met a real Indian before?"

"No."

"So, give him a chance."

"I will. Actually, I kind of like him." He closed his eyes, hating to say what he needed to say next. "I'll know in a day or two if I have a shot at Cora Stills."

"Sounds good."

Vic knew her words were meant to encourage him, but he heard a careful neutrality in her tone. An emptiness.

"Also," she added quickly, as if she was worried he might read her thoughts. "Was there anything useful in Liz's statement?"

Vic struggled upright in bed. "What statement?"

"I heard she gave one. When they first moved Liz out of the burn ward to the step-down unit. You didn't see it?" Her voice grew tight and anxious.

"I didn't know she'd given one."

"Pretty sure she did. Right before she went back into the ICU."

Vic squeezed his eyes shut. "Do you know who interviewed her?"

"No. I guess someone on the task force looking for Cora. Can you call someone?"

Something moved in Vic's gut. There was no task force, only Kevin. He didn't want to tell her that. "I can figure it out." Now it was his turn for his words to sound neutral.

For a moment, she didn't say anything. Vic guessed she was wondering why his excitement at the news was chased so tightly by despair.

"Okay. Vic, it's late, I have to go."

"Thanks for calling."

The air between them was empty and dry.

"Good luck, Vic." The call died.

Vic slid his phone back onto his bedside table. He stared at the ceiling for a time before turning off the television.

Chapter 20

He slept badly. In the deepest part of the night he blinked at the ceiling, reliving his phone call with Anne. He gauged the pauses in conversation, relived every shift in tone and topic. They all added up to the same thing. Whenever the conversation presented a chance to discuss their feelings, Anne pivoted away. It was as if she didn't want to know how he felt, or, he wanted to believe, she wasn't ready for that conversation yet.

He knew he was kidding himself.

He couldn't shake the feeling they were now different people. Instead of a shared sadness and linked comprehension of how each felt about Dannie's disappearance, they had internalized their grief individually. Chosen not to share it with each other.

He blamed himself for that. He stared into the dark. His months of drinking were more than just wasted time. They were the lost chance for he and Anne to face Dannie's disappearance together.

A tear skimmed from the corner of one eye to his ear. He swiped at it, angry at himself for those lost months, and, worse, at now feeling sorry for himself about it. He and Anne still had one thing in common, he told himself: They both wanted to know what happened to Dannie. Anne had never wavered about that, but he had. Lost in drink he'd been scared of what he might find. It was Anne who brought him around. Guided him to the right answer. As always, she'd known the heart of it, the same way she'd asked if he ever met an Indian, just as he started to criticize Jimmy. She knew how to reposition him, how to face him the right way. He loved her for that.

Always had.

But she was fading into the distance. Or he was.

Or they both were.

Find Cora Stills, he told himself. Find her. He wasn't sure he could bear to lose more.

At six he gave up trying to sleep and stumbled out of bed. He pulled the desk chair in front of the door and sat facing it. To the doorknob, he attached a feather-thin green elastic band given to him by his physical therapist. Starting with a lot of play in the elastic, he worked through the cycle of exercises designed to strengthen the muscles around this rotator cuff. The cycle finished, he shuffled the chair closer to the door, gripped the length of the elastic closer to the doorknob, and strained against the tighter resistance through two more cycles. Sweat beaded on his forehead as he concentrated. He shuffled the chair closer, shortened the elastic again, and forced himself to complete three more cycles.

Panting, he stopped, dropped the elastic and rotated his right arm, checking its range and flexibility. It ached in annoyance and he liked the accompanying stiffness. The exercises were working. Better, he felt grounded again, calm. He showered, dressed, sat at the narrow desk and dialed a number at police headquarters in Pittsburgh.

Even with the time difference it was an early call, but Kevin answered on the second ring.

"Vic?"

"Kevin. Glad I got you. Do you have a minute?"

"Sure, but I thought you were on mandatory leave." His first note of surprise gave way to suspicion.

"I am. Otherwise I'd be at my desk." Vic marshaled his thoughts, picturing Kevin sitting in his cube, his feet on his desk, not a blond hair out of place on his perfectly groomed head.

"What's up?" Kevin asked.

"I heard you're running the task force looking for Cora Stills. Any progress? Anything I can do?" He tried to keep his voice steady, as if it was the most natural thing in the world that someone two grades below detective would be in charge of finding a fugitive wanted for the attempted murder of a police officer.

"Sure. Making progress." Kevin's voice was guarded and Vic imagined him swinging his feet off his desk and hunching over the phone.

"Any good leads?"

Silence for a few seconds. "Vic, I thought you were on leave?"

"Oh, you know how it goes. When something happens with your partner you want to help. See if there's anything you can do. You know what I mean."

"Sure," Kevin said, his tone as flat as a cutting board.

Vic squeezed his eyes closed in frustration. His words were a mistake. Kevin had never partnered with another cop. He was the last remaining officer from Crush's experiment in hiring criminal justice majors directly from college. Kevin survived by working special projects, whenever Crush could think them up.

Vic closed his eyes, his thumb and forefinger pinching the bridge of his nose. He decided to come clean.

"Kevin, look, I heard Liz gave a statement. I was hoping to read it. I thought there might be something useful in there."

Silence spooled between them.

Vic hunched over his desk, the phone pressed tight to his ear. "Kevin. I heard you're on this alone. That's bullshit. You should have a team working for you. This is way too much for one person. I'm offering to help."

"You're on leave."

"Even better. We keep it between us. Look, I'm doing well. Shoulder feels good. Maybe I could help you figure out what to run down first. I can handle the shit work. Help you use your time effectively."

"Crush gave this to me. He believes I can do it."

Vic stopped himself from telling Kevin how the DA made Crush slow-walk the investigation, that Kevin got the job because he was the worst officer in the department. "Right. But ask yourself, why is that? This is a police officer who was injured. She's back in the ICU. We don't know if she's going to survive. Why you?"

"Because I can handle it." His words rushed together in anger.

Vic bit back what he wanted to say. He'd forgotten how incompetent people never understand their own incompetence, how hard they clutch any sign of being successful. "I wasn't arguing with you, Kevin. I know you're in charge. I just thought you might want some help, and I've got time on my hands." Vic hesitated. "Okay, I'll leave you to it." He waited, hoping he had sounded non-threatening enough. It was his last gambit.

"I'll call you if I need you," Kevin said, and the phone went dead in Vic's hand.

Vic dumped his phone on the desk, sat back, then stood. He cursed the window curtains a few times.

Someone knocked on his door.

Vic looked through the peephole, saw Jimmy outside, and opened the door.

Jimmy looked rested, his long hair wet and stringy from a shower. "What time you want to track down this Stills person?"

"Soon as we can do it."

Jimmy stood patiently, and Vic realized he was waiting for him.

Chapter 21

Vic and Jimmy found rubbery scrambled eggs and lukewarm take-out coffee in a small room near the front desk. Ten minutes later they headed west on Route 85 toward Arnegard. The sky was overcast but still towered above them.

Vic sipped his coffee. "You talk to Charlie Running Bear last night?"

Jimmy didn't answer for a few moments. "Yes. He thought it was funny. How you got handcuffed."

"Glad to entertain you guys."

"He said now you know how it feels."

Vic picked at the cap on his coffee cup. "I doubt that. That was just some young officer being stupid and showing his training didn't stick. I bet it's different when one of you guys gets handcuffed."

Jimmy gave him a sidelong glance and didn't say anything.

Twenty minutes later a sign welcomed them to Arnegard.

"Take this right," Vic said at the following intersection. "I liked your idea yesterday. Let's drive around. I want to get a feel for the place."

Jimmy dropped his speed and swung right onto a neighborhood road wide enough for three lanes. The concrete was so new the road almost gleamed. For the next ten minutes they crisscrossed residential streets, all of them as broad and new as the first road.

"What is it with these roads?" Vic asked.

"Fracking money." Jimmy was preoccupied looking at the houses.

Vic followed his gaze and saw how the houses—all of them little better than single story boxes clutching the ground—didn't match up to the shiny concrete roads. Yards were overgrown, facades half-hidden behind stubby, sprawling trees. Driveways were gravel or nonexistent. The last road of the town, the farthest from the main road, was lined with a string of mobile homes.

"Rig worker housing," Jimmy said as they passed. A few had white pickups parked alongside.

Vic nodded, counting front doors, and guessed that half the town was now rig workers.

They circled back into the residential streets. When Vic spotted Nadine Still's address, he guided Jimmy into a cross street and asked him to park. The front door of Cora Still's mother's house was about fifty yards away. He knew he was stalling for time, but he didn't care.

"Bad juju," Jimmy said. "Cops see me sitting here they're gonna ask why."

"I thought you said the cops were fired."

"Oh sure…and after that they probably hired the councilmen's cousins. They'll be worse."

Vic nodded, understanding Jimmy's point. "I just want a sense of what I'm walking into."

"You don't actually think Cora Stills is hiding there?"

"No way. She's too smart for that."

"So…" Jimmy didn't push it, and they sat in silence.

The wind buffeted the truck cab. Nothing moved in the house; the tiny gravel pull-off in front was empty. At one point, Vic's phone vibrated in his pocket but he ignored it. Another minute drifted by. A single pickup truck passed them, but otherwise the street was empty. Nobody walked dogs, nobody worked in the yards.

Jimmy shuffled in his seat. "How long do we sit here?"

"Okay. Pull up in front of the house."

Jimmy started the truck quickly, glad to be doing something. He parked in the pull-off and Vic slid out. At the front door he rang the bell. Instantly, his stomach contracted. He had no plan. He glanced about the yard, trying to gather himself. He saw tufts of grass, weeds, and humps of dirt from tunneling moles. The wind pushed at him. He only had one chance at Cora's mother, and there was so much riding on it.

The door remained closed. He looked through the small inset window, feeling like he might have bought himself time. No lights. He knocked. Still nothing. He turned back to the truck, looking at the grass near the pull-off. Partial tire tracks marred the ground. He climbed into the truck.

"Not home," he said.

"Good detective work. We got to go anyway."

Vic turned to say something but Jimmy cut him off. "Karl called me while you were banging on the door...he called you but you didn't pick up. He wants to interview you over lunch. We need to get going."

Vic nodded. He didn't mind. He needed time to think, to find a way to approach Cora's mother. She was his one chance and he needed to do it right.

Chapter 22

J immy guided the truck back into Watford City, to a diner on the main street. They chose a booth overlooking the parking lot. Jimmy pointed at a restroom sign and disappeared. Vic settled into the booth, surprised it was almost noon, given how early he had started the day.

His phone rang. He didn't recognize the number.

The phone was barely to his ear when Crush shouted, "What the hell is going on?"

Vic closed his eyes. He should have anticipated Kevin would tell Crush about his call. "I'm on leave. That's what's going on." He pictured Crush sitting ramrod straight at his desk, beads of sweat glistening on his shaved head, every muscle-flicker of his free-weights-sculpted arms showing through his white uniform shirt.

"North Dakota? What the hell are you doing there?"

Vic blinked and something shifted in his brain. He hadn't told Kevin he was in North Dakota.

Crush plowed on. "I got a call from the state police out there. Some investigator called Karl Swenson. Said he found you at a crime scene last night."

Vic shook his head. Something else he should have anticipated. Of course, Karl would check his credentials before interviewing him. As quickly, he understood why he hadn't recognized the caller. Crush was using his personal phone.

"I flew out to talk to someone. You remember Lily Bauer..."

"Of course I damn do!"

A waitress appeared at the booth, a carafe of coffee raised in an unspoken question. Vic nodded and signaled her to fill the white mugs.

"Okay," Vic continued. "Her ex-husband is a guy called Kent Bauer. I came out here to talk to him. I have a lead that he might know something about Dannie's disappearance."

"You're on damn mandatory leave!"

Vic paused, unsure why Crush was angry. "Right, and how I spend it is up to me. I'm paying for this trip. I'll be back at work in two weeks when my leave is up."

Crush was silent for a moment. "What lead?" He asked the question as if his brain cramped just thinking about what Vic might be doing.

"It's good enough to fly out here. Also, Cora Stills' mother lives near here. Figured I'd interview her about Cora, see if she knows anything. Way too much coincidence."

"Cora Stills is Kevin's investigation."

"C'mon." Vic felt his anger rise. "Kevin couldn't figure out who shoplifted a ham if the guy was eating it in front of him. You know that. That's why you put him on it. Because you do anything the DA asks."

Vic cut himself off. His anger had got ahead of him. Eva was sitting fifteen feet from Crush's desk, probably listening to their call, or at least Crush's end of it. Crush was smart enough to figure that out. If anyone overheard his call with the DA, it was Eva. He'd just given her up.

Crush took a couple of slow breaths. Then slowly, carefully, softly, he asked, "How do you know what I talk to the DA about?"

"Look, Liz is back in the ICU. She was almost killed and you put Kevin on it? Where's the task force? A few days ago, I went out to Stills' workplace. I was the first one to interview her boss. Seriously? That's first circle of acquaintances crap. Kevin doesn't even know where to start."

"Wait a minute," Crush said. Vic heard a shuffling sound and then a thump. Vic gritted his teeth, guessing that Crush had closed his office door. He'd worked out that Eva might be the leak and was taking precautions.

"What did you hear about my conversation with the DA?" Crush asked, his voice surprisingly gentle. Vic thought about the question. Crush hadn't focused on who leaked the information, but rather the content. His tone suggested he was bothered more about that than the leak.

"I heard he told you to slow-walk the investigation."

Crush stayed silent. He didn't deny it.

Vic understood Crush's silence. He was offering Vic a chance to explain himself. "Liz told me Cora Stills knew someone was coming to arrest her. That was how Cora got the drop on Liz, and why she had the house primed to burn down. The only people who knew a warrant was being prepared for Cora was me, Liz, the DA and whoever in his office does the paperwork. It's a real small group and the DA is in the middle of it. I need to find that leak."

"Uh-huh." Crush's intonation made Vic think he was aligning Vic's information with something else he knew or thought. Distractedly, Crush added, "Liz put that in her statement."

"You read her statement?" Vic couldn't keep the surprise out of his voice. Crush rarely followed individual cases that closely.

Jimmy slid into the booth, his eyebrows raised in a question. Vic held up a forefinger to stay quiet.

"Damn right, I did." Crush's voice recovered its bluster. "Liz was attacked. And why the hell were you asking Kevin for Liz's statement?"

Vic grinned. His first instinct was right. Of course Kevin told Crush about their call. He decided to come clean. "I wanted to see if she said anything else that might help when I talk to Cora Still's mother. That's all."

"Kevin is leading that investigation. You're on leave. You don't talk to him. He was right to refuse."

Vic bit down so he wouldn't say anything he regretted.

"Last thing, though," Crush added. "You're right. What you do on leave is up to you. I'm not going to ask about it. I'll say it again, how you spend your time is up to you. I just expect you to be at work the day your leave is up. Understand?"

Vic blinked. It almost sounded as if Crush was telling him that if he avoided Kevin he could go ahead. And he hadn't told him not to interview Cora's mother.

"Are we clear?" Crush threw out the question like a dart.

"We're clear," Vic answered. A moment later the call dropped. He put his phone on the table.

"Who was that?" Jimmy asked.

"My commander."

"Seemed like it. Sounded like a guy who likes to give orders."

Vic remembered the resources Crush put into the search for Dannie, how thorough it was. He hadn't considered, he realized, that Crush might not like the DAs instructions to slow-walk the Cora Stills investigation. That it might be eating at him. He wondered if Crush was looking for a way around the DA. He doubted it, but the sense of it was there.

"You order?" Jimmy asked.

"I was on the phone. Got you coffee."

Jimmy nodded toward the window. "Karl's here."

Vic followed the nod and saw Karl climb out of his car under a sky as dull as white marble. His pale skin looked waxy and the bags under his eyes like fresh bruises. Vic guessed he hadn't slept.

"There's a guy who loves his job," Vic said.

"You'd be surprised." Jimmy added milk to his coffee.

Vic was about to ask him what he meant when his phone dinged. He checked it to find a text message from Eva. He recoiled at what it might mean, but the text said simply *As requested.*

Attached was a file. Vic touched it open and saw Liz's statement. Excitement sliced through him. He closed it to read later.

"Good news?" Jimmy asked.

Vic watched Karl let himself through the door and turn toward their booth.

"It is." But he was thinking about the way Crush had chosen to send him the file. Not from himself. Instead, it was from Eva, from her personal phone, and she didn't mention Crush by name. He knew why. Crush was warning Vic that he'd guessed Eva overheard the call from the DA, that he knew Eva had taken his side. If an internal review ever targeted Vic, Crush would deny telling Eva to send the file. Eva would be blamed for sending it. It was an impressive display of Crush's legendary bureaucratic survival skills.

Or was it?

Another thought had him. Crush's decision to follow the DA's request to slow-walk the investigation might be good for his career, but it was bad for his reputation within the department. Every detective who worked for him wanted to catch Cora Stills. Vic knew he couldn't be the only one angry that Kevin was leading the investigation. Maybe, just maybe, Crush was telling Vic to keep investigating, that he didn't like the DA's request and hated letting down his detectives. Could it be, Vic wondered, that Crush's loyalty to the force and his detectives outweighed his ambition?

Jimmy slid along the booth seat to make room for Karl.

Vic poured milk into his coffee.

The day was shaping up.

Chapter 23

"Long night?" Jimmy asked, as Karl settled across from Vic.

Karl dead-eyed Jimmy and turned back to Vic. "You okay getting this knocked out?"

"Sure."

The waitress appeared and Karl gratefully watched her fill his coffee cup. They sat in pensive silence as each took a turn reeling off a lunch order. Karl ordered eggs and ham, and Vic guessed it was his first meal since the night before.

Karl didn't add anything to his coffee, just sipped it gratefully. He focused his blue eyes on Vic.

"You checked out," Karl said. "Tomkins Davis is your commander, right?"

"We call him Crush. I could have given you his direct number, kept you from digging around."

Karl gave a single vague shake of his head as if it didn't matter. "Crush?"

Vic smiled. "Long story. He'd just got the job and was angry with a bunch of us. Slams his fist on the table. He's a big weightlifting and nutrition guy and forgot he was holding an orange. Splat."

Karl nodded. "Better than Tomkins. It took him a few seconds to get his head around the fact you're in North Dakota." Karl watched him and Vic knew the interview had already started.

"I'm on leave right now. Line of duty injury. I decided to follow two leads that were out here."

"You're here on your own dime?"

"It was my partner who almost died."

Karl raised his coffee mug, drained it, glanced around and signaled to the waitress. "Crush said you got your partner out."

"Just."

"He also said the person your partner was there to arrest might know something about your daughter's disappearance."

"Right again."

The waitress appeared and refilled their mugs. When she finished, Karl slid out of the booth and looked at Jimmy. "You mind? I need to get into police business, now."

"I was there last night."

"I noticed. And you made sure you were close enough to hear what we said." His tone shifted during the sentence and Vic knew that Karl thought it was funny and didn't mind. "But this goes on tape."

Jimmy looked at Vic as he slid across the seat. "See? There goes the white man moving the Injun off prime real estate again."

"I owe you a beer," Karl said, as Jimmy passed him and took a seat at the counter.

"Oh sure. First relocate us, then give us firewater," Jimmy said over his shoulder, pointedly putting his back to Karl. Vic heard humor in his voice.

Karl tried not to smile, and Vic knew the banter was how they interacted. They were better friends than he first thought.

Karl sat down and punched the record button on his phone. He reeled off the date, time of day, place and a number Vic assumed was the case file. He pointed at his phone and Vic gave his name and threw in his rank and badge number.

"Walk me through last night," Karl said.

Vic took his time and described his arrival at the scene. How he was concerned the back yard wasn't taped off, investigated, and found the garden shed and drugged dog. He walked through the confusion that led to him handcuffed on the ground, and how he and Karl then investigated the neighbor's yard and the road beyond it.

When he was finished, Karl leaned close. "And why did you leave Pittsburgh to speak to Kent Bauer?"

Vic took a slow breath. "I have a source who suggested that Kent Bauer might know something about the abduction of my daughter. She was taken with three other women with the motive of trafficking them."

"Can you provide the name of the source?" Karl asked the question carefully.

Vic shook his head. "Sorry. Confidential."

Karl left it alone and followed up with several questions about Kent Bauer, including his years living in Western Pennsylvania. Vic offered to personally pull any files Karl needed and forward them.

The waitress arrived with their food and Karl announced a pause in the interview. He pressed the stop button on his phone. They ate in silence. Karl finished his meal in about six mouthfuls.

As soon as Karl sat back, Vic put down his hamburger. "How's it going?" He didn't think he needed to clarify the question.

Karl pursed his lips before spearing the last surviving hash brown on his plate. "Not much to go on."

Vic thought about that. "Can you tell me anything about how he died?"

Karl wiped his mouth with a paper napkin. The waxiness had fallen from his face. "You know," he said, "your commander said you've been a detective for what, twelve years?"

"Something like that."

"He said you're about the best he has."

Vic stared at him. He couldn't believe Crush told Karl anything like that. "He mention the time he suspended me?"

Karl smiled. "He did. He said you push hard. Sometimes things get bent and screws pop out. Once in a while something gets broken. But he also said you don't jump to conclusions too soon and you never take shortcuts."

Vic remembered his earlier suspicion that Crush wanted him to keep investigating Cora Stills. Here it was again. Talking up Vic to Karl was the typical kind of oblique tactic Crush would use to put Karl in a mind to help him.

"So far, Vic's been a bit of a dick," said Jimmy, standing at the edge of the table. Vic hadn't noticed him walk over.

A smile cracked Karl's lips.

Vic looked from one to the other. "You guys taking this act on the road?" He set his gaze on Karl. "I do have a couple of questions, if you don't mind."

Karl waved his hand at Jimmy. "Sorry, we need a couple more minutes."

"Of course you do." He turned for the counter.

"Back to how Kent Bauer died."

Karl let out a slow breath. "ME is working on it, but right now we think asphyxiation."

"He was strangled?"

"No ligature marks. His trachea was crushed."

Vic sat back. "Tough way to go. Takes time."

"They helped him along. Plastic bag over the head. We're pretty sure that was after the blow that took care of the trachea. He'd be too occupied trying to breathe to fight it."

Vic shut his eyes. "I don't get it." He opened them. "Was there a fight?"

"Nope. Looks like he was watching television, someone came up behind him and tased him. Zip tied his ankles and wrists while he was recovering. Then the larynx, then the bag over the head."

"That's complicated."

Karl nodded in agreement. "Yep. Seems like a lot of trouble."

Vic caught a vagueness in his answer and knew there was something more. He guessed Karl wasn't sure himself and wanted time to think about it. Vic considered the facts a moment longer. "Sounds like someone made it last awhile."

Karl looked away through the window. "I had the same thought. Like that was the point."

"So maybe revenge."

"I already interviewed the guys closest to him and a couple of women he hangs out with. Nothing so far."

"Debts? Gambling?"

"Looking into it now."

"You know," Vic said carefully, "that son he has in Pennsylvania? He's in jail and the boy's mother blames Kent for not helping the son out. But the ex is in jail herself, so her alibi is tight."

"Peach of a family," Karl mumbled.

Vic still had the feeling Karl wasn't telling him something. "Do you have anything else?"

"You'll like this. Crime scene guys were able to say the murderer came in through the back door. You were right, he left it unlocked when he put the dog out."

"Dog is okay?"

"He came around at the vets. It'll be a couple of weeks until we know what they used to drug him."

"That's something. The person cased the place, guessed the weight of the dog and gave him the right dosage of drugs to put him to sleep, but not kill him. Interesting thing to worry about, given what the murderer had planned for Kent."

Karl nodded. "I thought that as well, but I don't know what it tells me."

"Someone careful. But given the condition of the body, the motive is going to be the size of an eighteen-wheeler. Should be easy to spot. Do enough interviews and it'll probably run you over." Vic watched the waitress cash someone out. "Anything unique about the scene?"

"Every scene is different." Karl glanced at Jimmy, who was now lounging on his stool, watching the local news.

Now Vic was sure Karl was holding something back. "You know, when I come across something unique, I check other crimes to see if it pops up anywhere else."

Karl turned back to him, his blue eyes not giving anything away. "Must be nice to have a large force. Lots of resources to go file diving."

"Your case system online? Searchable?"

"Some of it. Last few years only."

"Never hurts." Vic had an idea. He swigged the last of his coffee and put the mug directly in front of him. "Different thing. I have a favor to ask."

Karl didn't say anything for a few moments, then, "You gave me the back yard. I'll listen to it."

"I want to interview Nadine Stills, mother of Cora Stills, the person who went after my partner. Problem is, I have no standing. She can tell me to jump off a cliff and I've got no recourse. The guy running the investigation in Pittsburgh is such a rookie his mother still straightens his hair with spit. Down the road he'll figure out he should talk to Cora Stills' relatives, but I have no idea when that will be. If I showed up with you, she'd do an interview."

"Normally we'd need something in writing for that."

"That's why it's a favor."

Karl picked up his phone. "I'll have to do it on my own time."

"That's okay. Jimmy and I stopped by this morning. Looks like she works during the day."

Karl gave a short nod. "Okay. Early evening tonight? I can probably get away at five. I'm staying around here tonight anyway."

"I'd appreciate it."

Karl slid his phone into his jacket pocket. "If I need anything more out of this," he waved his hand in a circle indicating the space between them, "I'll let you know. We can tack it onto what we have." He slid out of the booth and stepped to the counter. "Jimmy. I'll take Vic here out to do an interview tonight. You get a rest."

"Do I get the beers you promised?"

"If you lend me the money," he called as he headed to the cash register.

Vic stood as well. The day absolutely was shaping up. He reached around Jimmy and snagged his check. He guessed Jimmy was part of the reason Karl was willing to help.

As he waited for Karl to finish paying, he thought about Nadine Stills. An idea came to him. Jimmy walked up behind him as he gave their checks to the cashier.

"Actually," Vic said to Jimmy, "no beers for you tonight. I need your help with something."

Chapter 24

The knock on Vic's motel room door came a little after six o'clock. "Sorry about that," Karl said, when Vic opened the door. "Took longer than I thought to track someone down."

"You're doing me the favor. Do you still have time?" He rubbed his eyes. He'd reread Liz's statement seven times, trying to spot something, anything that would help him when he interviewed Nadine. Nothing had jumped out.

Karl shrugged. "As much as any other day. Jimmy called, he said you've got him doing something?"

Vic moved aside so Karl could step into his room. "I decided to act as if Cora Stills is hiding around here." He closed the door. "If that's true, after we talk to Nadine, she'll want to warn her. Cora's too smart to use a phone, so they'll have some old school way of getting in touch. I'll use the interview as the start of surveillance. If she goes anywhere, Jimmy will follow, and maybe we get lucky. If Jimmy and I work in shifts we can cover her."

Karl smiled. "Sit out all night on a long shot? I thought my job was bad."

"I'm pretty much down to long shots."

"Then let's get going. We can take my car if Jimmy's already there."

"He is."

Five minutes later they were headed west, directly into the sun. They drove in silence, Vic sunk into himself as he thought about the details of Liz's official statement. They crested a low rise and a shaft of sun shot underneath the visor. He blinked himself back into the present.

He looked at Karl. "When we were in the diner, it seemed like there was something else about the crime scene."

Karl kept his eyes to the road, his shoulders hunched so he could look under the visor. "This doesn't get out," he said finally.

"Understood."

Karl took his time. "Kent's hands and fingers were worked over. Badly bruised, skin split, some of the fingers broken. Someone hit his hands repeatedly."

It dawned on Vic what Karl was actually saying. "You think he was tortured?"

"Have to consider it."

"So. Tased, tied up, fingers smashed, then a crushed trachea, ending with a bag over the head."

"Like I said. Sequence of injuries like that, you have to consider it."

"It's also a lot of planning. Figuring out how to get into the house, take care of the dog, tase Kent and then work him over." Vic frowned at the road. "You said he was sitting in a chair. What chair?"

"Did I say that?"

Vic thought back. "You said you thought he was on a couch when he was tased."

"Right. Whoever it was came through the kitchen and up behind him. Tased him on the neck. That shocked him to the floor. We found him on his back, body under the coffee table and head sticking out, wrists zip-tied to the coffee table legs so his hands stuck up in the air."

Vic's stomach tightened. "Ugly."

"Right, his fingers were sticking up like golf tees. You can do the math."

Vic tried to see it in his mind's eye. "Do you have a photograph?"

Karl shifted in his seat. "When we get to Stills' house."

"If someone took that kind of trouble, they wanted Kent to tell them something or where something was."

"I thought that as well. Can't see someone doing it just for the hell of it."

"Maybe if they absolutely hated him, but my money would be on them wanting something."

They passed the first sign to Arnegard. Karl slowed to turn into the town's residential streets.

A car was parked in the pull-off outside Nadine Stills' house. It was an old Ford, grey squares of primer on the back door and above the rear wheel. Several rust spots speckled the trunk lid.

Karl parked in front of the house next door and dug out his phone. After swiping and pressing the screen a few times, he showed Vic a photograph. Kent Bauer was hard to see, most of his body underneath the coffee table. His head stuck out, covered in a plastic bag, his mouth a round black hole. His hands stuck up above the coffee table, the fingers black and, impossibly, pointing in every direction.

"He couldn't push up on the coffee table and go after his attacker?" Vic asked.

"Hard to see," answered Karl, "but his legs are zip tied to the table legs as well. Maybe he could roll over and take the table with him. But this is the kicker." He hesitated and Vic recognized a moment he'd felt himself, when he had to steel himself to say something. Karl's voice dropped. "See how his left hand doesn't stick up so high? Perp put an eight-inch nail right through his bicep into the floor. Only way to move was to rip himself free."

For a second Vic couldn't say anything. Finally, he leaked out a "Christ." He closed his eyes for a second and the image of a nail sticking out of a bicep flared under his lids. He jerked his eyes open. "The perp brought a nail and hammer with him?"

"Had to. Once Kent was tased, perp didn't have much time. Not enough to go looking for a hammer and get lucky enough to find a nail that size. I mean, it's so crazy you'd almost need to practice it."

Wind pressed against the car. Vic listened to it, guessing that Karl was doing the same. It wasn't strong enough to push the image out of his mind.

"Anyway," Karl said a few moments later. "I took your advice and found someone to look through old case files. Between the smashed fingers and the bicep, the case is unique. If it happened before it's going to stand out." He turned to face Vic. "You got a plan for this Nadine Stills?"

Vic strained to stay focused. "It'll have to be friendly. There's no fugitive warrant out for Cora yet."

"Somehow I doubt she'll roll over on her own daughter."

"Mainly I want to see how she reacts to us, see how defensive she is. If we rattle her enough to want to warn Cora, all the better."

"Good to go?"

"Might as well."

They both got out. Karl slammed his driver's door hard, and Vic knew it was a message in case Nadine was watching. He set his face to match Karl's and, shoulder to shoulder, they walked the path to the front door. Vic rang the bell.

The door opened within a few seconds and Vic knew Nadine had been waiting for them. Karl showed his badge and ID, and explained who he was. As Karl talked, Vic studied her. Cora and Nadine matched each other in height and broad shoulders, but Nadine's hair was a pale stringy brown, which made Vic wonder if Cora's red hair was dyed. Mother and daughter had the same green hooded eyes. The resemblance was strong enough to unleash something slithery in Vic's stomach. He clenched his teeth and swallowed it away. Nadine wore a loose navy-blue T-shirt over baggy, faded jeans. Around-the-house clothes. She smelled of stale cigarettes.

When Karl introduced him, Vic showed his badge and ID and asked if they could come in.

Nadine hesitated, her hand on the door, and Vic was reminded of his first conversation with Cora. They both held the front door the same way, their heads cocked down, thumbs absently working the wood of the door.

"Sure," she tossed off finally, and stepped back, in exactly the same way her daughter had. Karl shifted position to let Vic go first and he knew it was more than politeness, it was an unspoken message for Vic to take the lead. Nadine closed a door off the entry and turned through another.

"Thanks," Vic said, stepping inside.

The entry was barely five-by-five feet. A staircase rose steeply in front of him and to the right was the now-closed door. Nadine was already inside a small dining room. It held a table with six low-backed wooden chairs in a vaguely early American style. It was the kind of clunky furniture sold at discount stores. Karl circled the table and chose a seat that faced the entry. Nadine sat at the head of the table, her back to an arched opening that led to the kitchen. Vic glimpsed white cabinet doors and empty Formica countertops. He didn't smell anything cooking.

Vic sat across from Karl with Nadine to his right.

"What's this about?" Nadine asked.

Vic took his time pulling a notebook from his interior coat pocket and finding his pen. The silence spiraled in on them. Vic let it.

"Mrs. Stills." Vic flipped his notebook open and made a point of writing the date on a blank page. "I'm sorry to drop in like this during dinner time." He looked her in the eye. Her return gaze was blank. "I'm sorry, but are you married? Is your husband home or is he expected?"

Her lips curled. "I haven't seen him in twenty years. If he walked in right now it'd be because he got the house wrong."

"And do you have a daughter named Cora Stills?"

"You know I do." She said it sharply and clasped her hands together on the table in front of her. She shifted in her chair, as if settling in for a long session.

"And to confirm…" Vic worked his way through Cora's birth date and military service.

"That's her," Nadine said as he finished. Her tone was sharp, which told Vic something. She knew why they were visiting.

"And are you aware there is a warrant out for her arrest in Pittsburgh, Pennsylvania?"

"Yes."

"Okay." Vic made a mark in his notebook, mainly to slow down the interview.

"Have you been in contact with your daughter in any way in the last week?"

"I wish I had."

"So that's a no?"

Anger flickered through her green eyes. "I'm being clear."

Vic glanced at the credenza on the far wall. He needed more out of her than anger. "I'm sorry, Mrs. Stills." He lowered his voice and spoke as gently as he could. "I need a yes or no answer on this. I understand she's your daughter, but she's facing serious charges, possibly enough to bring in the FBI. It would be easier for everyone concerned if she turned herself in." He was concentrating so hard on picking his words and tone that it took him a moment to register the items on the sideboard. A short, carved statue in dark wood jumped out at him. Excitement sparked in his chest. It was African. He wasn't an expert, but he was sure of it.

He turned to Nadine. She was watching him with a light frown, as if annoyed that he wasn't paying her closer attention.

"No," she said tartly.

"Thank you. And when did you talk to her last?"

She rearranged herself in her chair. "We talk maybe once a week. The last time was about ten days ago. Check my cell phone. I was wondering why she hadn't called."

The last sentence sounded tacked on. Something added because she thought it might sound better. Vic let the silence tighten around them. "Yes, ma'am. Just so you know, as yet we don't have the legal authority to check your phone. Perhaps you could check it and tell us the last time you received a call or text from her?"

Nadine's mouth tightened, but she reached into the back pocket of her jeans and produced her phone. After a couple of taps and swipes on the screen she gave him a date and time.

"During that conversation, did she tell you anything about her situation or that she might be in trouble?"

"No. It was the usual conversation. What she was doing. How work was going."

"Do you have any idea where she might be today?"

She shook her head. "I don't. Not sure I would tell you if I did."

"I appreciate that." Vic liked her honesty. He wanted to look more closely at the statue but he didn't want her to know he attached any importance to it. He met her gaze. "However, I want to be clear that we believe she is in the area."

Nadine didn't blink or move. Karl's fingers were interlocked on top of the table. His thumbs moved, just once, repositioning one over the other.

"When Cora was growing up here, was there anywhere she liked to go? Favorite places?"

"Like we could afford to take vacations. Why the hell do you think she joined up?"

Vic noted that, again, she hadn't answered his question. He reached into his coat pocket, produced a business card and slid it face up across the table until it was in front of her. "I would appreciate it if you kept my card. My number is there. If she contacts you in any way, call." Then, gently, he added, "If you don't, you'll be in as much trouble as she is."

Nadine glanced at the card, white on the dark wood of the table, as if it was a splotch left by a passing bird. She didn't touch it.

Vic looked at Karl, who shrugged and stood up. Vic followed his lead. Nadine stayed sitting at the table.

"By the way," Vic added, as he put away his notebook. "Since you didn't ask, you should know we also want to talk to your daughter about human trafficking. It's something the FBI will want to discuss with her. Was she ever in trouble before this? I mean in high school or at any other time?"

Exasperation moved through Nadine's eyes, and Vic wondered if it was at the weight of the charges against her daughter, or her realization that she should have asked why they were looking for her daughter. "She's high spirited," Nadine said quickly. "So was her father, before he disappeared." She looked at Vic. "If someone is accusing her of trafficking, it's a lie. I won't say she's perfect, but that's ridiculous."

"I just want you to understand how serious this is. A charge like that has repercussions for anyone protecting a fugitive."

"If there's no more questions you can go." The statement was a freight train of anger.

"Yes, ma'am." Vic turned into the entry. Immediately he stepped past the front door and turned the knob of the door Nadine had closed before she let them in. Against the far wall stood an almond-shaped cow-skin shield. A line of African masks lay on a living room couch, staring at the ceiling. Open packing boxes sat on the coffee table and both armchairs. Vic tugged the door shut and turned to the dining room, just as Nadine appeared in the doorway.

"The door's right there." She nodded at the front door.

Thank you for your time," Karl said and opened the door. Vic followed him outside and down the path. Behind them the door banged shut.

Inside the car, Karl started the engine and turned to Vic. The smile on his face made him look younger. "Textbook stirring the pot, that was. I mean, you have no idea if Cora Still is anywhere near here."

Vic shook his head. "Well, as you said, she isn't going to give up her daughter. No point even trying. But when it turned out she didn't need to ask about the warrant and charges, you have to figure they've talked."

"Was there anything in the living room? You were blocking my view."

"Some stuff that belongs to her daughter. I saw it in Cora's house in Pittsburgh. She must have dropped it off. Nadine's lying about not seeing her in the last week."

"Maybe." Karl slid the car into gear. "Could have been shipped to her."

"It's possible."

"But if you wanted to make her antsy, it's done."

"I do. And now we watch."

Karl executed a U-turn. As they passed through the first intersection, Vic spotted Jimmy parked in his truck and gave him a half salute. He got a middle finger in response.

Karl chuckled before his tone turned serious. "I have a suggestion. Let's stop by the locals. I'll explain who we are and give them a description of Jimmy's truck and the tag number. That way they'll know why he's hanging around. People don't like Natives sitting outside their houses. Or is it Indigenous Peoples? I can never remember."

Vic nodded, more to himself. "Good idea." But he was thinking about the artifacts. He knew he should mention their significance to Karl, but he decided to wait. Maybe Nadine was stirred up enough to do something stupid. If she wasn't, the artifacts might be useful some other way.

Chapter 25

The local police turned out to be a young officer who lost the capacity for eye contact after Karl introduced himself as a North Dakota State Police Investigator. When Karl gestured to Vic and introduced him as a Pittsburgh Police detective investigating the attempted murder of his partner, the young man's neck reddened. In a rush, he spilled out how the chief and a senior colleague were fired by the town council a week earlier and he was holding the force together with a couple of part time officers. He took down the type and tag number of Jimmy's truck and Vic's rental and promised to pass the information on to the part-time officers.

Karl gave Vic a ride back to Watford and dropped him at his motel.

Vic slept fitfully until three a.m. and spelled Jimmy at four. Jimmy told him that Nadine stayed in her house all night after Vic and Karl left.

Alone in the tight wrap of his rental car for the next three hours he dozed, one eye on Nadine's house. She emerged at eight a.m., her head bent to the wind, and walked quickly to her car. When she pulled away Vic followed, as far back as he dared. She drove quickly and efficiently, the way people drive on their work commutes. Twenty minutes west of Arnegard, she turned right onto a gravel drive that led to a large well pad alone at the top of a grass-covered hill. She parked and walked inside one of the prefabricated buildings near the well head. Vic had to drive almost a mile to a gravel side road that led to an oil well. Like the majority of the ones he had seen, it was deserted, the horseheads bobbing lazily. He parked at the entrance, unsure if he was trespassing.

He texted his location to Jimmy and settled in to wait, the wind an endless exhalation. The sky glowed a dingy white, the seamless cloud-cover looking as if it rose vertically from the horizon. He munched on a nutrition bar, and at one point got out to relieve himself. The drilling pad where Nadine worked included a row of six pumpjacks, the large horseheads endlessly rising and falling like drunk birds constantly reaching for a sip of pond water. Another section included a series of ten upright holding tanks, each the size of a minivan. They connected, through a maze of pipes, to a tall exhaust stack topped by a steady plume of fire. From that distance, anyone walking from one building to another looked the size of a grain of rice.

The longer he sat the more his thoughts tracked one another. They spiraled, drew closer and fell away. The memory of Dannie the last time he saw her, how annoyed he was that girls her age wore leggings. Before she left the house, he'd insisted that she wear a long sweater or shirt to cover her behind. Dannie was still angry with him when she left for her friend's house with a curt "see ya."

The last words she'd ever said to him.

That memory belonged to a different world now.

He moved his legs to relieve the stiffness. Nadine's car remained parked. A persistent ache clutched his lower back. He chastised himself for not bringing the elastic bands to do his shoulder exercises. To chase away his memories, he made himself review, once again, the statement Liz gave to Kevin. He turned over every word, phrase, and sentence, searching for anything useful. This time, one specific line nagged at him. He held it up in his mind's eye, turned it, and looked at it from every angle. Nothing.

He spotted Jimmy's truck just after lunchtime, called him and guided him to where he was parked. Jimmy tucked in behind him, and they both got out.

"Need binoculars," Vic said.

"Not so bad. You got lucky. Out here it's sometimes three or four miles to another road or pull off." The wind whipped his long hair over his face, and he hooked it behind his ear.

"Nothing so far. Looks like she went to work and is actually working."

Jimmy gave a mock squint. "That sounds suspicious."

"Hey, this is a long shot."

Jimmy grinned. "I brought a book. How smart am I?"

"Just remember to look up and check on her once in a while."

Jimmy didn't answer, as if the comment was an insult. Vic decided it probably was. He changed the subject. "I read my partner's statement. She gave it to a detective a few days ago."

"Okay."

"She said that when she pulled into the driveway of Cora's house, Cora pointed a handgun at her. She identified the make and caliber but that's not important. Point is that Cora had a gun and probably still has it. More interesting is that after Cora handcuffed her to a radiator, she made a phone call. This was right before she torched the house."

Vic hesitated, and Jimmy nodded that he was listening.

"Anyway, she made this phone call, and my partner overheard Cora's part of it. Nothing is really useful, except at one point, Cora said, 'sure, Lewis and Clark.' That's it. Does that mean anything to you?"

"Half the crap out here is named for Lewis and Clark. Good thing my tribe saved their asses." Jimmy peered at him, and Vic had the odd feeling he wanted Vic to thank him.

Vic grinned. "You mean Sacagawea? Weren't you guys holding her as a slave at the time? I mean your tribe trafficked her from the Shoshone, right?"

The faintest of smiles tracked the corners of Jimmy's mouth. "See? Already back then we were acting like the white man." He glanced away. "Captive, not a slave. Then she married a French trapper. Her decision. Someone's been doing their homework."

"It's called investigating."

"More people should do it. Okay. My best guess? Lewis and Clark State Park."

Vic stared at him.

Jimmy shrugged. "Get on your computer and search on it. It's near Williston on Lake Sakakawea."

Vic didn't understand how he never thought to search on the phrase. "Huh," was all he managed.

Jimmy shrugged. "Does that mean she might be hiding out near there?"

"Beats me. But it might be something."

Jimmy grinned and turned back to his truck. "Get out of here, man. If I see Nadine heading to Williston, I'll let you know."

"Thanks."

Stiffly, Vic lowered himself back into his rental car and started the engine. As he pulled onto the road, he marveled at how some things are right in front of you, if you ever take the time to look.

Chapter 26

Vic and Jimmy exchanged shifts three more times, and Nadine did nothing more suspicious than commute between work and home, and once visit a supermarket. The next night Vic sat in his rental down the street from Nadine's house, watching the first milky glow of dawn in his side mirror. The dashboard clock read five a.m. He pressed his tongue against the backs of his bottom teeth. He knew what he needed to do, but getting it exactly right would be tricky. He'd been rehearsing it for almost an hour. He grunted encouragement to himself, picked up his phone and pressed a number on his call list.

"Captain Steven Klein," came the staccato response to the third ring.

"Skiv? Vic Lenoski from Pittsburgh. Figured you NCIS types would be at your desks already." The time difference meant that it was seven a.m. in Washington D.C. Vic guessed Skiv had been working for at least an hour.

"Lenoski. Tell me something I can use."

"Got a lead for you."

"A good one?"

"You want your African artifacts back?"

A distant thump and hard breath into the phone. "You have them?"

Vic guessed Skiv was now standing behind his desk. He'd hooked him, but now came the difficult part. "No, but I know where they are."

"Where!"

"Look, we need to work together on this."

"Yeah, yeah. Where are they?"

"No, Skiv, listen to me. I'm serious. You want the address you need to do this my way. Then we both get what we want."

"Are you interfering with an investigation?" His voice notched to just below a shout. "This is national security."

"Deep breaths. Hear me out. The address is the middle of the country, middle of nowhere. I'm guessing you'll send the FBI?"

"Damn right. What's the address?"

"Listen, will you? I need this done in two parts. First, a visit from the FBI. They review the artifacts, but they walk away without them. I need the artifacts to stay with the person who has them for seventy-two hours."

"Who the hell would do that? We confiscate what we see."

"No, you can't. That's my point. I need the person who has them to *think* they're going to be confiscated. The FBI needs to take photos and say they'll be back once they verify everything. I want the person who has them to get rattled and make a move, to contact someone. Do you understand? You can't just confiscate them."

"We *are* going to confiscate them. What you're asking is bullshit."

"If you go in and take them, there'll be no reason for the person to contact anyone, and I need them to. I can take the FBI to the artifacts, but I need your promise to wait seventy-two hours before confiscating."

Skiv's breathing was so heavy Vic felt like he was next to him in the passenger seat. "I'll give you a sweetener, something you can confiscate right now," Vic added.

"What?"

Vic glanced at his notebook and gave him the name of Cora's boss at the tile store. "Go into his office. There's an African mask on the wall."

"Okay. Sure. But what's the address with the rest of the artifacts?"

"No. You tell the FBI to come to my motel room and I'll take them there." The heavy breathing resumed. "You don't trust me?"

Vic rubbed his nose. "Not on this. No. You want them too bad. Look, play it the way I asked and we both get what we want. Do you understand?"

"Screw you, Lenoski. I'll give you forty-eight hours, not seventy-two. Where's your motel?"

"Skiv, when I tell you where I am, you're going to think you have the answer and the right address. You don't. This only works if I take the FBI to the artifacts, and they play it how I ask. This is the best lead you've had."

"Just tell me where you are."

Vic told him and almost heard the grinding of gears in Skiv's brain. Keyboard tapping sounds came over the phone. "Cora Still's mother. I gave you her address. Is that where they are?"

"No." Vic scrunched his eyes shut at the lie. "I told you, it's not what you expect. Send the FBI to me and I'll take them there. They take pictures and leave. And, okay, forty-eight hours. Deal?"

The air between them tightened like a guitar string. "Deal," he said finally. "I'll get the FBI there by tomorrow morning."

"Fine, just make sure it's before six."

"And if you screw me on this, if we lose them, I'm charging you with obstruction. You follow?"

"Cut the crap, Skiv. You and I both know that won't hold. I'm going to lead you to them. All I did was put some conditions on the recovery. In good faith, I also told you where you could find a mask. And don't forget they could be fakes. They might not be what you're looking for. You have to authenticate them."

Skiv took a couple of quick breaths.

"And who knows," Vic added. "Maybe this works out for everyone. You make your warlord happy. I get Cora Stills."

"I'll let you know when the FBI is going to arrive."

The call abruptly ended. "Don't go away mad…" Vic said under his breath to his phone. He smiled. Forty-eight hours was more than enough, he'd been willing to go down to twenty-four hours if it was needed.

Half an hour until Nadine left for work, but the day already felt complete.

Three hours later, Vic was parked on the same gravel access road near Nadine's workplace. He'd put the driver's seat all the way back and tied the elastic ribbon to the steering wheel. He worked through five exercise rounds to strengthen his shoulder, well past what the physical therapist had recommended. He measured his breaths, managing the burn from the muscles around his arm socket. Sweat dotted his forehead. Each strain against the elastic cleared his head. He finished the last cycle, let go of the elastic and worked his arm around. It was sore, but he was back to full movement. He needed to work the speed and heavy bags again.

His phone rang.

When he picked it up his hand bobbed up, unused to such light resistance. He decided that was a good sign. Karl's name showed on the screen. He slid the call button.

"How's Mr. Long Shot doing?" Karl asked.

"I don't know about long, but I'm shot."

Karl chuckled. "I get that. Jimmy called me last night about eleven. I guess he was outside Nadine Stills' house. He was bored out of his mind."

"I know the feeling."

"Still nothing? Or should I say Stills nothing?" He gave a breathy laugh, enjoying his joke.

Vic clenched his jaw. Karl sounded too happy for a guy with a nasty murder to solve. "What can I do for you, Karl?"

"Okay. Got something, not sure if it's anything."

"Anything's better than nothing."

"Remember you told me to look for other cases where fingers got messed up, that kind of thing?"

"Yes."

"Found one. I had one of our interns go file diving and she turned up something close. Not an exact match-up, but interesting."

"How close?"

"Happened a couple of months ago. Structure fire. One of those prefabricated work-site buildings burned down. Three people died inside; we haven't IDed them yet. Another person dead outside. He had smoke inhalation, but here's the good part. His fingers were smashed. Not like our Kent Bauer, this guy didn't have his hands tied, but his injuries might come from a similar weapon. And here's the three pointer. His trachea was crushed. Medical examiner thought the smoke would have killed him anyway, but that blow guaranteed it."

"Did you ID him?"

"We did. He worked for one of the frackers out here. He was off shift, so they're clear. What he did on his own time is up to him."

"Can I take a look?"

"Sure. Fire marshal is leaning toward the fire being accidental. Space heater fell over and the place went up. No sign of accelerants."

Vic worked his shoulder. "Has it been cleaned up?"

"Beats me. I don't even know who owns the property. The local Watford cops investigated. They listed the owner as someone offshore, but that's normal around here."

"Nice tax dodge if you can get it."

"I'll text the address. I can't send you the file, but if you stop by, I can show it to you."

"Thanks, Karl."

"No problem. Something to keep you going since you're Stills on stakeout." He huffed a laugh, not waiting to see if Vic thought the joke funny.

"About that." Vic pinched the bridge of his nose between thumb and forefinger. "You should know what's going on. I decided to make a move on Stills, so I called in a favor."

"How so?"

"Do you remember the statue on the sideboard in Nadine's dining room?"

"Sure, dark wood, looked old. Some half-naked African guy."

"Right, and when I opened the door to her living room, I saw a lot more."

"We talked about it."

Vic tapped the steering wheel. "Before I came out here, an NCIS guy told me Cora was investigated for stealing African artifacts while she was posted in Somalia. I'm thinking those are the artifacts, and Cora either drove them here from Pittsburgh or shipped them."

"That could mean Nadine lied to us."

"It might, but tough to prove. Anyway, NCIS is sending some FBI guys to authenticate them. When they show up, I'm hoping it rattles her cage enough to meet Cora. Supposedly, the whole bunch is worth maybe a million, so Cora won't want to lose them."

"Kind of a long shot again."

"Worth a try. Makes sense that after you and I visited, she didn't make a move. Cora probably anticipated people like us showing up, and she told her mother to sit tight afterwards. But the artifacts are worth too much money. They'll want to figure out if they can save them."

"I see that, unless they have a couple of burner phones to stay in touch."

"I thought about that. I'm hoping Cora outsmarted herself. She was in the military, she'll know how easily we can capture cell conversations. Also, if we search her mother's place and find one, her mother would be in shit. I'm betting they're doing this the old-fashioned way."

"If Cora is even in the state. When does the FBI show up?"

"Tomorrow, if everything goes right. I'll let you know. Can you send me the address of the place that burned down?"

"Sure. I'll text you."

After the call ended, Vic drummed his fingertips on the steering wheel. If Karl was annoyed about the FBI getting involved, he hadn't shown it. A moment later his telephone dinged. It was Karl's text, listing an address. He did a maps search, identified the location and scanned the road, anxious for Jimmy's truck.

Chapter 27

J immy arrived forty minutes later. Vic waved at him to stay in his truck, climbed in beside him and told him about his call with Skiv, and Karl's description of the body found at the site of the building fire.

Jimmy hooked a loose strand of hair behind his ear. "You want to stop watching her?" He sounded hopeful. "Go check this out?"

Vic thought about it. If Nadine had spotted his tail or contacted Cora, there was nothing he could do about it now. His best shot was the FBI visit. He cocked his head toward Jimmy "Do you think she spotted you?"

"No. She just went straight home from work. Never came out of the house while I was there."

"Same for me. Let's go check the fire."

"Now we're talking."

Vic followed Jimmy to the hotel, parked and climbed into Jimmy's cab. They headed east from Watford City, along Route 23. Fifteen minutes later, Vic squinted at the map on his phone.

"Should be somewhere around here."

"We keep going this way, we get to my Rez."

A minute later they passed a gravel road that led behind a grass-covered rise. Vic asked Jimmy to turn around and guided him onto it.

Jimmy picked his way between the deep ruts gouged out by hard rain and all-wheelers. Dust rose behind them in a plume.

Behind the rise they reached a flat gravel parking lot. At the center, waist-high posts connected by crime-scene tape marked the four corners of a square. Vic guessed it was the location where they'd found the body Karl had told him about. Beyond the square, edging the parking lot, stood the burned-out hulk of a large modular building, the white prefabricated type found on building sites. The roof was missing, the scorched walls burned down to three or four feet in height. Jimmy killed the engine. Without a word, they both got out.

Vic did a slow three-hundred-and-sixty-degree pivot. A line of tall poles followed the curve of the driveway and delivered an electrical line to a box on one end of the burned building. Somehow that part of the wall had escaped the fire. From the box, a second electrical line rose to three tall metal poles along the edge of the gravel lot. Each was topped by a floodlight. Despite the wind and chattering of the crime scene tape, the air felt dead. Vic couldn't reconcile the press of the wind and the sense of something gone.

"Looks like the stuff they set up in Iraq," Jimmy said, nodding at the building. "Halliburton crap. You could have a barracks, five offices and a situation room crammed into something that size."

"And someone wanted to know what was going on." Vic nodded toward a security camera nestled next to the floodlight on the center metal pole. He wondered if it still worked, if it was live.

They skirted the ten-foot square of crime scene tape and crossed to the left corner of the building. Someone had axed open a door. They stayed outside, staring over the burned wall into the interior. Inside was a mass of scorched, unrecognizable debris, marked only by the remains of a row of interior walls jutting horizontally from the back wall. They looked like a row of offices.

"Must have gone up fast," Vic said quietly. He breathed out to clear his nose of the flat ash-smell.

"They do. I've seen these thing go before. You said four died? Could have been more."

"Three inside, one in the parking lot." Vic's eyes were drawn to another square of crime scene tape inside the remains, near what looked like a larger room at the opposite end of the building. Tape had broken loose from one of the posts and trailed in the wind like a pennant. Vic followed the outer wall of the building around to the back and stopped when the taped square was in front of him.

It encompassed a small room, the charred remains of a couch set against the outside wall. This was where the three victims inside the building were found.

"Check this out," Jimmy called.

Behind Vic was another, smaller building, untouched by fire. Jimmy stood by the front door. Vic crossed the dusty space between the structures, following a well-grooved path.

"Someone kept this secured." He pointed at a large padlock on the front door.

Vic stared at the latching mechanism that held the lock. "Except that's been there since the beginning." He pointed at the screws. "See the rust? That didn't happen after the fire. Takes a year or longer for that to show up."

He stepped back and studied the front of this smaller building. Large slabs of plywood were spaced at regular intervals. Cut into the plywood, near the roof, were small sliding windows, each pane about eight inches high and ten inches wide. He pointed at the screws that held the plywood in place. "See that? Rust on those screws as well."

"Supply hut?" Jimmy asked.

"Something like that." Vic couldn't remember seeing anything quite like it before. It was as if someone had purposely locked down the building.

"I want to take some pictures." Vic stepped back, pulled out his phone and shot photos of the entire building, the windows and the padlock.

Together, they circled behind it. The back mimicked the front, except it lacked a door. About ten yards away stood a small building that looked like a miniature wooden outhouse.

"Pumphouse?" Jimmy suggested.

"Do you need wells out here?"

"Only if you want water."

Vic spotted an electrical wire leading from the back of the supply building to the smaller, outhouse-looking building.

"Take a look, will you?" Vic asked. He held up his phone so Jimmy would know that he intended to take more pictures.

"Sure."

They separated. Vic returned to the larger burned-out hulk facing the parking lot.

He took his time, shooting photos from various exterior viewpoints and studying the interior remains, until he had a rough sense of the floor plan. Based on the locations of the two front doors and the jutting wall sections, the building was designed to encourage people to circulate starting from the doorway on the right, which led into a large room that once held a bar, as the melted and smoke-darkened bottles showed. The space where the bodies were found adjoined the bar. From there, a hallway led down the center of the building, flanked by what looked like offices on both sides. He studied these smaller rooms, but the charred remains didn't provide any clues. The center hallway then bisected a second hallway that ran along the end wall, connecting the far front door to a back door that opened onto the path to the second, smaller structure.

He could guess the purpose of the building. He'd raided enough massage parlors when he was in uniform to recognize the layout. It was his next thought, that perhaps Dannie had walked those halls—been inside those small rooms—that he hated.

The thought froze him stock-still at the end of the building, staring at the yellow crime scene tape inside the charred interior. He forced himself breathe, to focus on the high sky and how the wind bent the surrounding grass. He wanted the wind to snatch the thought away. Slowly, he realized the landscape was familiar to him now. He was sensitive to how the wind moved over the low grass, to each variation of light. It was so different from Pittsburgh's narrow streets, steep hills and pinched, sharp-roofed houses. Its low, steel-grey skies.

The sense of belonging had to be different as well, he decided.

In Pittsburgh he always felt connected to things. It came from the way bridges linked opposite sides of rivers, how the meandering roads joined township to town to city. How the old, looming red brick warehouses and factory buildings fused him to the generations of Pittsburghers who forged a future with their hands, muscles and eyes. The purposeful, man-madeness of it all. The feeling—when he was growing up—that accepting and respecting these links was how he would come to belong.

Here, the sense of belonging wasn't to what people built and the problems they solved, it was to that press of wind, the shifting light, the arc of the sun in the sky. What mattered here, he decided, was accepting your place within the rearing sky and sweeping, wind-scoured land.

He guessed a different kind of strength was needed. That good and bad might have different definitions.

The hum of a motor broke his thoughts. It grew louder and a white pickup nosed into the parking lot. Black letters on the doors read O&G Supply.

The engine cut, the sound sucked away by the wind. Nothing moved, although to Vic's new sense of things, he knew that wasn't true. Clouds shifted, grass wavered. The yellow crime scene tape swung and shivered.

Vic crossed to the edge of the parking lot. The passenger door swung open and a short man with black hair slid to the ground, his jeans riding up on scuffed cowboy boots. He pointed at Vic.

"Hey!"

Vic waited. The man took a few steps toward him and stopped. He flared his chest and flexed his arms, his hands curled into loose fists.

"Who are you? This is private property!" The man's stomach overhung his belt and it wobbled slightly as he shouted, giving him a soft look that Vic decided was misleading.

The driver's side door slammed and gravel crunched. The driver circled in front of the truck. He was thin and tall, a grey, high-crowned trucker's cap tugged low on his forehead. Shaggy brown hair stuck out under the sides. While the dark eyes of the short man were electric, the taller man's eyes were hard to see. He stopped about five feet behind the shorter man, as if he was being careful. Waited.

Vic hadn't seen either of them before.

Out of the corner of his eye Vic saw Jimmy materialize around the opposite corner of the burned-out building, as if he rose from the ground or was brought by the wind. The two men were too focused on Vic to notice.

"Vic Lenoski," Vic called, to keep their attention away from Jimmy.

The short man walked half-way toward him, his steps pigeon-like. "What are you doing out here?"

"Gomez," the tall man called, although from the way he chopped off the last part of the word, Vic knew he hadn't meant to give away the name. He added, "This is private property. You have a reason to be here?"

Vic shrugged. "I heard about the fire. Thought I would check it out."

The driver closed the distance to Gomez. The wind lifted the edge of his blue jean jacket. Vic spotted a holstered gun.

"I don't get that," the tall man said.

He was near enough now that Vic could make out the face underneath the cap. His blue eyes were as faded as his jeans, the wrinkles beside them and down the sides of his mouth sharp and deeply grooved.

"Not much to get," Vic said. "I heard about the fire, that some people died here. I got interested."

"But why? Who gives a shit?" Gomez shifted lightly on his feet, sliding his right foot back. Vic tightened, knowing Gomez was preparing to charge.

"Someone always gives a shit," Vic said quietly, trying to calm Gomez with the tone of his voice. "Somebody dies, someone else hurts. Fact of life." He inventoried Gomez's face, wanting to recognize him the next time they met. Between Gomez's burning dark eyes he saw a hitch on the bridge of his nose. A break that hadn't properly healed.

Vic turned his gaze to the tall man. "What's your name?"

The man's jaw line hardened. "None of your damn business. What you need to know is that you're trespassing, and you need to leave."

"Who owns this property?"

"Same answer. None of your business." The tall man shuffled closer, Gomez mimicking his movement. They stopped a few feet away. "You going to clear off?"

Vic ignored him. "Simple question. Who owns this place? Then I'll go. By the way, I didn't see a sign on the way in. You guys need to post the perimeter if you don't want visitors." Now Vic was sure that the camera on the light pole still worked.

As if tracking his thoughts, Gomez asked, "Where's the injun?"

"I'm right here," Jimmy called from Vic's right.

Both men started and shifted their stances. Vic saw a jumpiness enter the tall man's eyes. Jimmy was too far away to keep in his peripheral vision.

Vic talked at the taller man. "I'm guessing O&G Supply owns this place, since you guys showed up in their truck."

"What you need to know is that it's time to go. Get your buddy and scram." He angled toward Vic, his right arm partially hidden. Vic thought of his own Glock, neatly placed under the passenger seat of Jimmy's truck.

Gomez took the tall man's lead and spun toward Jimmy. "You!" he shouted, and ran at him.

"Gomez!" shouted the tall man, but Gomez ignored him, his short legs pumping. The tall man's hidden arm moved and instinctively Vic skipped forward and punched him hard in the solar plexus. The man coughed and doubled over, his trucker's cap spinning to the ground. A handgun thumped to the ground. Vic circled behind him, grabbed his right arm and folded it up his back. The man grunted and dropped to one knee.

Vic glanced at Jimmy and saw him dip a shoulder as if he was moving to his right. Gomez shifted left in reaction, but Jimmy hopped to his left. When Gomez tried to readjust his right knee buckled and he staggered. Jimmy pivoted on the ball of his left foot and punched Gomez on the back of his neck as he wobbled by. The punch and his momentum carried Gomez over the low, burned wall of the building, arms flailing. He disappeared in a thud and puff of ash. Vic had to smile. Jimmy's fake was so convincing Gomez lost his balance; the pivot and punch a thing of fluid beauty.

Jimmy didn't even look where Gomez disappeared. He started for Vic.

"Fire up the truck," Vic called.

Instead, Jimmy crossed to the white O&G Supply truck, reached inside, turned and threw something into the grass on the far edge of the parking lot. Only then did he slide into his truck and start the engine.

Vic tugged the tall man's arm higher until he yelped. "Okay," he said to the man. "I want to be clear. You guys assaulted us. You know it, I know it, the security camera knows it. There was no damn reason for this." Vic shuffled to his right, turning the man, until he located the man's gun.

"We're driving off," Vic said. "No reason to chase us, not sure you can find your keys anyway. I see you again, I'm going to ask the same questions. If you'd answered them, we could have skipped all this."

Just on the edge of his peripheral vision, Gomez's soot-smudged face popped up above the half-wall of the burned-out building. He stood, swaying, and grabbed the edge of the wall to stay upright.

Vic shoved the tall man forward onto his stomach, let go and scooped up the gun. It was a Colt with a silver slide. A showy gun Vic didn't like. The man rolled and started to stand, but stopped when he saw Vic holding his pistol. Vic raised it but didn't point it at him. "I'll leave this for you by the main road."

Jimmy brought the truck around so Vic could open the passenger door while keeping the tall man in front of him. Vic backed into the truck and he and Jimmy bounced over the ruts to the main road. He tossed the Colt into the roadside ditch as Jimmy turned east.

They both checked their mirrors to make sure they weren't being followed.

"That went well," Jimmy said.

Vic rotated his right shoulder and found no pain or stiffness. It actually felt good. "Can't complain. Shouldn't we be headed the other way? Back to the motel?"

"Not after that," Jimmy said. "Not tonight. I have a place you can stay."

"Where's that?"

Jimmy smiled to himself, his eyes to the road. "Injun country."

Chapter 28

They drove for thirty minutes to a T intersection, where Jimmy took a right and less than a mile later turned left onto a two-lane road. A sign welcomed them to the Fort Berthold Indian Reservation.

"What's your plan?" Vic asked.

"My place, for now."

They crept past a clutch of houses near a large school and up a long hill. At the crest, Jimmy speeded up. The reservation stretched ahead of them, the hills steeper than around Watford. A few miles later they passed horses splotched with different colors. Ponies, Vic decided, watching them graze on the low grass of a valley. Moments later Jimmy turned right onto a single lane dirt and gravel road.

They snaked between two hills to a white frame, one-story house smaller than the first floor of Vic's home. It was flanked by two outbuildings, one only large enough for garden equipment, the second a small barn. An ancient tractor stood beside the larger building, gracefully rusting into oblivion.

"Home, sweet home," Jimmy said, cutting the engine. Red dust swirled past the car.

Jimmy opened the house door without a key and led Vic past a narrow galley kitchen. The living room was fronted by sliding glass doors and large windows that framed the rolling, grass-covered hills. The right wall of the living room held three doors, which Vic guessed led to bedrooms and a bathroom. The left wall was mostly hidden by books that stood upright on wooden planks threaded between cinderblocks. Vic wondered how the shelves didn't groan out loud from the weight. Vic remembered Jimmy quoting someone at the airport, and Karl's comment about Jimmy reading too much. It crossed his mind that perhaps the comment said more about Karl than Jimmy. He walked to the sliding glass doors and absorbed the view. Two steps down was a rough wood deck without a railing. In the distance, two ponies pawed the ground. One of them shook its head, its mane catching the wind.

"Ponies, right?" he called to Jimmy. "All the colors on them. They run wild here?"

"Pretty much." Jimmy was back in the kitchen, and Vic heard a refrigerator door open and close. "But we all know who owns which one."

"You ride?"

"Don't you? Drink?" Jimmy crossed to him and held out a plastic cup of water. After Vic took it, Jimmy sipped from his own cup. It crossed Vic's mind that he hadn't heard a faucet run, only the refrigerator and cupboard doors being opened and closed.

Vic swallowed. "That was a nice punch on Gomez," he said carefully. "Little deke, step, pivot and punch. Used his own momentum against him. Looked good."

Jimmy was silent. Vic knew this was a new situation for both of them. Until now, they'd been acquaintances of circumstance, but inside Jimmy's home the calculus was different. It was more personal.

"Couldn't believe he charged me like that," Jimmy said finally.

Vic smiled. "Not the smartest move."

"Better for me, though."

"Looked like it."

Jimmy's eyes glittered. "And you went all cop on the other guy. How'd you know about the Colt?"

"Saw it when the wind lifted his jacket. Then he shifted sideways to hide his draw. You always know what that means." He sipped more water, noting that Jimmy recognized the weapon's make. It felt like the conversation was milked out and that Jimmy agreed.

Jimmy looked at him. "Couple of things I should mention."

Vic waited.

"O&G Supply. Talked to some guys about them."

"Okay. Native or others?" Vic held his breath for a moment. He was moving into phrases and vocabulary that were new to him. It made him uncomfortable. He didn't want to insult Jimmy by using a word only whites would use, or sound like he didn't know what he was talking about.

"Both." If Vic had spoken out of school, Jimmy let it go.

So far so good, Vic thought. He waded ahead. "I saw a bunch more drilling sites on your Rez. I guess I didn't expect that. Does O&G work here as well?"

"Sure. All over. That's the point. It's why we're better off here, not at the motel."

"How's that?"

"The guys we met today...they work for Ewan Fleck. He owns the company."

"I saw Fleck's photo on their web site."

"Did you make the connection?"

"He looked familiar, but that was it."

Jimmy stared through the window. "His dad is Chief Fleck. Runs the Watford City Police department. Him you already met."

Vic followed Jimmy's gaze to the hills outside. "How the hell did I miss that?"

"When Lou handcuffed you, I heard the conversation. The chief never introduced himself. And you were too busy getting pally with Karl."

Vic absorbed the words. Jimmy was right. He'd been focused on talking to Karl. He wondered why Jimmy brought it up, and guessed at the answer. "You're saying Chief Fleck runs interference for O&G Supply?"

"Big time. That's why you need to stay here. He's the grease that makes the white world around here run smoothly. As soon as he finds out we fought O&G guys, he'll show up at your hotel and kick you back to Pittsburgh."

Annoyance crept into Vic's throat. "Explain that."

"Easy. Chief Fleck sits in the town council meetings. He reports to the mayor, and they go way back. All best buddies. It's simple math. The state issues drilling permits, but local officials have lots of ways to get them revoked. Maybe the county auditor claims he never got the company's drill-date notification. Or a report goes to the state saying the company isn't capping their test holes correctly. Maybe the local municipality delays issuing LoadPass permits, so the company can't drive a rig or tanker truck on local roads. You want to avoid all that, you sign a three-year maintenance contract with O&G. After three years, if you don't renew with O&G, oops, there's a busload of state environmental inspectors all over your drill sites. Extraction stops, air tests get run, wastewater runoff checked, your company gets hit with months of downtime. Meanwhile, our Ewan Fleck, owner of O&G, is holding these huge parties every month...in this mansion he built west of Watford. The mayor, council, local county officials and the drilling companies all show up. Lots of fun. Booze, girls, you name it."

"Envelopes for the mayor and county officials?"

"Damn right, just no one's proved it. These guys are old fashioned. Cash for everything. The drilling companies don't care, for them it's just the cost of doing business."

"And anyone makes trouble for O&G, they get the chief in their face."

"Exactly. By now the motel's front desk knows to call Chief Fleck the second you show up."

Vic turned to him. "Thanks. Since I'm here, anything I can do? Buy you dinner?"

Jimmy kept his gaze to the hills, a half smile on his face. "Did you see a bunch of restaurants on your way out here?"

"Exactly none."

"Right. So, red beans and rice." Jimmy swigged his water. "I'm vegetarian. Get used to it. But right now, I gotta make a phone call." He pointed to the center door on the right wall. "Bathroom. Only flush if you shit, I gotta be careful with water."

Vic stared at him for a second. "No running water?"

He shrugged. "That's a luxury. I put a tank in the attic, but it's a pain to fill. I use it for showers and shitting only. Keep your showers short."

Vic almost made a joke about Jimmy using his motel bathroom and stopped himself. "Wait a minute, you have no running water, but your cell phone works?"

"It's a mystery, isn't it? It does, as long as you're near a road."

Jimmy let himself onto the deck and closed the door behind him. Vic stood in the living room, his eyes running along the bookshelves. He noticed a space that held two framed photographs and crossed to them.

He'd expected family, but the first photograph showed three young men in football uniforms, kneeling at the center of a football field, helmets on the ground in front of them. The young man on the left was Jimmy. Vic didn't recognize the man in the center, but the man on the right was Karl Swenson. The pale skin and shock of blond hair hadn't changed. Their expressions were stern, dedicated. The kind of frowning seriousness high school athletes adopt to show their commitment. Captains, thought Vic. Something they both neglected to mention. Not only did they play together, they *were* the team.

The second photo was an army squad standing shoulder to shoulder. Their faces were dirty, boots and knee pads coated with dust, uniforms deeply wrinkled at the armpits and elbows. Half of them wore wrap-around sunglasses and looked like hawks. They cradled their weapons as if they were babies. Like the football photo their faces were stern, but strain was chiseled into their cheeks and jaw bones, the idea of laughter hammered out of them. Jimmy was at the center of the line, perhaps half a step ahead of the others. The men on either side of him leaned toward him, just slightly, as if they were protecting him. Trusted him.

Vic knew what that said about Jimmy.

He pivoted slowly, taking in the room. He saw no other photos, nothing hanging on the walls. Just the concrete block and plank bookshelves as high as his shoulders.

His phone rang. He recognized Pittsburgh's area code and answered.

"Vic?" It was a hoarse voice that sounded as if it was reaching through time.

Vic blinked. "Liz?"

"Damn right."

Vic was buoyant. "Where are you? What happened? Levon said you were back in intensive care."

"I got too much to do for that kind of crap." She coughed and Vic heard her muffle it. "What's going on?" she rasped.

Vic squeezed his eyes shut, ordering his thoughts. "No good news so far."

"What do you need me to do?"

"Can you work? You just got out of the ICU."

"You gonna tell me what I can and can't do?"

Vic was suddenly smiling. It was Liz again. She was hoarse, hiding what it cost her to breathe, but it was Liz.

"Okay, okay. Shoot me for worrying about you."

"Tell me what you got, Vic. I'm sick of this damn hospital. People running around with their faces looking like it's the end of the world."

Vic brought her up to date. Jimmy meeting him at the airport, finding Kent Bauer dead, maybe tortured. His visit with Nadine Stills, their ruse with the African artifacts to see if she would break cover and lead them to Cora.

"Jesus," Liz said. "You been busy. What can I do?"

"What *can* you do?"

"Levon brought my laptop. I can research."

"Ewan Fleck." He spelled the name for her. "His name keeps coming up. His father is the local Watford City police chief. I need everything you can find on him."

"Got it."

"When you have something, give me a call." He hesitated. "Good to hear your voice, Liz."

"Ain't *my* voice. Feel like I swallowed sandpaper."

"You know what I'm saying."

Vic ended the call and slid the phone into his pocket, feeling buoyant. The patio door ground open.

Jimmy raised his chin to him. "Charlie Running Bear says hello."

"Same to him, I guess. But I was thinking. It barely took twenty minutes for Gomez and the cowboy to show up when we got to that site."

"Right."

"I'm guessing the camera on the pole must be working."

"Looks like it."

"And they're protecting that site. They don't want anyone near it. Now, why is that?"

Chapter 29

A
s Jimmy chopped and sautéed, Vic read book titles on the bookcase, finding an assortment of history texts about the American west, politics, gardening, translations of Greek classics, American Indian history, a single long shelf of law books, and, oddly, a collection of poetry translated from Polish.

"Polish poets have it going on," Jimmy called to him, seeing Vic leaf through one.

"I've never heard of these guys."

"One of them won a Nobel. Czeslaw Milosz. Poland went through the German occupation, Russian occupation. They spent a lot of time thinking about exile, how to live under occupation, what's good and bad about it. What it destroys, how you live." He flicked Vic a sly grin. "Easy to relate to."

Vic nodded and slid the volume back on the bookshelf. His degree was criminal justice and he never felt comfortable when conversations turned to writers and what they said. He always had the feeling he was missing something, or the rules kept shifting.

Jimmy hadn't lied about dinner. It was red beans and rice with vegetables. Vegetarian food was new to Vic, but he liked it. As they finished, Vic's phone rang. He didn't recognize the number but answered anyway.

"Vic Lenoski?" asked the voice on the other end.

"Yes."

"Special Agent Lewis with the FBI. Agent Croyle and I are on our way from the Bismarck regional office. We're supposed to look into stolen African antiquities, whatever the hell they are. You owe us an address."

"Sure. When do you want to door knock?"

"First thing in the morning. This is a national security thing. I hear you're being a pain in the ass about it."

Vic stared at the ceiling for a moment. "You guys ever hear of interagency cooperation?"

"Sure. I'm the agency and you need to cooperate."

"Okay. Now I get why you're posted to Bismarck. Meet me in the parking lot of the Days Inn in Watford City. Seven a.m. I was hoping earlier but I'm staying pretty far away, now. Look for a purple Chevy."

"Better if you just give me the address now. Easier for everyone."

Vic hesitated only a second. "No. I'm a pain in the ass, remember? See you at seven." He hung up before Lewis could respond.

"Sounds like a champ," Jimmy said.

Vic rubbed his face. "I'm sure he's better in person."

He wasn't. When Vic and Jimmy pulled into the Days Inn parking lot, a tall, dark-haired man in a blue suit, white shirt and black tie pushed himself off Vic's purple rental car and tapped his index finger on the face of his watch.

"How'd he know it was us?" Jimmy asked.

As Jimmy slid his truck into a space beside the rental car, Vic replied, "He's been doing that to everyone who pulled in since six this morning."

They crossed to Agent Lewis, who waited for them to come to him, arms folded over his narrow chest. A car door slammed nearby and a short, thick-chested man in suit and tie joined them. Agent Croyle. They shook hands all around.

"We don't need you," Agent Lewis said to Jimmy, as soon as the introductions were finished.

"You want the address, he comes with us," Vic said quickly. "We'll be in our own cars, so you don't have to talk to us. Jimmy's gonna stay behind after you guys leave and see if the suspect goes anywhere."

"Bullshit on that. We watch her. You got some stupid requirement that we can't confiscate the artifacts for forty-eight hours, fine, but we watch her. I'm not losing this stuff. Washington is all over this case."

Vic doubted Washington was all over anything at all, as a general rule. "Sure," he said after a moment. "I'll give you the route she normally takes to work. But I want to know if she meets anyone." He pulled out his phone and showed the agents Cora Stills' DMV photo. "And I really need to know if she meets this woman. This is the whole deal. This is Cora Stills, Nadine Stills' daughter. Cora's a fugitive. We're doing things this way round to see if Nadine'll contact her. Cora assaulted a police officer, my partner."

Agent Lewis bent down and studied the photo. He straightened up. "Can you text that to me?"

"Sure thing." Vic found himself liking Lewis a little better. He forwarded it to the number Lewis called him from the night before. When Lewis's phone dinged, he tapped on his screen a few times and a moment later Agent Croyle's phone vibrated. He too studied the photo.

"Got it," Croyle said. "She dangerous?"

"She's armed, a handgun we know of. Like I said, she tried to kill my partner." Vic then explained Nadine's normal route to work and work hours. "If she does anything else, it's suspicious."

"We'll need your car," Agent Lewis said to Vic when he finished.

Vic looked at him. "Explain that?"

"I told you we'd do the surveillance. Agent Croyle is doing the day shift, he'll need your car. I have shit to do, I'll need our agency car."

"Who's doing night surveillance?" Vic asked him.

"That's up to you guys."

Vic fought down the urge to say it must be nice for the FBI to have their nights off, but he wanted to split the surveillance with Jimmy anyway. He nodded agreement and a minute later Jimmy and Vic led the two agents toward Nadine's house.

When they reached Arnegard, Jimmy and Vic parked around the corner from Nadine's house and Vic joined Jimmy in his truck. They watched the FBI agents knock on Nadine's front door. Agent Croyle gripped a square black case that Vic guessed held a digital camera.

It took Nadine a couple of minutes to open the door, clutching a robe closed at her throat. They'd woken her, which was the plan. Vic watched the agents show their IDs. Nadine emphatically shook her head. She stopped when Agent Lewis pulled an envelope from his jacket pocket and held it in front of her. Even at that distance, Vic saw Nadine's hooded eyes widen.

"What the hell is that?" Jimmy asked.

"Search warrant, I would bet."

"They can get one just for *suspecting* she has the artifacts?"

Vic remembered the long shelf of law books in Jimmy's house. "That's why he mentioned National Security. That argument gets them anything they want. It'll be a Federal warrant."

Jimmy shook his head as if warning himself to stay quiet.

Nadine stepped aside and the agents followed her into the house. The door closed.

"This'll take awhile," Vic said. They'll photograph everything and then email the photos to experts and NCIS to confirm they're authentic. Mind if I make a phone call?"

Jimmy shrugged, his eyes on Nadine's front door.

Vic brought up the web browser on his phone and searched local real estate agents. He settled on one in Watford and dialed the number.

"Can I help you?" a perky voice asked.

"Gee I hope so," Vic answered, trying to sound naïve. From Jimmy's glance he guessed it wasn't working. "I'm new in town, just moved here, and I'm looking for some property. I heard about one and I was wondering if it was for sale."

"We can help with that! Where is it?" The young woman sounded so excited Vic struggled not to roll his eyes. He gave her the address of the burned building he and Jimmy visited the day before.

"I'm not familiar with that one. Can you hold? I'll ask around."

As country music filled his ear, Vic considered the sky and how the clouds rose in ballooning columns across the horizon.

"Why hello," said a male voice. "I'm Walter Noss. I understand you're interested in some land east of Watford?"

"Exactly." Vic settled into his role and repeated his story. New to the area. Looking for land.

"And your name, sir?"

"Tomkins Davis," Vic said, grinning at the fun of using Crush's real name.

"And do you work for one of the fracking companies?"

"I do."

"Wonderful, which one?"

Feeling stupid for making such a simple mistake, Vic slapped Jimmy on the upper arm to get his attention. "Which fracking company I work for?" he echoed out loud, for Jimmy to hear.

Jimmy mouthed "Enerhill."

"Why, Enerhill," Vic said slowly, as if repeating the name of a jewel.

"Oh, well then, welcome to North Dakota," Walter said, with more oil in his voice than might be under the entire state. "Now, where is this property you're interested in?"

Vic gave him the address of the site from the day before. "I heard they had a fire, or something. I liked the location. Perhaps they want to sell? I can tear down the burned building and build over it."

"Well, that particular property isn't on the market. Perhaps you could stop by the office, I could suggest some other locations." Vic heard the clicks of a keyboard on the other end of the line, and guessed that Walter was looking up sites.

"Well, like I said," Vic said slowly, giving him time to search, "I like the location. Right where I wanted it. Looked like it had some land to it, and I want a good spread."

"When you say a good spread, do you have a budget in mind?"

Didn't take him long to get to it, thought Vic, surprised at himself for using the word 'spread.' Jimmy twisted toward him, staring, a half grin on his face.

"Well, nothing too big. Wouldn't want to spend more than a few million. All in." The line was silent but the clicking on the keyboard speeded up. Vic smiled to himself. He'd worked briefly, early in his career, with Sergeant Wroblewski, a legend at undercover work. During their short stint together Wroblewski gave him several pieces of advice. One was that if he got in a jam and had to lie, to tell the biggest lie he could think of. "Small lies don't work," Wroblewski told him. "It's like you're hiding something. People smell that. Tell a big lie. It's backwards, but it makes people respect you. It works."

And now he was an executive for a company he'd never heard of, looking to spend several million dollars on real estate.

"Well," Walter said, as if he'd just focused his gun sights on an elephant. "I found the property you mentioned. As I said it's not on the market and I'm unfamiliar with the owner. It's a company registered in Panama. Can you wait a moment?"

"Sure."

Jimmy gestured for him to lower the phone. Vic covered his phone's microphone and waited for him to speak.

"Just three million?" Jimmy asked.

"Stock market's been down lately."

"Sir?"

Vic dropped his hand. "Yes?"

"I just talked to my office manager, and I have some good news. He's familiar with the owner, he says he's seen the name on sales documents."

"Great."

"And you'll be familiar with the owner, in fact, I'm sure since you already work with his company."

"How so?"

"It's the parent company of O&G Supply. They service most of the companies in this area. And, of course, they are owned by Ewan Fleck. We've handled several transactions for them. I could reach out and see if he's interested in selling, what the acreage might be?"

"Why, Walter, that would be outstanding. Why don't you do that? Please use this number." Vic made up a telephone number on the spot. "Unfortunately, I'm changing cell providers. Let me know once you talk to him?"

"I will, sir, but I still think you should come into the office. With a bit more discussion about your interests, I could find you several properties, in case this one falls through."

"Well, let's hope that doesn't happen." Vic hung up.

The wind buffeted the truck. The door to Nadine's house remained closed.

"Wow," Jimmy said. "Jerk FBI agents, federal warrants and lying cops. Why does all this feel so familiar?"

"You have a better way?"

"I would have called Karl. He put you onto the place, right?"

"He did, but he told me he didn't know the owner. We got that figured out now, although it was obvious after yesterday. But that makes me think of something else. When did the fire happen?"

"A couple of months ago."

"Okay." Vic pressed Karl's number on his phone and listened to it ring.

"Is that Lenoski?" Karl asked after the third ring.

"It is. Question for you. That property you put us onto yesterday, the one with the fire?"

"Yes?"

"Jimmy and I took a look. It's still as is from the fire. Why is that? Was the scene released back to the owner?"

"Let me find out. I'll call you back."

As Vic hung up, the front door to Nadine's house opened and Agents Lewis and Croyle emerged. They walked single file down the front walk, the camera bag bumping against Croyle's hip. They climbed into their car and pulled away. Vic and Jimmy waited, and a minute later their sedan slid to a stop behind them. Croyle got out and walked to Vic's side of the truck.

"How'd it go?" Vic asked through the open window.

Croyle smiled. "Your NCIS buddy thinks that African stuff is the real deal. I'll stay on her. If I see her talking to anyone, I'll let you know. Sorry about your partner. I hope she recovers. I get why you're doing it this way."

"Does your partner?"

Croyle tightened his jaw and watched his partner drive off. "He's from Miami, got posted up here after some case. Makes me wonder why. He doesn't like the weather, the scenery, the air, you name it. Anyway, I grew up in Billings. Home turf for me and I like it. I'll keep an eye on her. You guys can split the night shift."

"And why isn't Lewis doing night? I don't get that."

"Said he needs to be available to liaise with DC."

Vic smiled and handed over the keys to the Chevy. "Right. I guess you couldn't do that from your phone while you sit surveillance in a car."

Croyle met his gaze, his blue eyes laughing. "That would be doing two things at the same time. Tall order for him."

"Thanks." Vic held out his hand and they shook.

As Croyle headed to the Chevy, he called over his shoulder, "Okay, you guys take over at six. I'll leave the keys at the front desk for you."

"Sure."

"Then get out'ta here. I need a line of sight on the house. Your truck is blocking me."

"No problem," Vic said.

As Vic and Jimmy pulled away, Vic's phone rang.

"You'll like this," Karl said, when Vic answered.

"Like what?" He put the phone on speaker for Jimmy to hear.

"I called the detective working the fire case. The scene *was* being held."

From the way Karl emphasized the word 'was,' Vic guessed what was coming next. "But not anymore?"

"Nope. The detective got a call this morning from Chief Fleck in Watford. Chief was screaming at him, saying it had been two months, they needed to release the scene."

"And your detective did," Vic finished.

"Yes, he did." Karl paused. "You guys were out there yesterday?"

"Yep."

"Now that's some timing for you."

"Yes, it is," Vic said. "Thanks, Karl."

Jimmy and Vic drove in silence, until Jimmy said, without taking his eyes from the road, "If that security video was working, and the Chief saw it, then he knows it was you and me at the scene."

"Yep."

"Wanna bet how fast they run bulldozers through the site?"

166

Chapter 30

With little to do until they started surveillance that evening, Jimmy and Vic stopped at a supermarket in Watford for groceries and returned to Jimmy's house. At ten o'clock Agent Croyle texted Vic, saying Nadine Stills was at work. He told them Agent Lewis was watching the house, in case Nadine had asked someone to remove the artifacts while she was gone.

"Didn't think of that," Jimmy said, when Vic told him.

"Me neither. It's almost like they've done this before."

"Makes them almost sound competent," Jimmy grinned. His phone rang and he stepped onto the deck to take the call. Vic looked about the living room. He was acclimating to the small space. He wondered how Jimmy came by the house, and if he owned it. But the rooms held no photographs of family and he hadn't spotted any sign of a girlfriend. To be on tribal council, he guessed Jimmy needed to be connected to the community and from a trusted family. Yet there were no signs of that. And while the living room had a comfortable feel, the spare room where he slept the night before held only a single bed across from a stack of cardboard storage boxes, a stuffed Army backpack and a large gun safe. There was a transience to it all that troubled him, as if Jimmy didn't really want to unpack and needed the option to leave easily, if he wanted.

Outside, Jimmy bent sharply at the waist, bobbed back up again and made sharp, cutting motions with his free hand. An argument. A moment later he lowered the phone and drove his finger onto the face of it hard enough to poke a hole in a two-by-four. He stuffed the phone into his jeans, grabbed an empty plant pot from the corner of the deck and sent it spinning into the hills.

Vic watched silently. Until that moment Jimmy had never shown an ounce of anger, and Vic had decided he was someone who intellectualized when his emotions ran hot, rather than embraced them. The phone call had knocked him out of character. He watched Jimmy suck in a couple hard breaths before letting himself through the sliding door.

"Let's go," Jimmy said curtly.

"Where to?"

"I'm supposed to show you something." Jimmy almost spit out the words.

"I guess you don't like the idea."

"Get in the damn truck." Jimmy crossed the living room and went out the door.

"Good talk," Vic said to his back, and followed.

Jimmy jerked the truck onto the road. Vic let him drive, waiting for him to calm down. Just outside the reservation Jimmy turned right and sped along the two-lane road, passing the left turn to Watford. It was new territory for Vic.

After fifteen more minutes, Vic said carefully, "Haven't been out this way before."

Jimmy didn't answer, and when they reached a T-intersection turned right. The next sign indicated the mileage to New Town and the Four Bears Casino.

Vic gave it a few minutes more, but when the casino appeared, he said sharply, "Jimmy, where are we going?"

At the next traffic light Jimmy veered right into the casino parking lot. He pulled into a space, cut the engine and turned to Vic, one hand still on the steering wheel. "I disagree with this." His voice was flat and controlled, the anger compressed.

"I don't know what you disagree with. I don't even know who you talked to on the phone."

"Charlie Running Bear."

"Okay."

Jimmy tried to crush the steering wheel in his fist, his knuckles painfully white. He spoke past him. "He wants you to meet someone. Last night he didn't think it was a good idea. Now he does. I don't know why the hell he trusts you."

"He's never met me. It's not about that."

Jimmy released his hand, the palm white from his grip on the steering wheel. "This puts you into Rez problems. I don't think it's any of your damn business."

"Maybe he thought about it some more and thought I might be good for the Rez, somehow."

"No! This has to do with that Levon Grace guy. Charlie can't keep his thinking straight. He's putting this Grace ahead of the Rez. And this isn't even his goddamn Rez."

Vic waited a moment then kept his voice purposely calm. "Okay. I need some help with this. Why would he put Levon first?"

Jimmy glanced at him. "You don't know?"

"No. I told you at the airport. I didn't even know Charlie's name until you showed up."

Jimmy shook his head. "Understand this. Charlie Running Bear lost his legs in a bang and slam…"

Vic interrupted. "You lost me."

Jimmy took a breath and pushed his hair behind his ear. "Iraqi militia tactic." He breathed deeply and took hold of the steering wheel again. "Bad guys set up an IED, but it's part of an ambush." His voice took on a new quality, as if he was talking from a distant place. "Bang goes the IED, our column stops, we get out of the Humvees to help the wounded, and they slam us. RPGs and small arms fire on the guys getting out of the Humvees. Get it?"

"Yes."

"Anyway, Charlie is in the Humvee hit by the IED. Column stops, guys hop out to help, and the bad guys open up."

"You were there?"

"No. But your buddy Levon Grace was. Anyway, so Charlie's Humvee is a mess. Two guys in the front seats are dead. This was before they armored the Humvees. Firefight is bad. Our guys go to ground so they don't get shot, put fire on the bad guys. Except your Levon. He runs down the column, gets to Charlie's Humvee, pulls him out. Tourniquets his legs. Then he lays down fire so Charlie and the other guy in the back seat don't get shot. When it's over Charlie and the other guy get airlifted out. Without Levon, Charlie's dead. No one else helped him."

"Sounds like Levon."

Jimmy's breath whistled as if he was letting off steam. He wiped his mouth with the back of his hand. "Right. But you see the problem? Who does Charlie put first? This Levon or his Rez?"

"Maybe he thinks both. What does he want me to see?"

"Not what, who. Someone started living with us a couple of months ago. That's where I'm taking you."

"And why this person?"

Jimmy was silent for a moment. "Easier to show you." He started the engine.

"Before you do that," Vic said quickly, "when we met you told me Grace's name was ironic. I don't know what that means. Explain it."

Jimmy was still. Finally, he gave his head a single shake. "Not up to me. I could lie and say it was ironic that Levon Grace was the guy who called Charlie, which led me to you, but that's not it. Look. War zones, there's rumors about everything. I mean everything. One rumor was about him. What he was into, what got screwed up. It was ironic, given his last name. That's why I remember it. But it was all rumors. Maybe true, maybe not. I don't know. I spoke out of turn. You need to ask him."

Jimmy put the car in gear, took a right out of the parking lot and crossed a bridge over Lake Sakakawea. They drove the main street of New Town and turned right, passing a sign welcoming them into the Fort Berthold Reservation. Vic remembered from the map how the reservation spanned both sides of the lake. Jimmy concentrated on the road. Vic wondered if this was some personal compromise Jimmy made with what Charlie Running Bear wanted. He would take him to meet this person, but provide no background information. Given Jimmy's anger, Vic knew it was better to let it rest. He shifted on the seat. He wasn't sure what any of this had to do with Cora Stills.

Half an hour later Jimmy slowed the truck and turned into a dirt track marked by a parked pick-up truck. They rumbled past it and followed the road into the treeless, grass-covered rolling hills. They skirted a small rise and a sprawling single-story house swung into view. Two other buildings were scattered on the property, one a barn, the other a low, domed building covered with tarps. Thin trails of smoke rose from a jagged hole in the roof and a nearby fire pit. Three ancient pickup trucks were parked near the barn, and Jimmy parked at the end of the row.

"Wait here." He crossed to the house and thumped on the door. When no one answered he returned to the truck.

"They must be in there." He pointed at the low, domed building.

Vic stared at the tarps. "Whatever that is." As he grew used to the silence, he heard a slow, muffled drumbeat.

"Sweat lodge," Jimmy explained.

"I've heard of them." Vic peered at the structure, interested.

"Religious ceremony," added Jimmy. "We wait until they're done. Shouldn't be long."

Between the lodge and house, perhaps fifteen yards from Jimmy's truck, a sixty-gallon metal drum stood on a platform. What looked like a piece of hose pipe hung from the base of the drum.

Vic decided to try again. "It would be helpful if I knew who we were meeting."

"I've never met either of them. I just have a description."

"Helpful. Thanks." Jimmy seemed unfazed by the sarcasm.

It was five minutes before a flap of the tarp shifted and a slight woman with long grey hair crawled out. She rose, walked to a nearby fire pit and, using a branch, spread the embers as if she wanted the fire to go out. The drumming ceased.

Moments later, the flap moved again and another woman crawled out, her long black hair swaying as she stood up. A shapeless, oversized dress in faded blue hung from her shoulders. Vic guessed she was in her twenties. She stretched the small of her back as another woman emerged. The second woman was tall and round, her face beet red. As Vic watched, the first woman crossed to the sixty-gallon drum, stopped, said something to the second woman, and snatched the dress over her head. She was utterly naked. Vic's breath caught. She was beautiful, every curve of her proportioned, her chocolate-brown nipples and the clutch of hair between her legs a perfect triangle.

She stepped under the metal drum, twisted something on the end of the pipe and raised the hose over her head. Water cascaded over her breasts and stomach, glittering in the sunlight.

Jimmy leaned over the steering wheel, his eyes intent. The large woman said something and laughed.

"The one in the shower, I think that's her," Jimmy croaked.

Vic blinked and focused on the face of the woman in the shower, but it was raised to the stream of water, her long black hair shimmering and swirling against her skin. The large woman stepped closer, took the hose and held it for her. Her hands free, the woman lowered her face and wiped water from it. Vic's breath froze in his lungs.

He'd seen her before.

He knew her.

Her photograph had hung on the wall of his dining room for months.

His hand scrabbled for the door handle and caught. He staggered out of the pickup. "Susan!" he shouted, regaining his balance. He strode toward her. "Susan Kim!"

He couldn't take his eyes from her face. She seemed to register him but didn't react. Vaguely he saw the grey-haired woman running from the fire toward him. The large woman holding the hose twisted in his direction and scowled.

"Vic!" Jimmy's voice from his left.

Vic stumbled on the uneven ground and righted himself. It was Susan, he was positive. The large woman twisted something on the hose and the water stopped.

"Susan Kim!" Vic shouted.

Halfway to her he was wrenched to a stop by two arms around his chest. They lifted him and swung him back around to face the truck.

"Stop!" Jimmy's voice hard in his ear.

Somehow the grey-haired woman was in front of him, wrinkled face tilted up. She shouted something he didn't understand. He tried to break free but Jimmy's arms were a straightjacket. He managed to twist his head around to see Susan Kim accept a towel from the large woman, as if she had all the time in the world. The elderly woman spoke sharply this time.

"Vic." Jimmy's voice thundered in his ear. "Stop! This is a religious ceremony. You don't interrupt."

"She's taking a shower!" Vic strangled out. "That's Susan Kim, she was taken with Dannie. My daughter." He tried bouncing on his toes to get free but Jimmy's arms tightened. At the top of his lungs Vic shouted, "Susan! I'm Dannie's father. Do you know where she is?" He wrenched to his left and managed to face her.

Susan didn't blink. She finished wrapping the towel around herself and stepped from underneath the makeshift shower. She looked lost in thought, as if trying to solve a puzzle.

Jimmy and the elderly woman exchanged sharp words in a language Vic didn't understand. His brain reeled at the sound of it.

"Vic." The way Jimmy said his name sounded like a knife stab. Holding a handful of the back of his shirt, Jimmy let go and circled in front of him, his free hand pressing into the center of Vic's chest. "Look at me."

Vic blinked. Over Jimmy's shoulder he saw the hills, the blue sky. He tried to center on the black-brown of Jimmy's eyes.

The elderly woman slid away and Jimmy leaned close, a few inches from his face. "Vic," he repeated, "listen to me. Maybe that is Susan Kim. We don't know her name. We don't know how she got here."

Vic heard himself speaking, the babbling of it. "It's her. Ask her. I have to talk to her. She'll know what happened to Dannie."

"That's what I'm saying."

He focused. "What?"

"Vic. Get this. She doesn't talk. It's why they had her in the sweat lodge. She hasn't said a word since she got here."

Chapter 31

Something inside Vic released. He knew he was moving his jaw, his tongue, his lips, but no sounds came out. Finally, "What do you mean?"

"Exactly that. She doesn't talk. She's been like that since she got here. We're treating her."

"I don't understand, she just showed up?"

"Pretty much."

Jimmy's non-answer registered in his mind, but he was too distracted to focus. By now the large woman stood partially in front of Susan, protecting her. A figure exited the sweat lodge and stood by the flap. Vic glanced at her and saw someone short with a mass of black hair, the downward tilt of her head hiding her face. She was lost in the oversized dress she wore, her bare forearms bony. A girl, he thought, no more than fifteen.

He blinked and looked toward the shower. "Susan," he called. "I talked to your brother, Paul. He wants to know what happened to you. He's worried to death. We've got to tell him you're safe."

The same deadpan stare. Desperation rose inside him. He looked at Jimmy. "Can she write?"

Jimmy conferred with the elderly woman, who shook her head. "We tried that. No. She draws sometimes, but it's just lines and circles. It makes no sense. At least not yet."

Jimmy's words circled back inside his brain. "You're treating her?"

"Yes. That's what we do here."

Vic stared at Susan, who returned his gaze, her soaked hair now compressed into a black rope over one shoulder. Vic thought he saw some kind of recognition or understanding in her eyes, but he wasn't sure. The elderly woman left Jimmy and crossed to her. Vic watched as she urged Susan toward the house.

"You're treating her," Vic repeated.

Jimmy turned to him. "Yes. She is," he nodded at the grey-haired woman guiding Susan. "Kelly Redfeather. She studied psychology in college. This is her specialty. She takes in traumatized women. Victims of abuse and trafficking. Works with them. She has her own way of doing it. Part scientific and stuff like the sweat lodge. The old ways."

Vic looked at the lodge, at the girl standing by the door flap, her face still hidden by long black hair. She seemed frozen in place. Fourteen years old? Fifteen? He registered the meaning of that with a shudder. He looked away and shifted from one foot to another. He was aware of a sweetness in the air he hadn't noticed. Woodsmoke. He watched the large woman and Kelly reach the house and shepherd Susan inside.

"The drawings you talked about…" He heard the desperation in his voice. "You said lines and circles? Korean, maybe?"

Jimmy was quiet for a few beats. "You think we don't know what written Korean looks like?"

Vic's insides hardened. He looked into the distance for anything that might help him. It was just grass covered hills, the few trees sucked into cuts between them. The sky a crater above. No movement. No life. He closed his eyes. Reached inside himself and found only a few words. They came out in a whisper. "Sorry. I just need something. Any god-damned thing." His blood felt thick. "This case. Everything I find gets slammed back in my face."

"You helped already. You told us who she is."

"I'm not leaving her. Her family needs to know she's here. She's alive."

Jimmy raised his eyes. "Give us a bit longer before you do that. She's traumatized, that's why she doesn't speak…Kelly said…she doesn't respond to anything, doesn't interact with people. She turtles when men are around. She needs time and a safe space. You shouting at her isn't going to do it.

You're making it worse."

"I get that." But it was Anne he was thinking about. How to explain one of the trafficked women was alive, when he knew nothing of Dannie. This felt worse, somehow.

The large woman came outside, crossed to the girl at the sweat lodge entrance and guided her by the shoulder toward the house. Vic felt sunlight on his face.

Slowly, the implications of finding Susan, and this place, sank in. Dannie might still be alive. The idea twisted in him. He'd refused to let himself believe it for so long, forced himself not to believe it. He'd take the side of statistics and his own experience. Despite that, the possibility that she might be alive had stubbornly refused to leave him. It was oyster grit. He'd forced himself to ignore it, at the same time aching for a pearl. He tamped down the thought. "Is there a lot of this?"

"What do you mean?"

"Trafficking. Women being abused."

"Too damn much. All the tribes."

"Who polices it?"

"Everybody and nobody. That's the problem. Tribal police, state, local, FBI. Indian reservations are jurisdictional nightmares. White hurts an Indian or the other way around, who investigates? Does it happen on Rez land or not? Whose courts do we use? Built-in prejudice on both sides. Mistrust each way. It's exhausting. We argue and nothing gets done."

"And people know that and take advantage of it."

"Always have. Right from the beginning. It's been going on forever." He waved his hand at the house. "When I joined the council, I started pushing money to these kinds of programs. You fight the jurisdictional problem and that becomes your life…and meanwhile people get hurt every day. Me, I decided to catch them as they fall. Try and get them back on their feet."

Vic slid his hands into his pockets. He looked at Jimmy's truck, an idea forming in his mind. "So that's why Charlie Running Bear wanted you to help me."

Jimmy looked at him but stayed silent, waiting.

"Charlie has a dog in this fight. I saw the newspaper articles. He's an activist. I bet he's after the people who do the trafficking, while you're working the victim's side. You guys yin and yanged me. You're two sides of the same coin." His anger rose. "I bet Charlie saw me as motivated, a white cop, someone who wouldn't put up with all the jurisdictional crap. He knew I'd just wade in. Shake everything up. Put a spotlight on all the problems for him."

Jimmy still didn't say anything, but after a moment his brown eyes brightened. "You're missing something."

"Like what."

He nodded toward the house. "Read your history. Every big change comes from the bottom. We help those women, get them back to living some kind of life, who do you think they become?"

This time Vic waited, not sure of Jimmy's direction.

"The people who demand the problem gets fixed. They're the victims, but if they survive, they get fierce. They know how terrible it is. They felt it...lived through it. It's totally personal for them. They won't be ignored." Jimmy smiled. "They become warriors."

Vic stared at him. "You guys think you have it worked out."

Jimmy shrugged. "It's a start."

"I'm still not letting Susan out of my sight."

"You have to."

"No way. I stay right here." He crossed his arms over his chest, knowing he sounded like a spoiled child and not caring.

Jimmy looked at the sky for a moment and sighed. The wind fell, and in the quiet he heard a soft chiming sound. Jimmy heard it as well, and together, they pivoted and looked in the direction of the noise. Jimmy's truck. Both doors were open, the sound the ignition key alarm. Jimmy crossed to the truck and reached inside for the keys before walking around to shut the passenger door. He returned to Vic.

"If you feel like you need to stay close to Susan, and I see why, I'll ask if you can stay nearby. No way you can stay in the house. But we have to go soon if we're going to spell those FBI guys and watch Nadine. I doubt the

FBI like to miss dinner."

"Thanks."

Vic walked back to the truck and leaned against the passenger side. Jimmy watched him for a few moments, took in the skyline, and crossed to the house.

Vic watched Jimmy and Kelly talking at the front door. He tried to piece things together. He thought he now understood why Charlie wanted him here. Charlie was making sure he was invested. He'd never expected Vic to recognize Susan, that was just a bonus. But that led him to think about Jimmy's neat slide away from explaining how Susan Kim arrived on the Rez.

Kelly ducked into the house and Jimmy started for the truck. As Vic waited, he thought about how small the house looked against the hills, and how tiny he felt. How lost among the sky and hills they all were.

"She'll let you stay, just not in the house."

"Okay."

Jimmy pointed at the barn. "I explained how Susan was taken with your daughter. She said you can stay there if you want to be on premises. But she's got conditions. You don't approach or speak to any of the women. Especially Susan. You stay out of their way. And never, never let yourself be alone with any of them."

"Works for me. What about tonight?"

"I'm not done. I didn't tell her you're a cop. Don't let that slip. No way she'll let you stay if she knows that. The local cops ignore us or worse. Now here's my main point. She didn't want to do this but caved because I'm on tribal council. You screw this up and you screw me up. Understand?"

Vic took a slow breath. "I do."

Jimmy nodded, as if he had checked a box in his mind. "Watching Nadine Stills, for tonight I'll take the whole night. You stay here. FBI takes the stuff from Nadine tomorrow, right? After that it won't matter about her... Susan is who you want to stay close to....right?"

"Exactly." Vic heard himself say the word, surprised at how soft it was. Nadine seemed like a distant memory, Cora as well. It would be a waiting game, now, until Susan started speaking again. Until she could tell him what happened. And he needed to think. If Susan was alive, Dannie might be as well. But where?

"Let's take a look in the barn," Jimmy said. "See if you need anything. I've got about enough time to go home and grab anything you're missing, bring it here, then spell the FBI boys."

Vic nodded and followed Jimmy to the barn.

Chapter 32

Vic wasn't sure about staying in the barn until he got inside. At some point, someone had removed the gates to the four stalls, cleaned them out and replaced the floors with brown-painted plywood. Composition board was screwed to the stall sides for privacy. Each space was large enough to hold a single bed, a bedside table topped with a small lamp, and an old wooden dresser. Vic didn't see how anyone could open the drawers without collapsing onto the bed.

"Not good in winter," Jimmy said, "but it's okay this time of year." He pointed to a door at the end of the building. "There's a porta-potty out there."

Vic wanted to make a joke but didn't have it in him.

Jimmy nodded to the open space next to the double doors at the front of the barn. "You saw the long table and chairs when we came in? Use that for eating. Kelly Redfeather said you're on your own for meals."

"That's fine." It came out sounding annoyed. He didn't mean it, and he felt bad.

Jimmy looked at him, a sliver of outside light running up his body from a gap in the boards of the outside wall. "Hey, you wanted to stay here. We can go back to my place."

"No. Sorry. That sounded wrong. But I do need to get back into the motel. I've been wearing the same clothes for two days."

"We can do that tomorrow. Kelly understands why you want to keep Susan in sight. She's trying to help you. But you have to give the women here space. That's why Susan went straight to the shower like that...she wasn't expecting us."

Vic nodded. "I get it."

"Okay, then I'm headed out. I'll bring you a sleeping bag and dinner. Try to stay in the barn as much as you can."

Vic gathered himself. "Thanks. And if you're stopping at your house, do you have a cleaning kit I could use on my Glock? It's due." He leaned closer. "And you need to explain how Susan got here. How did that happen?"

"It's complicated."

"That's not an answer. You know it isn't."

"Look. I'm not in a position to tell you. Not my call. She got away from the traffickers and someone vouched for her. That's how she ended up here."

"Still not really an answer."

"Can't help you." Jimmy gave him a hard look and turned for the door. Vic fought down his anger and followed him, stopping in the doorway. He watched Jimmy cross to his truck, open the driver's door and stop. Jimmy stared through the gap between the truck's body and door. Vic followed his gaze. Susan stood on the house porch, her arms folded over her chest. She wore baggy jeans and a white shirt, her still-wet hair over her shoulders and down onto her forearms. Her eyes were locked on Jimmy, who didn't move. It was as if he didn't want to startle her. Vic felt himself folded into the moment with them, the air a held breath, the sky still, the hills poised somehow. The moment stretched, until a bird swooped between the house and truck, releasing them. Susan turned, slowly, and let herself back into the house. Jimmy gazed after her a few moments longer, then slid into the truck.

Vic watched him drive away. He didn't understand what just happened, but it felt significant. He relaxed, and took his first breath since he'd noticed Susan on the porch.

Chapter 33

Two hours later, when Jimmy returned, he held a duffel in one hand and a Styrofoam food container in the other. Vic opened the lid to an unidentifiable mish-mash of red, brown and white food.

"What is this?" he asked, keeping his voice civil. He didn't want to sound like he was complaining.

Jimmy dropped the duffel on the table and looked over his shoulder. "New Town's best. Fusion, maybe?"

Vic side-eyed him and saw a smile. Jimmy shrugged. "It was on the floor of my truck. Slid around."

Vic closed the lid and placed the container on the table. "Food is food. Did you bring anything for my Glock?"

Jimmy pointed at the duffel. "With everything else. And I gotta go, or those FBI guys watching Nadine will be pissed."

After he left, Vic placed the duffel in the room where he intended to sleep. At the table he found an outlet to charge his phone and sat down to eat. Around the second or third fork-full of semi-cold white rice he recognized the tastes of cilantro and cheese. No meat. Mexican, he decided, followed by the conclusion that Jimmy's brand of vegetarianism included forcing it on others.

He ate as much as he could, mainly to fuel himself, then found the elastic straps and went through the sequences of exercises for his shoulder. It felt strong and unaffected by the fight. As he finished, someone knocked lightly on the door.

Vic opened the door to Kelly Redfeather. She held a reusable water bottle out to him. He thanked her and accepted it. She slipped into the barn and sat down at the long table. Vic took the nearest chair.

"My name is Kelly Redfeather."

"Jimmy told me. I'm Vic Lenoski." They shook hands.

Sitting, she seemed even smaller. Her face was weathered brown, the lines around her mouth and eyes cut by a knife-edged wind. Her brown eyes were deep and spaced apart, her chin prominent, and with her grey hair she projected a kind of maternal trustworthiness. He could see how traumatized women might respond to her, how anyone would, really.

Her eyes locked onto him. "You're sure about this Susan? I mean her name?"

"Susan Kim. Yes. I've been staring at her photo for months. Are you sure she can't speak?"

She gave him a disgusted look and tapped her hand on the table. A jumble of thin silver bracelets jangled. "I've been doing this for thirty years. Loss of vocalization has happened before, it'll happen again. It's psychosomatic. Same way people who witness something bad can temporarily go blind. It's a defense mechanism the brain uses. She'll get it back, I just don't know when. Tell me about her. It might help me with her recovery."

Vic explained what he knew about Susan's family life, her education, her work as a stripper and her abduction. How she and the other three women were held in a barn for transport, and how her training helped her injure one of the men.

Kelly gave him a tight smile. "Martial arts explains a couple of things."

"Her brother told me Tae Kwon Do. Fifth degree black belt, or something."

She nodded. "Last week she started going outside every morning and doing routines. I thought they looked like some kind of martial arts."

"Patterns or forms. My daughter trained for a year or two."

"Are they common in Tae Kwon Do?"

"Yes. More than sparring."

Kelly nodded. "That's good, then. She's reconnecting to herself. Reclaiming her identity."

Vic liked her tone of voice. It was firm and confident. Someone who trusted her own abilities.

She studied him. "You understand she may know very little about your daughter?"

"They were together."

"Maybe, but first rule of trafficking is to split up the girls. Don't let them make alliances or band together. Drug them, more often than not. They want the girls as alone as possible and dependent on whoever is running them, not each other."

Vic sat back. He hadn't thought of that. "But she must know something. They drove out here in the same van. And you're sure you can't communicate with her somehow? Hand gestures or something?"

"Loss of vocalization is always different. Sometimes they are mentally fine, they just can't talk, other times they are so traumatized they can't talk or relate to anyone in any way. It's a spectrum, and I'm not sure where she is on it. Not yet. She seems pretty sharp mentally, though, she just isn't communicating. Just don't expect anything soon."

Vic fought down his frustration. "Can you tell me how she came to you? It's odd she would end up here."

"Yes and no." Kelly's eyes flashed. "No one really polices abuse here. I started this place maybe twenty years ago, and I've had a couple hundred girls and women come through. This is normal for us. I wasn't about to kick her out over some detail like whether or not she's Native. And the council felt she deserved it."

"What does that mean?"

Kelly stared at him in silence. The table was pushed against the outside wall, and from tiny gaps between some of the wall planks, Vic saw the light outside had faded. A tendril of wind reached him.

"Jimmy's on council. That's up to him." She rose and stepped to the door. "In the morning, make sure you stay inside. I told you Susan does her routines or patterns then. That young girl you saw today at the sweat lodge imitates her. They do them together. I don't want that interfered with. Am I clear? When you reverse how traffickers split up girls, put them together, it helps their recovery. It helps them re-socialize. Deal with the shame they feel."

Vic rose as well. "I'll stay out of sight." Another thought came to him. "Wait. You must be familiar with the places the women were put to work. They must talk about it. I need to know where to look."

She hesitated. "Logically, yes, but it doesn't work that way. The traffickers move the girls around. They know they're breaking the law, so they try and stay ahead of it. Anywhere I've heard about is probably closed by now." She frowned. "Susan hasn't said anything, of course, but the girl she came with told me their place caught fire, that was how they escaped."

Vic's heart skipped a beat. "When was that?"

"A couple of months ago. But that's all I know."

"Jimmy and I looked at a place that burned. Not far from here."

"Well, there you go." Kelly stared at him, as if considering saying something more, but thought better of it and let herself outside. She closed the door behind her.

Vic tried the lamp at the end of the table. It worked, although only enough to shrink the darkness into the roof joists and corners. He stood for a time, wondering if he should call Anne. He knew he should, but rationalized it away, telling himself he needed more to tell her. The truth was he couldn't face making the call. He drank water, his dinner a dead weight in his stomach, and went to his cot to lie down.

When he awoke, the barn was pitch black except for the glow of the lamp by the door. He sat on the edge of his cot for a moment, waiting for his head to clear, then went to the front of the barn and found his phone. It was just after midnight. Taking his phone for its flashlight, he went out through the back.

The sky was littered with stars, the moon half full and white. He stopped to let his eyes adjust to the darkness. The wind was still, the air smelled of something he couldn't quite place. Sage, perhaps. Two stones clinked as if something had knocked them together, but when he cocked his head and waited, he heard only the whisper of the wind. Gradually, the looming shadow of the porta-potty separated from the darkness and he went inside. On his way back into the barn he listened again, but heard nothing.

He turned on the lamp beside his bed and opened the duffel. He found a hard-cover gun case lined with foam that contained a cleaning kit. He moved to the table and lined up each item from the case. He smiled. For all of Jimmy's vegetarian and intellectual interests, his army training hadn't lapsed. He had everything he needed.

Ten minutes later, his Glock disassembled, he was using a solvent-dipped Q-tip to clean the slide when his phone rang. He used the first knuckle on his middle finger to answer the call and switch the phone to speaker.

"Vic?" Liz's voice still sounded hoarse and overworked.

"Liz, what the hell. It must be two in the morning there."

"I ain't taking those knock-you-out pain killers. I'm awake. I work now so I don't get nasty looks from the nurses. And you need to know. This Ewan Fleck boy, his story ain't being told in public records."

"Okay." Vic held the Glock's slide up into the light, looking for powder residue.

"Lives clean. No criminal record. Even pays his taxes."

"Son of a police chief. Makes sense."

"Anyway, still working through the properties he owns." Liz stopped and Vic heard muffled coughs. When she came back on the phone, her voice was hoarse. "It's his company that's interesting. I need a warrant for his financials, but I found a bid he put in for work with the state of North Dakota. Public record, pretty detailed. According to that he doesn't pay himself much. I mean minimum wage kind of level."

Vic placed the slide on the table. "That makes no sense. Where does he live? Someone said he has a big house outside Watford."

"He does." Liz gave him the address. "He owns a bunch of other properties, most of them in Watford City."

Vic remembered how small the town of Watford was. "You got a list?"

"Of course."

He recited the address where Kent Bauer had died. "How about that one?"

"Yep, on the list."

"Kent Bauer lived there."

"Well what do you know? Company housing."

Vic knew it could be legitimate, but it could also be a reward for something. There was no way to know. "Can you email me the list? I might drive by them."

"Sure, but this is what's interesting."

"What?"

"His properties are all owned by a holding company."

"Pretty usual out here, I was told."

"Right, but his name is on the holding company. He's not trying to hide it at all, which *is* different. Says he's pretty much legit. But then I added up the assessed values of his properties. Guess what? Almost six million. And that's just what I can see."

Liz dissolved into muffled coughing. Vic thought about what she was saying as she recovered her breath. When the bout ended, he said, "Now where'd he get the money to buy that many places?"

"Right. Like I said, his story ain't being told. Six million in property with almost no income? Good deal if you can get it."

"Thanks, Liz. That helps. You should get some sleep."

"One other thing."

Vic waited.

"Someone from the DA's office stopped by. Hana? That girl with the country club hair? Asked me how I was doing all nice, like. I didn't buy it for a second. Then she said she figured I was talking to you, and she had a message she wanted me to pass along."

"Hana's been straight with me so far."

"Well, a girl that good-looking could tell you anything and you'd buy it. Anyway, she wanted you to know Lily Bauer cut a deal. Confessed to starting the fire in Gretchen Stoll's bedroom and that it got out of control, didn't mean to kill her, blah blah. And this Hana was real specific that you know Lily's son got released on time served. He's out. Press conference about the confession tomorrow. I'm guessing no one mentions her son getting released. DA must be in pig heaven."

Vic smiled. Hana had pulled the strings. "I guess that's progress."

"I'd rather it went to trial," Liz mumbled. Her voice tightened as if she was fighting a cough. "Anything on Cora Stills?"

"Not yet."

"Okay, I gotta go."

Before Vic could answer, Liz broke into a coughing fit and hung up. She wasn't ready to work, Vic knew it, but he understood how much she wanted to take part. Slowly, he got back to cleaning his Glock.

His mind wandered as he worked. Kelly Redfeather. Her comment about the burned-out building, how Susan Kim and the native girl escaped. He thought of Dannie and went cold. Suppose she was there as well. He forced himself not to think about it and slowly, one piece at a time, reassembled his Glock. And then he thought about the security camera footage. If the company still had back-ups, he wondered if Dannie might show up on it. It was something to ask about.

His phone rang. His hands still oily, he repeated the knuckle presses to put it on speaker.

"Vic? It's Jimmy." His voice was high and excited.

"What's up?"

"Nadine Stills went out. I followed her to Lewis and Clark State Park. She's in a trailer on the edge of the park."

Vic leaped to his feet. "Tell me where."

"From the entry to the park, you take the first right and follow that road until it's dirt. Bunch of mobile homes. Five of them. Nadine's in the one closest to the road." He was speaking so quickly he almost ran his words together.

"Did you see Cora Stills?"

"You said she was a redhead? I think so. Whoever answered the door had red hair. But I couldn't park close. It's a two-lane road and no one is on it. She would've seen me."

Vic bounced on his toes, frustrated. He was stuck on the Rez with no car. "Okay." He wiped his mouth with his sleeve. "Hide. Whatever you do, don't let either of them see you. Don't follow Nadine home, just come back and get me. Fast as you can."

"What if she goes somewhere else?"

"Did she know you were following her?"

"No. I parked in a different place outside her house. When she came out, she looked right where I used to park. I think she knew we were staking her out, but didn't see me. Driving out I stayed back."

"Good. She might stop somewhere else on her way home, but it'd be worse if she sees you following her. Stay out of sight and let her go. Then come back and get me. We'll get her tonight."

"Nadine's back out. She's moving."

"Get your ass hidden." He ground his knuckle on the disconnect button.

Chapter 34

Vic punched the air and swore out loud at being stuck on the Rez. They'd found Cora, he was sure of it. Every instinct told him to get moving, to get out there and ram down the door to her trailer. He paced in front of the table, his heart pounding. Frustrated, he wiped his hands on a cloth, went outside and washed his hands the best he could with the last of the water in the bottle.

Back at the table he slid the Glock into his clip holster, attached it to his belt, and waited.

Wind pushed against the slats of the barn and leaked through the spaces between them. He kept glancing at his phone, willing Jimmy to call. He needed to do something. He texted Liz a quick note.

Might have found Cora. Will let you know.

No response. He checked the time. Almost two-thirty. He considered notifying the FBI agents, but knew if they arrested Cora it would be weeks before he could interview her. The same went with Karl. He got up and paced, the silence oppressive, time moving slower than tree growth.

It was almost three-thirty before a truck motor betrayed the quiet. He stepped outside. As soon as Jimmy pulled up, he yanked open the truck door and slid in.

"Let's go."

Jimmy killed the engine. "Good news."

"Tell me on the way."

191

"Give me a second, will you? I'm beat. Listen. I sat tight after Nadine left. Whoever is in the trailer stayed there, at least for the half hour I waited. I wanted to make sure they didn't take off."

"Okay." Vic wrestled down the urge to shout at him to get going.

"And Nadine went straight home. I swung by her house coming here. Her car was parked in front."

"Jesus, you drove through Arnegard?"

"You know how small it is. It's not like it's out of the way."

"How long will it take to get there?"

Jimmy shrugged. "First, I need to take a piss, then we head back. And you need to think about something. We drive right by your hotel. We could stop and get your car."

"I want to get her before she disappears."

Jimmy slid out of the truck. "I get that." He ducked down to look into the cab. "But we pick up your car and change shirts. You need to do that. Especially the shirt." He slammed the door.

Vic struggled with Jimmy's suggestion. When he got back, Vic said, "Okay. Yes. I need my car. I can't get stuck without one again. Let's go, but make it fast. That means we knock on Cora's door about five. She'll be dead asleep and out of it. Good time to catch her." Vic frowned as another thought came to him. "Unless you told Charlie Running Bear you'd found her, and he wants her for some reason."

"I did tell him, but he has no reason to grab her. Or have his guys do it."

"Charlie has guys?"

"When he wants to get stuff done, sure. He can't do it himself because of his legs. I told you he was active in the pipeline protests. I meant his guys were."

Vic was quiet a moment, thinking. That information felt important, somehow, but he didn't know why. He brushed it away. "Let's get going."

It took almost an hour to reach Watford City, Vic seething the entire way. He kept repeating to himself that he needed his car. The motel loomed ahead, moths the size of hummingbirds slamming themselves at the oversized LED lights along the roof. Jimmy parked by the side door, but it was locked and Vic's keycard didn't work. He double-timed to the front door and approached the dozing night manager. Sure enough, agent Croyle had left his car keys at the front desk for him. Vic took the elevator to the second floor.

When he stepped into his room, something felt out of place. He turned on one of the lamps and stared. His suitcase was on the bench where he left it. He checked the bathroom; his toiletries looked untouched. In the bedroom he lifted the lid of his suitcase. His dirty clothes were inside, exactly as he'd left them. Carefully, he nudged his gun case. The latches were undone. He never left it unlatched, even when it was empty. He checked inside but it looked as it always did.

It bothered him, but he didn't have time to sort it out. He snapped the latches into place and went to the closet. As he changed, he caught a whiff of himself. Jimmy was right. In the bathroom he coated his underarms with deodorant before tugging on clean pants and shirt.

He let himself out of the room and pushed the elevator button. The doors beeped, opened, and Vic stared into the faded blue eyes of Watford Police Chief Fleck.

"There he is," the chief said, stepping off the elevator and bumping Vic with his chest, forcing him back into the hall.

"Chief." Vic took another step back to put room between them. He guessed the front desk clerk wasn't as sleepy as he looked, but that didn't make sense. The chief had arrived too quickly for that.

Chief Fleck kept his voice low and hard. "First you show up on my crime scene, now you're trespassing on private property and assaulting local citizens."

"I don't know what you're talking about."

"The burned-out building on G&O land. Private property. And then you take a run at the guys who came to kick you off?"

"Not true. Did you see the security footage of the incident? I defended myself, plain and simple."

The chief blinked and Vic wondered if he didn't know about the security camera, or if he was surprised Vic knew about it. At the same time, he guessed that if the footage did exist, within an hour it would be deleted. "Glad to stop by your office and answer any questions," he said quickly. "Kinda late at night right now."

"And what are you doing out this late?"

"Just headed back to the Rez to get some shuteye."

"You're not sleeping in your room here?"

"Maybe tomorrow."

Vic watched the Chief calculate something. "I'm thinking you've about spent as much time in town as you need to."

"Still got a couple of things to look into, Chief."

Fleck's eyes narrowed. "I don't think you're listening to me."

"I hear you loud and clear. You want me out of town. I said I'm glad to leave, I just need to do a couple of things first."

"Uh-huh."

Something felt off. If the chief was going to arrest him, he would have arrived with another officer. And his tone of voice had turned more conversational than confrontational.

The chief rocked on his heels. "Around here people don't trespass on private property. We need to discuss that. My offices, before you head home. I need a statement."

"Sure. But, so we're clear, the property wasn't posted. I didn't know we were trespassing. If there was a sign, I would have respected it."

"You got an answer for everything, don't you?"

He spread his hands. "I wish I did." Fleetingly, he thought of Dannie.

"And keep away from that Jimmy Pronghorn. That boy is trouble."

Vic stayed quiet. He had purposely not mentioned Jimmy, and yet the Chief knew about him. Now Vic was sure that someone had given the chief a detailed, and probably misleading, description of the fight.

They stood in silence, the flat light of the hallway around them. Vic could feel how thin the carpet was under his feet.

"Chief," Vic said carefully. "How did you get here so quickly? You got a room here or something? I mean, I wasn't here ten minutes."

The chief relaxed. "I spotted you guys when you turned off Route 23." A note of pride lingered in his voice. "I was getting gas. Figured you were heading here."

It was a fifteen-minute drive from Route 23 to the hotel. The speed limit was twenty-five and Jimmy, as he tended to do, had stuck to it. Vic had kept his jaw clamped shut the entire way to avoid urging him to speed up. Now, he was glad Jimmy followed the posted speed.

Breaking the silence between them, the chief said, "Call my offices to set up a time to give a statement." He turned to the elevator doors and pressed the button. They opened immediately. Vic stayed in the hall and waited for the doors to close. Something nagged at him. It was all too pat. If the chief wanted him in his office, he could have called. He didn't like how the chief knew about Jimmy. And then he realized that if the chief saw them on the road, he knew Jimmy was with him. He spun on the ball of his right foot and jogged down the hall to the stairwell. He trotted down the stairs, popped out on the first-floor hallway and pushed through the side door into the parking lot.

Ahead of him a plump, black-haired man sat on the ground, his legs straight in front of him, his back against the driver's side wheel of Jimmy's truck. The front of his white T-shirt was saturated with blood. Vic blinked, trying to process what he was seeing. Gomez. The man who charged Jimmy the day before at the burned-out building. A dull thud came from the other side of Jimmy's truck. Fist to flesh. Vic ran toward the sound. When he swung around the front of the truck, the lean man from the day before had his left hand around Jimmy's throat, his right cocked to punch.

Vic barreled into him, right shoulder low, right arm clamped against his chest. The man bounced off the side of a truck and into the lane between parking spaces. Vic was on him instantly. He dragged him upright against the truck and punched hard, a right and a left, into his midsection. The man huffed out a breath and slid down the truck into a sitting position, legs in front of him, just like Gomez. Snot ran from his nose and his hands flopped like beached fish.

Vic strode back to Jimmy. Somehow, he was still upright, but his head wavered back and forth as if he was high. Blood dribbled from the corner of his mouth and his eyelids were at half-mast. Vic tugged open the cab door, got his arm around Jimmy's chest and helped him inside. "We need to move," he hissed. With Jimmy folded into the seat, he slammed the door and ran around to the other side of the cab. He grabbed a handful of Gomez's T-shirt, dragged him off the wheel and clambered into the cab. The keys were in the ignition. He started the truck, reversed out of the space and bounced out of the parking lot.

Vic concentrated on driving, constantly checking his rear-view mirror. He wanted to jam his foot onto the gas but he held their speed just five miles an hour over the speed limit. It felt like they were crawling, but finally signs for Route 23 appeared. He guided the truck through the intersection and sped up.

"Assholes," Jimmy groaned, from beside him.

"You doing okay?"

Jimmy's head was still down, hair hiding his face. "Never better." He took a shallow breath. "What the hell took you so long?"

Vic glanced at the sky. It was pitch black, the moon a vague glow behind clouds. Across the horizon, flames plumed from wellhead exhausts, as if whatever was underground was pushing so hard to get out the flames could barely keep up. "We got played." He checked his speed. "Chief found me when I came out of my room. Kept me in the hallway. He was buying time for those guys to work you over. I knew it didn't feel right."

Jimmy made a sound like a wounded bear and shifted upright in his seat. He pushed his hair behind his ears and wiped his mouth with the back of his hand. He checked the glove compartment, found paper napkins and held a wad against the side of his mouth.

"I'll stop next place I see, get you some gauze."

"How did they get on us so fast?"

"I asked the chief the same thing. He said he spotted us when we turned off 23 toward Watford. I bet he called his buddies as soon as he got behind us. They still made it here fast." He tapped the steering wheel with his hand. "I found out Ewan's company owns a bunch of houses in Watford. I bet they were holed up in one of them. Watford's so small they could make the hotel in a few minutes."

"Lucky us."

Vic saw Jimmy explore his chest and abdomen with his free hand. He probed in a couple of places, testing the extent of his bruises.

"How'd you get Gomez down?"

Jimmy shook his head. "I was in the driver's seat. They pulled up behind me and Gomez charged, just like he did last time. Came right along the truck. I saw it in my side mirror. I timed his run and opened my door. Dumbass ran right into it. He went down, I got out and gave him a couple of shots so he'd stay there."

Vic chuckled. "The other guy?"

"I was worried he'd have a gun. Remember last time? I didn't see where he parked after he dropped off Gomez, so I guessed and tried to put the truck between us. I guessed wrong and ran right into him. He belted me pretty good before I could defend myself. Then you came along."

Vic spotted a sign for an all-night convenience store. "I'll stop here and get you some ice and stuff."

Jimmy nodded.

After he parked and cut the engine, Vic looked at Jimmy. "You still up for Cora Stills? How you feeling?"

Jimmy nodded slowly. "I'm good. If it gets hairy, I won't be your guy, though. You'll need to handle it yourself."

Vic smiled. "You've done enough for tonight."

Jimmy stared at the darkness on the other side of the windshield. "Sure feels that way."

Chapter 35

Vic crisscrossed aisles in the convenience store. These stores were nothing like Pittsburgh. They were supermarket-sized buildings under nonsensical, sterile brand names so focus-grouped and buffed they only meant something in PowerPoints. They sold everything from fishing gear to thirty kinds of frozen pizza, cheap lingerie to car parts. He passed long counters of take-out food, found the first aid section and grabbed gauze, cold packs and Ace bandages. He was halfway to the cash register when his feet slowed. He stopped. The fluorescent lights buzzed somewhere high above him.

It wasn't, he thought, that Chief Fleck had orchestrated an ambush. It was how he'd done it. He'd given Vic a warning by hurting someone close to him. Jimmy had little to do with why Vic was in North Dakota, but that didn't matter. And Vic made another bet. He guessed the chief handled it that way because it was a twofer. Warn Vic, and hurt a tribal council member. He was sure of it. And that meant it was ingrained in the man. A bad so natural and instinctive it was a wavelength of bad, a broadcast. The worst kind of bad. Not the kind that drags someone down, the kind that drags everyone down.

He started toward the cash register. Chief Fleck was like all those pipes spouting fire, he thought, venting what usually burns underground. He shook his head. Jimmy's references were getting to him.

He paid and crossed the parking lot.

Will I ever get my damn car back? he wondered.

He dropped the plastic bag with the first aid supplies on Jimmy's lap and started the truck. Jimmy pointed in the direction to go without speaking. They moved into the night, alone on the highway. Jimmy shrugged out of his T-shirt, manipulated an ice pack to activate the cooling chemicals and used an Ace bandage to hold it against his ribs.

"Hate rib punches," he muttered.

Vic knew the feeling. They took the longest to heal, as if the bone was bruised, not the skin and muscle.

Jimmy manipulated another ice pack, wadded the inside of his lip with gauze and used his bundled shirt to hold the ice pack against the side of his mouth.

They drove in silence for thirty-five minutes, circling the lake and driving along the northern side. In time, Jimmy extricated the gauze from his mouth.

"Coming up," he said in a clipped way, as if he didn't want the cut on his lip to break open. He tossed the ice bag into the footwell and unwound the Ace bandage from his chest. He added the second ice bag to the first and awkwardly tugged on his T-shirt.

A green state park sign appeared, and Vic slowed to make the turn. They followed the park entry road downhill, the lake looming ahead, black ink with a skin of light from the half moon. It reminded him of Liz's hospital room that first night he spoke to her. That same consuming darkness kept at bay by feeble light.

"The wine-dark sea," Jimmy said softly.

Vic glanced at him, wondering what he was talking about.

Jimmy stared straight ahead. "Read Homer at all? *The Iliad* and *The Odyssey*? Homer keeps talking about the wine-dark sea. I was reading it in high school and saw the lake one night. I thought that was what he meant."

"It looks black, not red."

"Yep. It's a mystery. Turn right."

This new road followed the contours of the lake's northern shore. As they circled around an inlet, Vic glanced out of his window and saw a jam of bleached logs bobbing gently in the water, the trunks stark white against the dark water.

They followed the road up a short rise. Just as they crested the top, another vehicle rushed toward them, brights on, hogging the road. Vic yanked the wheel. The passenger side tires thumped onto dirt and Vic held on, controlling the truck's slew. The other vehicle rocketed past. "Shit." Vic teased the wheel and brought them back onto the road. "What the hell was that?"

He glanced at Jimmy, who was frowning at the windshield.

"Did you get a look at it?"

Jimmy hesitated. "Pickup."

"Surprised anyone would be out this late." Vic glanced at the dashboard clock. It read 12:10. He knew that wasn't right. "Does anything work on this truck?"

"Engine. Brakes. You need more, I mean really? Up ahead." They passed a cluster of cabins facing the lake, but Jimmy pointed at a distant, L-shaped gravel access road lit by pole lights. Five squat and angular mobile homes edged the short side of the L like a skirt hem.

"Where did you park?"

"Does it matter now?"

"I guess not." Vic slowed the truck and executed a three-point turn in the mouth of the access road. Facing back the way they had come, he cut the engine. They slid out and met behind the truck.

"First one?" Vic whispered, and Jimmy nodded.

They started up the road, automatically stepping onto the grass at the driveway's edge to silence their footfalls. Vic led Jimmy to the mobile home's front door.

Jimmy shuffled to one side and swung his arms to test his movement. Vic climbed the three steps and raised the heel of his left fist. His right hand freed his Glock from his side. He held it pointing at the ground.

He thumped the door with the heel of his fist and it swung inward as if he'd kicked it. He darted to his left, hiding his outline against the sky and thrust his gun forward. He sighted along the Glock into the black interior of the trailer.

Silence.

"Cora Stills!" Vic shouted.

Nothing stirred. Vic called again. He hesitated, then reached inside with his left hand and felt along the wall. He touched a light switch and with a quick suck of breath, flipped the toggle.

Light flooded the room. From the corner of his eye Vic saw a kitchen to his right. He peeked around the door frame, surveying the living room over the sight on the slide of his Glock. He tracked over a couch, armchair, heavy wooden coffee table and wall-mounted television.

And Cora Stills.

She was flat on her back, crammed into the narrow space between the couch and the coffee table, her head wrenched viciously to one side.

Vic cursed, rage shooting through him. He stepped into the room and spotted a corridor that led to the rest of the trailer. "Stay outside!" he shouted at Jimmy. Glock at arm's length, leading the way, he shuffled past Cora's body and down the hallway. He cleared a bathroom and bedroom.

He came straight back to the living room, kneeled by Cora and placed two fingers on the side of her neck. Her skin was warm but nothing pulsed under his fingers. The front of her neck was oddly depressed, the red of bruising already beginning to appear.

"Shit!"

Jimmy was standing beside him, now.

Vic sat back on his heels, his mind reeling. He stared at Cora's red hair, her empty green eyes. She was wearing sweatpants and a T-shirt. Sleeping clothes. He stood up. "Shit!" He looked at Jimmy. "Outside."

They walked down the steps. Anger overwhelmed Vic and his mind tilted. He strode toward the darkness of the rolling hills. At some point he stopped. He was too late. He breathed hard to steady himself. It felt as if everything inside him had been snatched away. All this way for nothing. He struggled to compose himself. Finally, angrily, he walked back to Jimmy. "Your buddy. Karl. The state police guy. Call him."

Jimmy's phone was already in his hand. He scrolled using his thumb and pressed the screen. Vic held out his hand. Jimmy frowned but passed him the phone.

Somewhere on the fourth or fifth ring a groggy voice said, "Jimmy?"

"No. Vic Lenoski. From Pittsburgh. I'm on Jimmy's phone."

"What happened?" Karl's voice sharpened.

"We found Cora Stills. And you got yourself another murder scene."

"Is Jimmy okay? What the hell happened?"

"Jimmy's fine. He tracked Cora here, came and got me, but she was dead when we got back. Still warm. I cleared the house and we're outside."

"Do the locals know?"

"We're in a state park."

A creak as if Karl was swinging his legs over the edge of his bed. "Okay, yeah, that would be us. You guys okay?"

"No, I'm goddamned not."

Silence for a split second. "I bet. You guys stay put. I'll get things moving." He drew in a quick breath. "You went to see Cora Stills at four-thirty in the morning?"

"Oh, is that what time it is?"

A longer silence. Vic guessed Karl knew he needed to be careful about what he said next. Finally, "If you guys aren't there when I arrive, I'm putting warrants out on both your asses. You read me?"

"One hundred percent." He explained their location, ended the call and handed the phone back to Jimmy. "We wait."

They did, Vic twenty feet from the mobile home's front door, pacing. Jimmy inside his truck, tending his bruises. Vic tried to clear his head. Kent Bauer murdered. Susan Kim unable to speak. Cora Stills dead. Everything was sliding away from him. He felt himself following, spinning downward, faster, his stomach rising into his mouth.

At some point, red and blue lights burst over the distant crest where he'd run off the road to avoid the pickup. Less than a minute later a state police cruiser ground to a stop at the end of the gravel road.

A uniformed officer got out, checked with Jimmy in the truck and then with Vic. From the doorway he stared inside the trailer but didn't go inside.

"EMTs should be here soon," he said, and started stringing crime scene tape.

Karl arrived fifteen minutes after an EMT exited the trailer and called a medical examiner. The neighbors woken by the commotion were back in their mobile homes, chased inside by the uniformed officer.

Karl leaned through the driver's window and talked to Jimmy for several minutes before walking the driveway to the trailer. Vic met him ten yards from the front door.

Karl nodded to him. "Let me take a quick look so I know what we're talking about, then you give me a preliminary and you guys can get out of here."

When he returned, Vic walked him through the whole story. How he used the FBI to flush out Nadine Stills, Jimmy tracking her to the trailer. The drive out. The pickup that almost ran them off the road, and how it might be connected to the murder. What he touched inside and outside the trailer.

Finished, he waited for Karl to stop writing in his notebook. When he did, he looked up. "You left out the part about two guys jumping Jimmy."

"Wasn't sure if Jimmy wanted to bring that up. Mostly, I figured Jimmy wouldn't press charges, so there wasn't much point."

"He's pretty pissed. I know Jimmy. The quieter he gets, the more you need to pay attention."

"Noted."

"And you're right. He's not a press-charges guy." Karl shifted his head as if he had a crick in his neck, his blond hair shining somehow in the moonlight. "You didn't see the truck that almost ran you off the road?"

"Too busy trying not to wreck."

He nodded, stuck his notebook in his jacket pocket and turned to the lake. Vic followed his gaze. The lake stared back, an unblinking black eye.

Still focused on the distance, Karl said, "You're gonna get a reputation."

Vic pinched the bridge of his nose. The time of night, the failure, everything that was snatched from him, it all bubbled inside him. "I don't think I care."

"I didn't say what kind of reputation." Karl turned back to him.

Vic met his stare. "Still don't care."

Karl smiled. "So. I'm gonna call your commander. Tomkins or something?"

"Crush."

"I'll tell him you tracked down Cora Stills, found her, but somebody took her out before you guys talked. But he can tell your partner, and your department, that Cora Stills got justice. He can stand down his task force."

"There wasn't a task force, just one rookie asshole. That's part of the reason I'm out here. But I'm sure he'll call a press conference."

From Karl's frown Vic knew the lack of a task force bothered him. Then he chuckled. "Press conferences. They all do, don't they?"

Vic wanted to laugh, but he felt as if he was losing his balance.

"One other thing." Karl fell silent.

Vic waited.

"I'll need an official statement from both of you guys, but I got a day or two. Be glad Jimmy is with you, or I'd be looking hard at you." A smile flickered over his lips. "But this raises another question. You gonna stick around? Just interested. I mean the longer you're here, the worse my work load."

Vic barely heard him. He was overwhelmed with a single thought. He knew he should have decided earlier, but with Cora gone, he had no choice. It scared him to ask, he hated to ask. He focused on Karl. "Do you have a DNA swab test?"

Karl frowned. "Always."

"Then you need to swab me." Karl stayed silent and Vic pushed ahead. "Remember that burned out building you told us about, before Chief Fleck got you guys to release the site?"

"I remember."

"You also said you have bodies but no identities."

"Still true."

"You need to swab me and see if I match any of the bodies. It's possible my daughter was there. Unless your ME identified all the bodies as male."

Karl shifted on his feet. "We got both male and female remains."

"Then swab me. Eliminate me as related to the bodies." Vic heard the way he positioned it to Karl. He'd made the same suggestion to suspects and witnesses countless times. He'd just never been on this side of it. Never realized how terrible it sounded.

"You sure you want to go there?" Karl asked.

"I've got nowhere else to go. I'm out of options. I've been telling myself for months that she's dead. I just never believed it. But I have to know. I need to be sure."

Karl stared at him for a few moments, turned and walked to his car.

Vic watched him, cursing himself for letting Jimmy talk him into stopping at the motel. He was sure that whoever almost ran them off the road killed Cora. Fifteen minutes earlier and he could have stopped it.

He'd arrived too late for Kent and Cora.

His leads were gone, sliding away like everything else about him.

Chapter 36

When Karl finished taking the swab, Vic crossed to the truck. Jimmy was behind the wheel.

"You good enough to drive?" Vic asked.

Jimmy stared at him. "I need something to do. And you look worse than me right now."

Vic didn't argue. He walked around to the passenger side and climbed in. The sliding down feeling was stronger. His stomach pitched, he felt it in his mouth. Jimmy guided the truck down the road and over the rise. The lake reappeared, black under the half moon, the sky littered with stars. Jimmy tracked the shoreline with its logjam of bleached white tree trunks. On the opposite bank plumes of fire reached for the sky. Vic kept spinning downward, exhausted, his breath trailing out of him, his eyes locked on the water, his mind reeling. Not wine-dark. The thought saturated him. Blood. The black of dried blood. But viscous somehow, the logs the bleached bones of the dead. The fires an earth-wail at the sky. The lake rushed to meet him. It was in him, he was in the lake. He couldn't stop it. Black blood, white bleached bones, the earth broken open, raging fire. He sagged against the door. Every part of him scattered into the blood lake. His bones bleached. The last of him plumed upward, fire into the night.

He was swimming up out of something black, thick and viscous, his lungs aching. He crested hard, gasped. He breathed, blinking at milky light. A distant pink skyline. The emptiness inside him now an ache in his gut.

"Welcome back," a voice said.

He detached himself from the truck door. His right arm shuddered with new blood flow. He turned his head, a twinge in his neck.

Jimmy stared back at him. The left side of Jimmy's mouth was swollen, a black scab the size of a carpenter ant on his lip. His hair was pulled behind his ears. He sat at a slight angle, his right hand on the truck wheel. Vic guessed that had to do with his ribs.

"Dawn," Vic said vaguely, orienting himself.

"Bound to happen."

He stared through the windshield, looking for landmarks. "We're almost back where Susan Kim is."

"Figured this is where you'd want to go."

"Right." But he didn't want to be there, he realized. He just wanted to be done. With everything. To go back to Pittsburgh. The part of him that cared was lake blood now, leeched out of him. He felt it right into the bleached white of his bones.

He rearranged his legs, shook blood into his right hand. "Not sure what the point is, anymore. Last night took it out of me."

Jimmy frowned. He opened his mouth, gingerly, as if he didn't want to upset the ant on his lip, then thought better of speaking. He slowed the truck and swung onto the gravel road that led to Kelly Redfeather's property. They passed the pickup parked at the end of the driveway.

Vic thought of Kelly. He didn't want to disrespect her. "We need to get out of sight. I promised Kelly."

Jimmy nodded. "We're good. Still early." Jimmy guided the truck behind a hill, the house unseen in the distance.

Vic glanced at the dashboard clock and chastised himself for forgetting it was broken. Jimmy thumped his foot on the brakes and they lurched forward in their seats. Vic snapped up his head. Ahead, a pickup sat crosswise on the road, blocking it. A heavy-set, long haired man sat in a beach chair in the truck bed, an AR-15 cradled in his arms.

Jimmy ground the truck to a stop. Beyond the barricade truck a second man rose from a beach chair in the bed of a second pickup, scoped rifle in hand. Beyond the two trucks was a custom Chevy van, white with flashy

207

detailing along the side.

"Okay," Jimmy said. He threw the transmission into park.

"What the hell?" Vic asked. Vaguely, he noted that Jimmy didn't turn off the engine. That felt like a message, and he shifted to make it easier to reach his Glock. Flexed more blood into his fingers.

The man cradling the AR-15 spit a stream of tobacco over the edge of his truck. The second man dropped from his truck as easily as a cat and sauntered toward them. Unlike the overhanging belly and rounded shoulders of the man with the AR-15, this man was lean, his movements considered and measured, his body angular and shoulders pointed. Like Jimmy, his black hair was center parted and reached well down his back.

Jimmy rolled down his window. The man leaned his elbows on the window frame, still cradling the rifle. For a split second, the lens of the scope caught the milky morning light and Vic thought the sky had winked at him. A loose smile played over the man's lips, but his brown eyes were steady.

"Jimmy." His gaze never left Vic.

Vic shifted his hand to the butt of his Glock.

"It's okay," Jimmy said, his voice careful. He glanced at Vic then turned to the man in the window. "Joe Ironcloud. It's been a while."

"Yes. It has." The man's stare never left Vic.

Vic saw the side door of the van slide open. Near the roof, a slab of metal slowly unfolded outward and lowered itself into position level with the van floor. A man in a wheelchair rolled onto the platform. Vic had seen the thick chest, bulging biceps and the long black hair before. "Charlie Running Bear," he said quietly, as the elevator began a slow churn downward, carrying the wheelchair to ground level.

A second man climbed out of the passenger side of the van, and Vic lost his breath.

Levon Grace.

"Why don't you boys get out," Joe said, still watching Vic. "You know, we can pow-wow." He topped off his sarcasm with a snide grin, straightened and stepped back from the door.

Jimmy looked at Vic and said softly, "We call him Charlie Wheelie Bear now." He cut the ignition.

Vic wanted to smile but didn't have it in him. He stepped out of the truck.

"Been wondering what you were up to," Levon called to Vic, as he and Jimmy crossed to Charlie Running Bear.

"Coming up short," Vic replied. Levon stepped to him and wrapped him in a hug, the first time they'd ever greeted each other that way. It revived Vic, just a bit. Levon waved a hand toward the van. "This is Charlie Running Bear."

"I figured." He looked down at Charlie, who watched him back with brown, flinty eyes. "I saw your photo in a story on the pipeline protests."

"They should have taken pictures of the security team they brought in. Head bangers. They were the dangerous ones, not us."

Vic studied Charlie's legs. They ended mid-thigh. His hands rested in his lap, his fingers and wrists gnarled and thick, as if he spent a lot of time hitting baseballs with a telephone pole. Charlie was watching him, Vic realized, waiting. He had the feeling Charlie was used to people sizing him up.

People wondering what else Iraq did to him.

"I appreciate you asking Jimmy to help me," Vic said to him. "Can't say Jimmy feels too good about it right now, though."

One of Charlie's gnarled hands waved dismissively. "Those parking lot boys are just the usual shit, but the protests took it to a whole new level. He tells me you're not having much luck."

Vic looked at Jimmy. He was standing nearby, his legs spread wide, as if he expected an earthquake and wanted to keep his balance.

Vic turned back to Charlie. "I guess Jimmy talked to you."

"He did." A door slammed on the van and the driver circled behind Charlie's chair. She was short and stocky, with a cast of face that matched Charlie's. She stopped behind his chair.

Charlie waved at her. "My sister, Louise. She helps me get around." He indicated Levon.

"We picked up that guy in Bismarck. Figured we might be able to help you out."

Vic glanced at the heavyset man in the pickup, cradling the AR-15. "Not sure how. I'm tapped out. The two people I wanted to talk to are dead. Cora Stills was my best lead, but I got there too late." Vic heard the emptiness in his voice. There wasn't even a trace of desperation.

Charlie Running Bear didn't say anything, just stared at him for several seconds. Then, carefully, he turned and looked at Levon. Vic saw the question in Charlie's eyes and knew the look. Charlie was asking something like, *is this guy worth anything? You told me he was, but I don't see it.*

Levon nodded down the driveway. "Vic, let's talk a bit." When they were about twenty feet from the others, Levon turned to him, his brown eyes darker than Vic remembered. "What's going on? I talked Charlie into coming up here to help. You're acting like you're in some other state."

Vic stared at the road gravel. "I'm out of options. Everything I've been doing the last year, squeezing leads out of nothing. Everything's come up empty."

"You've got Susan Kim. You found one of them."

Vic frowned. He'd never told Levon the names of the missing women. And then he knew. Liz did. Liz was talking through Levon.

"Liz asked you to come out?"

"More like she told me. You told her to look into Ewan Fleck. She did, and twenty minutes later she told me to get out here, fast as I could."

Vic took a breath. "Look. Susan isn't talking. I might as well go home. Wait until she does." He looked up at the sky. "And when I get home with nothing, Anne's gone. My job's probably gone. The DA will make sure of it. He probably already knows I coached Lily and Denny on their plea deals. I'm done."

"But you've still got a lead."

"What?"

"Ewan Fleck."

Vic stared at him. "What do you mean?"

"Liz kept at it after she talked to you. Starters, he's got a closed juvie file. He also got tossed out of the University of North Dakota. Charged with rape. The woman dropped the charges, but they still didn't let him back in. What does that tell you?"

Vic watched the eastern horizon sky turn peach-colored. "Someone paid off the woman." It was an ancient story, one he was tired of hearing. He followed the line of thinking. "I guess if the university kicked him out, they knew he was guilty and it was bad enough they couldn't swallow it."

"Right. Then there's his finances. She already told you about that."

"Not enough. Just skeletons in the closet." The image of the white logs in the black lake rose to him. "Nothing to do with us."

"Maybe. But what about this? Watford City High School. Cora Stills and Ewan Fleck. Same class."

Something flickered in Vic's gut. "Connects them, doesn't link them."

Levon smiled and reached into his T-shirt pocket. He handed Vic a grainy black and white photo. "From their senior yearbook. Entrepreneurs of America club. Seven members. Oh. Look who's in the club."

Cora's hair was much longer in the photo, her smile crooked. Levon tapped the boy standing next to her. "Meet Ewan Fleck. The one with his arm around Cora's shoulders."

"Freaking Liz," Vic said softly.

"Freaking Liz is right. No wonder you always clear your cases. But it gets better."

Vic felt the blood in his veins, thick somehow, the viscous black of the lake. But moving again.

"Liz checked all the members of the club. Turns out that one," he pointed at a boy standing at the edge of the photo, "was arrested two weeks before graduation for dealing pot. Did two years. Cora went into the Army right after graduation, and our friend Ewan? Missed the last two weeks of school. His diploma was mailed to him."

"They were dealing pot together?" Vic blinked. "And Cora plea-dealed her way into the Army instead of jail?"

"Yep. And Ewan walked. There's your favorite police chief pulling strings. Liz tracked down the high school principal. Retired in Florida. She couldn't get him to stop talking. He went along with the police chief and swept it under the rug. It's been eating him for years."

Vic shook his head. "Entrepreneurs of America."

"I told Charlie all this on the way out here. He had something to say. You know who organized the counter-protesters and pipeline guards at the Standing Rock protests a few years back?"

"Ewan Fleck," Vic guessed, the name sliding into place as easily as a chambered round.

"Oh yeah. And that's just the start."

Chapter 37

Vic knew Charlie was watching them as he and Levon walked back to the van.

"Ewan Fleck," Vic said, when they reached him. Jimmy shifted on his feet and Joe Ironcloud shrugged his shoulders as if he was loosening himself for the start of something. "Tell me about him."

Charlie nodded to Levon, a thanks-for-straightening-him-out gesture. "Running maintenance for the drill rigs is where Fleck starts. From there it goes to everything the workers want and need. Every god-damned thing. Drugs. Prostitution. I told you. He hired the head bangers to protect the pipeline company last summer. They beat up our organizers, screwed with our trucks, gave bullshit stories to the media."

"You guessed I'd connect him to my daughter?"

"No. But most stuff that smells is connected to Fleck. And we got the same problem. A few months ago, six of our teenage girls disappeared—right off the Rez. Just like that. The only thing that made sense was the timing."

Vic thought he knew the answer but still asked the question. "How so?"

"We were talking about starting the protests again. It was a warning. You natives screw with the pipelines and the drillers, we're gonna take your daughters. Put them on their backs for the rig workers. So back the hell off. That's why I asked Jimmy to meet you. Figured he could help you move faster, and you could go places Jimmy and I can't. I wanted to know everything you found out. Who was involved, where our girls are. I want it to stop."

"You're jumping to conclusions." Jimmy stepped forward. "You don't

213

know our women were taken as a warning."

Charlie pivoted his wheelchair toward him. "Jimmy, I love you like a brother, you know that, but sometimes you got your nose too far into a book. Remember how it went with the protests? First the fake stories to the press. Then some of our guys worked over. After that our trucks screwed with—on our land. Then the girls taken. Those aren't individual acts. It's escalation. It's a language. You yell at me, I punch you. You threaten me, I beat you up. You shoot at me, I take your women. Get it? It's the same language they been speaking to us for three hundred years. Our ancestors thought learning English was enough. Fact is we learned the wrong damn language."

"You think going to war fixes it?" Jimmy's eyes blazed.

"Who said go to war?" Charlie's voice compressed and turned hard. "I'm thinking more like cut the head off the snake."

In the silence that followed Vic inhaled what Charlie was saying. That bad could be a language: unspoken, precise as grammar, every sentence a diagram of rage. He thought of those bleached logs, the bones, the water like black blood.

But cut the head off the snake?

In Pittsburgh, in that other life, he would have told Charlie to stand down. Back-pocket it. He was shocked to discover that urge was gone. He liked the feel of where Charlie was going. The freedom of it. The way it curled in him like a need.

Still.

His old life wasn't completely gone. He knew the importance of things that don't fit, the things that are different. How important they are to the truth, every time.

That was his own belief.

He looked at Charlie. "You're forgetting something. I show up and two people die. One is close to Ewan, the second works for him. We need an answer to that, because I bet it's related to the missing women."

Charlie grabbed the large wheels of his chair, tugged. The small front wheels dangled in the air. A wheelie, just like a thirteen-year-old.

"Convenient, huh? Like someone's covering their tracks."

Vic grappled with that idea. "Doesn't makes sense."

Charlie dropped himself to the ground. "How so?"

"I'm not official. Cora and Kent could deny everything. I can't make them talk. I stir the pot and add some risk, but they can handle it. Cora was tough enough."

Levon shoved his hands into his jeans. "Cora was on the run. Ewan might see her as a threat. If she was caught, she could give them Ewan's trafficking to get a deal."

Vic thought about it. "Maybe. But she was killed second. If Fleck, or whoever it is, thought she'd plea deal, she'd be dead the moment she showed up. On top of that people on the run go to a place they feel safe, and she came here. But we can check that. If Ewan Fleck owns the trailer where she was staying, she had nothing to worry about." Saying it out loud made him sure. "But I feel like there's something else going on."

Charlie broke in. "But it always comes back to Fleck, doesn't it?"

Vic had to agree that much was true. "We need to talk to him, but it's got to be the right way."

Charlie nodded at Joe Ironcloud. "We'll help."

"Liz gave me his address," Levon said. "I know where he lives."

Charlie yanked on his wheels and did another quick wheelie. "I say tonight. I'll put my guys on him, track him so we know his movements. We'll go over there now. Catch up with you guys late day."

Vic heard himself say, "Tonight works." Somehow it needed to be nighttime. He was too far past the normal way of doing things, of the channels dictated by lawyers and review boards, their incomprehensible dialect of procedure and law.

Charlie nodded a silent message to the man standing in the back of the pick-up, cradling the AR-15. He folded his lawn chair, lowered the tailgate and dropped heavily to the ground. They all watched him maneuver the truck off the road so Jimmy's truck could pass.

Ten minutes later, Vic and Jimmy were inside the barn.

Jimmy pointed at one of the rooms and went to lie down. Vic sat at the

215

table, thinking. Perhaps fifteen minutes later he heard the distant slam of a screen door. He found a crack between the planks of the barn door and looked out. Susan Kim, in dark leggings and a loose sweatshirt, her black hair in a ponytail, picked her way to the side of the house. As he watched, she stretched her arms, then her legs and back. Another thud of the screen door and the girl he'd seen outside the sweat lodge joined her. She was dressed in a similar way, the movement of her arms and legs as awkward as the motion of a colt. The girl imitated Susan's stretching movements, then her switch into a Tai Kwon Do pattern. Even at that distance, Vic saw how Susan sank into the routine, her eyes almost closed, the movements as instinctive as choreographed. The young girl tracked her movements, with quick glances to stay on form. The day woke around them, the sky rose.

The screen door slammed again and Kelly Redfeather took a seat on the porch next to a young woman Vic hadn't seen before. He watched Kelly lean close and talk to the woman, saw how she touched her arm sometimes. And then a quick laugh. The woman looked at Kelly, as if seeking permission to smile or laugh with her. Kelly touched her shoulder, lightly, and was rewarded with the woman's smile.

Charlie was right about the language of bad, Vic thought. But there was more to it than that. Kelly's smile, her touch, the way she committed her land and buildings. The years she spent to reach this day, the women come and gone. And how Susan—even with her eyes half-closed—slowed the pace of her pattern so the young girl could mimic and learn the movements. All of that meant something, too. Watching from inside the barn, alone in the gloom, he saw in front of him, right there, the language of good. He'd dealt with bad his whole life, surrendered to it. Charlie's words were a truth to him. But maybe, just maybe, something good could rise from bad, something exactly as resilient and powerful.

Perhaps it was always there, if you took the time to look. If you trusted it to be there.

He turned from the door.

Maybe.

But first, Ewan Fleck.

Chapter 38

Vic's phone rang at noon. Liz. Taking the call, he said, "Good job on Ewan Fleck."

"Thank the internet. I figured out his high school graduation year from when he got kicked out of college. Everybody's yearbooks are online, now." She coughed roughly, but her voice sounded stronger. "Levon told me Cora Stills was dead when you found her."

"I got there too late. Again. Levon's with Charlie Running Bear now. They're trying to get eyes on Ewan Fleck."

"You go careful with Fleck, Vic. He's a guy with a lot to lose. And his dad will be trouble. He made sure his son walked free a couple of times."

"He already had some guys take a run at Jimmy."

"Jerk." She breathed, a husky whistle, and took a moment to recover. "You remember that Hana person from the DAs office? She stopped by to see how I am."

"Nice of her."

"She's got a plan, that one."

"Okay." Liz didn't seem put out about Hana's visit this time, or show any need to insult Hana's hair. He felt good about that. Hana was winning Liz over.

"She wanted me to tell you something. I don't know what you guys talked about, but she said she overheard some of the prosecutors. I guess the DA likes to do these reward parties, when a case goes well. Maybe have some girls come in and dance for them. Males only. I'd say it pisses her off."

"I bet it does, but not for the reason you think. She's telling us maybe

217

there *is* a link between the DA and Cora Stills. Cora was fired because she used women from the strip club for private parties and didn't tell her boss. Kept the money for herself. If he knew Cora, that explains the bullshit with the warrants and how Cora knew you were coming. He leaked it to her."

Silence for a few moments. "Somebody needs to nail him on that."

"If anyone can, it's Hana. But with Cora dead, I doubt it."

"Well, like I said, she's got a plan. She was *real* specific. She said I was to tell you she'd take care of it. Exact words were, 'tell Vic, leave this one to me.' And something else, Vic. You haven't called Anne?"

Vic took a slow breath. "Not in a couple of days."

"You found Susan Kim and didn't tell her?"

"I've got nothing to tell her about Dannie."

"Anne came to see me, too. Wanted to know if I'd talked to you. I'm not telling you how to run your marriage, Vic, but get off your dead ass and call her."

"I get that." Vic sat at the long table and rubbed his free hand over his face. The connection between them was relentless. "I'll call her after I talk to Fleck. Hopefully, I'll have something by then. Can you help me with one thing?"

"Sure."

He gave her the address of the mobile home where they found Cora Stills. "Check who owns that. I'm thinking it might be Fleck."

"Sure." Her voice went tight. "Okay, I gotta go. You take care, Vic."

"I'm so good at it." As he touched the disconnect button, Liz dissolved into a fit of coughing.

He put down his phone and thought about Ewan Fleck. He needed a way to get him talking. Something. Otherwise Ewan would just nod and play dumb.

He needed something to trade.

Jimmy padded toward the back of the barn and Vic heard the backdoor thump closed. A few minutes later Jimmy was back and sat across from him at the table.

Vic studied his scabbed and swollen lip, the red welt on his forehead.

"Looking good."

"Screw you." He compressed his words to keep from reopening his split lip. Working his head around he stretched his neck muscles, then settled an angry stare on him. "You know we can't go to war with Fleck, right? Cutting the head off the snake. That's garbage. It won't change anything."

Idly, Vic tapped the button on his phone and watched it light up. "I was pissed enough to agree with Charlie this morning, but I've been thinking about it. I'm not doing anything to Fleck unless I can prove he trafficked."

"He's not going to admit it. Not a chance."

"Not outright. But there might be another way." Vic took a breath. "I need to lie down."

Jimmy shrugged and gestured toward the cots.

Vic stretched out, but his mind kept working, thinking about Ewan, testing scenarios, until he drifted off to sleep.

Vic awoke later that afternoon to the sound of engines. When he walked to the front of the barn, Jimmy was looking through the partially open door.

"Charlie and his guys," Jimmy said.

"Kelly Redfeather lets them onto her property?"

Jimmy stayed by the door, hands in his pockets. "Charlie raises money for her. He's also funding a place like this one on his Rez, so he gets a pass. Places like this are always scrambling for money."

"Charlie's a complicated guy."

Jimmy turned to him. "Not really. He likes to get things done and isn't particular about how he does it. He came back from Iraq that way. You want a hammer, he's your guy. I keep telling him he needs to think things through. I mean seriously think them through."

Vic joined Jimmy at the door, and they watched the van and one of the pickups park. The van door opened and the elevator started. Levon slid out of the front seat and waited beside it.

"Tell me something," Vic said slowly. "Those two pickups of Charlie's, either of them almost run us off the road last night, by Cora Stills' place?"

Jimmy smiled. "No. I thought of that too, but no."

"You remember what the truck wasn't, but you can't describe what it *was*." Jimmy's eyes turned cold. "Looks that way, doesn't it?"

Vic held his gaze and stayed quiet. Jimmy was lying, he was sure of it. He just didn't know why. Outside, the wheelchair elevator was flat to the ground and Charlie pushed away from it, rolling across the rutted driveway to the barn. Louise came up behind him and took hold of the handles. A couple of times, when the chair struck a rut, she pushed down so the front wheels rose and Charlie rocked the large back wheels to get himself free. They did it automatically and as a team, the movements practiced. Levon followed their progress. The large man with the AR-15 trailed behind. From the strap over his shoulder, the weapon was against his back now. He carried a cardboard box at chest level, one hand under the bottom.

Inside the barn, everyone arranged themselves around the table. The large man thumped down the box. From inside, he produced sandwiches and bottles of water and juice.

"Let's eat," Charlie said.

Vic had forgotten how hungry he was.

The first few minutes were everyone unwrapping their food and taking bites, until around a mouthful Charlie said, "Joe Ironcloud has eyes on Fleck. We can hit him tonight."

"Hit him how?" Jimmy asked.

Vic put down his sandwich.

Charlie waved his free hand. "Only way he understands. We go in hard and lay into him. Make him talk."

"No damn way," Jimmy shot back. "Attack a white guy in his own house, off the Rez? When his dad is police chief?"

"Damn right. Gets everybody's attention," Charlie shot back. The man who carried in the box nodded, a hopeful grin on his face.

Vic felt Levon's eyes on him, telling him to speak. "I think I've got a way," Vic said.

Everyone turned to him.

"Jimmy's right. The problem is Fleck has no reason to talk, so he won't. You go in your way and when everything's done, you'll be the bad guys."

Charlie shrugged. "What else is new? Doesn't make him innocent. And the message will be sent."

Jimmy cut him off. "We need to stop that kind of thinking. We need more than sending messages."

"Listen," Vic moderated his tone, hoping to defuse the argument. "I've been thinking about this all morning. We need to work from the things we have on him. Use those against him."

Charlie's eyes flashed. "We know he's the guy."

Vic met his gaze. "Actually, we don't. But we have angles on him. For starters, Cora Stills came here to hide. I've got my partner checking, but if she was in a trailer owned by Fleck, he's incriminated. An accessory."

Levon—his sandwich demolished—balled up the paper wrap. "Even if he does own the trailer, which is fifty-fifty, he can say he didn't know she was on the run." He arced the paper ball toward a garbage can near the door. They all watched it swish home.

Except Vic. The movement of him throwing drew his eyes to Levon's neck. He was wearing a T-shirt, the first time Vic had seen him wear a shirt without a collar. And over the top of it was a necklace. The strap was a leather thong, holding something brass with a silver ring around the center. It took a moment for Vic to realize the brass was actually two shell casings, the silver at the center a line of solder joining them together. When he lifted his eyes, Levon was watching him.

"He can say that," Vic said, dragging himself back into the conversation. "But think of it from his point of view. Suppose he *is* involved. In that case, he knows Cora Stills was trafficking, and he knows Susan Kim is out there somewhere. That means he's got a loose end and a witness. He needs those to go away."

A slow smile crossed Jimmy's lips, stopped by the tug of his scab. "Now that's something, but the loose end turned up dead."

"Right. But, let's say we go in there and offer a trade. Tell him we can make sure Cora's involvement never sees the light of day, and his witness—Susan Kim—will disappear. For a price, because he'll understand that. Then we don't need him to admit anything, we just need him to accept the offer and pay the money. He does that and he's implicated. It's an admission of guilt."

Charlie reversed his wheelchair from the table and returned. "Too subtle. We need to get in his face."

Levon's forehead creased into a frown. "How do we make that happen?"

Vic shrugged. "I keep coming back to one thing."

"What?" Jimmy asked.

Vic pointed at his own chest. "Me."

The table fell silent. Charlie cocked his head. "Why you?"

"Neither Fleck or his dad know I'm out here looking for Dannie. Chief Fleck never asked when I met him at Kent's house. I visit Ewan Fleck and say I'm a cop. I tell him I chased Cora Stills here on a trafficking charge. I show I know what I'm talking about by telling him how Cora took the women and transported them. I describe the women, name them, and say I know where Susan Kim is. I tell him all that and he knows I'm not making crap up. And when he knows I'm not bullshiting him, I tell him I'll take a deal. I'm willing to go back to Pittsburgh and report that Stills is dead, the trail's cold, there's nothing more to find. But I only do that for cash."

Jimmy leaned forward. "Doesn't that put Susan in danger?"

"He doesn't know she can't speak and he doesn't know where she is. I'll tell him I cut a deal with her, that she's willing to keep quiet for fifty thousand dollars. Me, I need one hundred and fifty thousand to go back and shut down the case. Two hundred thousand all in. And I bet he has the cash sitting in his house."

Jimmy frowned. "Why so much? It'll scare him away."

"And why would he have it in the house?" Charlie shifted forward in his wheelchair, and from the gleam in his eye, Vic knew he was interested. Levon was sitting back with a slight smile on his face.

"Jimmy said he's old school. Pays off everyone with cash. My partner said he reports very little income. My bet is he takes a lot of his maintenance contracts in cash. That's not money you put in a bank."

"The prostitution is cash," Charlie cut in. "Drugs always is. We know that already."

"Okay." Jimmy jammed his index finger onto the tabletop. "But why ask for so much? It's too risky. Suppose he can't put his hands on that much."

"Maybe. But I know someone who did a lot of undercover. He always told me, if you have to lie—and you always need to—make damn sure you lie big. I believe him on that. This isn't the same thing, but it's close. That, and if I ask for a lot, it tells him my evidence is good, that I know I can put him in jail. So he damn well better pay for it."

Jimmy stood up and walked a small circle, his head down, a frown on his face. Vic waited. After a few laps he stopped. "But how are you going to sell it? Fleck needs to think you're the kind of cop who would take money to look the other way."

Vic grinned. "I have an idea, there. Let me worry about that. But I think I can sell it."

"Good enough for me," Charlie said. "I mean, as a start."

"I have a question." Levon's forehead furrowed. "What happens afterwards? I mean, suppose he bites, gives you the money. Then what?"

Vic chose his words. He guessed he might lose Charlie with what he said next. "I give it to Karl of the North Dakota State Police. Let them chase it."

Charlie frowned and his knuckles—where they held his wheelchair wheels—turned white in the gloom of the barn.

Jimmy shook his head. "That doesn't work. You arrest him on that he'll just say it was a misunderstanding. It's your word against his."

"The money isn't what gets him arrested. You use that for probable cause, and on that you can put together a task force, drop in undercover guys, tap phones, line up search warrants, you name it. I bet six months after we deliver Karl the cash, they'll have enough solid evidence to blow up his whole network. They won't even need the cash as evidence. We're playing the long game."

Vic looked at Charlie. His eyes were turned inward. "Charlie?" he prompted.

Charlie met his gaze. "I still think it's too clever. And we can't wait six months. We still got six missing women."

"Knowing their names helps the state police. They can target them. That's easier than just doing surveillance. They can do one-off raids as they locate them and get them back."

The room fell silent, each person thinking.

Levon broke the quiet. "I like it."

Jimmy sat down. "I'm in."

Charlie nodded. "I'll try it. I'd still rather kick in the door. But we're gonna cover you. No way you go into his house without back-up. And if it goes to shit, we do it my way." He punched an oversized fist into the palm of his other hand.

"Okay. Just keep in mind this could go a bunch of ways. Fleck might not be the guy, for starters. Or maybe he thinks I can't keep Susan quiet. Or he denies everything. But I think I know enough about how Cora trafficked the women to convince him I'm his get-out-of-jail-free card."

"Might be enough to make him shoot you and drop you down a well," Charlie said quietly.

"Maybe. I need to position it right. Make sure he understands someone will come looking for me, and that person won't cut a deal."

In the silence around the table Vic's phone dinged. He checked it, and found a text from Liz.

Sorry. No go. That trailer where you found Cora
is owned by some guy who works one of the well heads.

Vic slid the phone into his pocket without saying anything. He didn't want the others to know, they might see it as a bad omen. He wasn't too worried. From everything he'd seen, Ewan Fleck was a careful guy who kept himself well insulated behind other men and his father. He would have to make do with what he already knew.

Chapter 39

The conversation turned ragged, now that the decision was made. Vic stepped through the back door of the barn. He walked a little way into the rolling hills and texted Eva, Crush's secretary, asking her to have Crush call him.

As he waited, he stared into the hills. The day felt stretched out, tired. The darkness he'd felt in his veins the night before was still there, even after the arrival of Levon and the discoveries about Ewan Fleck. He didn't feel any closer to Dannie, to understanding what happened to her. He was still lost.

The ring of his phone jarred him into the present. He looked at the screen and saw that Crush was calling him from his personal cell.

Just like him. Keep it all unofficial. And then he realized he was doing it too. He'd reached out to him via Eva, instead of calling him directly. That pretty much summed up the way they circled one another, always at arm's length.

He slid the button on his phone.

"Vic?" Crush's voice was cautious.

"Yeah..."

Crush cut in. "That investigator from North Dakota called. You found Cora Stills?"

Vic pinched the bridge of his nose with his free hand. "Yes. Too late, though."

"That ends it. That's good."

Vic could tell from the distance in Crush's voice that he was thinking the DA would be happy about that particular outcome. A happy DA was good for his career.

"You should know," Crush continued, "that the FBI is taking credit for the collar, even if she was dead. Apparently, there were a couple of agents investigating her mother, and when North Dakota updated her warrant they showed up and took over the scene. FBI is also saying they found a bunch of African artifacts stolen by Cora Stills. They've already got a press conference lined up."

"I bet they do." Vic was too tired to protest.

"The North Dakota State Police Investigator told me that, actually, you and some native guy found the artifacts. And Cora. He made that point very clear."

"We did, but that's fine. I don't care. They can have it. None of that helps me."

Crush was silent. Vic knew that ran against everything Crush believed. A bust like that? He'd write his name all over it.

"Okay," Crush said, and even in the single word Vic heard annoyance and impatience. "You wanted me to call."

"Thanks. I have a…" he stumbled on the word and had to take a breath. He closed his eyes and forced himself to say it. "I have a favor to ask."

Silence. "What?" Crush sounded stunned.

"I've got someone I need to interview, but it might come back to you, and I need a favor."

"Why would I do you a favor?"

Vic kicked a foot into the low grass. "Hear me out. If a local police chief from up here calls—a Chief Fleck from Watford City—I need you to bad mouth me. Tell him you already suspended me once, I'm drunk all the time." Now that he was talking, it came out in a rush. "Tell him I'm a pain in the ass. I don't follow orders. That you're lining up the paperwork to fire me."

"You want me to trash you to a police chief?"

"Yes. It's important." And suddenly, for the first time in a couple of days, Vic found himself grinning. "And you can ad lib. C'mon, Crush, you're dying to do this. You know you are. If he calls, have at it. You'll feel great. I need to sound like the worst cop ever walked the earth. Burned out. Crooked."

Crush coughed, and Vic figured he was hiding his excitement. When he spoke, his words were measured. "There's a reason for this?" Then, just as quickly. "No, I don't want to know. I get a call for a reference from this chief in North Dakota, I trash you." The sound of his breath streamed over the phone.

Vic pictured him in his office, his white shirt skin-tight to his bulky gym muscles. He would be staring through the window toward the Ohio River, the top of his shaved head bright, his mind straining to understand what Vic wanted him to do. Why he wanted him to do it. Looking for a trap.

"Okay," Crush said finally. "A free pass to trash you."

"That's it."

"Then that's what I'll do. And Vic?"

"Yes."

"It's always Commander Tompkins to you, do you understand me?"

Vic smiled. "Yes, sir. I do."

He pressed the button to end the call. The grin was still on his face and he didn't know why. He didn't even mind calling Crush 'sir'.

Chapter 40

At six o'clock, Levon and Charlie started for Ewan's house, locked in an argument about riding horses. Charlie wanted Levon and Joe Ironcloud to approach the house on ponies from the north, while he and the rest of his crew stayed on the road south of Ewan's property. Levon hadn't ridden before, which made Charlie all the more determined to get him on the back of one.

Levon had yet to see the humor in it.

Two hours later, Jimmy swung his truck through the parking lot of Vic's hotel and let Vic out beside his purple rental Chevrolet.

Vic climbed out of the cab and looked back in the open window. "Let me grab my stuff and then I'll follow you in my car, but I need to make one stop on the way. Nearest supermarket."

Jimmy nodded, and Vic went through the motel's side door and up to his room. The last thing he wanted was to let the front desk clerk see him. He would call later to check out.

With his car loaded, he followed Jimmy to a supermarket. He returned from shopping with a pint of whiskey, and standing in the parking lot, spilled some on his shirt and pants. He gargled a mouthful and spit it out.

Jimmy watched him through the open window of his truck. "You want Ewan to think you're a drunk?"

"I want him to believe I'm a guy who'd take money." He climbed into his Chevy.

Forty minutes later, Jimmy slowed as they approached a driveway, raised his arm through the open truck window and pointed over the cab roof. Vic slowed and turned between two brick pillars.

Two hundred yards of driveway brought him to a modern split-level of stone and oversized windows. There wasn't an oil derrick anywhere in the surrounding hills, a first since he landed in Williston. He parked and slid the pint bottle into an inside pocket of his sport coat. He made a point of slamming the door and staggering just a bit, in case someone was watching.

Four garage doors faced the driveway. To their left, natural stone steps led toward the house. Vic planted each foot carefully, taking his time, exaggerating a concern for his balance.

The path led to double front doors. Vic leaned on the bell so he didn't have time to reconsider. Chimes echoed, saturating the house.

A short, heavyset woman with an apron over jeans and t-shirt answered the door. Her hair and eyes were black, her face pale.

"Ewan Fleck," Vic said quickly, before she could ask a question.

She lifted her head, like a bloodhound catching a scent. *So far so good*, Vic thought.

"Who are you?"

"Tell him Vic Lenoski. Pittsburgh Bureau of Police. I have something for him."

"What?" Her eyes flicked to his empty hands and back. "What do you have?"

"I have ID."

"You said you have something for him."

"I do." He gave her what he hoped was a winning smile.

They stared at one another, the woman's irises jumping about like bats searching insects at twilight. Vic hoped he'd strewn enough confusion. "Just a minute." She thumped the door shut and a deadbolt clicked.

Vic studied the wood grain. The wind shushed around him. He wondered if Levon was on a pony somewhere to the north. He decided he needed a photograph of him on horseback to show Liz.

The deadbolt clicked and the door swung open, the woman standing to one side.

Vic stepped over the threshold. She closed the door and motioned him along the hall. They passed a cathedral-ceilinged living room on the left, large enough for a couple of tennis courts. Two of the walls were glass. She took the next left, into a modern kitchen about the size of the first floor of Vic's house. A great room stretched away to his right, all floor-to-ceiling windows like the living room, except the southern wall, which was dominated by a stone fireplace and chimney that stretched to the ceiling.

Between the kitchen and the great room was a large island topped by a granite counter. Behind it sat a thick-shouldered man. He placed a smart phone among three others on the counter and looked Vic up and down with cagy brown eyes.

From his thinning hair, Vic guessed late thirties. In the eyebrow ridge and deep-set eyes, he recognized Chief Fleck.

"This is Mr. Fleck," said the woman to Vic.

"Hey," Vic said, and stretched across the counter to shake Ewan's hand. He didn't take it.

"Make it fast," Ewan said. "Rosa said you have something for me. Who are you and what do you want?"

"I do." Pointedly, Vic looked at Rosa. After a moment Ewan nodded to her and she disappeared into the hall. The house absorbed her—footfalls and all—as if she never existed.

The corners of Ewan's mouth were turned down. "So?"

"Vic Lenoski. Pittsburgh Bureau of Police."

"Good for you."

"I'm out here looking for Cora Stills. Found her last night." He leaned forward and smiled like he was sharing a secret. "Dead."

Ewan didn't move, he didn't even blink. "Like I said, so?"

"She works for you. Helps you that she's dead, I'd say. But you're not out of the woods. Not by a long shot."

Ewan gave one of the phones, a flip phone, a spin. Watching it, he said carefully, "I know everyone on my payroll. She was never on it. Not even sure I know who she is." He looked past Vic to the kitchen doorway. "She ever on my payroll?"

"Nope."

Vic turned. Leaning against the doorframe was the same man Vic had seen at Kent Bauer's house, the driver of the white pickup who was friendly with Lou, the Watford City patrolman. He was as tall as Vic remembered, loose and in control. That same feeling of command. He raised his chin at Vic in recognition, a slight smile on his face.

"We've met," Vic said, without any real point, buying time, although he now understood why Ewan lowered his phone as he walked into the kitchen. The house was so large they needed to text one another.

The man shrugged. "Not really. Last I saw you were face down with some cop sitting on your back."

Vic decided to draw Ewan out a bit. "Right. Shit training. Whoever runs that Watford City force doesn't know their ass from a hole in the ground."

Silence. The man in the doorway looked at Ewan. Vic followed his gaze and saw the muscles in Ewan's jaw ripple in anger.

Good. He wanted Ewan off balance. He waved a hand, making sure the movement was a bit loose. "Maybe she isn't on your payroll, but you know her." Vic slowly opened his jacket with two fingers so they could see him reach into his jacket pocket. He removed the yearbook photo and slid it across the granite to Ewan. "This might help."

Ewan picked up a pen that lay across a paper pad and drew the photograph closer. Stared at it. Vic filled the time by looking around the kitchen. The back wall was a long stretch of countertop, broken only by a modern stainless-steel range and oven combination the width of a small car. Newly remodeled, he realized. Vic glanced at the man in the doorway, and turned back to Ewan.

When Ewan looked up, Vic said, "I need to tell you a story."

Ewan sat back and folded his arms over his chest.

"So, this is how it goes. Pittsburgh." Vic pointed at his chest. "Where I'm from. We been watching Cora for a while. Turns out she managed a strip club for a time." Again, he smiled like he was passing along a confidence. "I know the guy who owns the club. Thuds Lombardo. Used to be a big-time gangster, but he went straight. That's a good story, too. Anyway, *your* Cora decided to fill an order for you. Four women. A blond, a redhead, an Asian chick and a brown-haired girl. All of 'em looked young. I even know their names..."

Vic heard the man behind him shift position, but Ewan made a small motion with his hand for him to stop.

Ewan spoke carefully, putting a warning into the words. "You're making shit up. I have no idea what you're talking about."

Vic swayed slightly. "Hear me out. There was Dannie, Chrissie Stutz, Carole Vinney, and Susan Kim." A thought arced through Vic's brain like fire. If Ewan knew Dannie's last name, he might connect them. He hadn't thought of that. Quickly, he added, "I know this because I talked to their mothers. Oh, and this morning? Susan Kim told me the same thing."

Ewan's forehead clotted with lines and a flush of red showed on the skin in the V where the top of his shirt was unbuttoned. His gaze flicked toward the other man and back to Vic. "Look, buddy, I have no idea what you're talking about. Time for you to leave."

"Really?" Vic pointed at the photograph. "Really? You and Cora Stills were buddies from way back. Back when both of you, and that other guy on the right of the photo, got busted for pot. Entrepreneurs of America. Now there's a club. One guy went to jail and Cora chose the army. Plea deal. But you, you walked. Now which good old boy police chief helped you do that?"

Ewan jerked to his feet. He was taller than Vic expected, rangy, but a sag of belly said he was letting himself go. The man from the doorway drifted into Vic's peripheral vision, his face strained.

Ewan drove a finger onto the counter. "Look. That was high school. Okay. I remember her from back then. Haven't seen her since. End of story."

They stared at each other. Slowly, Vic shook his head. "Funny, you saying that. I think you've seen her since. In fact, I know you have. And that's gonna bite you. But her being dead is an opportunity. For both of us."

"You're full of shit."

"See, there you go. You haven't heard me out."

"I don't have to do squat."

"Except hear me out. I mean, dude, you're an Entrepreneur of America. A business deal guy. Pretty impressive what you do. Servicing all those oil wells and fracking companies. All their workers. Shit. Those workers. You can help them build a pipeline all day and lay pipe all night. You got all of it covered. Am I right?"

Silence.

Outside, darkness had fallen. Lights sprang on around the great room, on some kind of timer.

One of the cell phones on the counter vibrated. Ewan stabbed the button to send the call to voicemail. He licked his thick lips. "Okay. Now, you need to understand. I don't know what the hell you are talking about. No idea. Like I said before. Time for you to go."

Vic leaned forward. "Right. I'm out of here. Can't wait. But that's a problem for you. I get back to Pittsburgh, I've got two choices. Door number one, I tell my commander the trail ends with Cora. She's dead, no new leads, done. Or...." He pressed his jacket over the pocket that held the pint bottle, as if he needed to reassure himself it was there. "Or, door number two, I go back and tell the FBI there's a trafficking case to be made. Cora Stills arranged transportation of four women out here, to you. And I can deliver one of those four women. A living, breathing witness. I bet the FBI can crack you open in less than two days. And your dad won't be able to do a thing to get you off, this time."

The man to Vic's right spoke up. "You're finished here, cowboy."

Vic didn't move.

Ewan watched him, his brown eyes slits. There was something feral about him, in the whole way his face had transformed, the round bulk of his shoulders. "I told you. I haven't seen Cora Stills in years."

Vic smiled at him. "That's all you got? I can prove you've seen her lately. I tell the FBI and they eat you alive."

The man to Vic's right stepped over and grabbed a handful of Vic's jacket behind the collar. "We're done."

"Wait." Ewan blinked. Nobody moved. With the gathering darkness outside, Vic could see Ewan's back reflected in the great room windows. He told himself not to stare at the automatic holstered to Ewan's belt at the small of his back.

Ewan tilted his head. He smiled, as if pretending to enjoy a joke. "Explain that to me. Me having seen Cora Stills recently. How are you so damn sure? I think you're the one bullshitting me. I smell a shakedown. And if you are, you're gonna have a rough night. Whatever kind of cop you are."

Vic waited and the man holding his jacket let go. Vic straightened his coat, letting Ewan see his belt holster. He looked at the ceiling, then tromped on the floor. "Terrazzo tile. Good stuff. Lasts forever, at least that's what the people in the tile shop where Cora worked told me. And guess what. Back in Pittsburgh? I got a copy of Cora's purchase order for this very tile. Her signature on it. Describes this floor tile, that backsplash," he gestured with his thumb at the counter behind him. "Even those blue inset tiles in the backsplash. Special order from Italy. I'd say Cora showed up here with all that tile in a white van, not that long ago. And I might be wrong," he glanced at the other man, "but I bet the van's driver was Kent Bauer. I would have confirmed that if I got to him an hour earlier."

"Probably fifty places in North Dakota I could buy this tile."

Vic spread his arms. "Sure. And all the FBI needs is a purchase order they can confirm with the store. Done. But man, Cora got you such a big discount. The employee discount. Guy who owns the place called her a discount queen. You just need a receipt. You have one, right?"

"Even if that was true," said the man next to Vic, cutting him off, "why the hell would Cora do any of the things you're talking about? I mean for Ewan?"

Vic kept his face serious, not wanting to give away he'd noticed how easily the man said Cora's name, how familiar he was with pronouncing it. He turned to him. "She's saying thank you." He turned back to Ewan. "Just a guess on my part, but when you guys got busted for pot, someone arranged a deal for her to go into the Army. I bet that was your dad. Chief Fleck, working his magic. You walked and she got a deal. The FBI can check that with the judge, and if he's not around, your high school principle knows. He's retired, and he can't stop talking. But that third guy? They threw the book at him. Because someone had to go to jail, right? But Cora never forgot that. She's eighteen years old, jail would scare the living shit out of her. And I bet you laid it on. Told her you talked your dad into getting her the deal. She would be thanking you every day. Forever."

"You're making shit up."

His answer was so fast Vic knew he'd guessed right.

Vic smiled. "No. I think I nailed it. Saving her from jail meant she'd do anything for you. Discount tile. Grab some girls off the street and drive them clear across the country to you."

Silence again. Vic leaned toward the counter. There was another possibility he didn't want to consider. Perhaps Ewan had something on Cora, that he'd forced her to do his errands. He pushed the possibility out of his mind. "Okay, Ewan. I'll play. You don't know what I'm talking about and you haven't seen Cora in years. But how about I tell you my deal? Listening doesn't hurt you. Doesn't prove a thing. And I've sure got you interested, don't I?"

Ewan didn't move, as if he was scared he might give something away.

Vic spread his hands. "Let's make a deal. I already told you the FBI is behind door number two. That's easy. Door number one and everyone walks free, but you gotta trade." Vic hesitated, Sergeant Wroblewski's voice in his ear about lying big. "Fifty thousand for Susan Kim. She's scared and just wants to go back to Korea. Lose herself. Then one hundred and fifty thousand for me. Because I'm near retirement and that's enough to make me damn forgetful. Then I go away and you never see me again. Door number one means no one ever opens door number two. Done."

Ewan was as rigid as his floor tile.

"I'll even make it easy," Vic said softly. "You don't have to say a thing. I'll come back tomorrow night. And then you tell me. Door number one or door number two. Oh, and if you're thinking there might be a door three, that maybe everything would be better if I just disappeared, you need to know people are waiting. If I don't show up tonight, or tomorrow with Susan's fifty thousand, she has the number of an FBI agent I know. The same one who's investigating the Cora Stills murder and confiscated all of Cora's stolen art shit from Africa. And my commander is expecting me back. If I disappear, one way or another, you're through door number two."

Silence. Vic saw the calculation in Ewan's eyes. "Anything else?"

"That's it."

Ewan glanced at the other man and a small smile curled his thick lips. "See? Told you it's a shakedown. Big time. If I actually did any of the shit you're talking about, I might be worried."

Vic smiled and spread his hands. "However you want to play it. I'll be back tomorrow." He backed to the doorway, watching Ewan's hands, then pivoted and walked swiftly down the hall to the front door.

The night was cool and hit him like a good jab. His forehead went cold and he realized he was sweating. He forced himself to slow down, to take his time on the steps to his car. He reversed into a turn, drove to the main road, took a left and accelerated toward the Rez and Susan Kim. A couple of miles down the road his phone rang.

Jimmy.

"I'm about a mile back," he said. "No one followed you out of the house…I watched. You're clear. How'd it go?"

Vic blinked at oncoming headlights and watched them rush past. "I guess we'll know tomorrow."

"Yes, we will."

After they hung up Vic dug the pint bottle out of his jacket and took a short swig. Just a tiny one, but he needed it all.

Chapter 41

It took almost two hours for everyone to reach the barn. Levon arrived walking stiffly, Charlie following in his wheelchair, a grin he couldn't wipe from his face.

"You a horse soldier, now?" Jimmy asked, as Levon entered.

Joe Ironcloud followed them in. "For a first time, he was pretty good. We could make a brave of him."

Levon glanced back and forth between them. "A pain in the ass, that's what it was."

"Wait 'til tomorrow," Charlie grinned. He swerved his chair in front of Vic. "Where are we?"

"I go back tomorrow night. With a little luck he coughs up the money."

"He'll be ready for you tomorrow. First time in you always have an advantage. It'll be different. He's gonna have a plan."

"Yep."

Looking around, he saw Charlie's bodyguard settle himself at the table, his AR-15 in front of him. Louise was missing.

"I will say this," Levon said to Vic. "Coming in from the north like that does give us good line of sight. I watched the whole thing through a rifle scope. I saw you back away from him at the end. When did you figure out Ewan was packing?"

"When it got dark, his back was reflected in the window."

"That other guy, have you seen him before?"

"Yep." He glanced at Jimmy. "One of the guys we saw at Kent Bauer's house. Seems thoughtful. And both of them are disciplined. I tried to get

Ewan mad a couple of times, just to see how he'd react, but he didn't bite."

"Is that better for us, or worse?" Charlie asked.

Vic was tired suddenly, like the day was snatched out of him and all that remained was night and sleep. "I don't know," he said quietly. "I could argue it either way. We just wait, now, and go in tomorrow."

Charlie tapped his finger on the arm of his wheelchair. "Okay. We left Louise watching the house. She has the truck, the rest of us came back in the van. She'll call when they go to bed. Figured it might be interesting to know who came and went after you left."

"Thanks." Vic nodded toward the refurbished stalls. "I think I'm done for tonight." He rose, but a thought came to him. He turned to Charlie. "Kelly Redfeather?" Native names still felt odd in his mouth, but he was getting used to them. "She and I talked, but I thought of a question I should have asked. Can you ask her if she'll see me again?"

"Sure," Charlie said. "Too late now, though."

Vic thanked everyone, walked down the aisle between the stalls and stopped. He wanted to lie down, but he knew he had one more call to make.

He stepped away from the back door, the evening cool, the stars so numerous it was almost overwhelming. He picked the top name from his speed dial list.

"Vic?" asked a tired voice.

"Anne. You still up?"

"I am." Her voice was dull and flat. Empty, more than anything else.

"I just wanted you to know, I found Cora Stills."

Silence for a few moments. The wind pushed against him, gently, a cool, clean smell.

"And?"

"Someone got there ahead of me. They'd killed her."

The gentle sound of a breath being released. "So that's the end?"

"No. There's something else. I found Susan Kim. The Asian woman abducted with Dannie. She's being counseled. She's so traumatized she can't speak."

238

"She can't tell you anything about Dannie?"

"Not yet. Maybe one day."

Anne was silent. "So, really, we haven't learned anything."

Her tone wasn't accusatory, she just sounded exhausted.

"Well, progress, but nothing substantive. Not really. One day, I'm hoping."

Silence again. The breeze moved through the darkness like something that couldn't be tamed or changed. A ghost, he thought.

"It's good you went, Vic. You needed to do this."

"I've got one more person to push. It's a long story, but I think he organized everything. Cora was working for him, or felt she owed him. But he's well protected. I don't know, I'm trying to make him incriminate himself. Maybe. I'll know tomorrow."

"And then you come home?"

"And then I come home. If I think there's a case, I'll hand it off to the locals. But it could take months for them to nail him." He didn't want to talk about it, he realized. "You sound tired, Anne. Long day at work?"

"Yes, but that's not it. I like the work, it gives me energy. And then I come home, I'm tired, and my mother goes to bed early. I start thinking about things. I always end up remembering Dannie. It hurts."

Vic leaned against the barn wall, everything about him folded around his phone. "I know. The same happens to me."

"And there's nothing I can do." She paused. "I go through this every night. The same thing. I can't stop myself."

Vic couldn't bring himself to say anything. Finally, "In the airport, on my way out here. I realized it's not just about losing Dannie. It's also about everything she was going to be. I suddenly understood that."

For a long time, Anne didn't say anything. Then, "Vic, like I said. I'm glad you went out there, even if we didn't learn anything. We needed to try everything. But you found Susan Kim."

"Well, depending on how things go tomorrow, we might not be done. But I'll come back."

"And do what?"

Vic found he didn't have anything to say. He didn't know what he was going to do. The thought of working for Crush seemed impossible. That same feeling he'd had before leaving Pittsburgh returned, harder and deeper than the first time. "I have to think about it," he said slowly.

"So," she said softly, "lots to consider. Maybe that will get my mind out of doing this every night."

"Let's hope."

In the quiet that followed the breeze wrapped around him, tried to pull him into the sky.

"Yeah. Let's hope," Vic said finally. "Goodnight."

"Take care, Vic. Take care."

Chapter 42

Vic rose early, the narrow cot leaving a crick in his back. He took his time tying his shoes and stretching his bad shoulder. As he walked to the front of the barn, he passed Jimmy, Levon and Charlie, all sleeping. Charlie's wheelchair was parked beside his bed.

At the table at the front of the barn were Charlie's bodyguard and Louise, who must have arrived after he went to sleep.

"Charlie told me to ask Kelly Redfeather if she would speak to you," she said to Vic. "She will. Meet her on the front porch of her house at ten. She has an activity planned for the girls, so they'll all be inside."

"Thanks. Charlie said you watched Fleck's house after I left. Anything?"

She shook her head. "One guy left maybe an hour after you did. Fleck went to sleep around midnight. At least all the lights were off by then."

"Thanks."

She shrugged and looked down at her phone. Vic wanted to strike up a conversation, but she wasn't interested and he wasn't sure what to say. Instead, he pointed at a loaf of bread, a box of donuts and a jar of peanut butter in the center of the table. "Breakfast?"

"Just don't eat the glazed donuts. Those are for me." The voice was husky, and Vic realized it was the first time he'd heard the bodyguard speak.

"Never crossed my mind." Vic opened the donut box and slid out a sugar and cinnamon one. Four of the dozen, he noted, were glazed.

As he ate, he pushed the barn door ajar and looked out. Susan and the girl were doing their Tae Kwon Do patterns by the house. He finished the donut and slid out his phone. Snapped a photo.

At ten o'clock, Vic let himself out of the barn and crossed to the house. He heard voices inside, but Kelly wasn't anywhere to be seen. He sat on one of the porch chairs and waited. A few minutes later Kelly maneuvered past the screen door, holding two mugs of coffee. She offered one to Vic.

"Thanks. All we had was bread and peanut butter. And donuts. I need something to wash it down."

"Garth wanted the glazed ones?" She sat on the chair opposite him. "I swear that's all he eats. That and barbecue."

"His name is Garth? The guy always carrying the AR-15?"

Kelly stared into her coffee mug and said with a sigh, "His mom really liked country music."

Vic let the comment go. He knew the meaning of past tense and didn't feel entitled to ask about it. He sipped his coffee and looked at her. The morning light was kind to her, adding life in her face. He guessed she simply preferred being outside and was happier when she was. "I was warned not to touch the glazed ones. By a guy with a weapon."

She sipped her coffee. "See? Life isn't that complicated, really. I'm pretty sure we all overthink it."

"I always thought the complications started when we stop being happy with where we are."

She folded her hands around the mug. "Wise words for a cop."

"Ah. Jimmy told me not to tell you about that. You found out anyway."

She looked at him, her brown eyes level. "Charlie told me. Is that why they took your daughter?"

"Probably not. I think she just filled a requirement for them. Blond hair. Young."

She looked away across the grass, past the collection of pickups and the barn to the rolling hills. Wisps of clouds striated the sky. "It's always what you least expect."

"I got soft," Vic said quietly. He wasn't sure why, but he felt the need to confess to her. "I didn't think the stuff that I dealt with every day would reach into my family. I thought if we were all in my house, we were safe. I was kidding myself."

"You can't beat yourself up about that. You can't think that way. If you do, you go nuts." She turned to him, her brown eyes patient. "You wanted to talk to me."

"I did. I asked you earlier what the women might have told you about where they were kept, where they had to work."

"Right, and I told you, it shifts too quickly to matter."

"I should have asked if they heard any names. If they talked about anyone. Who they might remember."

Kelly frowned slightly. Vic waited, his eyes drawn to the sky. From inside the house came the sound of voices, as if the women were playing some kind of game, working together on something. Someone laughed, the sound so clear he knew the window behind him must be open.

"The problem is the men stick to first names and nicknames," Kelly said slowly. "They aren't stupid."

"Then let's start this way. How about Ewan Fleck? I talked to him last night."

Her face hardened. "The man-with-no-head."

Vic frowned, not understanding. Kelly smiled to herself and looked toward the hills. "You have to understand our mythology. The man-with-no-head is an evil spirit. Some say he has a mouth on his shoulder. There's a story he tricked his way into a single woman's home. Fed on cooked fat placed on her belly, and that immediately afterwards she gave birth to twins and died. I think of him as our bogeyman."

"I'm not sure I follow."

"Oh, there's nothing to follow, really. It's just a story we've told children for hundreds of years. There's no need for it to make sense. To me, it's about all of us understanding we have the same fears. That someone might trick their way into our lives, destroy our women, that things created from evil can live on. It helps us understand one another, see how we are all the same. That no one is alone with their fears." She sipped her coffee, her eyes still on the skyline. "I put Fleck in that category. Someone evil, more myth than real. Someone who trades on everything that scares us. But he doesn't run the women. Not directly. He isn't the one to beat and rape them if they

243

misbehave." She looked at him, her eyes frank. "There always seems to be enough men willing to do that."

Vic fought down a tickle of disgust in his throat. "Could you write down all the names you've heard in the last year? Nicknames, real names, it doesn't matter."

"I can."

"And the women you treat say Ewan Fleck is the boss."

"Yes. He's the one in charge. It's one of those things in the air that everyone senses." She looked at him. "Like a myth. Or a bad smell."

The voices inside were quieter, more task-oriented somehow.

"Okay, that helps me. I'm going back to see him tonight. I have to know how far I can push him when he says he's not involved."

"He's lying," she said gently.

Vic rose. "Can you put that list together by this afternoon? It might be helpful when I see him tonight."

"I'll have it after lunch."

"Thank you. And thanks for letting me stay in the barn. I guess Charlie and his crew stay sometimes? They seem comfortable here."

She rose and collected his empty mug, her silver bracelets jangling softly. "For goodness sake, Charlie's stayed here before. After the pipeline protests. He needed to keep himself out of the picture for a while."

Vic smiled. "I don't think Charlie is the kind of guy who could ever keep himself out of the picture."

"You're a quick learner, Vic Lenoski." She gestured toward him with one of the empty mugs. "Your friend, Levon Grace. He did us a favor by saving him. Two hundred years ago Charlie would have been a war chief. A great one. Men like Jimmy are important and play a role, but Charlie Running Bear is the type we can never get enough of."

She hooked the handle of the screen door with her little finger and let herself inside. The door slapped shut behind her.

Chapter 43

The list was only eight names long. Kelly had added some physical description alongside a few of the names. From that, Vic guessed the man with Ewan the night before was Walker Trill. He was, from Kelly's crabbed writing, the man closest to Ewan and the one he relied on the most. The only one with a last name.

Vic tapped the paper about halfway down. The nickname Macho. No one knew his real name, but Kelly's notes identified him as short, Mexican, and the man most likely to assault the women. Her note said that everyone warned her about him. Vic bet that was Gomez, the man Jimmy had twice put down. He wondered if it was the same man Susan Kim had hurt while she was in Denny Halpin's barn. He hoped so.

That afternoon, Vic's phone buzzed. A text message from Eva, Crush's secretary.

Crush asked me to tell you. He got a call from a Watford City police chief. He wanted a reference about you. Crush said he gave you one you could be proud of.

Vic smiled and texted back a thank you. Crush couldn't help himself. Still using Eva as an intermediary. Still being vague about what actually happened.

The guy was a political animal.

He thought about the meaning of the text. It could be a sign things would go well tonight, or an unknown. The real question was how much the chief knew about Ewan's activities. Was he oblivious, did he suspect them, or did

Ewan work at the Chief's direction? Was the Chief doing his son a favor by calling Crush, or was he planning something? Vic closed his eyes. It was too late for that kind of thinking, too complicated to work out.

It was too late for anything but going back to Ewan's house.

And finally, in the end, he didn't care.

Garth went out at five o'clock and returned with Mexican food. He handed a new pint of whiskey to Vic.

As they ate, Charlie distributed walkie-talkies to everyone and made each person repeat his role for that night. At seven o'clock, Levon and Joe Ironcloud left to collect their ponies for the ride in from the north. Charlie, Garth and Louise would cover the house from the south. Jimmy would be positioned to the west, ready to drive to the house if help was needed. At eight-thirty Jimmy and Vic set off, Vic following Jimmy's pickup. A corner of the fabric bed-cover on Jimmy's truck was unsnapped and flapped in the wind.

As they cleared the reservation and took a left onto Route 23, Vic's phone rang.

"Hey," Jimmy said. "Karl called. Asked if you're around. He wants to talk to you. There's a lake overlook between New Town and the casino, right before the bridge. I told him we'd meet there."

"Sure." Vic wondered if Jimmy had told Karl what they were up to. He hoped not. Vic knew the best way to put the state police investigation into play was to dump the money on Karl's desk. Karl wouldn't have a choice, then.

Just past New Town, Jimmy's turn signal flickered and Vic followed the truck up a short, steep drive to a parking lot. The lake stretched in front of them, the sun's setting beams sparkling on the water. The sky ran the gamut of pink to peach, a band of violet star-studded night above the sunset. Karl's cruiser was parked to one side, facing down the access road. As they arrived, Karl climbed out of his vehicle and waited, legs spread, sport coat flapping in the wind.

Vic and Jimmy parked next to one another. When Vic got out of his car, he snapped down the corner of the truck's bed cover. They crossed to Karl and shook hands.

"Jimmy, can you give us a minute?" Karl asked.

Jimmy nodded. They watched him cross the parking lot and face the lake, his arms folded, hair whipping in the wind.

Karl turned his blue-eyed gaze to Vic. "I wanted to let you know as soon as I could."

"Let me know what?"

Karl glanced at the ground.

Something shifted in Vic and he was suddenly tense. "What?"

Karl looked up and met Vic's gaze. "Your DNA test, we got a preliminary back. Full test takes a couple more days, but I thought you should know."

"What?" The word was out of his mouth quickly, but he already knew.

"You're a familial match to one of the sets of remains we found in the fire."

Vic couldn't breathe. "You mean Dannie is one of the bodies from the fire."

Karl held his eyes. "We think so."

Vic stepped to his right involuntarily, as if he could sidestep the news. Not have it stick. Yet it was already inside him, squeezing. "You're sure? One hundred percent?"

Karl kept his gaze level. "I made them double check the sample. No screw up. We'll do a second check with dental records, once we have them. There's no good way to tell you, Vic. But I wanted to tell you myself. You shouldn't get a form letter."

The thing squeezing Vic's insides ground down and he staggered back a step, the wind a freight train in his ears. He caught himself.

"I'm sorry, Vic," Karl said carefully. "Can I do something?"

Vic was aware of Jimmy watching them. "No," he heard himself say. "I'll call my wife. Let her know."

Oddly, Karl held out his hand. On some level, Vic knew Karl just wanted to reassure him, offer a lifeline, but a handshake felt ridiculous.

Still, he responded.

"Thanks, Karl." He crossed to his car. Somehow, he opened the door and sat behind the wheel. In the side mirror he saw Jimmy and Karl talking, their heads bent to one another. Jimmy glanced in his direction, bright eyed. Moments later he tapped on the driver's window.

Vic gathered himself, started the car and pressed the window button. It was barely six inches down when Jimmy said, "Vic, I'm sorry. What can I do?"

Vic stared straight ahead. "Nothing. I expected this." But he hadn't. He'd let that tiny grit of hope that she was alive stay inside him. But he'd known all along he was lying to himself. And now that grit was growing, rough and hard.

The wind hurtled through the empty window like insane laughter. Jimmy ignored the way his hair streamed over his face. "We'll call off going to see Fleck. No problem."

Vic listened to the wind over the rumble of the car engine. "No." He stared at the lake. "We're going."

Chapter 44

Jimmy clambered into his truck and reversed out of his parking spot. Vic followed. At the intersection they took a right onto the bridge. Vic grew numb. He glanced at the passenger seat and saw the pint of whiskey. He scooped it up, twisted off the cap and forced down a mouthful, in one burning gulp. His eyes watered. Halfway across the bridge his brain started to swim. In his mind he saw the gravel lot in front of the burned-out building, the low scorched walls. The square of yellow tape inside. A guttural whine filled the car, his own voice. The road blurred and he wiped at his eyes with his shirt cuff, spilling whiskey on his pants.

He swigged again, a smaller slug, and thought: Ewan Fleck. He screwed the top on the bottle and tossed it onto the seat. The casino flashed by on his left. The sun, glued to the horizon, burned his eyes. He yanked down the sun visor. One more chance at Ewan Fleck. The whiskey roiled his stomach. That's all he wanted. Well heads littered the land around him. Everywhere, slow-dipping oil derricks fed Gordian knots of piping. Exhaust stacks raged fire at the sky.

Ewan Fleck. The name was stuck in his brain like a three-inch nail.

Jimmy's turn signal brought him back to himself. He'd gone somewhere in his mind, he didn't know how long they'd been driving. Jimmy pulled onto the shoulder, Vic behind him. He remembered the lake stretching to the sunset, Karl, a glimpse of the casino. And now this.

Jimmy walked back to him and Vic let down his window. Jimmy placed his arm on the roof of the car and leaned down to him, his hair swinging in the wind. "You sure you can do this?"

Vic stared straight ahead. "No. But it's tonight or nothing."

Jimmy was silent for a few moments. "Hopefully you spit out whatever whiskey you put in your mouth. You stink of it."

A fierce urge rose in Vic's throat, begging to taste whiskey again. To take the bottle and drink it down. "I'm good." He was lying, and Jimmy would know it too. Before Jimmy could say anything, he added, "I'm doing this. I want to get this guy."

Jimmy tapped the car roof with his hand several times and straightened up. "Okay. You know where he lives. I'm going to find a place to hole up. Vic, you need help, something goes wrong, two clicks on the walkie-talkie button. Don't say anything. I hear the clicks and I'll come. Last thing we need is Charlie hearing you're in trouble. He'll go in shooting."

Jimmy stepped away from his car. As Vic waited for him to get into his truck, he saw the twilight fading, giving way to darkness. That felt right to him. A dump truck thundered by and Jimmy pulled into its wake. Vic gunned his car's motor to follow.

The lights atop the two pillars flanking Fleck's driveway were lit. The fierce pull in his throat was growing, demanding whiskey. He guided the car along the driveway and parked near the garage doors. He sat for a few moments, his hands on the steering wheel, afraid that if he removed them, he would grab the bottle and drink.

The moment didn't pass as much as he steeled himself to withstand it. His car window was still down. Carefully, he picked up the pint bottle, unscrewed the cap and tipped some into his mouth. He swilled twice and spit through the window; greedily swallowed what little was left in his mouth. Slowly, he let himself out of the car.

His walkie-talkie squawked, Charlie telling everyone to take positions. Vic turned the volume to zero. The last thing he needed was Charlie barking commands while he talked to Ewan.

The front door loomed ahead of him. He wasn't quite sure how he covered the distance from his car. He pushed the bell.

The door opened as if someone was waiting. Walker Trill. They nodded to one another and Vic stepped inside, gathering himself. He was hypersensitive to everything around him, to the seams separating the floorboards, the line of brass studs across the back of the living room's leather sofa, the mother-of-pearl snaps on Walker's white cowboy shirt.

"Walker Trill," Vic said carefully, trying to soften his acuity. Adrenaline fought his whiskey buzz.

Trill didn't seem surprised. "Clever boy. Okay, Vic Lenoski. C'mon through." He led Vic down the hall to the kitchen.

Ewan sat at the counter on the same stool as the night before, his array of phones in front of him. The maid who opened the door for Vic the night before was at the sink, washing dishes.

Fleck watched him enter. He looked amused, and Vic had trouble meeting his eyes. This was the man who murdered his daughter. Who caused everything to happen from the moment Dannie stepped out of Vic's house to visit a friend. The Glock on Vic's side felt heavy, as if it wanted to be lifted free, aimed.

The trigger pulled.

"Rosa," Fleck called, "I can finish up. Why don't you head upstairs? We won't need you again."

The water stopped running. "Yes, Mr. Fleck."

They all waited as Rosa wiped her hands. Vic evened his breathing. Without a glance, Rosa passed him and disappeared into the hallway. Her footsteps disintegrated into silence.

Cautiously, Vic skimmed the great room windows until he spotted the reflection of Fleck's back. His handgun was holstered in the same place as the day before. He breathed once again, through his mouth this time, summoning confidence. He knew he needed to sound sure of himself, as crazy certain as he could. He looked at Ewan. "So, you got the money?"

Fleck leaned back. "Right to it, huh?"

Vic bored a look into Fleck. "We aren't friends. This is a business deal. Now, you got the money or not?"

"We should talk about this a little." Walker's voice was right in his ear, and as he finished speaking his hand slapped down on Vic's left shoulder, pinning him, his other hand pushing down on his Glock through his sport coat. It was effective, designed to hold him in place and freeze his Glock in its holster.

Vic knew better than to argue.

After a moment, Ewan said, "You can see why we need to be careful, here." He reached behind him and produced his SIG. He placed it on the counter in front of him. "Don't move now. Walker here is going to take your gun. Then we talk." His face was passive. He nodded at Walker.

"We good?" Walker said into his ear.

Vic nodded. He stayed still as Walker reached inside his jacket and removed his Glock. He slid it over the counter, circled in front of him and ran his hands over Vic's chest and back, down his arms and up and down his legs. He removed the pint bottle from his jacket pocket and put it on the island counter. Reached onto Vic's left hip and removed the walkie-talkie. He stared at it, then at Vic. "Why is this on? You're in North Dakota, not Pittsburgh."

Vic shrugged. "Habit."

With a quick twist of the dial he clicked it off and nodded to Ewan. Walker slid the walkie-talkie near the Glock and stepped back a few paces. "Phone." He nodded at the counter.

Vic dug his phone from his pocket, taking his time, and placed it on the island.

Walker motioned again. "Unlock it."

Vic did so, and stepped back. Walker picked it up, swiped through a few screens, and tapped on it. Vic bet he was turning off the GPS and checking the voice recording function.

Walker placed the phone on the counter and crossed his arms, legs spread. "Hypothetically, not saying we will, but say we make a payment. Who says you don't come back in a year and want more?"

Vic shrugged. "I don't work that way. We make the deal, we drink on it. Done."

"Maybe." Ewan sat back and put his hands behind his head. "But a year from now you'll be out of a job. That money won't look so good then. You'll need more." A small, knowing smile curled his lips. "We talked to your

252

commander. He wants you fired. He says you're drunk all the time, he already suspended you once. He's getting ready to fire you. You're not even supposed to be out here. You're so far up shit creek you're an asshole."

Vic silently thanked Crush. "See. You just answered your own question."

"Explain that," Walker said.

Vic had a read on them now. Walker was the careful, methodical one. Ewan the loose cannon, the risk-taker. "What you guys actually figured out by talking to my commander is why I asked for so much. You think I don't know he's after me? All bullshit, by the way." He pointed an unsteady hand at the bottle on the counter. When Ewan nodded an okay, Vic unscrewed the cap and took a swig. His throat screamed for more. With an effort he put it back on the counter. "He hates me. I close more cases than anyone. I spent six years making him look good. He's full of shit. Anyway."

He paused and squinted, as if trying to remember the topic.

"Oh, yeah, you already answered your own question. If I'm fired, I got no protection. Without my job I got no credor...credibility. FBI doesn't listen to me. Staties don't listen to me. I'm just a drunk, pissed off guy. I come back here asking for more money, it's door number three. You guys plant me in the hills. Who the hell comes looking for me? No one. No, this is a one-time. While I still got someone to come looking for me if I don't come home." He looked from one to the other. "I'm a lot of things, but not stupid."

"Still, we'd feel better if we could talk to Susan Kim." Walker looked at him evenly, his voice reasonable. "You can see why we'd want to."

Vic shook his head. "Deal breaker. She wants money and nothing to do with you guys. All she wants is a plane ticket to Korea."

Ewan toyed with the butt of his SIG, pushing it back and forth. "We just have your word that you know where she is."

Vic was silent a moment. "Check my phone."

As Ewan and Walker glanced at one another, Vic said, "Look in photos. Want me to do it for you? Last photo I took."

Walker picked up the phone and swiped through a couple of screens. Expanded something. He walked around the island and handed it to Ewan.

"I took it this morning."

They glanced at one another and a look passed between them. There was something more about the photograph, but Vic didn't know what. Walker took the phone back and tapped a couple more times. "Taken today," he said.

"Okay." Ewan cocked his head toward the great room and Walker crossed to a series of cupboards flanking the fireplace. Vic didn't follow his movements, he just waited, watching Ewan's SIG.

Walker came back with a black nylon duffel. He placed it on the counter and unzipped it. Inside were bundles of bills.

"How much?" Vic asked.

"What you asked for. Fifty thousand for Susan, one-fifty for you. Or however you plan to split it. Hundred-dollar bills."

"Now we're talking." Vic grinned at them. "We should have a drink."

"No." Ewan frowned. "You should get out of here, then go drink all you want. And understand something. I ever see you again, I guarantee you it's door number three." His voice lowered. "And one more thing, cops come after me for any reason, any time from now, and wherever you are, it's door number three. Get it?"

"Bullshit. If it's three years from now, that's on you, not me. I'll destroy the evidence I have on you, but if they come after you then, it'll be for crap you guys did since. And trust me on this, guys like you always get caught."

Fleck rose from his stool as if he'd just sat on a tack.

"Take it or leave it," Walker said to Vic, quickly, and Vic knew he was used to managing Ewan's temper.

Ewan opened his mouth to speak but the front door banged. Ewan looked in that direction and shouted, "Who's there?"

With a sweep of his hand Walker grabbed the bag and dropped it on Ewan's side of the island. He stuck Vic's Glock in the back of his jeans as Ewan holstered his SIG.

"It's me," came a voice from the hall.

Heavy footsteps, and Chief Fleck walked into the kitchen, his belly overhanging his utility belt. He pulled up short when he saw Vic. He looked at Ewan for an explanation.

The silence was thick enough to eat, until Walker spoke up. "Hey, Chief. You remember Vic Lenoski, right? I asked him over to tell Ewan what he found at Kent Bauer's house. That back-yard shit. Ewan wanted to hear the story."

Chief Fleck looked at Vic. "Uh-huh."

Vic saw him doing the math. The chief knew Walker was lying. The question he was asking himself was how much he really wanted to know. Vic guessed he debated that question a lot when it came to his son. His eyes hardened and he looked at Ewan. "I stopped by to tell you something. The place that burned?"

Ewan nodded.

"I got a call a little while ago. State police turned it into a crime scene again. Turns out they identified one of the victims. A woman." He looked at Vic. "She's a DNA match to this guy. He's the father. I guess they already told you that, Lenoski."

Vic tried to say something but his voice froze. He managed a nod. The bottle on the counter shouted his name.

"Noooo shit," Ewan said. He sat back on his stool, his glittering eyes locked on Vic.

"I thought you guys were going to bulldoze it?" the chief asked.

"We haven't done it yet," Walker said. "It took us a while to free up a dozer. Equipment just got there a few hours ago. That was tomorrow's job."

"Well, now you leave it alone. Beats me what they hope to find, but you guys don't touch it." He stared at Ewan. "You read me?" His voice was sharp.

Ewan tore his gaze from Vic. "Sure. We don't touch it."

Walker tapped the countertop with the heel of his fist. "I'll pull the equipment out of there in the morning."

The chief nodded slowly and looked at Vic again. His mouth was tight. "You found what you were looking for. Tomorrow you come see me, make that statement, then you head home, right?"

Vic found his voice. "Sure."

"Sorry to hear about your daughter. I guess she was a runaway?"

Vic wet his lips. "Trafficked."

The chief didn't move for several seconds. He turned back to Ewan and stared at him.

"We didn't know that," Walker said.

The silence lengthened. Chief Fleck looked from Ewan to Walker and back at Ewan again. He wanted to ask the question. Vic could see how it was eating at him. How someone trafficked ended up on Ewan's property. Vic saw him start to shape the words, then glance at Vic and hitch up his utility belt. "Do nothing to that site." He stared at Ewan to make sure he understood, then turned to Vic. "And you see me tomorrow and then get your ass home."

"Tomorrow." Vic avoided his gaze.

"I'm out of here." Chief Fleck gave Ewan another calculating look and turned for the hall.

When the front door slammed Ewan placed his SIG on the counter. He looked at Vic, his eyes burning. "Forget to mention that detail?"

"Didn't think it was any of your god-damned business. And it doesn't change our deal."

"Oh, but it does." Ewan leaned toward him. "Now I gotta wonder why you really want the money. You have to be thinking I killed your daughter, one way or another. And you want money instead of throwing me in jail?"

"I don't buy it," Walker said softly.

Vic's armpits and the back of his neck were hot. "I told you. Me and my commander don't get along. I'm not giving him you on a platter. Screw him getting all the glory. I'd rather have the money than do that. The deal stands. You want the evidence I found to go away, I walk out of the house right now with the bag."

Ewan rose from his stool, almost thoughtfully. He walked around the counter until he was directly in front of Vic. They were about eye-to-eye, each six feet tall. Vic sensed how much younger Ewan was, the muscle-tightness in how he carried himself, despite the belly. He was keenly aware of the SIG on the counter.

Ewan studied him. "You stink."

Vic waited.

256

The uppercut was slow to develop.

It wasn't as bad as raising a fist, drawing back and punching, but pretty close to it. Vic saw Ewan's right elbow tighten, his right shoulder drop. He might as well have told him the punch was coming. The moment Ewan's fist lashed upward Vic dipped to his right. The uppercut cut the air by his left ear. He danced back. From the corner of his eye he saw Walker raise the Glock from the counter and level it at him.

Ewan stepped back to regain his balance from the miss. Vic stutter-stepped forward and drove a fist into Ewan's stomach, just below the rib cage. Ewan gagged and coughed at the same moment. Staggered. Vic ducked to his left and came up behind him, grabbed his collar and twisted him around so he was between Vic and Walker.

A crashing sound froze them all. A divot the size of a saucer marred the countertop. A distant gunshot echoed through the kitchen. Walker's gun arm dipped and he twisted his head, following the sound. Vic tracked his gaze and saw a jagged five-inch hole in a nearby window, cracked glass spilling off it like spider legs. Black night oozed through the hole. Walker took a step toward the window, his brow furrowed, as if trying to solve a puzzle.

With a splat the back of Walker's head disintegrated, blood and brains splotching the countertop and far wall. He dropped as if someone had chopped off his legs. Somehow, Vic's Glock stayed in his hand. Vic connected what happened. Two shots, the first misdirected off the countertop when it shattered the window, the second directly through the hole and on target.

Ewan bucked against him, got a hand on his wrist and rolled him over his shoulder.

The space was too small for Vic to fall and his back slammed into the kitchen island. Pain screeched through his rib cage. Facing each other they went into a hug, tight, Vic feeling like he was backed against the ropes. Instinct and training took over. He dropped his arms and threw two sharp uppercuts. The second connected squarely with Ewan's jaw, staggering him. Vic skipped sideways and put everything from his hips up into a right cross.

Ewan's nose opened like a red flower and he sagged to his knees, blood streaming over his chin.

Vic grabbed his walkie-talkie, twisted the off-on knob and pressed the talk button twice. He dropped it on the countertop and picked up the SIG. Aimed it at Ewan, who was on his knees, hands trying to stop the blood leaking from his nose.

Heart hammering, Vic sucked air. He backed along the island, stepped around the end and checked Walker. He was piled on the floor, what was left of his head sunk almost to his lap. His hands rested palm up on the floor, as if he was in some kind of convoluted yoga position. His right hand still gripped the Glock. Vic glanced at the hole in the window. Joe Ironcloud. Him and his damn scoped hunting rifle.

It had to be.

Vic checked Ewan, who now had an arm on the island as he tried to pull himself upright. Vic stepped over the blood spatter on the floor and twisted his Glock from Walker's hand. He jammed it into his holster. He circled the island. Ewan was on one knee, still bent at the waist.

"Stay down," Vic yelled, so loud it surprised him. But the shock of the gunshots and Walker's death were unspooling in his brain. What it all meant.

Ewan sank back onto both knees.

Breathing hard, Vic stepped around Ewan and pocketed his phone and pint bottle. Holding his Glock in one hand and the walkie-talkie in the other, he stepped into the doorway, so he could watch Ewan and the front door. Don't let Chief Fleck be first through the door, he thought. He wasn't sure what he would do if he was. He needed Karl. He might have a chance if Karl was first.

The front door crashed open and Joe Ironcloud stared down a handgun at him. He lowered it. "You good?"

"No." Vic checked Ewan. He was up, bent over the kitchen island, blood smeared on the floor and countertop.

Joe hustled down the hallway and looked into the kitchen. "Well, shit."

"We need to call this in," Vic said urgently. "Plan is screwed."

Joe stepped closer to Ewan. "Maybe your plan."

258

"No. We call this in before it goes totally to shit. Get Karl out here. State police. They'll keep Chief Fleck on a leash. This is out of control."

Joe pivoted toward Vic and raised his handgun to Vic's forehead. His eyes glowed like a cat's in a flashlight beam. "No cops. None. Your plan went to shit. Now it's our turn. That was the deal. I'm going to find out what happened to our women. Where they are. You understand?"

He pressed the barrel into Vic's forehead.

Vic felt himself, crazily, push back against the barrel. "No! We need an ambulance. We can't run from this. Chief Fleck knows I'm here. He saw me. They come for me they come for you. I'm not protecting you."

Joe laughed, high and shrill. His eyes danced. "Chief Fleck won't be saying anything to anyone. Not anymore." He drove the gun barrel forward and Vic staggered back into the hallway. Joe lowered his gun, aiming it at Vic's gut, and held out his free hand.

"Phone. You don't talk to anyone. Or you end up same place as him." He nodded in Walker's direction.

Vic dragged in a breath and handed over his phone. As he did the front door banged open and Levon stepped inside, sighting down Joe's scoped hunting rifle.

Joe stuck his head into the hall, saw Levon and turned to Vic. "See? You call the cops and it's your buddy goes to jail. He shot Walker, not me. You that kind of guy? The kind who'd jail a friend who saved your life?"

That first memory of Liz lying in her hospital bed flashed through Vic's mind. Her white bandaged arms. He thought of Jayvon. His chest ached.

He couldn't give Levon up. Joe was right.

Levon lowered the rifle and walked toward him. His face had the same skeletal look he'd had after shooting the man attacking Mary Donahue all those months before. "You okay?" Levon searched his face.

"No."

In the kitchen, Joe grabbed Ewan's hair, raised Ewan's face and slammed it onto the granite countertop. Ewan's arms stroked like a swimmer's and he collapsed onto the floor. Joe dragged him upright by the hair and talked into his face. Smacked his cheek with the barrel of his gun.

Levon stepped into the kitchen. He looked at Walker's remains and turned to Vic. "You need to get out of here."

"We can't run from this."

"Maybe not me. But you need to."

Vic wiped his mouth with the back of his hand. The open front door loomed at him from the end of the hall, a black rectangle of sky calling.

Levon leaned closer. "Vic, look at me. You got into a fight with Ewan, the other guy trained a weapon on you. I couldn't hear what you guys were saying. I took it at face value. I fired."

Ewan was on the floor, Joe talking rapidly into his walkie-talkie. As Vic watched, Joe holstered his gun and pointed at Ewan. "Watch him." He stepped past them into the hall, pulled open a nearby door and disappeared down a flight of steps.

"Vic, what the hell happened?"

Vic blinked. Jimmy was walking up the hallway toward him. Vic hadn't seen him come in. Jimmy looked into the kitchen and his face twisted in anger. "What the hell? Chief Fleck is dead out there. Shot in his car."

"Joe," Vic said, more to himself. "Everything was working until Chief Fleck showed up. State police impounded that building again, the place they found Dannie's remains. He wanted Ewan not to touch it. He told Ewan my daughter was inside. Ewan heard that, he guessed I was playing him. Came after me." He gestured into the kitchen. "We need to call Karl. Get this sorted." He heard the lack of conviction in his voice. He glanced at Levon, who was looking at the floor, the rifle barrel pointing at the ground.

"What's that?" Jimmy raised his nose like a bloodhound.

Vic smelled it as well. "Something's burning."

Joe popped out of the doorway. "Time to clear out. House is going up. Let's go."

"You set the house on fire?" Jimmy shouted at him.

Joe smirked. "Charlie told me. We gotta move." He pointed at Ewan. "He told me where to find our women. Turns out the son of a bitch can't keep counsel. Too damn scared. We need to get them before his crew hides them."

A whooshing sound came from below and smoke bellowed out of the basement doorway. A fire alarm shrieked and the air turned acrid. Jimmy, Levon and Vic glanced at one another.

"Suit yourselves," Joe said. He handed Vic his phone back and hurried for the front door. Over his shoulder, he called, "Plenty of shit down there to burn. Decide fast."

Vic made up his mind. He stepped into the kitchen, grabbed Ewan under the shoulders and dragged him into the hall, headed to the front door. Jimmy picked up Ewan's legs by his jeans and they struggled along the hall.

"Wait," Vic panted. "There's someone else here. Rosa or something. I saw her earlier."

They lowered Ewan to the floor.

"Upstairs." Vic started up the staircase, hearing Levon and Jimmy behind him. He looked down the second-floor hallway. It was wide, with three doors on each side. "Jesus." He stepped to the first door and yanked it open. A bedroom. Levon brushed past him, still holding the scoped rifle, and checked the en-suite bathroom. When they returned to the hallway Jimmy was closing the door on the opposite side of the hall.

"Clear," he called.

They worked down the hall to the last door. Vic reached for the handle and saw a thick deadbolt. It wasn't locked, but what flashed through his mind was why it was there in the first place. He swung open the door.

Rosa crouched on the far side of the room in front of a crib, flanked by a double bed and large dresser and changing table. She held a knife in her right hand. The room smelled of talcum powder.

"The house is burning," Vic called to her. "You need to get out."

"Not with you. I go with Mr. Fleck."

"He's downstairs. The house is on fire." Levon pushed past him and Vic saw Rosa's eyes widen at the rifle in his hands. Jimmy followed in Levon's wake, looking around the room. The fire alarm in the hall shrilled to life.

Rosa twisted and reached into the crib. Lifted out a baby. "Leave us alone," she shouted. "I will kill her!" She faced them, the knife blade to the child's throat, her thumb all that separated the blade from the white flesh. Her eyes burned.

"Rosa," Vic struggled to moderate his voice. "Listen to me. We have to get out. The house is on fire. You hear the alarm?" Smoke belched from the ventilation system, thickening in the room. The baby wailed, its tiny legs struggling against Rosa's belly.

"Mr. Fleck told me not to take the baby out of this room!" She screamed the words at him.

Jimmy said something in a different language, and Rosa glanced at him. When Jimmy finished, she said, "I don't care. I work for Mr. Fleck. We aren't on the Rez."

"I'll take you to Kelly Redfeather." Jimmy's voice rose a notch. "You know her. You can take the baby with you."

In the distance something popped and a grinding sound echoed from the vents. Another fire alarm joined the chorus.

"I'll take the child, Rosa."

The low, smooth voice came from someone Vic didn't know. He turned. Susan Kim stepped next to him and stopped. Her hair was pulled back in a long braid. She was dressed completely in black, with what looked like a black quiver slung over her back. She swallowed, as if surprised she could speak, and licked her lips. "I have to save the child. You know that, Rosa."

Jimmy stepped sideways, his eyes wide, staring at Susan's profile. She warned him back with a wave of her hand.

Rosa couldn't take her eyes from Susan. "Mr. Fleck. He warned me."

Susan cut her off. "Ewan is dead. It's just us, now."

Rosa straightened, her eyes wide.

Susan crossed to her and plucked the child from her arms. Rosa made no move to stop her. She dropped the knife.

"Get out of the house," Susan said to Rosa.

Rosa scuttled through the door and into the hallway.

The child pressed to her chest, Susan turned. She looked directly at Vic. "I promised Dannie I would save her baby."

Chapter 45

"Dannie's..." The word stuck in Vic's mouth.

"You can talk..." Jimmy's sounded awestruck.

They all stared at one another. Downstairs something shattered. A window exploding, Vic registered vaguely. He'd heard the sound when Cora Stills' house burned.

Levon folded the rifle into his arms. "We need to get out of here."

Jimmy took Susan's arm. "Follow me." Locked together, they darted through the doorway with the child. Vic stood rooted to the spot.

"Vic!"

Levon tugged his arm. An instinct kicked in and he followed.

"Figure it out later," Levon called over his shoulder. "Move."

Vic reached the top of the staircase. Dark grey smoke swirled up the steps, rumbling toward the ceiling, and Levon disappeared into it, moving swiftly. The house lights flickered and extinguished. Vic grabbed the handrail and started down, holding his breath, his eyes stinging.

At the front door he stumbled over Ewan Fleck. Vic knelt beside him and felt for his carotid artery, but in the darkness all he could do was probe the neck. He couldn't find a pulse and his fingers came away sticky with blood. Somebody grabbed his jacket and tugged, and he scrambled into the night, the air suddenly clear and pure.

"We can't get caught here," Levon said in his ear. "I saw a security panel, fire call will be out."

In the driveway, Jimmy's truck jumped to life, the headlights splashing the driveway with light. He saw Susan climb into the passenger seat, still cradling the child.

"Go," Levon said in his ear. "Meet at the barn." He pushed and Vic stepped toward his car, but stopped.

Vic turned in time to see Levon jog across the grass and into the night. For a second he shifted from one foot to the other, then stepped over Ewan's body and back into the house. Crouching, he scuttled down the hall, eyes burning.

In the kitchen he felt his way around the island, stretching out his arm in the darkness and smoke until he touched the fabric of the duffel bag. As he dragged it toward him his breath gave out. Smoke rushed into his lungs, coating the inside of his mouth. Gagging and coughing, he dragged the bag down the hall and staggered outside.

His breath coming in painful whoops, he reached his car. Inside, he found his keys and wrenched on the ignition. As he turned the car toward the driveway, his headlights slewed over a police cruiser. Chief Fleck was bent over his steering wheel, the windshield splattered red.

He gunned the motor and swerved down the driveway, searching for Jimmy's truck. On the highway he turned left and floored it, his lungs aching. He went on a coughing jag and spit phlegm out the window. His speed reached eighty in what felt like a moment. He kept his foot pressed down on the accelerator, and a few miles later spotted Jimmy's taillights. A fire truck, sirens and light blazing, shot by in the other direction. He pulled in behind Jimmy's pickup, matching his speed. His headlights showed three adults in the cab, two of them bent over something. One corner of the fabric cover of the truck bed flapped in the wind. He watched the two bent forms as he drove, his mind blank for a moment.

Rosa, he guessed, finally. Jimmy driving. Rosa and Susan Kim.

The two women caring for his granddaughter.

Chapter 46

They reached Kelly Redfeather's farm an hour later, bouncing up the gravel driveway to the barn. Vic was out of his car before the engine died. He pulled open the passenger door to Jimmy's truck. The baby was sleeping against Rosa's chest.

"Can you still talk?" he asked Susan.

She nodded. "Yes. I think I needed to see Lettie. It just came back."

Vic sucked in a breath. "Lettie?"

Susan swung her legs out of the truck, and Vic had to step back to give her room. Rosa gingerly slid along the bench seat after her. From his peripheral vision, Vic saw Kelly coming toward them from the house.

Susan shrugged. "That's what Dannie named her."

"And you promised to save her?"

She nodded, gently stroking the child's cheek with the backs of her fingers. "Dannie and I didn't see each other much after we left Pittsburgh. They kept us drugged most of the time. I just got a couple of chances to talk to her right before I escaped."

Kelly reached the group and stood on the periphery, her eyes darting from one person to another.

"Who's the father?" Vic bent closer and stared at the baby's tiny features, or at least as much as he could make out in the dark.

"This can wait until tomorrow," Kelly said sharply. "You all stink of smoke. I'm not asking what happened." She nodded at Rosa. "Rosa, you and Susan bring the child inside, we have a bassinet. It won't be the first time we've had a baby here." She turned to Jimmy and Vic. "You two sleep in the barn;

265

we'll sort this out in the morning. And tomorrow you leave. Charlie called me. He said he'll be back in the morning and that I need beds. Is everyone clear?"

Jimmy and Vic watched the three women start toward the house, but after a few steps Susan Kim stopped and turned back to Vic.

"Ewan Fleck," she called. "The father." She glanced at Jimmy, an oddly shy look on her face.

They watched the three women let themselves into the house.

"Rosa," Vic said. "She's one of yours?"

"One of ours? Funny way to put it. Sort of. As much as anyone." Jimmy turned and walked down the row of snaps on the truck bed covering, clicking each one closed. "Grew up near here and went to high school in Watford. Her grandmother lived on the Rez. I'm betting she met Ewan Fleck in school."

"Did you know Susan was in your truck?"

Jimmy finished with the snaps. "Nope. I don't know when she got in. Or how she knew she should."

Vic nodded. He wasn't sure either, but an idea of it was forming in his mind. More of a scenario, really.

"Ewan Fleck," Jimmy said, as he led Vic into the barn.

"I sure as hell hope not," Vic answered.

They washed as best they could in the single tap on the outside of the barn. Vic was tempted to use the jerry-rigged shower where they first saw Susan, but decided it would be overstepping. Twice he suffered coughing jags, and again when he lay down on the cot. He thought about calling Anne, and decided he didn't know enough yet. He needed to be sure about Lettie before he told her. It would be too hard if the child turned out not to be Dannie's.

For both of them.

He couldn't bring himself to believe Lettie was his granddaughter. Not yet. He desperately wanted to believe she was, but he needed to be sure.

He couldn't sleep. His mind kept returning to Lettie, and as quickly to the deaths of Kent Bauer and Cora Stills. To Ewan. They were connected, he just needed to align what he knew correctly.

He finally fell asleep not long before dawn. When he woke, Jimmy was already up. The barn door was ajar and he was sitting just inside the barn, hidden from the outside, with a perfect line of sight to Susan and the teenager as they completed their morning patterns. Jimmy couldn't take his eyes from them.

It was eight-thirty when Charlie's van ground down the driveway and parked in front of the barn. It was followed by the two pick-up trucks, one driven by Garth, the other by Joe. The doors to the vehicles swung open and the men climbed out, along with Levon, followed by Louise and five young women. The women all wore sweats and T-shirts, as if pulled from their beds without time to dress. Vic guessed they were between seventeen and twenty.

Kelly and Rosa came from the house immediately and herded the women into a group. When Vic and Jimmy stepped from the barn, Kelly crossed to them.

"I need those beds, now."

"They're yours. But I need to talk to Susan Kim."

Kelly frowned. "I'll see if she wants to. I won't make her."

"Tell her I want to talk to her and Jimmy. Together. That might make a difference."

She nodded and headed to the house. Jimmy glanced at him, but didn't say anything.

"Rosa," Vic called.

Rosa said something to a young woman, pointed toward the house and crossed to him. Vic was aware of Charlie, Joe, Garth and Louise watching. Levon followed Rosa, the same strained look on his face as the night before.

When Levon drew close Vic stepped in front of him and lay the palm of his right hand on the back of Levon's neck. "Thank you, Levon."

Levon reciprocated, his own hand on the back of Vic's neck. They lightly touched foreheads.

They stood that way for a moment, before Levon said quietly, "You know what Liz would have done to me if you didn't come back?"

They dropped arms. "That's twice," Vic said softly. "Through a window both times. Hell of a shot. Both times."

Levon nodded slowly. His eyes turned dark and unhappy. "That's me. That's what I do. For better or worse."

Vic wanted to say more, but turned to Rosa. "Can you confirm that Lettie is Dannie's daughter?"

Rosa frowned. "I don't know who Dannie is. I helped the child's mother give birth to her, if that helps. I'm a midwife. I took care of Ewan's girls, that's how I know Susan."

Jimmy joined them. "Do you have a photo of the mother?"

She pulled a phone from her jeans pocket, swiped through some screens and showed Vic a photo. "That's the mother. Ewan called her Baby."

Vic stared into Dannie's blue eyes. They were focused on the camera, a torn smile on her face, the baby against her chest. He couldn't speak and was glad when Levon did it for him.

"Do you have any other photos?"

She shrugged. "Four or five."

Vic shuddered but found his voice. "Send them to me. They'll be the only photos that child has together with her mother."

Rosa hesitated, but nodded. Vic gave her his phone number and a few seconds later five photographs arrived. The screen door on the house slammed and Kelly walked toward them, Susan in her wake. Kelly said something to Susan, gestured at him and joined the cluster of young women milling by the van, followed by Rosa. When Susan reached him, Vic drew Jimmy and Susan away from Levon, who watched, halfway between both groups.

Vic studied Susan. She stared back, unblinking.

"You've got a problem," Vic said.

"I don't know what you mean." The wind rose and swirled her long hair.

"Your brother provided a DNA sample when you disappeared. Hair from one of your brushes. He was desperate to find you, he wanted to do everything he could."

She watched him, waiting.

"And here's the thing. Jimmy, here, is friends with a state police investigator. The one looking into Kent Bauer's death. I think he's a pretty thorough detective. And that means he's going to find your DNA in the backyard shed, where you waited for Kent to come home. So you could tie him up and torture him, before you killed him."

Jimmy's eyes widened. Susan's whole body tightened but she stayed silent.

Vic saw her reaction and pushed ahead. "He won't figure it out right away. He won't think to run the DNA through the missing person's database for quite a while. But, like I said, he's a thorough guy. He'll get to it eventually."

"I don't know what you're talking about," Susan's voice was a whisper.

"Don't insult me," Vic snapped at her. "But you planned that murder carefully. Maybe you'll get lucky and he won't find your DNA. But Cora Stills? That was spur of the moment. The FBI are looking into that one, and I bet you made a mistake somewhere. You had to move too fast. And I know you were at Cora's house. Jimmy even saw you." Vic glanced at Jimmy in time to see him look down, redness along his cheekbones. "Or maybe he just recognized that pickup Kelly keeps at the end of the driveway. The one that almost ran us off the road. That was spur of the moment, because you had to reach Cora before Jimmy and I did. You knew we were going because you heard my phone conversation. You were outside the barn. I had my phone on speaker, and there's enough gaps in the barn wall that you can see Pittsburgh from inside. That's how you learned where Cora was. I was sure I heard someone outside when I went to the bathroom."

Susan raised her eyes to him.

Vic didn't see any denial in them. "I'm guessing the FBI will link you, they're pretty thorough. And then yesterday? You eavesdropped on me again when I talked to Kelly on the porch. You heard we were going to Ewan's. And you hid in the bed of Jimmy's truck."

"What are you going to do, arrest me?"

"She's on the Rez," Jimmy said quickly. "You have no authority here."

"Hear me out." He looked at both of them. "The way you killed them all. Smashed hands. Crushed windpipe. I couldn't see Ewan when I left the house, but I touched his neck to see if he had a pulse and I felt the damage to his windpipe. He was alive when Levon, Jimmy and I went upstairs. Beat up, but alive. Then you show up. We go downstairs, he's dead."

"Joe Ironcloud," Jimmy said quickly.

"Maybe." Vic looked at Jimmy. "It took me a while last night to think it through. But when you crossed the room to take the baby from Rosa, I saw you had a kind of quiver on your back. I didn't know how to factor that in. And then I remembered something from Tae Kwon Do. Your specialty."

The wind moved among them. Garth said something to Charlie and he shrugged. Kelly stood next to Charlie, frowning at them, as Rosa shepherded the young women toward the house.

"Escrima. Filipino short sticks. Each a little under three feet long, a weapon you can make by cutting a wooden broomstick in two. Designed to smash fingers and toes, break the jaw, crush the trachea."

Susan and Jimmy stayed silent. Vic wasn't sure why he was still talking. Something left over from the days before Dannie disappeared. He was aware of the distant hills, how someone could walk toward them and be lost forever.

Finally, Susan shifted on her feet. "So, like I said. What are you going to do?"

Vic closed his eyes and opened them. "I just don't get one thing. You couldn't talk. How did you think you'd get Kent to tell you anything?"

She shrugged. "Beats me. But if someone can't talk, maybe they write a question on an index card. Show it to them."

Vic let that sink in. "Okay, I have a question, and a piece of advice."

Susan waited.

Vic gazed at her. "Why you did it. The guy in the parking lot after the fire. I get that, you needed to escape. But Kent Bauer. Cora Stills. Ewan Fleck?"

She stared back, unflinching. "I told you last night."

He nodded. "Because you promised Dannie you would save her baby?"

She gave just the slightest of nods.

Slowly, Vic saw the sequence. "Let me guess, you started with Kent Bauer, because you were working your way up the food chain to Ewan."

"I didn't know where Ewan lived, but I knew he had Dannie's baby. Dannie told me that before we tried to escape. Bauer worked for Ewan and drove us here, and we spent the first night in his house. I started there. But before he told me Ewan's address some people knocked on the door. Dannie had also told me that Cora visited Ewan sometimes, so I went after her, but Cora pulled a gun and I had to fight her off."

"And then you hitched a ride with Jimmy last night." Vic breathed slowly. "How did Dannie end up with Ewan in the first place?"

"He picked Dannie out of our group when we arrived. Took her to his house and kept her there for almost a year, locked in a room. Until she had the baby."

Vic remember the deadbolt on the outside of Lettie's bedroom door. "And then he threw her out?"

"Said her body was different. He sent her to work with us. Dannie figured out how to set the fire and use it to get out. But the guy who ran the place bolted the door before we all escaped. Sally and I were the only ones who made it."

"Sally is the young girl who follows you around?"

"Yes. We got to the road and flagged down a native driving a truck. He brought us here."

Vic looked at Jimmy. "Did you know that?"

He shook his head. "Not all the details. Just that they were dropped off here the night of the fire. People don't like to talk about what happens to their daughters. It's private. But Sally told us Susan helped her escape, so we let her stay."

"You said you had a piece of advice?" Susan asked, carefully.

Vic drew in a slow breath, his lungs still heavy from smoke. "Yes. Stay on the Rez. Figure out a way. I mean the rest of your life. Me, FBI, state police, no one can touch you here." He looked at Jimmy. "You're on the tribal council. You can figure that out."

Jimmy reddened. "Maybe."

"Cut the crap, Jimmy, you want her to stay. Don't play hard to get."

Susan allowed herself a quick glance at Jimmy from the corner of her eye.

"I don't understand this," Jimmy said. The wind whipped his long hair over his face and he hooked it behind his ear. "You're a cop. You'd look the other way on this? All of this?"

Vic stared at Susan for a few moments, then turned to Jimmy. "I don't know what's good or bad anymore."

Jimmy cut him off. "Don't give me that. You still believe in the law."

Vic felt the press of the wind, the upward draw of the sky. "I suppose. But listen to me," he said gently. He was sorting out his thoughts as he spoke, but he knew he was right. "Susan killed four people. Low-lifes, sure, but still." He looked at Susan. "That said, the law can't solve this one. Not fairly. I've worked in law enforcement my entire life, and I can tell you right now, the prosecutors will look at what laws you broke and solve for that. They'll charge you with murder and set the punishment. Crime and then punishment. That's what they do. But I'm thinking that with you, that process is already done, just backwards. You being kidnapped and trafficked was punishment, then came the crimes. I'm calling it a wash. For you to be punished, then commit crimes just to be punished again makes no sense to me. Not anymore. More than that, and this has been bugging me a lot, I want to see some good come out of what happened to Dannie. I want to know and believe good can come from bad. I *need* to believe that. If you can set your life straight from here, on the Rez, I'm okay with it."

Before Jimmy could say anything, or perhaps before Vic could change his mind, he turned and walked over to the others. Levon fell into step beside him. Vic looked at Kelly. "I'm putting my stuff in my car. Then him..." he pointed at Levon, "and I are going to take my granddaughter and drive back to Pittsburgh."

Kelly's eyes flashed. "That child isn't going anywhere with two grown men."

"My wife will be waiting for her in Pittsburgh. My wife is Lettie's grandmother, like I'm her grandfather. My wife and I are going to bring Lettie up. She's blood. We *should* bring her up."

The wind pushed around them all. Kelly shook her head. "I need to talk to your wife. Make sure about this."

"I'm calling her right after this. You can get on the phone."

Charlie straightened in his wheelchair. "You can trust him, Kelly. That guy there?" he nodded in Levon's direction, "he already saved my life. Last night he saved that guy's life." He gestured at Vic, "If Levon trusts Vic, I do too."

Kelly was still for a moment, then gave the slightest of nods. Vic could see she didn't like it, but he didn't really care.

Vic stuck his hand out to Charlie. "Appreciate the help," he said. "But not the part that happened at the end. We didn't need to do that."

"I warned you we'd do it my way if yours blew up."

Vic wanted to say something, but let it go. He shook hands with Garth and Louise. When he got to Joe Ironcloud, he stuck out his left hand to shake.

Joe stared down at it, confused.

Vic hit him with a right cross that bounced him off the van and onto the seat of his pants. Blood spilled from a cut in his eyebrow. He blinked, his eyes wobbling as he tried to collect himself. Vic leaned over him.

"Never, ever, put a gun to my head. You understand me, asshole?"

Chapter 47

With Lettie asleep in a borrowed car seat and the rental pointed down the driveway, Vic climbed onto Kelly's porch. Charlie's van was gone, as was one of the trucks, Garth driving. Joe no longer had it in him to get behind the wheel.

Vic knocked and waited on the porch. From the other side of the door voices called to one another, excited, happy.

Kelly opened the front door and watched him from the other side of the screen.

"Going away present," Vic said. With his foot he lightly kicked the black duffel bag next to him on the porch. "A gift from Ewan Fleck. This is where it belongs."

Kelly looked down at it. "Does it bite?"

"No. More like a tapeworm. But I think you can handle it."

He returned to the car. Just before he got in, he looked over the car roof toward the house. Kelly was standing on the front porch, the duffel unzipped, a wad of bills in her hand. Vic gave her a little wave and swung behind the wheel. He checked the mirror as he drove away. Kelly was following their car, her hand shading her eyes from the sun. It might have been a salute, but he knew better.

"This is going to be a trip," Levon said.

"We take our time. It's gonna take a couple of days." Vic turned at the end of the driveway and accelerated. "In fact, plenty of time for you to explain what the hell happened in Iraq. Why Jimmy thinks your last name is ironic."

Levon was silent for at least another mile. Finally, staring through the windshield, he said, "I found out what I do best is the worst thing about me."

Vic waited for him to continue, but a mile slid by, and then another. "I might need more than that."

Levon turned his face to the countryside streaming by the side window.

Another mile, and Lettie began to fuss. Vic glanced at him. "Okay. Don't tell me. But tell Liz. She knows there's something eating you. She needs to know what she's signing up for. She's a big girl, Levon, she can handle it. She'll surprise you."

Two long days later, late afternoon, and the relentless flat of Ohio was broken by the distant rise of the Allegheny Mountains.

Western Pennsylvania.

Vic was surprised at how good the landscape looked to him, how he felt comfortable and centered again. As night fell, they drove through the tunnels, Pittsburgh leaping to light in front of them. The rivers glittered. Vic dropped Levon off at the hospital where Liz was recovering, although from the conversations she'd had with Levon as they drove across the country, Vic guessed she would be released soon. Thirty minutes later he eased the car into his driveway, the lights inside his house blazing onto the front lawn.

Anne met the car before he cut the ignition. She climbed into the back seat to look at Lettie. Vic watched her face. She fought tears, gave her lips a quick press with two fingers and touched Lettie's cheek with them. Blinking, she slid Lettie from the car seat and carried her into the house. Vic dragged his bags into the living room. At the bottom of the stairs waited a large roller bag.

Anne's.

He hefted it. He knew she'd left it there for him to carry upstairs. He lugged it to the upper landing and saw Anne changing Lettie's diaper. She'd reconfigured Dannie's room into a nursery.

"Spare room," Anne whispered.

Vic nodded and rolled the suitcase into it. The bed was mussed and another bag was dumped on it. Vic didn't mind. Anne was back in the house.

When he came into the hall, she was closing the door to Lettie's room. "She's out like a light," she said softly.

"I gave her a bottle near Cleveland. She fell asleep right after that."

Anne stared into his face. "Let's go downstairs."

Vic got himself a glass of water but Anne didn't want anything. They sat at the card table in the dining room.

"What's the plan?" Anne asked.

"I think one day at a time."

"You know what I mean." She pointed at a FedEx envelope. "That came today."

Vic sipped his water. "There's loose ends. I have to talk to a North Dakota State Police investigator. He's been calling me for two days straight and I told him I'd call when I was home. He has questions for me. I'll talk to the mothers of the women who were kidnapped with Dannie. If they provide DNA samples to him, he can probably identify their daughter's remains."

"And after that?"

Vic looked at the ceiling. "I take care of Lettie."

"We have jobs."

Vic met her gaze. "I'm finished. I can't go back there. Not now. It wouldn't be right. I'd like to spend my days taking care of Lettie while you're at work."

After a moment, her light frown shifted to a smile. Vic knew she wanted to know what happened in North Dakota, but had decided to let it go. For now. "Are you sure?"

"I am. Maybe, when Lettie is a little older, I'll find something to do."

"I'll help with her, too. But you understand that I only moved into the spare room."

"I'm just glad you're back."

"We've a long way to go, Vic." She rose, but reached out and cupped his cheek with her hand. "But maybe there's hope for us yet."

At the doorway she turned back to him, a smile on her face. "Wish I'd seen it."

"What?"

"You and Levon, driving back. A couple of lugs like you, driving across

276

the country with a six-month old baby." Her eyes glistened. "And thank you, Vic. Despite all of this, thank you."

Vic listened to her footsteps on the stairs. She'd mentioned hope. That worked just fine for him.

He thought about that drive back. The entire way, he and Levon never said a word about the night at Ewan's house. What happened. He knew they never would. Levon might have pulled the trigger, but he'd put the gun in Levon's hands and pointed where to shoot. He might as well have pulled the trigger himself. He couldn't call himself a cop any more, and he damn well wouldn't let Levon take the blame for something he did. He would have to live with that.

Forever.

The windowsill caught his eye. Anne had replaced them, the fifteen photographs of Dannie, one for each year of her life.

He had one more to add. The photo of Dannie and Lettie.

His chest seized. Tears streamed down his cheeks. He hadn't let himself think about Dannie the whole drive back; now he couldn't escape it. He pressed his hand over his mouth to stifle a sob. His entire body shook with the force of his tears.

How long? With his eyes squeezed shut, he didn't know.

A deep shudder, finally, and he was able to breathe. He wiped hard at his cheeks. Upstairs, a short wail, as if Lettie sensed his pain. It was followed by the light thumps of Anne's footfalls into the nursery.

Vic took slow, deep breaths. Settled himself.

It would be like this forever, he knew. The hurt. The struggle back.

It was another few minutes before he reached for the FedEx envelope and tore it open. A smaller envelope slid out with a large yellow sticky note on the outside. In small, crabbed handwriting, he read:

Karl asked where we were that night. I told him you and I
went back to the Rez after he told you about Dannie.
We stayed the whole night. Kelly Redfeather confirmed it. Checked for Lettie's
birth certificate, there wasn't one. I fixed that. Rosa gave me the date.

Your friend, Jimmy

PS. Susan says hello, Joe Ironcloud doesn't

Vic reread the note. *Your friend*. He smiled at that.

Of course. Jimmy had pull on the tribal council. He opened the envelope and slid out a formal document with a North Dakota seal. On it was the name Lettie Lenoski, born February 26, father unknown.

But Vic did know, and one day, if she asked, despite everything, he would tell her.

Acknowledgements

I've been very lucky for the help and support of many people as I wrote and rewrote the early drafts of this manuscript. Caren Knoyer, Howie Ehrlichman, Janet McClintock, Jen Collins, Steve Sharpnack, Sylvia Adams and Barb D'Souza all read and critiqued early chapters, giving me the confidence to keep going. Carol Silvis, Anne Slates, Sharon Wenger, Louise Lamanna and Darla Grieco read the entirety of my first draft in fifty-page increments, and I took their comments and suggestions to heart. A more polished second draft was read by the novelists Annette Dashofy, Mary Sutton (who writes under the pseudonym Liz Milliron) and Jeff Boarts, who offered succinct and valuable insights, in addition to humorous and well-timed reminders about my tendency to repeat words and lose track of character names. As always, Verena Rose of Level Best Books provided a thorough review and continues to be strongly supportive of my work, and I am truly grateful for her confidence in me. Last but not least, I'd like to thank the readers of my final manuscript, Shawn Reilly Simmons of Level Best Books, Glenn and Doty Mauney, and Steven Hastings, who helped me fill in the remaining potholes and smooth the lingering wrinkles still in need of attention. I'm incredibly thankful for everyone's generosity, time and effort.

A Note from the Author

Anyone familiar with North Dakota's Route 23 corridor between Routes 85 and 83— including the Fort Berthold Reservation, New Town, Watford City and Arnegard—will know immediately that I took enormous liberties describing the geography, topography and road configurations of these areas. I took these same liberties with my descriptions of Lewis and Clark State Park, the North Dakota State Police, the Watford City Police Department, the oil and gas industry in North Dakota, the Pittsburgh Bureau of Police and Allegheny County District Attorney's Office. While these places, towns, cities and organizations do exist, they were all altered according to the needs of the story, and my own whims, and as such are entirely fictitious. Further, any similarities between the characters and events in this narrative and real persons, living or dead, is entirely coincidental.

About the Author

Peter W. J. Hayes was born in Newcastle upon Tyne, England, and lived in Paris and Taipei before settling in Pittsburgh, Pennsylvania. He worked as a journalist, advertising copywriter and marketing executive—including six years as Chief Marketing Officer for a multinational corporation—before turning to mystery and crime writing. He is the author of the Vic Lenoski police procedural series, and is a Derringer-nominated author of short stories. He is also a past finalist for the Crime Writers' Association (CWA) Debut Dagger award. He can be found at www.peterwjhayes.com.

CPSIA information can be obtained
at www.ICGtesting.com
Printed in the USA
LVHW041524120820
663008LV00003B/252